Cries of victory erupte... monster flew away. The tr... mundane battle with new ...

As the shouts subsided, Tarl looked slowly about, surveying the walls for damage. His mouth fell open as he was struck by the reality of what had occurred. The entire city of Phlan, walls and all, was in an impossibly huge cavern.

"Look, Master Tarl! Someone has stolen the skies over Phlan!"

The cleric took a deep breath. "No one has stolen our skies, friend. They've stolen us."

FANTASY ADVENTURE

# Pools of Darkness

**James M. Ward and Anne K. Brown**

# POOLS OF DARKNESS

First Printing, February 1992
Printed in the United States of America.
Library of Congress Catalog Card Number: 91-66510

9 8 7 6 5 4 3 2 1

ISBN: 1-56076-318-3

TSR, Inc.
P.O. Box 756
Lake Geneva,
WI 53147 U.S.A.

TSR Ltd.
120 Church End, Cherry Hinton
Cambridge CB1 3LB
United Kingdom

To my wife, Janean, and my kids, Breck, Jim, and Theon, because sometimes they're way cool.

—J.M.W.

To my dear husband, Richard, whose undying faith and love are more than I ever could have hoped for.

—A.K.B.

# PROLOGUE

"Not again! It won't happen again!"

Eyes ablaze with uncontrolled fire, the god sprayed bolts of lightning on all who cringed before him. Those that missed showered through the sky and onto the innocent and unsuspecting population of Faerun. Merchants, farmers, and mothers with small children ran for cover.

"I've played by the rules. I've organized, I've attracted worshipers, I've even granted a few of them special privileges! I'm getting nowhere in this realm and I'm fed up."

The god slammed his fist on the arm of his throne. As he glared at those assembled around him, his eyes sent waves of fear among the creatures who looked on.

"Something must be done! I will not lose one more worshiper! What is it going to take for those pathetic humans to respect and fear me? Any ideas?" he hissed.

Those in the audience chamber cowered. Many found themselves unable to meet his gaze. This being might have been attractive if not for his terrific temper and uncontrolled wrath. A handsomely sculpted face, broad shoulders, and a graceful gait could not conceal the anger and chaos that dwelled within.

No one answered the lord, though they all knew someone was going to pay for the silence.

Boom!

A blast from a smoldering censer above the god's head transformed seven high priests into piles of smoking ash. The aroma of burned incense overpowered the chamber.

Crackle!

Withering beams of darkness sprayed from the god's hands and dissolved six huge pit fiends from the planes of Gehenna into swirls of dust rolling across the polished granite floor.

Ssst!

A split-second of concentration changed five of the god's powerful evil wizards into pillars of salt in five different cities around the realm.

The god ranted, shouted, raved. No creature in the chamber could escape the tirade.

Several huge, warty fiends, more animal than human, foresaw their immediate futures and threw themselves at the feet of the god, shouting in unison.

"Bane, redeemer, boss, exalted one, you gotta get tough with those bums. You got the power. You got the magic. You just gotta make 'em notice you."

"Notice me? Isn't it enough that my agents create strife throughout Faerun? Isn't it enough that the hatred they foster has corrupted whole cities? What does a god have to do to get a little attention down there?"

Bane again slammed his fist on his throne. The intense rumbling of the chamber sent nearly every two-legged creature in the room crashing to the floor.

"You're doin' it right, but you need a new approach," the fiends groveled. "We'll help ya, and we'll get some wizards and some demi-powers to help ya. Before you know it, you'll have all the power and followers you want. All it takes is a little godlike act directed at some of those cities. We got a plan. . . ."

"Why didn't you say so before? I've been waiting for you so-called advisors to advise me! Get on with it!"

Bane slammed his fist on his knee, and a female sorceress who had tired him for a long time was struck by a lightning bolt. When the smoke cleared, nothing remained but a few scraps of charred silk from her gown.

The warty fiends leaned in close, but not too close, to their raging lord.

"Well, boss, this is how we see it. . . ."

# ❦1❦
## City in Turmoil

What started as a day of humid sunshine smelling of damp earth and the scent of things green and growing turned quickly into a day of severe, threatening weather. By noon, the brilliant blue sky was obscured by ominous, dense clouds. Black, boiling thunderheads followed, moving in with unnatural speed.

The citizens of Phlan had endured worse, and they took the storm in stride. Livestock was corralled, shutters bolted, and children were ordered to play indoors.

By suppertime, the countryside was drowning in torrential rains and hail. Intense winds blew clapboards off houses, tore branches off trees, and knocked over anything that wasn't securely fastened to the ground. Worst of all was the lightning that ripped through the sky and the thunder that shook buildings to their very foundations. Not even the oldest citizens could remember such a day. The druids who had predicted the sunny weather that morning were completely confused by the change in conditions. Nothing in their divinations had even hinted at bad weather.

As evening wore on, the storm's intensity grew. Lightning strikes set fire to a half-dozen homes, although the flames were drowned by the driving rains. Small trees were uprooted and tossed about like kindling.

Despite the late hour, few residents slept. Those who

were safely home and not assigned to guard duty on the city's walls found it impossible to sleep amid the clamor of rain and thunder and the buffeting winds. Most whiled away the hours in front of fires. The only thing to do was to wait for the storm to blow itself out.

Even with a full contingent of guards on the walls and most of Phlan's citizens wide awake, few were aware of a strange, magical force creeping over the city. From far across the continent, an invisible, silvery energy was forming a misty ring outside Phlan's impenetrable stone walls. The energy gradually grew and melded into shimmering tentacles, burrowing under the walls and around fieldstone foundations. As the force swelled, it formed a magical network beneath every structure in Phlan, wrapping around cellars and encircling storage pits. The invisible stranglehold tightened under the city as the storm pounded from above.

In one of Phlan's most famous residences, a sorceress paced the floor. A purple nightdress swished about her legs as she moved from window to window in the dimly lit room. From the top floor in her tower, she could normally see the entire city, but tonight the driving rain obscured lights in homes only fifty yards away. Blasts of lightning were the only reassurance that ·the rest of Phlan hadn't blown into the Moonsea.

"Come to bed, Shal. The storm will blow over whether you're awake or not." The voice of the wizard's sleepy husband drifted from beneath warm blankets, tempting her weary body.

The sorceress gripped the window sill. Her fingertips whitened as her grasp grew tighter. Frustrated, she stalked across the room to flop down on the bed.

"I can't sleep! This storm has my brain all stirred up. I feel as if I have thunder and lightning rattling through my veins." Shal rolled onto her side to face her husband.

Tarl propped himself up on one elbow. "I think you and the rest of the wizards in town should arrange a place to meet during storms like this. Then you can climb the walls together. Or levitate. Or fly around the room. Or—"

Tarl's words were snuffed out by thunder. Shal jolted, then sighed. "Magical powers are a wonderful thing, but when one's body is a channel for energy, storms like this can be brutal. You're lucky that clerics don't have this problem." The sorceress rolled over and buried her head under the pillow.

Tarl clamped his eyes shut as a lightning bolt tore across the sky. Blinking from the glare, he lifted a corner of the pillow and spoke softly to his wife. "Can I make you some tea or warm some milk . . . hey! What's the matter?" He pushed away the pillow and gently pulled Shal close. Enormous tears rolled down her face, and her body shuddered. Tarl shifted to sit up, holding his wife and rocking gently.

The cleric pushed away Shal's red tresses and whispered in her ear. "You've been through worse storms before, my sweet. What's wrong this time?" He continued rocking as the wizard sobbed, then gasped for air.

"I don't know. I feel . . . strange." Tears still rolled down her flushed cheeks.

"Are you sick?" Tarl asked, worried. His hand moved to her forehead.

Shal shook her head. "It's true, I've been through plenty of storms, but this one feels . . . *different.* I can't explain it." She buried her face against Tarl's arm.

Her husband kissed her hair gently, but he was genuinely alarmed. Few things scared Shal. After all the adventures and monsters she and Tarl had faced together, they both had nerves of steel that matched their tall, athletic bodies.

"What can I do to help, Shal? Can I get you anything?" Tarl stopped rocking and helped his wife sit up.

The sorceress shook her head. Sniffling, she looked at Tarl. "I guess all I can do is wait." She leaned against his muscled shoulder.

A loud bang startled Shal, and she leaped off the bed. The balcony door had blown open in the wind and was now swinging wildly as rain sprayed into the room. She sprinted across the chamber and caught hold of the door. After slamming it shut, a louder crash echoed in the chamber. The wizard stamped her foot as she saw that all six panes of glass in the door had shattered. "By the gods," she shrieked. "You'd think after ten years, I would have learned to control this magical temper of mine." She tiptoed among the shards on the slippery stone floor, and Tarl cringed as he watched her walk around the broken glass. Water blew in through the open door, and the curtains whipped wildly.

Shal shouted to Tarl over the wind. "Stay there so you don't cut your feet. I'll fix this in a jiffy!" She ran to her spellbook and began flipping pages. The water that dripped from her fingers and hair evaporated on contact with the magical tome. "Mend, mend . . . here it is." She closed her eyes in concentration.

A second time, the wizard dashed across the room and stepped around the glass to stand near the door. The sorceress repeated the words of the spell, and as Tarl watched, a purple mist flowed from her fingers and surrounded the fragments of glass. The pieces rose from the floor to assemble themselves into their proper positions. The six windows were restored and completely sealed. Shal closed the door carefully, locked it, and leaned her back against the panes. She was soaked to the skin, her nightdress clinging to her.

"Great trick, don't you think?" Shal was capable of magic of tremendous power, but still took delight in using spellcasting to conquer mundane chores. And the incident had temporarily distracted her troubled mind.

Tarl clambered out of bed and reached for an enormous towel. The sight of her body outlined under the wet, purple fabric was too much for him. "I think I know a way we can use up some of your excess energy," he said, a gleam in his eye.

Shal smiled as she grabbed the towel and rubbed it through her hair. Stripping off her wet gown, she wrapped the towel around her firm body. With a simple spell, she warmed a bottle of red wine, then poured mugs for herself and Tarl.

Her husband sat on the bed, beckoning. Shal always enjoyed the sight of his white-blond hair brushing his tanned shoulders. Handing him a mug, she sipped some wine. The wizard's towel dropped to the floor as lightning and thunder continued their assault.

* * * * *

Up on Phlan's protective wall, even the most seasoned guards trembled as lightning seared the black sky. This was the worst possible kind of weather for guard duty. But everyone knew the importance of the night watch. Besides, midnight would bring replacements and the warriors could go home to warm fires and dry clothes.

"Yeeow!" shouted a young soldier as a lightning bolt struck the ground only thirty yards from him. The red stone wall didn't so much as shiver from the blast. Two old guards, seventy years if they were a day, snorted and snickered as they paced in the downpour. The novice guard's look of surprise turned sheepish as he turned away from the grizzled oldtimers.

An ancient hand clamped down on the youth's shoulder, startling him. Whirling around, he stared at the two weathered, wrinkled faces. The taller of the two men spoke.

"Lookee here, Ston. The boy's beard ain't even growed in yet! And the poor fella's stuck on the wall on a night like this. What's yer name, son?" The face squinted at the fledgling.

"Uh, Jarad, sir," the boy stammered.

Now the shorter man spoke. "Well, Jarad, me lad, this be my friend, Tulen. Call me Ston. A boy like you needs someone old and wise to show you the ropes. Well, yer lucky, cuz you got two someones like that right here."

Tulen finished his friend's thought. "Stick with us, lad. We're nearly as old as these stone walls and we've seen just about as much. Save yer neck, it will, if you follow our lead." The ancient guards chuckled and turned to lean on the wall, one on either side of Jarad. As the wind whipped their gray beards and water streamed down oilskin ponchos, Ston and Tulen took advantage of their captive audience to tell tales of legendary battles.

The crusty guards were in the middle of the story of how Phlan came to be guarded by rings of walls when two wizards approached. Ston and Tulen chortled as they saw that the mages floated a few inches off the puddled stone. Invisible magic ovals surrounded the men, keeping them absolutely dry.

"Lookee what we got here," laughed Ston. Even Jarad had relaxed enough to chuckle.

"You ought to try the rain, youngsters," Tulen mocked. "It might wash the stink of sulphur and brimstone off you." The warriors exploded into a fit of laughter.

The first mage, dressed in mustard-colored robes, turned to his companion with a worried look. "Tarsis, do I stink of brimstone?" His companion, wearing a rust-orange cloak, looked first at his friend, then at the howling warriors.

"Don't pay any attention to them, Charan," he snapped. "They wouldn't know what to do with half our powers. And they obviously don't understand magic."

A lightning bolt as large as had ever been seen struck the center of the city. The thunder that accompanied it knocked Jarad and Ston off their feet. Tulen and the wizards cowered from the blinding light and the blast.

Suddenly all was still. The rain and wind stopped. Lightning no longer streaked overhead. The eerie silence that enveloped the city frightened even the old guards. Both drew swords and peered into the darkness.

"I'm goin' for Rakmar and his catapult crew!" Ston hissed. "Tulen, put these wizards to some use! Sound the alarm! And let's get some light on whatever's out there!" The stodgy warrior waddled down the wall with remarkable speed.

Tulen popped open a covered niche in the stone wall and reached for a crossbow and a pail stuffed with bolts. The missiles were enchanted with magical light that would break the inky blackness. Handing Jarad a crossbow, he ordered the youth to start firing. "Shoot high and long. Yer not trying to hit anything. We gotta get some lights out on the plains so's we can see what's comin'." Tulen himself started firing bolts as rapidly as he could load them. All along the wall, other warriors did the same, and soon the field beyond the walls was peppered with circles of bright light. Nothing seemed to be moving out in the darkness. Not a drop of rain fell from the sky.

"I don't get it," Jarad complained. "The rain stopped, so you're sounding the alarm?"

The old warrior answered without disrupting his loading and firing rhythm. "I'll explain later. Stick with me, kid. We're in for something ugly."

In the unnatural silence, the sound of boots on the wet stone announced Ston's return. Throwing off his poncho, he reached for a crossbow and started firing onto the field. "The word is out. The militia's up in full force."

Tulen sighed in relief and fired the last bolt from the bucket. The men hauled out three pails of normal bolts, loaded their weapons, and peered over the wall, waiting.

\* \* \* \* \*

In the wizard's tower, husband and wife lay wrapped in warm blankets and each other. Tarl could feel Shal's pounding pulse, but she was calmer than before.

"Tarl, we've seen a lot of adventure in our lives, but are you ever unhappy that we never had children?"

The cleric was taken aback. This subject had a way of popping up when he was least prepared. He tried to soothe Shal although he wasn't sure of his own feelings. "If the gods want us to have children, we'll have children."

"But we—"

"Shhh. Don't think about it right now. You need to relax and try to sleep." Shal opened her mouth, but Tarl pressed a finger to her lips. The wizard gave up and settled into his arms.

The tower suddenly shook as a colossal lightning bolt struck the center of Phlan. "Did you feel that?" Tarl asked. "Really, my love—"

"Shut up, Tarl! Let me out of bed!" Shal whipped back the blankets, jumped to her feet, and paced over to a wardrobe. "Oh gods, something horrible has happened. I just know it. Tarl, get dressed. We have to go outside." The sorceress was already tugging a robe over her head. The cleric blinked at her, confused.

"Shal, it's all right. It's only the storm."

"It's not the storm! Something dire has happened. I can sense it. Please, please put some clothes on. We have to go out. Hurry!"

Tarl shambled over to his wife, whose eyes were filling with tears. "It's alright, sweetheart. I believe you. We'll go out." He yanked on breeches and a tunic and pulled on a pair of boots. Reaching for a heavy warhammer, he took his wife's hand and led the way down the stairs.

"Listen," she said ominously. "The rain stopped."

* * * * *

Phlan's walls were a flurry of motion. Troops moved through drills they had practiced dozens of times. All around the city walls, the fields and grasslands were dotted with magical lights that would betray the approach of any enemy. Tar-covered logs stood ready to be lighted and dropped on foot soldiers who might attempt to climb the wall. Baskets of sharp caltrops were scattered onto the ground, waiting to pierce the feet of advancing troops. Catapult teams loaded and cranked down enormous buckets of rock without waiting to catch first sight of the enemy.

"Hssst. Ston! See anything?" Tulen's voice was a gravelly whisper.

"Nothin'. That's what scares me."

"Uh . . . gentlemen," Jarad stammered. "Where did the

moon go?"

"What?"

"The moon. It's gone. It was hard to see anyway—what with the storm and all—but the clouds have broken and, uh, it's completely gone."

"He's right, Tulen. Look up. No moon. No clouds. Whooo, I've got a baaaaad feeling about this."

"Steady yerselves, men. Yer as nervous as bridegrooms. We're tougher than anything that's out there."

"Ha!" Ston spat. "Sorcery! I know it is. I can feel it. Give me critters to fight, and I'm happy. Orcs, skeletons, even a dragon or two—I'll battle 'em—but keep that magic stuff away. It's too creepy. Why, I remember—"

"Shush!" Tulen ordered. "Listen!"

As the men squinted over the wall, hundreds of soldiers materialized within the circle of lights. The soldiers did not ride out of the darkness; instead, they sprang up as if growing from the grass itself.

"I knew it! I told you! Sorcery!" Ston gurgled.

"Shut up and start firing!" Tulen punched his friend. "We've been in worse!" Already, two bolts had whooshed out of Tulen's crossbow.

Farther down the wall stood the city's largest gates. Named the Death Gates by Phlan's citizens in honor of the thousands of monsters and mercenaries who had died there over the years, they were usually the hub of any battle.

As enemy warriors swarmed toward the walls, they were greeted by barrels of hot oil pouring down from above. As the liquid spread, wizards flew high out of reach of the attackers, casting spells to ignite the oil. Blazes flared; grass, walls, and soldiers were caught in the flames. The enemy troops were driven back by the intense heat.

The volley of crossbow fire never ceased. As more attackers arrived, more and more of the enemy fell to the expert aim of Phlan's crossbowmen.

When the flames along the wall died, the enemy renewed its press. The city's heavy artillery teams ignited the tar-coated logs and dropped them over the wall. Dozens of enemies were crushed and burned, and dozens more were turned back.

\* \* \* \* \*

Far from the field of battle, far from danger, the wizard who commanded the enemy forces watched the assault. He was gleeful—an odd thing since his troops were dying in great numbers and his forces had not yet struck a telling blow. The denizens of Phlan did not suspect the worst: the wizard's magic had stolen the entire city and dropped it into a cavern deep below his tower. Bane would be pleased. The wizard would gain more power than he ever dreamed possible.

It only remained to conquer Phlan's citizens and strip away their souls using the pool of darkness. He assumed those tasks were to be the easiest parts of his plot.

His troops were formidable. Humans were shoulder to shoulder with pig-faced orcs. Scaly lizard men fought alongside bug-eyed goblins and hobgoblins. Every soldier was tough and battle-hardened. They had the proper respect for their leader, a Red Wizard from the faraway land of Thay. The troops had been offered an enormous amount of gold for an easy mission. In addition to their payment, they would be allowed any loot they could carry away.

The wizard pounded a fist. "Where are my fiends?"

Instantly a black mist formed next to the angry sorcerer. Within moments, it writhed and coalesced into a twelve-foot-tall ebony horror, whose rumbling voice startled the wizard. "Your bidding, Lord Marcus?"

The Red Wizard glared at his servant. "We're looking bad out there!" he hissed. "Summon your minions and get busy! Those weaklings can't stand up to the power of a pit fiend and his hellish followers. Your unit alone should scare them into surrender! Now go!" Marcus pounded his fist again. His face flushed crimson to match his robes.

The winged monstrosity nodded at its master. It flexed its banded muscles and stretched its arms and feet, revealing sharp talons larger than a man's hand. Green ooze dripped from two tusks protruding from the beast's mouth. As the liquid splashed to the ground, wisps of smoke arose from the blackened earth. Although the creature resembled a gargoyle, anyone could see that its power was a hundredfold greater. The monster's crusty skin creaked and scraped as it called out for its minions. Black sparks leaped from its body.

One by one, other black forms from the bowels of the Nine Hells arrived. Foul clouds of mist formed around the pit fiend, swirling into solid forms. Dwarfed by their master, the three-foot-tall beasts were nonetheless horrifying to behold. Vaguely human in shape, each had spiky wings and a tail. The monsters hopped about on sharply taloned feet as a smell like charred flesh filled the air. Each of the twelve creatures carried a sharpened black trident. The mob slobbered and hissed in anticipation of the impending onslaught.

The Red Wizard's rage turned to a gloat. "Spinagons! What fine creatures! These beasts will terrify the puny mortals! Now go! My prize will be the souls of Phlan, and I do not intend to wait!" Marcus's eyes blazed, and he waved a hand at the hideous assembly. The pit fiend flapped its wings and lifted off the ground, its minions following closely.

\* \* \* \* \*

The defenders of Phlan were turning back their attackers with ease. Bodies piled up outside the walls, while less than a dozen city guards had been pronounced dead by the priests. Many of Phlan's wounded were healed by clerics and soon returned to their posts. Those who were seriously injured were carried to churches that stood ready to serve as infirmaries.

Catapult teams tirelessly fired and reloaded their weapons. Archers delivered a constant stream of arrows into the charging enemies. Wizards arrived from all over the city and hovered high above the battle, casting spells of fire, lightning, ice, and magical energy. The hobgoblin troops in the enemy forces broke ranks and fled the field.

At the Death Gates, cries of triumph rose over the clash of battle and carried down the walls.

"Tarl's come!"

"Master Tarl is here to help save the city!"

"Tarl is fighting at the Death Gates!"

The cleric blushed at the accolades and turned to his wife. "By the gods, when you're right, you're right! We've got trouble! Go find yourself a good spot and rain purple death on whatever's out there!" He reached up to kiss Shal's cheek. His wife magically elevated to join the other wizards high above.

Heading toward the stairs leading to the top of the wall, Tarl paused. "Blast it. Brother Anton took the Holy Warhammer of Tyr to the Ceremony of Spring, and I sure could use it now. But this one will have to do." Gripping his hammer, he charged up the stairs. Nearing the top, a glowing blue warhammer appeared in his hand, replacing the one that had been there only moments before. "What? I'm the only one who can summon this weapon, but I didn't call for it yet. At least, I don't think I called for it." Looking at the familiar weapon, Tarl shrugged. "Well, you're here now! Let's make Tyr proud!" The cleric of the god of justice dove into the fray.

The clash and fury of battle was so great that most defenders didn't notice a faint glowing mist forming high above the city. The wizards were the first to see it. Half a dozen spells were cast at it to discern its nature.

The mist appeared to have no other purpose than to provide light. As the cloud grew, its intensity increased until the city was lit as brightly as if it were midafternoon. Puzzling as that was, the spellcasters continued to shower spells down on the attackers. Then one of the sorcerers far out over the field shouted a cry of alarm.

In the distance, thirteen black spots appeared high in the air. As they closed in, flapping wings could be detected. A new cry arose from many of the wizards. "Fiends! There are fiends heading this way!" The sorcerers flew toward each other and arrayed themselves into a gigantic sphere, each facing outward. In this formation, they could attack the beasts from any angle of approach.

Facing the front of the battle, Shal aimed four purple lightning bolts toward the attack force. The wizards around her continued to rain their own magic onto the enemy. In Phlan, it was common for wizards to adopt a particular hue to use as a magical signature, so streaks of blue, yellow, orange, pink, and red streamed from the assembled mages in a beautiful but deadly display.

Below, on the city's wall, Ston hollered at his friend.

"Lookee, Tulen! Purple magic! Lady Shal has arrived, and she's blastin' those critters!" The ancient warrior fairly hopped with excitement.

"I thought you hated sorcery, you old goat!" Tulen chided.

"Fool! Of course I hate it, but not when it's on our side!" Ston chortled and fired his crossbow.

"Lookee what else we got, Ston! Big trouble overhead!" The grizzled warrior pointed to the swarm of spinagons and their massive leader. "Time for some fancy shootin'! Pay attention, Jarad, me boy!"

The oldtimers took aim, waiting for the creatures to approach. They stood perfectly still, fingers on triggers. At last the beasts drew near, and the men could release their missiles.

Both bolts whizzed toward the monsters, scoring their marks. Instead of sinking deep into the black flesh, however, the bolts bounced off and tumbled to the ground. Other arrows, catapult loads, and hurled daggers found their targets but also careened away. The monsters didn't so much as miss a wingflap and returned the favor by firing poisoned tail spikes at Phlan's troops.

As the leather-winged monsters flapped boldly toward the weakened defenders, a magical assault took shape, streaming toward the incoming horrors. Magical bolts of every size and color seared toward the unholy mob. A third of the energies fizzled uselessly away, but the remainder hissed and popped against the fiends in a rainbow of death. A purple streak blasted two spinagons, bowling them over and knocking them helplessly to the ground, where they exploded in a shower of cinders. A yellow and a blue streak each destroyed another spinagon. The mass of fiends broke formation and flapped around the sphere of wizards, hurling poisoned tail spikes. They bounced off the enormous shield of magical protection that surrounded the wizards and crumbled to dust.

A quarter of an hour and dozens of spells later, the last of the spinagons tumbled to the ground. The pit fiend roared in anger, circling to retreat. Its minions had wounded some of the defenders, but this city was proving to be unusually tough. Half the citizens should have run in fear at the mere sight of the creatures from the Nine Hells. But even the fiends' dreaded magical attacks had been deflected with little harm.

The seething pit fiend flapped away from Phlan, back toward the waiting Marcus.

Cries of victory erupted from the walls as the last monster flew away. The troops turned toward the more mundane battle with new energy.

Moments later, the soldiers that remained on the battlefield also broke ranks and turned to run. Catapult loads and arrows followed them until the soldiers were beyond the perimeter of lighted crossbow bolts. The cheer that arose in Phlan was deafening.

As the shouts subsided, Tarl looked slowly about, surveying the walls for damage. His mouth fell open as he was struck by the reality of what had occurred. The entire city of Phlan, walls and all, was in an impossibly huge cavern.

"Look, Master Tarl! Someone has stolen the skies over Phlan!"

The cleric took a deep breath. "No one has stolen our skies, friend. They've stolen us."

Shal settled out of the air to stand next to her husband, confirming his statement with a nod. Though their situation looked grim, both adventurers knew that the danger had only begun.

# ❧ 2 ❧

## Chilling Dreams

One hundred miles to the north of the spot where Phlan had stood, a seasoned ranger camped in a tight grove of pine trees amid the violent gales and lightning. The warrior slept soundly despite the weather, but haunting images of danger played through his mind, causing him to toss and turn.

"Shal! Look out!" The ranger sat up in the darkness, screaming, as lightning struck a nearby pine. "Tarl! There's something—" He stopped as he realized that he didn't know what he was about to say next. Rain sprayed through the evergreen branches and rolled off the canvas propped over the ranger's bedroll.

Three times in the last four weeks, Ren had dreamed the same nightmare. Now his head dropped into his hands, and he rubbed his forehead, as if clearing the images from his mind. His pulse thumped in his temples.

Ren shook his head hard. Water spun off his hair in all directions. Despite the lean-to, he was wet from head to toe. The relentless wind drove the rain under every leaf and into every crevice.

"Why do I keep having that dream?" Ren spoke aloud, even though no one was around to hear. Reaching for his sword, he scanned the trees and listened, alert for any passing orcs that may have heard his scream.

Several tense moments went by, but no creatures approached. Satisfied, Ren arose in the darkness and packed his wet gear. Even the equipment inside his backpack was damp. The rain and storms hadn't let up for over four weeks. The seasoned ranger wondered if he would ever dry out again.

His mount, a huge war-horse named Stolen, shook its wet mane and flicked its tail. Then Stolen stood stoically as Ren loaded the saddlebags and patted the massive horse. "Stolen, old boy, it's probably better that we're awake. The orcs will be out, crawling these woods. Time to get busy hunting them." As he swung onto the war-horse, he thought to himself, What a time to be having nightmares. Just when I've got a job to do.

A little more than four weeks earlier, Ren had petitioned the council of Glister to settle a nearby valley. Like most rangers, Ren didn't believe in the ownership of land. A person could settle the land, care for it, even drive out unwanted creatures. But the land would outlast anyone who might claim to own it. Ren merely asked for the right to live there undisturbed.

After several long hours of verbal parrying and thrusting with Glister's council, he had come away with an agreement. If Ren eliminated the bands of marauding orcs that terrorized the region, he would be awarded a charter to live in the valley in peace. The council had offered the ranger the use of Glister's own troops, but Ren preferred to work alone. Now he trotted through the forest on his war-horse, quite alone and quite wet.

Ren sighed as he thought of the Glister council. He had done his best to make a good impression. The ranger had walked into the chambers that morning in a suit of gleaming chain mail of fine elven craftsmanship. His magical daggers, called Left and Right, were visibly sticking out of his dragonskin boots. A two-handed long sword hung in its sheath across his back, and a shimmering elven cloak of displacing was draped over one arm. His gauntlets, equipment belt, and bracers, also made of dragon hide, were shining and well oiled. Standing six-foot-six, the ranger's impressive equipment and his gray-peppered beard spoke volumes about his skills and experience. But if Ren was a man of action, he had always been a simple speaker. Looking back, the ranger wondered if his mission might have been easier if he had appeared slightly less capable.

"Like the way I look now," Ren muttered. His hair and beard were shaggy and plastered to his head by the rain. His elven chain mail was caked with mud, as were his dragonskin boots and gauntlets. Grass and pine needles clung to the mud and stuck to his wet leggings. Even the huge war-horse looked bedraggled. "Well, maybe the enemy will underestimate my fighting abilities," he said half-heartedly. Stolen trotted through the trees.

Ren had been pushing the war-horse as hard as he dared in the darkness. He had scouted the land carefully earlier that day and knew where the orcs were gathering. Leaving Stolen in a circle of trees, the ranger crawled to a rise high above the encampment.

Slowly the ranger peered over the hillock. A ring of watchfires illuminated the valley. What had been a small brook flowing into the lowland was enlarged by the rain into a wide stream, but the marshy conditions didn't seem to bother the orcs. They were beginning to arise from soggy tents, gathering about a central bonfire.

"Ren, you sorry thief, what have you gotten yourself into now?" He groaned as he tried to hold his grip in the mud and keep his face out of the water. He tried to console himself by thinking that the mud covering him would serve as a useful camouflage.

As he watched, more and more orcs joined the circle around the fire. As the surveillance wore on, Ren's mind wandered to his recurrent nightmare. The ranger hadn't thought about Shal and Tarl for months. The three of them were good friends, but their paths had diverged after they'd killed the evilly charmed bronze dragon controlling an army of orcs and ogres that were menacing Phlan. When Shal and Tarl became lovers, Ren felt out of place. They had parted friends and sent messages back and forth, but ten years had passed in the meantime. Ren hadn't seen his friends in three years.

The images from the nightmare lingered. He could see Shal and Tarl looking a little older than the last time he'd seen them. The two were in Denlor's Tower, in their bed. An enormous, gut-wrenching earth tremor and a crash of thunder was shaking the place. Shal leaped out of bed, naked, and ran to a grab a purple cloak filled with pouches. Tarl followed, pulled on his clothes, and reached for his shield and warhammer. The nightmare shifted to reveal Shal casting streams of violet energy at an unseen enemy and Tarl fighting something dark and horrible. Ren's own screams always awakened him before he could learn what terrors his friends faced.

The first time he had dreamed about Shal and Tarl the ranger was disturbed, but this third nightmare left him truly shaken. Ren wasn't one to have visions of any kind, so he was terribly afraid for his two friends.

Now he cursed the charter to which he had agreed. Ren was forced to devote all his energy to clearing out the orcs until the job was done. If he hadn't given his sworn and signed word to terms made clear on the vellum he carried, he would have dumped the responsibility, forsaken his quest to settle the valley, and sought his friends to make sure they were safe.

After the second dream, Ren had begun taking risks he normally wouldn't have taken. Any skilled ranger could battle five or ten orcs without fear. An average warrior orc stood about five feet tall and was usually armored in anything it could steal from its victims. Orcs liked using arrows and slings rather than getting close to the enemy to battle with swords or axes, so at close range most of them were lousy fighters.

But the ranger knew from experience that orcs liked to travel in packs, and the larger the pack, the bolder the orcs. Because Ren was worried about his friends, he'd started attacking packs of ten to thirty orcs. The ranger's tactics were particularly reckless, but the size of the orc bands made such attacks especially dangerous. A few orcs always managed to escape and warn other bands, so that eventually the hunter had become the hunted.

In the weeks that followed, Ren had discovered many traps set by the orcs, although his keen eyes and sharp tracking skills helped him avoid the cruder snares. Ren had spent the last two decades in the woods, and only the elves and the native woodland creatures were more skilled at moving stealthily through the forests.

Ren had considered returning to Glister to lead its troops into battle against the orcs, but he would have suffered an unbearable delay. By the time he arrived in Glister, organized the militia, and led them back to the hills, he would have lost more than five days. All his scouting would have been for nothing—the orcs would have moved away and set new traps. Besides, Ren trusted his instincts and disliked worrying about the welfare of companions.

Forcing his mind back to the task at hand, Ren peered over the hill. He caught sight of seven different totems, each representing a different orc warband. Ren was well aware of this custom, because he had captured sixteen such orc totems and hidden them back on the trail. Later on they would be proof to the council that the ranger had done his job.

Squinting through the rain and darkness, the ranger saw captured dwarves in slave pens at one end of the camp. The dwarven warriors had obviously been tortured; their long beards and hair had been hacked off. Something would have to be done to save them, and quickly. He would have to devise a plan to free the dwarves or, as a last resort, put them out of their misery before the orcs subjected them to painful deaths.

Three of the larger orc totems concerned Ren. These were different from the others he had encountered. They were centered in the middle of heavily guarded tents. Half-orcs roamed around them.

"Now there's a completely different breed," the ranger muttered to himself. "I hope the next time I want to sign a charter a lightning bolt comes down and—"

Crash! A lightning bolt split the sky, and the rest of Ren's sentence was lost in the thunder. The rain poured more heavily, drumming on Ren's armor. He clamped his mouth shut and thought better of saying anything more. He was in no position to push his luck.

Ren sighed. Half-orcs. These crossbreeds were taller, smarter, and fiercer than their cousins. The totems told Ren there were at least three powerful bands of half-orcs in the valley, heavily armed and well organized. The ranger looked around for any nearby guards. Half-orcs were usually smart enough to post perimeter guards.

A lengthy scan revealed one guard crouched under a tree about fifty yards away. Hunkered down under its tarp, it wasn't paying attention to anything but the rain. Ren didn't have to worry about that one immediately.

Then the ranger spied a band of hill giants. They were hard to miss, since none stood shorter than twelve feet tall. Hill giants weren't known to be very bright, but what they lacked in brains, they made up in muscle. They lived by terrorizing communities of humans and other "smaller" people. Primitive in appearance, each sported overly long arms that, combined with their stooped posture, meant their knuckles nearly scraped the ground. Their low foreheads resembled those of apes. Ren had fought a few hill giants in his day. He knew they were slow and not impossible to kill, but taking on this large of a contingent—he counted nearly forty—would be nothing less than suicide.

The ranger groaned. He had no other choice but to turn back to Glister and form a small army of men and dwarves to take to the valley. But if he left now, the captured dwarves would surely suffer unspeakable horrors at the hands of the orcs. On the other hand, if those forty dwarves with their armor and weapons were on Ren's side, the story might be different. Forty dwarves and a skilled ranger might conquer the monster army.

"Now what do I do? You'd better think of something in a hurry, ranger. Hmmm. Now that's not a bad idea," Ren muttered under his breath. "I'll kill the guard, and meanwhile, I'll think up a typically brilliant plan to kill an army of orcs, half-orcs, and giants all by myself." The confidence he heard in his voice was greater than the confidence he felt in his gut.

Crawling through the mud on his belly and then on hands and knees, Ren made his way to the brush near the orc's tree. He was grateful for the rain and thunder that hid the sound of his movements. Rising to his feet but keeping low, he cautiously approached the guard, planting each foot solidly so as not to slip in the mud.

The orc had chosen his position well. His post overlooked the north end of the valley and was in view of two other trails leading to the camp. Had it not been for the rain, Ren would have been an easy target.

The ranger was within thirty yards of the orc when the mud gave way under his feet and he fell with a loud splash. The orc leaped to its feet with bow in hand. It nocked an arrow before Ren could react.

Too late the orc learned a lesson about soggy bow strings. They behaved a lot like wet noodles; neither hurled killing arrows very far.

The look of surprise on the orc's ugly face as his arrow hit the ground at his feet was nothing compared to the expression on his face when, a moment later, Ren's two-handed sword cut him in half. Ren's blood was pumping at his brush with death.

The ranger grabbed the arrows from the orc's quiver, ran through the mud to his war-horse, and drew out his longbow. Ren wasn't as skilled with the longbow as other rangers. In contests, he'd seen skilled bowmen hit discs of wood hurled up in the air one hundred and fifty yards away. Ren could never hit such targets from more than seventy-five yards. The orcish arrows he had stolen had to fly only one hundred yards, but their targets were stationary and much larger than a four-inch circle of wood.

The ranger's bow strings were coated with beeswax and were safely dry inside a pouch. Ren knew they would be effective for a short time, even in the rain. If his plan failed, the warrior had nothing to lose. He ordered Stolen to follow quietly, then walked to the ridge.

The storm was at its worst. Lightning shattered the sky, thunder rattled the valley, and rain poured down in sheets. The ranger peered down the hill and discovered a clear line of sight to the orcs as they huddled together in clumps. Partially sheltered by a white oak, Ren launched arrow after arrow into the small army below. He hurried the attack to prevent his own bow from becoming useless and to give the impression of multiple archers confronting the army.

The effect of a black-feathered orc arrow arriving out of nowhere and thunking into the chest or leg of another orc was more than Ren could have hoped. Like a swarm of angry bees, the orcs screamed and began drawing weapons. Ren knew the only thing orcs hated as much as dwarves and humans were other orc tribes. As the arrows landed amongst them, the creatures naturally assumed they were being attacked by some other orcish tribe in the valley. Ren saved the last few arrows for the hill giants. These stupid beasts quickly decided they were being double-crossed by the orcs.

In moments, monsters were fighting with monsters and the valley was a swarm of battling giants and orcs. As Ren fired the last arrow, he worried about what to do next. If he rushed down to free the captives, it might distract the orcs and giants and force them to join together. If he stayed on the hill, he might be too late to save the dwarves.

Ren watched the struggle. The half-orcs made short work of the smaller orcs, and the battle quickly switched to half-orcs against giants. The swirl of melee moved to the south end of the valley. The orcs were hampered by the mud and the stream cutting through the valley, but the giants barely noticed these obstacles. Every strike by a giant crushed an orc warrior. The giants had to suffer dozens of orcish blows before teetering into the mud.

Ren saw his opportunity. Mounting his horse, he charged down the hill, waving his sword. The razor-sharp edge sliced through the bindings on the slave pens and the gates popped open.

"Run for your lives while the fools are busy." Ren shouted. But the ranger had forgotten about the hatred these dwarves held for their captors. Every one of the forty wounded, exhausted warriors picked up an orcish weapon and shield, and charged straight into the battle.

The mounted ranger was left without a choice. If the dwarves were determined to fight, honor demanded he be at their side. But astride his horse, he was at a disadvantage against the giants. Leaping off his mount, he left the horse in the shelter of the slave pens. Gripping his sword, he charged into battle behind the dwarves.

Amid the clamor of battle, a chant arose. In all his years of battles, Ren had never fought side by side with dwarves. He now learned that some dwarves go to their deaths singing.

The unarmored dwarves chanted a steady, low hymn of battle and bravery. The rhythm of the song coordinated the dwarves' attacks and united them into a single killing force. Hill giants and orcs alike were confused by the sudden influx of the dwarven fighters and by their apparently joyful song. The dwarves seemed charged by the tune. Every evidence of weariness evaporated. As Ren rushed into the fight against the hill giants, he heard the pounding of the rain, the grunts and groans of monsters, clanging weapons, and above everything, the amazing dwarven song. And most remarkably of all, he found himself energized by the tension in the air.

The battle became a swirl of arms and legs, but mostly giant legs. Ren swung, hit, dodged, and jumped without thinking. The dwarven voices carried him along. He never slowed. The blows from the ranger's sword found many targets and often ended the lives of the giants he struck. The dwarves had to work much harder with their orcish weapons, but the giants constantly missed the short, ducking creatures. The stocky warriors dodged in and out between the legs of their foes.

For a long time, it was impossible to tell which side was winning. Being a practical man, Ren was ready to lead the retreat if it looked like his allies were in trouble. But after a time, there seemed to be more and more dwarves and fewer giants battling. Ren became the lead figure in a wedge of death boring through the ranks of the giants and half-orcs.

And then only one hill giant was left. Panting, Ren moved toward the armored foe. The singing stopped suddenly, and the ranger heard a gravely shout behind him: "Back off, human. This one's mine."

Ren looked over his shoulder to see fifteen dwarves, all that remained of the forty that had entered the fray.

The speaker was the biggest and strongest of the lot, but obviously battle-weary. In one hand he held a shield too large for his short frame, and in the other hand he grasped a hill giant's spiked club. Even Ren would have struggled to wield such a club. The dwarf swung the weapon in his hand like a small mallet.

"He and his tribe stripped our mine and killed many of my people. I will have the final revenge on him. And nothing will stop me."

The tone of his voice and the fire in his eyes left no question that anyone arguing would become his enemy. Ren lowered his sword and backed away.

The dwarf began his chant. The remaining dwarves took up the song, but stayed a respectful distance away from the two opponents.

The last giant was also obviously some type of leader. The sixteen-foot-tall creature was armored from head to foot in bronze plate mail. The armor surprised Ren, since hill giants weren't normally intelligent enough to make use of anything more complicated than animal skins for clothing. It must have been made or stolen from a band of ogres or evil humans. Ren was also curious about the baton of bronze the hill giant carried.

Between the dwarf and the giant, there was no fencing, no circling, no testing each other's skills. There was only raw hatred, spawned from generations of conflict with the other's race. The dwarf threw down his shield and ran at the giant as fast as his stout legs could bear him. The hill giant tossed away his shield too and smashed at the earth with his baton. Huge sprays of mud and water flew into the air with every blow. Both foes lunged at each other with all their might. The baton sailed toward the head of the dwarf, and the dwarf's club crushed the chest of the bending giant. Both were dead before they hit the ground.

Ren shook his head over the waste of the dwarf's life. It was as if the warrior wanted to die in battle to remove the stain of being captured by an enemy. There was no logic to the sacrifice, but hatred was rarely logical.

Another gravelly voice diverted his attention. "Human, what is your name?"

"Ren o' the Blade. What are your friends doing?" he asked, watching the remaining dwarves moving slowly around the battlefield.

"We never leave a battlefield without killing any wounded enemies or those faking death. It is our way. We owe you a debt of steel and blood. Such things aren't taken lightly by my kind."

A thought came to the ranger. "If you feel you owe me a debt, I'll consider it settled if you'll take these orc totems to the human settlement of Glister. I've hidden more totems in the woods. If you'll collect them all and present them along with this charter to the council there, I'd be most grateful. You can tell them Ren has accomplished his mission. Will you do this?"

"We would do this and much more. We have heard about the ranger who kills orcs for the right to settle in the Valley of the Falls. Know this day you have become a warrior brother to all our kin. We will spread the word about you to our brethren." The dwarf bowed respectfully. Ren flushed at the honor.

For the next few hours, Ren helped the dwarves bury their dead. The orcs and giants were left to the elements. At first, Ren thought about looting the bodies of the orcs, but he knew the dwarves would view such actions as dishonorable and disgusting.

"By the gods, I'm tired," the ranger said.

"It is the weariness of battle and victory. We feel it also. But we dwarves welcome the exhaustion. It feels good because it makes us feel alive." A throaty, hoarse chuckle came from the dwarf, and Ren realized it was the first time he had ever heard one laugh.

"For all eternity, we will make sure the Valley of the Falls belongs to you and your children, Ren. On this you have the promise of the dwarves." The dwarf spoke so solemnly that the ranger couldn't doubt the sincerity of his new friends.

Ren exchanged hearty handshakes with the dwarves and mounted his war-horse. He galloped through the woods without looking back. He would return in a few weeks after finding Shal and Tarl and enjoying a long, peaceful visit. His mind told him he would find them safe and well, but his heart nagged that something was terribly wrong in the city of Phlan.

# ♣ 3 ♣

# City of Unrest

In the war-torn streets of Phlan, residents were busy with last-minute shopping and trading. Evening approached. Although night and day were artificial in the gods-forsaken cavern, the citizens knew darkness might mean a new battle at the city walls. They wisely observed a self-imposed curfew and rarely ventured out after dark.

Among the hustling villagers was a tall, white-haired man. The whiteness of his hair belied his age, but his muscled frame erased any question of his youth. He had spent the day inspecting the city walls, troops, and weapons.

He ducked into a bakery, accidentally slamming the door behind him with a bang.

"Afternoon, Tarl. You sure know how to make an entrance," chuckled a slender, elderly woman. "Usually the bell above the door is enough for us to know you're here."

Tarl smiled, embarrassed. "Sorry about that, Celie. I've got a lot on my mind lately. But I'll sleep better knowing our troops are well-equipped and morale is high. Now, do you have any tarts left to improve *my* morale?"

The woman behind the counter rattled off the list of her remaining baked goods. Tarl made his selections, and Celie began to load them into his basket. "You really should be heading home, Celie, while people are still on the streets. A woman your size could be carried off in a hurry by one of those fiends that attacked a few days ago." Tarl never failed to wonder how a woman who had been a baker all her life could stay so thin.

"You're my last customer, Tarl. Once you're on your way, I'm going to bolt the shutters and head for home. My cats will probably be wondering where I am." Celie added up Tarl's purchases.

Without a word, Tarl went to latch the bakery's shutters. Their stout oak wouldn't be much good against fiends or magical fire, but bolting the shutters somehow felt right amid the chaos of life in the cavern. When Tarl was finished, Celie scolded him. "Now, you know you didn't have to do that. I'd have gotten to it."

"Can't have anything happen to the best bakery on the Moonsea, now can we? And I'll be walking you home, Celie. No arguing."

Celie made a face, though she knew Tarl was right. Tarl paid for his purchases, then Celie asked if he wouldn't mind locking the back door for her. While his back was turned, she slipped a large poppyseed cake, his wife's favorite, into his basket.

They locked the shop together, then headed into the streets. Celie's home was a little out of the way, but Tarl didn't care.

As they walked, Tarl told Celie of his pleasure at the readiness of the troops. He could see the relief on her face as he described the city's condition.

"Phlan has never looked stronger. We may be stuck in some magical hole, but we're prepared for any type of battle. The priests have all been blessing buckets and buckets of arrows and crossbow bolts. They're the best thing next to magic to destroy fiends.

"The walls are solid and weren't damaged at all when we were transported here. We lost less than two dozen men and women during the first attack. Our food stores look good. I'm certain we can weather this disaster like we have the other battles that have found Phlan."

With Celie safely inside her cottage, Tarl gripped his basket and turned for home. Despite the late hour, Tarl stopped to help Celie's neighbors shutter their windows and rescue a cat trapped on a roof.

As Tarl hurried through the streets, he noticed a crowd gathered in a tiny square. Wondering what would keep these folks out in the streets at such a late hour, he approached.

Tarl recognized an ancient warrior named Garanos standing on a stone bench, addressing the crowd. The people seemed restless, but they were listening intently. Garanos was a renowned hero of Phlan and perhaps its oldest warrior. His tone was proud and inspiring.

"Even the flight of dragons three centuries ago did not destroy our city. We refused to surrender, in spite of the horrors and the sieges. We have always been a strong, spirited people. Our ancestors accepted disasters as a way of life, but fought hard and conquered even the worst enemies.

"No wizard or scholar in all of Faerun could explain why hundreds of dragons would take to the skies and wreak devastation on the countryside. But Phlan survived and rebuilt after the dragon attacks. That was before my great-great-grandfather was born. Phlan became an important trade center and sailing port. Merchants came to depend on our waters. But we all know that this progress was not without a price.

"The influence of humans stirred up the creatures living in the older ruins of Phlan. But even the nightly raids that killed hundreds did not cause Phlan to collapse. Our relatives banded together to save their city. Hordes of creatures streamed down from the north, from the Dragonspine Mountains and the Grey Land of Thar. Still Phlan refused to yield. Our city became an armed camp. Fortifications were built. The rings of walls that we now call home were constructed to stop the attacks of monsters. Those walls have protected us for decades, and they protect us still."

Garanos noticed Tarl standing at the back of the crowd. He shouted to the cleric to join him. Those who watched also began chanting Tarl's name. Flushing slightly, Tarl wound through the throng and stepped up onto the bench.

"Noble citizens," Tarl began, "you have every reason to be proud of Phlan's past and be hopeful for her future. Time and war have reddened our stone walls, but like those stones, we must stand firm.

"For the past three hundred years, since the flight of dragons, our city has grown stronger and prospered despite repeated attacks. Armies of slavering, headhunting orcs, squads of evil mercenaries, and packs of enchanted monsters all have tried to breach Phlan's defenses. Attacks have come night and day, in rain, snow, and fog. But our ancestors never surrendered.

"Serving on the walls in defense of the city became a high honor in which every citizen took pride. Phrases like, " 'I was at the wall during the breaching of the full moon,' or 'I was at the wall during the hydra attack,' became common badges of courage. Sections of the walls still bear names like Orc's Bane, Denlor's Last Stand, Beholder Massacre, or Bonemarch.

"I inspected the northern gates, those we call the Death Gates, only this morning. They stand as strong as ever. Many of you oldtimers will remember the history of those gates. They started out as the North Gates. They were renamed the Black Company Gates after five hundred mercenaries died battling a horde of ogres. Then the name became the Goblin Spine Gates after an army of goblins and orcs tried to rip them apart and storm the city. Ogre Gates, Fire Giant Gates, and Beholder Gates were all used at one time or another to mark the horrors that have attacked Phlan. Eventually, they became known as the Death Gates. The name stays with us and feels right to all those who defend the city."

Tarl stopped as an old wizard floated out of the sky and landed on the bench beside the two men. The crowd applauded as they recognized Auranzath, a powerful wizard and self-appointed town historian. Orange robes and a black beard fluttered around him.

"See here now," Auranzath croaked. "It sounds to me like you folk are runnin' like scared chickens! What would your grandpappys say? They saw times worse than this and never complained! They had a job to do and they did it!" He waved his staff toward the southwest corner of the city, and his voice became animated before the captive audience. "You all know of the Broken Tower. But how many of you really know its story? That tower guarded the docks and the beach entrance to the city. The wall that ringed the tower was a favorite point of attack for monsters. Horde after horde, like the waves of the Moonsea, crashed against the tower walls. Armies of monsters used battering rams and powerful magic to try to break through. Three times the walls broke. Hobgoblins, goblins, and hill giants streamed through the breaches, expecting easy loot and frightened prey! But each time, the monsters found another wall. From inside Phlan, a wall of steel and living flesh pushed into the monsters! The attackers were forced back, leaving their dead in the Broken Tower. Warriors, filled with pride, would later be heard saying they had been part of the victory at the Broken Tower. My great-great-Uncle Ezra was one of those! If he were here today, he'd be telling you to buck up! Show some pride! Show whoever stuck us in this damned cave what we're made of!"

The wizard thumped the bench with his cane as the crowd cheered. Garanos grinned at Tarl and Auranzath. Above the noise of the mob, he confided in the two men. "These fine people seemed ready to surrender everything! It was going to be a tough fight to inspire them. Thanks be to the gods for sending you two along!" The trio smiled at the noisy crowd, then Tarl raised his hands for attention. When the mob settled, he ordered them all home with instructions to prepare for the following day and the coming fight. As the throng dispersed, Tarl thanked Garanos and Auranzath for their efforts. Grabbing his basket, the cleric headed for his own section of the city.

The citizens had a right to be upset. No one knew how or why the city had been abducted, and the horror of it was only beginning to take its toll.

A hundred yards ahead of Tarl stood his home—one of the most renowned places in Phlan. Denlor's Tower had seen conflict after conflict in the years of war. It was the outermost northeast point of the city. A wizard named Denlor had constructed its magical, blood-red walls overnight in the middle of the creature-infested ruins of old Phlan. The tower was designed as a symbol of strength and a challenge to attackers everywhere. Denlor's Tower also became a magnet for both evil and good spellcasters. Clerical and magical defenders of Phlan had flocked to the tower, trading lightning bolts, fireballs, mystical vapors of death, and other destructive magics in the darkness. After years of constant defeats for the evil shamans and wizards, Denlor was treacherously assassinated. Soon after Denlor's death, another powerful wizard arrived and took over the defense of the tower. Although new names were suggested for the structure, the sorceress insisted that the old one stand. No one argued with a sorceress who could slay dozens of orcs with a wave of her hand.

Tarl sighed as he thought about the first time he'd met Shal Bal of Cormyr, the sorceress who ruled the tower nowadays. Back then she was having some problems dealing with Denlor's death and other magical mishaps. Tarl was suffering from the loss of some of his fellow clerics. They made an unlikely pair, but together with Ren, another new-found friend, the trio conquered their own personal torments and helped rid Phlan of hundreds of monsters in the process. That was ten years ago. It seemed like yesterday.

The cleric blushed slightly as he thought of the way that the threesome's exploits had become famous in Phlan. They were honored heroes of the town. Any of them could have easily risen to be a ruling councilman, but these were honors they always refused. All three wanted only peace for Phlan and themselves.

The streets of Phlan were nearly deserted by the time Tarl entered Denlor's Tower. The door banged shut behind him, and he turned to secure the lock. "Shal?" he called up the spiraling stairs. Gripping his basket, he raced up the stairs, two at a time, in search of his wife. He found her upstairs in her reading room. As he unpacked the basket, they discussed a topic the cleric had come to dread.

"Tarl, First Councilman Kroegel wants you to join the

council. I think it's a good idea. Your temple leaders think it's a good idea. Phlan needs a strong leader on the council, and you're the best man for the job. If you don't take it, we might get stuck with Gormon on the council. And the only position he's suited for is chief of sanitation."

Irritated, Tarl paced around the reading room and into Shal's spellcasting chamber. He thought much better on his feet, and he needed to think clearly right now. He wasn't good at resisting his wife. "Shal, you know why. You've been asked to join the council as many times as I have. Please, let's not fight about this. We both know I'm a priest, not a politician. Besides, now that I'm Phlan's military advisor, I'll never get any rest. I can't juggle both positions."

"Rest! Is that all you think about is rest? If ever Phlan needed you, it's now. Fiends and armies are threatening the city!"

Tarl stopped his pacing and went to her side. He tried to put his arms around his beloved wife.

"Don't even try it, cleric," she snapped, shaking him off. Tarl was a big man, six feet tall and all muscle, but an old mishap with a magical wish had left him shorter than his wife and less muscled. When she didn't want to be touched, she usually got her way.

Shal's purple robes swished about her with a life of their own. Tarl smiled, thinking that something magical probably did give her clothes some animation. His mind wandered as he thought how wonderful it would be to spend some time as her clothing, wrapped around her firm body and feeling her every move. He sighed but was abruptly brought back to reality.

"Tarl, we aren't through arguing about the councilman's position." Shal spoke in her most authoritative voice, waving a finger at him. It was the same finger that had launched purple fireballs and lightning bolts to halt ogres and giants in their tracks.

"Look, Kroegel gave me until the end of the week to give him my answer. Can't we forget about this for a while? Let's enjoy this peaceful interlude while it lasts. We both know an attack could come at any time." Tarl had discovered the poppyseed cake in his basket and now held it up for Shal to see. Taking a bite, he teased her. "Mmm, I'm really hungry!"

Shal saw through his diversion but allowed herself to succumb. She suddenly realized she was ravenously hungry. Striding over to her husband, she broke off a piece of cake and wrapped her arm around his waist. "Don't think you'll get out of this discussion so easily next time," she said softly.

"I know you far better than that. I wouldn't think of it." He kissed her hair, and the couple sat down to dine on the bread, cheese, and apples from Tarl's basket.

Shal grew more and more quiet as they ate. Finally she looked at her husband with wide eyes. "Tarl, I'm scared."

The cleric leaned close and wrapped his arms around the sorceress. "As long as I'm here, there is no force in this world that can hurt you. What's scaring you?"

Shal sighed. "Just being here in this hole is enough to frighten anyone. Not knowing how or why we're here makes it worse. But I've used all the detection spells I know and haven't learned anything. The other wizards in Phlan are in the same predicament. You'd think that we'd be able to figure something out. I know that some- where out there is a great evil ready to pounce on Phlan, and we're almost powerless to do anything about it."

This worried Tarl. His wife usually showed more confi- dence. "Come with me," he whispered.

He led Shal through her casting chamber to their favorite balcony. Denlor's Tower was high enough to survey most of the city, and part of the Moonsea, too, had they not been deep in some cavern.

"Shal, what can I do to do to make you feel safe?" He could feel her tension and wished he could just rinse it away with a warm bath and a mug of tea. But this was more serious, and Tarl knew it. "I don't mean the kind of safe the farmers get when they lock the door at night. Or the kind of safe my Aunt Dorinna gets when she puts that disgusting smelling mud all over her face."

His last comment brought a giggle. "Your Uncle Arnis really hates that stuff. You don't like it much either, do you? Lately, I've been thinking about trying it. Maybe it'll keep me looking young." Tarl rolled his eyes, but was glad to see some humor coming from his wife. He held her close.

"I want to make you happy—as happy as our lives will allow. It's hard being in the front of battles all the time. Half the time when we're hurling spells and fighting side by side, I'm terrified at the thought of you facing the same blades and awful creatures I face."

Shal's chest heaved. "I'm sorry I'm so upset. This whole mess is getting the better of me. The best we can do is to keep looking for a way to rescue the city."

Tarl stroked his wife's hair and gently led her back inside. "What you need is a good back rub," he whispered. Shal smiled and sat down on the bed. As she tugged on her robe, a voice sounded in the street below.

"The alarm!" Tarl said, disappointed. He and Shal dashed about to gather weapons and prepare for battle. "Sorry, love. I'll have to owe you that back rub."

Shal laughed as they hurried out the door. "Don't worry. I won't let you forget! Now, let's go see if we can't quash our enemies once and for all!"

# ❦ 4 ❦

# Dark Castings

Impenetrable darkness filled the casting chamber at the top of the magical tower. In the cool blackness, a horrid pit fiend basked in the silence. It flapped about the chamber with its twenty-foot bat wings, drooling and slobbering. The room's stale air held the salty-sweet smell of blood that the fiend savored. It inhaled through flared nostrils, drinking in the foul scent. The heinous killer, summoned from the Nine Hells, was thrilled with his new assignment and accommodations. In all his soulless existence, he couldn't remember a better opportunity or one that promised more fun.

Marcus, a Red Wizard from Thay, had foolishly summoned the fiend to the Prime Material Plane to help do the bidding of the god Bane. The fiend and the wizard were to add their personal touches to their god's plan, and if all worked out right, in a few years two new evil demigods would be loose on Toril.

"Aaargh," the fiend groaned in pleasure. "It's good to be back on this plane, regardless of the outcome of the battle. Ah, better wars will come. *Latenat!*" Green sticky goo dripped from the fiend's foot-long fangs. The acidic slime oozed to the ground and sizzled, making coin-sized pits in the black granite. Similar indentations covered the entire floor.

The massive bulk of the twelve-foot fiend zipped

quickly around the room as it cast powerful spells. Its black bat wings glowed red as the beast conjured several unique protection spells. Giant taloned hands evoked detection and communication spells simultaneously, and as the spells activated, each talon became red-hot, the color of molten metal. The creature barely noticed the heat.

The fiend circled the chamber repeatedly, in exactly the same loop every time, but followed no markings a human eye could detect. The creature's bare feet, humanlike despite their three foot length, emitted streams of hot, jet-black sparks. A single spark would have burned right through the flesh of a normal creature, but each fist-sized flare bounced off its crusty, ebony skin.

"Power, that's what it's all about! Now that Marcus the fool has summoned me to this plane, I can accomplish what I have been planning for a thousand years. *Latenat!*"

The fiend's wings blazed with magic. It summoned more inky darkness and wrapped the blackness around its flesh like a coating of soot. Again the creature savored the scent of blood in the air, inhaling deeply.

"I'll use the power Bane has given me and give him some of the souls he wants. But I will keep the souls I need to grow even more powerful. Nothing can stop me. Nothing! *Latenat!*"

The horrible creature swung its talons against the nearest wall, punching huge holes into six-foot-thick marble. The stone crumbled to the floor with no effect on its harder-than-steel talons. The fiend sneered at the rubble as it continued gesturing. Suddenly twin spheres of blue energy surrounded each talon-studded fist.

A strain was evident in the fiend's voice as it completed the incantation, but no one was present to hear. No one with the slightest intelligence would have wanted to be near while such a pit fiend tried to communicate with its god. Few people could walk away with their sanity intact after viewing such a spectacle. The spheres of energy on the fiend's fists spread with every magical urging.

"*Kazaranthan!*" the monster hissed. The blue-white energy spread from its taloned hands to the tops of its thick, corded arms. "*Kallendurm ankerath!*" it spit. The spheres spread from its arms to the muscled chest that made the girth of a bull look puny. "*Gorgathen tellenl aunduen!*" A gasp of pain spewed from the creature with the last of the magical words. The spheres expanded over the rest of the fiend's body, covering its massive tree-stump legs and heavy, black-veined wings.

The final effort sent the creature to its knees in pain. "I hate that spell. *Latenat!*" it mumbled. The blue spheres touched without combining, and the fiend became completely engulfed in a protective ward. The enchanted being planned to cast one more spell of protection before summoning the attention of its god. Worshipers of Bane offered sacrifices so they would avoid the attention of their god, and the fiend knew how dangerous it was to ask for direct contact.

The creature gestured at the floor. Only magical vision would have noticed the golden lines rising up from the granite surface. The pattern made by the shimmering enchantments forced more energy into the fiend.

"Aaaahh, surely there is nothing able to stop me now. *Latenat!*" Gasping, the creature reveled in the massive power and pain it felt. Mystical energies coursed through its unholy veins, swelling them to the bursting point. The gigantic creature grinned a fangy grin.

More gestures and magical words started the process of summoning another creature, this one from the Elemental Plane of Earth. The wall in front of the fiend pulsed with malevolent energy. Ominous fractures crept over a steadily growing bulge in the marble surface. The jet blackness soon outlined a nineteen-foot humanoid form. Rocky protrusions exploded out of the black marble. "Come forth to your master! *Latenat!*" the fiend commanded. A nearly indestructible earth elemental fractured itself from the wall with a loud crash and stood before the fiend that commanded it.

A voice like stone grinding on stone boomed in the chamber. "I'm not pleased to be here." Few creatures had the nerve to speak in such a manner to a fiend.

Elementals summoned by ordinary wizards were ten-foot piles of rock able to crush walls and a wizard's enemies. This elemental was a prince of its kind, and its massive rocky protrusions were diamond-hard. A keen intelligence dwelled in the creature—an intelligence and a rebellious spirit lacking in its smaller brethren. "What is your desire?" demanded the grating voice.

"You are my shield and voice, creature. You will cast my spells and speak as I speak. *Latenat!*" The fiend left no chance for error in voicing its command. It directed the elemental to turn toward another wall. Every gesture, movement, and breath of the fiend was instantly copied by the elemental.

With this last precaution, the fiend felt truly safe. It checked its many layers of mystical defensive energy and discovered them to be sound. It checked the enchanted controls over the elemental and found these as solid as the diamondlike materials from which the elemental was made. The fiend reinforced the protections on the single magical entrance to the chamber in which it dwelled; it would not be disturbed. Slobbering at its success, the fiend was now ready to commune with its god.

The fiend's lips moved to call forth its master, but the

sound issued from the elemental. "Bane, my master, I beg you, hear me."

"AAAAAAaaaaaahhhhhhhh!"

An abominable howl filled the chamber, swirling in and out and around the two figures. A tiny, dazzling dot of light blinked on the wall in front of the earth elemental. The dot cut through the numerous layers of magical darkness in the room, denying any concealment. The blazing energy grew in size and bathed the elemental in a blast of light as intense as the sun. The pit fiend ducked behind the girth of its guardian, grateful that its own skin wasn't exposed to the blistering, hot light. The fiend's control of the elemental allowed it to see through the elemental's eyes; luckily, the dazzling light didn't harm the rocky servant.

"Tanetal, my diabolical child, I am so glad you called me." A booming, sugary voice grew in volume as the light grew in size. Soon the entire wall in front of the elemental was blasting forth a beam of energy so intense that the moisture in the air began steaming away in a mist.

"Lord Bane, you are all," the elemental spoke in the voice of the pit fiend. "I have carried out all your instructions. Phlan is in your power, and the pool of darkness is ready to give you many souls. What more can I do to answer your bidding?" The fiend raged silently at the groveling supplications that hid its true feelings. Its god had spoken its real name. If any other creature heard the name Tanetal, it would be able to control the pit fiend. Among all fiends, true names were never used. The elemental would now have to die, for it had heard the name—but, not until after this conversation was over.

"Fool! Dead thing! You think you have carried out my plan! You worm, you are less than the slime of worms!

Where is my city?" The blast of anger from the god snuffed out all the protections that the fiend had spent hours creating in the chamber. Fortunately, its personal wards were not eliminated. The chamber and the huge magical tower shook with the wrath of the god. The earth elemental didn't even twitch. The fiend still cowered behind its massive body.

Now an enormous ball of light formed in the chamber. It writhed and took the shape of a seven-foot-tall, bald human with a long black beard and mustache. This visage was what Bane allowed his worshipers to see when the god felt the need for direct contact with creatures on the Prime Material Plane.

"Well?" the god-voice boomed.

The deity's glare was too much for even the diamondlike surface of the elemental. The creature burst into a billion shards. The fragments that hurled toward the god were pulverized into harmless soot. The rocky projectiles hitting the fiend ripped its flesh to shreds and sent the creature to the floor, writhing in pain, despite the protective energies that still wrapped around it.

"That's much better, my dear drooling son. I do so much like communicating with you directly. Let me tell you what has happened with my plan so far." The face softened. The pit fiend was instantly drawn in awe and adoration to the god's every word.

"All the cities of the Moonsea that I wished for my own, except yours, have been collected. They were ripped from the earth and are now in the plane of Limbo. While a few cities are still trying to resist me, their pools of darkness are transforming the human souls into my minions. In a few months, I will be able to put these cities back in their places around the Moonsea and my worshipers will fill the land to overflowing, thus increasing my power in Faerun.

"Listen!" shrieked the god. With that, the many layers of magical defenses around the fiend vanished, all except the blue spheres of protection.

"You poor excuse for an imp!" Bane's voice was earsplitting. Now the blue spheres burst with a stoneshattering boom. Not only was the tower rocked, but the land around the massive structure reeled with the anger of the god.

"Do you want to tell me why Phlan isn't where it should be?" Each word of the god blasted the fiend harder and harder into the floor. The very stones under and around the creature sank and molded themselves to the monster's body. Its massive frame started to melt from the energy it was absorbing.

"Master! Please! Mute your righteous wrath before I perish and am unable to do your will! *Latenat!*" The fiend sniveled at the pain that racked its body.

The god smiled and reduced his power to a fraction of what it had been. The fiend still squirmed.

Bane's light was completely blinding. Crusty layers of flesh peeled off the arms of the fiend. It wrapped its body in its wings, which blocked the searing heat temporarily, although soon the wings would be burned husks embracing a skeletal frame.

"AAAAAAaaaaaahhhhhhhh!" The voice of the pit fiend finally convinced Bane to convert the burning light to a cool radiance. The forces blasting the creature to the floor changed, picked the fiend up, and healed it completely. Huge chunks of black rock fell from the flesh of the fiend and crashed with loud echoes to the floor. The fiend gasped as it spit out its explanation.

"I purposely shifted Phlan to a huge cavern below this

tower, using the power of the pool of darkness to transport it. It will now be easier, for you in all your greatness, to shift it back again when all the souls have been pulled from Phlan. All this was done only for you, noble master. All was done to make you more powerful here in Faerun. I know what great effort you expended to pull the other cities away. Was I wrong, most noble of gods? *Latenat!*"

"No, my loyal toadling. I don't know yet what you intend, but the souls of Phlan must be mine at the precise moment when I gather those from all the other cities. So hurry up with your plans. Summon me again when our work is accomplished, Tanetal."

With that, the light vanished and the god was gone. The fiend groaned in relief with the disappearance of the intense pressure on its body and mind. Whatever happened, Phlan would have to surrender its human souls to the pool of darkness, or bits of the fiend would certainly be scattered over this chamber, like bits of the elemental it had summoned.

\* \* \* \* \*

The fiend wasn't the only creature present in the mage's tower. In other parts of the fortress, equally evil activities were underway.

"Fiends," the Red Wizard said imperiously, "arise. I have a mission for you."

Three abishai, one black, one green, and one red, flapped down from their golden alcoves in Marcus's throne room and shuffled over to the wizard. If it were possible to read the expressions on the faces of the ghastly creatures, it would be obvious they didn't like taking orders from a mere human.

Of the many types of fiends, abishai were among the lowliest. Their distant cousin, the pit fiend, was the most powerful of their kin. The abishai's bodies showed disgusting similarities to their more powerful relatives.

Like pit fiends, abishai looked much like hideous gargoyles. Thin and reptilian, they possessed long, prehensile tails and great bat wings. Standing seven feet tall, their true heights were deceptive due to their crouching, bobbing gaits. These monsters were powerful, much stronger than goblinkin, and about as intelligent as an average human. And each abishai was more than a match for even the most powerful of wizards. A man wiser than the Red Wizard might have had the sense to be fearful.

"My pit fiend has given you three to me to use as I wish. You will guard my tower night and day. Fly out from the tower three hundred miles and circle the entire area. Kill anyone or anything that might cause me trouble."

The three fiends grumbled in irritation.

"None of this!" the wizard shouted, waving his ringed hand. "I, Marcus, have power over you. Now go!"

The abishai flew across the room and out of the chamber. As they went, each vowed silently to serve the pit fiend Tanetal for a thousand years, but only if they were allowed to dismember the wizard and rip out his organs one by one, keeping the insolent spellcaster alive during the fun.

No, the red abishai thought, I must offer to serve Tanetal for five thousand years. It was the most intelligent and powerful of the three, and it knew that such a plan might successfully exclude its lesser brethren from the delight of torturing the Red Wizard.

Unaware of the hidden feelings of the abishai, Marcus gloated as he sat on his throne. Invisible among the Red

Wizards of Thay, he'd been of their lowest rank and was paid no attention by other wizards in the sect. Marcus's only claim to fame was a smidgeon of power granted to him after he became a follower of Bane. From that day on, his star had been on the rise. And a dark star it was.

A high priest of Bane had given Marcus the means to summon the pit fiend to Toril's plane of existence, as well as the name of Tanetal. This evil priest had also told Marcus of Bane's plan to take over the cities of the Moonsea and fill them with possessed humans who would worship Bane and make the deity the most powerful god in Faerun.

When Marcus summoned Tanetal, he was startled but overjoyed by the massive power of the pit fiend. The creature's mere touch had given the wizard awesome mystical abilities. And in a snap the fiend had summoned the lesser fiends, the abishai, to serve Marcus in any way the Red Wizard desired.

"Oh, that was a glorious day when Tanetal became my servant. We raised this tower and later we stole the entire city of Phlan. All I must do now is conquer the city with the mystical minions I command, and all will be pleasing to Bane. I will be granted powers beyond those of mere mortals. What more could one wizard ask?" Marcus hissed and seethed in distorted ecstasy.

Over the next hour, Marcus gave instructions to clerics of Bane and then to the commanders of the mercenary armies. Phlan would fall—of that he had no doubt—and all would be perfect. True, the city had resisted the first attack of Marcus's army. The residents were surprisingly well prepared for battle, and powerful wizards lurked within the city, including one female who cast the most damnable violet lightning bolts. But they would fall; they would be defeated.

Marcus smiled as he thought of the day that the people of Phlan would be submerged into the pool of darkness under the red tower. The evil wizard and his pit fiend would absorb a fair share of the power from those souls, and Bane would never notice the energy missing from his pool. The fiend had been explicit and had carefully described this part of the plan. Bane would get eight out of ten souls, and the rest would be enough to make Marcus a demigod. The very thought of this made the Red Wizard quiver.

Now the mage cleared his throne room. All the orders had been given, and his war plans would proceed perfectly. Marcus's gray, stormy eyes scanned his golden domain. He had worked hard to tastefully decorate the walls, floors, and ceilings of his rooms in red gold. He didn't realize that he was the only creature who found them to be in good taste.

His eyes fell on the four fiend alcoves. The residents of the first three had already been sent on their mission, but the fourth held a charming creature, another race of fiend. What had his pit fiend called it? Ah, yes, an erinyes.

"Erinyes, come over here, sweet child." Marcus's voice dripped.

This creature's small size, a mere six feet tall, and its youthful, feminine form belied its age of over twenty-two thousand years. It looked nothing like the abishai, but instead resembled a human female with feathery wings. Nonetheless, it had come from the seventh level of the Nine Hells. In its long lifetime, it had learned how to manipulate those who tried to manipulate it. Stepping from the alcove, the creature lifted lustrous green eyes to the scrawny human on the throne and stretched seductively.

"My master, the damnable pit fiend, shall be made to pay for this some day," it whispered. Moving milky-white hands and arms, the erinyes caressed itself from throat to thigh and fluffed out ten-foot white wings. All the while, it gloated as it observed the reaction of the foolish human.

"You woke me, noble wizard. Please give me a moment to compose myself before coming closer." Soft white hands, wishing for nothing less than to snap the bird-neck of the wizard in front of it, carefully adjusted an oiled leather corset and short skirt. It knew just the right amount of perfectly formed milky-white flesh to expose.

The erinyes knew Tanetal's plan well. When the time was right, it would strip the soul from the spellcaster. The pit fiend and the erinyes would then become demi-gods using the souls kept from Bane. All the erinyes had to do was what came naturally to the seductive creature. It glided over to the loathsome wizard.

"You are looking wonderful today, noble Marcus. What can this poor little girl do for you?" The erinyes batted its eyes, moved suggestively toward the throne, and wet its ruby lips with a seven-inch long tongue. It filled the room with a musky scent that it had perfected several thousand years ago.

Suddenly, the chamber shook.

The wizard's eyes grew wide in fear. "*Consheltuen!*" he spoke in haste.

Marcus activated three defensive spells in succession. His skin became steel hard. Three different red energies swirled about his form, forming shields meant to prevent fire, arrows, and low level magic from harming him. A scarlet shield appeared in front of the sorcerer, knocking the comely erinyes to the floor.

"Ooof!" the erinyes groaned. It was slammed to the

floor before its wings could break the fall. Reaching out in irritation, its tender fingertips began to weave the pattern for an inky spell of cancellation. Realizing that such an act would reveal too much of its powers, the erinyes stopped. Marcus couldn't know that his life might be ended so quickly.

"Marcus, do not be concerned." A pout formed on the erinyes's perfect lips. Looking very sad, it knelt at the feet of the Red Wizard. "It is only your pet, the fiend, in the casting chamber. I am sure it only wants to give you more power." The smile on the erinyes's face fooled Marcus completely.

By the gods, I hate these puny humans, the erinyes thought to itself. It added a few centuries to the tortures it planned for the pit fiend.

"You are right, my dear," Marcus purred, looking down at the demure winged creature.

The wizard truly enjoyed dominating this feminine creature. He would have to thank Tanetal for this gift. The erinyes was so understanding, so giving of all its talents. The wings were a wonderful bonus; so soft to the touch, so delicious. Briefly, Marcus considered having his pit fiend summon a few more of these creatures. He leered as he pictured himself among a bevy of such beauties, then turned to the erinyes.

"Let's get on with more interesting matters, shall we?" Marcus smiled down and reached out.

The erinyes smiled back at him and stretched out delicate ivory hands capable of ripping him limb from limb. It forced control upon itself so as not to attack this idiot, not yet anyway. It allowed itself to be led across the room. The tower shook again, this time more violently.

"That's enough!" the wizard shouted. He hated interruptions. "There is only so much I can put up with." The wizard marched toward the upper floors of the tower, leaving an uninterested erinyes behind. Marcus's body began to glow red with the many protective spells he cast on himself. It simply wouldn't serve his purposes to seem less than awesome in front of his pit fiend.

The erinyes watched the scrawny wizard leave and was pleased. It could barely sense the greater fiend above in the spellcasting chamber. It knew something powerful must have attacked the pit fiend, even if Marcus was too dim to realize it. It didn't want to be nearby when Tanetal and Marcus had their discussion.

The erinyes amused itself by magically destroying the wizard's bed, the vials of oil and glowing candles it had summoned for the pleasure of the stupid man. It could always create more. It half wished this wizard were a little more inventive; he might actually be fun if he weren't such a bore. Humans were so dull in all of their activities and always did things the same way. Sighing, the erinyes fluttered back to its alcove to doze and wait for another summoning.

Marcus sputtered as he levitated up the secret stairs leading to a hidden door in the spellcasting chamber. The power the fiend had given him made him almost twice as powerful as before. He inventoried the spells of protection surrounding his body and was pleased to see that all were functioning with full effect. Six different spells created a red aura about him. His skin reflected a lovely shade of crimson. His flesh was as hard as stone.

The wizard's mood improved slightly. "Yes," the wizard sighed, "everything is going perfectly. Maybe I should ask Tanetal to enhance my physical power. I think the erinyes might be even more impressed with my physique."

Marcus unlocked the secret door, his spells bathing the

chamber in red light. The fiend was on its knees, surrounded by a ring of huge, charred black diamonds. The spellcasting chamber was in ruins.

"Look what you've done to this place! There are holes in two walls, there's a pit in the floor, and what in the world is that white goop on the wall over there?" Marcus seethed at the gigantic beast.

The fiend slowly lifted its head to glare at the human. This wizard had summoned the fiend to his plane and held it by its true name. The greater fiend was bound by magic to do what the Red Wizard commanded. But what was left unsaid by the sorcerer allowed the fiend to do a great deal else on its own.

"I have spoken directly with Bane. Such communication is not without its risks. The god is not pleased with us. *Latenat!*"

"Not pleased?" Marcus said, backing up and licking his lips nervously. "Well, uh, we must do something at once. What shall we do? How can we make Bane the Glorious smile on us?"

"I think," the fiend said as it rose, "we must send the people of Phlan into the pool of darkness. Then we will be all right. How are the war plans? Remember, I am to be the guardian of this tower and you are to command the forces attacking Phlan. This was your idea, because you thought you could easily handle the defenders of Phlan. *Latenat!*" The fiend sounded as if it questioned Marcus's abilities.

"Of course I remember," the wizard snapped, staring at the white blaze marks on his chamber wall. "I have given the orders for the second attack and I go now to lead it. There shall be no problems, no problems at all."

"For both our sakes, I hope you are right. *Latenat!*"

# ❦ 5 ❦

# Wizardly Eye

Dusk. It was coming early, as it had been for several weeks. Despite the moist warmth of the spring air, the early nightfalls gave the feeling of approaching winter. The days should have been lengthening as summer approached. But the weather was just plain odd, and no one could figure out why.

The woman in the woods noticed it too. She gritted her teeth as she observed the lengthening shadows. Looking to the overcast sky, she calculated the time until sunset, then returned to her work in earnest.

"Come on, catch! C'mon . . ." Sparks flew from the flint and steel, into the tinder she had gathered. The woman puffed gently on the sparks, cupping her hands around the weeds to keep out the wind. Another puff brought a smolder, a crackle—and a bright flame. A few more twigs crisscrossed over the grass would do the trick— soon the campfire crackled and popped at the dry pine branches and logs. The woman leaned back with a sigh, basking in the warmth on her face.

She could have easily flicked a finger and produced a steady, hot flame at the end of a digit, but the woman preferred to conquer nature by human means whenever she could. Like many wizards, she was neither strong nor muscular. She knew the limits of her physical strength, and practiced using her mundane talents to their best advantage.

The sorceress checked the pile of wood she had gathered, reassured there was enough to last the night. With darkness setting in so early, the only intelligent action was to make camp just as early. Getting caught in the forest in the dark without food, water, or firewood was downright dangerous. Although it cut the day's travel short, stopping early to set up camp had been the only sensible thing to do.

The woman turned and sat on a fallen tree. She scanned the woods for a sign of her companion, but all was quiet. "Gamaliel, where are you?" she asked softly. She knew better than to shout in an unfamiliar forest, possibly alerting an enemy or wild animal to her position. As usual, she would just have to wait until he returned. Gamaliel was her best friend, but he could be infuriating. She was getting tired of his habit of running off into the woods, leaving her to set up camp. There was work to be done, and she was annoyed at being left with all the chores while he was having fun doing gods-knew-what.

The sorceress swept her waist-length hair forward over her shoulder and began pulling out the burrs, bits of grass, and leaf fragments that had collected there during her trek through the woods. The fire hissed and simmered at her feet, and for the first time all day, she began to relax.

Normally, the woman braided her hair every morning, to avoid such a tangle. "Those blasted goblins," she muttered as she tugged at a stubborn knot in her hair. "If they could have waited twenty minutes to attack this morning, I wouldn't be having this problem." She sighed. "But I guess I should be glad that my hair is the only thing that's a mess, and not the rest of me. Or Gamaliel."

The attack had come at dawn. A band of goblins returning to their lair had cut short her morning routine. There had been only nine goblins, and a quick choice of spells, coupled with Gamaliel's attacks, had dispatched them easily. They both escaped without injury, but that incident had set the tone for the entire day. Monsters seemed to be leaping out from behind every tree, eager to make a quick snack of the sorceress and her companion. She encountered more creatures this single day than she had the entire previous week. Oh, well, maybe that meant her quota was filled. . . .

The sorceress added more wood to the campfire. She scowled at the darkening sky, then swung her hair over her other shoulder, continuing to pull out bits of debris. Her hair shone red in the firelight, redder than usual. It was a deep, rich color, not exactly brown, yet not bright red either. It was a mixture of amber and rusty shades, and always looked different depending on the light. It nearly glowed in the light of the fire.

The flames of the campfire grew brighter and crackled louder. The woman relaxed further. Her hair was nearly done. The fire would soon be ready to cook supper. After cooking, she could collapse into her bedroll. What a day it had been. The fire warmed her sore muscles and lulled her tired mind.

The crackling fire was enough to obscure the sound of leaves rustling in the brush behind the sorceress. A great cat had made its way to the clearing and made no other sound as it watched her. It sat back on muscled haunches, eyes wide, contemplating its next move. The cat sniffed the air.

The animal crept soundlessly to the edge of the small clearing and stopped. Tawny fur glowed golden in the firelight, and green eyes stared at the woman's silhouette against the blaze. The murky daylight was nearly gone except for a pink smear on the horizon. The cat circled the clearing until it was behind its prey.

The huge feline was in position. It silently dug its back claws into the earth, twitched its haunches, and flared its nostrils. In the span of less than a heartbeat, it was airborne. Over two hundred pounds of feline launched through the air without the sorceress ever hearing a warning.

The next thing the woman felt was a great thud against her back and the whump of her chest hitting the ground. It nearly knocked the wind out of her, but her instincts drove her to roll quickly to face her attacker. She saw white fangs and piercing green eyes, felt the cat's hot breath on her face. She gasped for air, then spit out the words as fast as she could find them.

"Will you cut that out? How many times have I told you not to pounce on me like that? By the gods, one of these days, Gamaliel . . ." She propped herself up on her elbows, removing an enormous paw from her chest. The cat leaned in, touching his damp, pink nose to the sorceress's cheek. He purred at a volume the woman found both ridiculous and infuriating.

"You are such a . . . a . . . a cat!" Undaunted, the huge feline rolled off his mistress and lay on his side in the grass, exposing the ivory fur on his belly. Stretched out, he was longer than the woman was tall. He touched her lightly with a paw.

"Oh, so now you want your tummy rubbed. I don't know why I put up with you sometimes." Although she ought to ignore the cat, her hand automatically moved to his great chest and began rubbing. The cat rolled onto his back, still purring at a tremendous volume. He stretched, then relaxed, four paws flopping in all directions. The woman laughed at the sight. He lay with his ivory belly exposed, his dark brown paws hanging limply. A bright pink nose shone from his deep brown muzzle. The heavy gold chain with the jade pendant around the animal's neck accented the richness of his fur. The sorceress thought he was a beautiful cat, with his tawny body and dark brown ears, face, tail, and paws.

"All right, you ferocious beast. You've had your fun. Time for supper. I'll set up the bedroll, and you can find us some dinner." The cat lay motionless, blinked, then flipped over and stood. "And Gamaliel, we've had fish the last four nights. Do you think you could find us a nice rabbit or something for a change?"

The cat stared at his mistress as if offended. His words found their way to her mind. *If you're dissatisfied with my hunting, mighty sorceress, perhaps you'd like to provide us with some dinner. I'd like to see you hunt in the dark. Besides, I happen to like fish.* The cat turned his head and sniffed at the breeze.

The sorceress leaned over and scratched the cat between the ears. "You know I'm not complaining about your hunting. We've never gone hungry, even in the barest climes. But if it were up to you, we'd have fish for breakfast, fish for lunch, and more fish for dinner. We humans like a little variety. So how about a change of pace? I think you owe me after that prank of yours. I just combed all the twigs out of my hair, and now I have to start over again, thanks to you."

The cat looked at his mistress as if she had just asked for dragon steaks. His thoughts reached her again. *Oh, all right, Evaine. Meat it is. I'll do it, if you'll stop your whining.*

"My whining?" she choked. "You're the biggest baby on

four paws." She slapped his flank lightly, then added, "Okay, Gam, see what you can find for us. I'm getting hungry. The fire should be ready when you get back." The cat rubbed his nose against Evaine's cheek, purring, then bounded off into the growing darkness. She heard his movements in the brush for only a few moments, then all was silent as the cat began stalking.

As she spread out her bedroll on a heap of pine needles, Evaine reflected to herself that she no longer regarded her mental conversations with Gamaliel as unusual. At first, she had felt self-conscious about conversing with an animal, especially out loud. But that was several years ago. After all they had been through together, she hardly regarded Gamaliel as an animal any more. Most wizards had familiars, but few shared such an intimate bond with them. Before Gamaliel, Evaine had traveled with a small barn owl familiar that she cared for deeply, but the relationship never developed the way this one had. She and Gamaliel complemented each other and learned from one another. They had become an indivisible team. She could never imagine life without him.

Evaine added wood to the campfire, then walked the perimeter of the clearing, sprinkling a magical powder and murmuring the words of a warding spell. A pale green glow followed her in the grass, then slowly dissipated. After the day she'd had, she wasn't taking any chances on getting ambushed in the night. If she were with more companions, they could all take turns keeping watch, but she and the cat both needed their sleep. Gamaliel's senses were keen, and he usually detected intruders, but there was no reason to take chances.

The sorceress sat on the bedroll and pulled out her spellbook to begin studying. Her hands slid over the green leather cover. This tome was another old friend, her most prized possession. The magic contained in its pages had seen her through some tough times and had survived all kinds of dangers, from fires to dousings of water to dragon breath. She knew of wizards whose spellbooks had been destroyed, practically stripping them of their powers. Evaine shuddered at the thought of trying to survive without hers. She was lucky to have a companion like Gam, who would stick by her no matter the danger.

Evaine sometimes considered learning more mundane methods of combat, in the event that somehow she lost her magical skills. Like most wizards, she was good with a staff and a dagger, but learning the techniques of swords and axes would mean giving up the study of magic almost entirely. And Evaine always found herself on some intellectual quest. Even if she committed herself to the study of combat, her nature would force her to return to her books in no time. Magical study was too much a part of her, as if it had been woven into her soul before she was born.

Evaine took a few deep breaths, then began to concentrate. She opened her tome and started memorizing the spells. The sorceress became lost in concentration. Years of study had allowed her to focus her mind quickly and completely.

Evaine didn't know how much time had passed before she was startled by a sound directly in front of her. She looked up, slamming the book shut, expecting an ambush.

Two gleaming eyes stared back at her.

*You really should be more careful, out here alone. What if I had been a band of orcs?* The cat's message was teasing. He was obviously pleased at startling her. If cats could laugh, this one would have been howling.

"If you had been a band of orcs, you'd either be lying on the ground looking like charcoal or you'd be running for the nearest stream. I've placed a ward around the perimeter of the clearing. And to answer your next question, you didn't smell the magic because I've been working on a version of the spell that's virtually undetectable, even by magical creatures like you. I see that it worked. So much for trying to outfox the fox, eh Gam?"

Gamaliel blinked at her, looking hurt, but Evaine had seen his practiced look too many times before. This cat was unique, all right. Ignoring his ploy, she changed the subject. "Let's see what you brought us."

The cat carried a small brown rabbit—*and* a gleaming silver trout that weighed close to twenty pounds. Both were held carefully in his huge mouth.

"Way to go, hunter. I see we have some variety on the menu tonight." She took the rabbit from him and scratched his chin. Gamaliel carried the fish to the other side of the campfire.

She knew the answer to her next question before asking it, but posed it anyway. "Um, Gamaliel, do you want that cooked?" The cat didn't respond, but he answered her by wordlessly starting on his dinner. She shrugged and turned to prepare the rabbit for the fire.

By the time supper was cleaned up, Gamaliel was already snoozing on the bedroll. Evaine rubbed him gently, coaxing him into making room for her. She had banked the fire into a heap of glowing coals that would provide heat the entire night but not enough light to give away their whereabouts. The bedroll was warm from the fire and the dozing cat. She crawled under the blankets, grateful for the comfort after her adventurous day. She would sleep soundly with her warding spell in place and the giant feline snoozing between her and the dark trees. If anything were going to attack her, it would have to get through her magical protection as well as two hundred pounds of muscle, claw, and fang.

A few stars flickered through the cloud cover. Evaine made a mental list of the work she and Gam would have ahead of them over the next few days. "Phlan. We'll be in Phlan in a couple days, Gamaliel. Then we can find the pool of darkness and figure out how to destroy it." She grimaced at the thought of another pool. Hunting the evil artifacts and destroying them had become her vocation, but each such endeavor came with its own anxiety.

Sleep cut her planning short. As Evaine drifted off, she murmured to the cat, "Afterward . . . maybe you and I can take a little vacation, away from monsters and evil pools."

*     *     *     *     *

Evaine slept so soundly that she didn't hear Gamaliel get up from the bedroll and creep into the woods at first light. He was back after only a short time, carrying another enormous fish and a fat quail. Evaine was still sound asleep, so the cat padded over to her, purring loudly in her ear. She awoke with a start, but was pleased to see her companion. Sitting up, she hugged him around the neck and got a wet face from his muzzle. He was still damp from fishing, and it was then she noticed the fish and the quail.

She laughed. "You certainly are efficient, Gamaliel. This is the closest thing to breakfast in bed that I've had in a long time. But I suppose we should get moving."

*Some of us are early risers, Evaine. We don't waste the whole day sleeping late.* The cat's green eyes sparkled.

Gamaliel couldn't resist putting on airs at every opportunity. He and his mistress both knew the sun was barely up.

Evaine was used to his attitude, and didn't mind his feigned arrogance. "You and those green eyes. I always know what you're up to. When you're mad or upset, your eyes turn golden. But when you've just stuffed yourself with fish or had a fun romp in the woods, they're greener than any emeralds." After all the years she had spent with the cat, this singular feature still amazed her.

The sorceress patted the cat's head, stretched, and crawled from her bedroll. She built up the fire, cleaned the quail, and put it over the fire to roast. Gamaliel had learned long ago that poultry cooked quickly, and he knew to hunt for it when time was short.

While the bird cooked, Evaine brushed her long hair and braided it. Then she shook out the blankets and rolled them up. Gamaliel finished his fish, then scattered their remaining firewood with his great paws. Their gear was nearly packed by the time the quail was ready to eat.

Evaine gulped her breakfast. While she cleaned up, Gamaliel amused himself by pouncing on dry leaves blown by the wind. The sorceress chuckled at his antics. She always marveled at his grace despite his huge size. And she always laughed at his playfulness. Despite his intelligence and attitude, he could romp like a kitten when he wanted to.

With their belongings packed and the campsite clean, Evaine again walked the perimeter of the clearing, this time disarming the magical ward. Always careful, the sorceress left nothing to chance. Gamaliel followed her, obliterating her footprints efficiently with his claws.

Then the pair set off in the direction of Phlan.

The forest was thick, and the only paths through the trees were those made by animals. Gamaliel led the way, finding the easiest route through the undergrowth. It was slow going. But even with the goblins and other monsters that stalked the woods, it was still safer than taking a major road. A single female traveler, even one with a big cat, was an easy mark for bandits and other troublemakers. Though Evaine could take care of herself with her magic, she didn't wish to attract attention or tangle with the wrong enemy. She had serious business ahead, and she would need all her strength and energy for her upcoming mission.

Evaine and Gamaliel traveled until the sun reached its zenith—or what they assumed to be the sun's zenith. The clouds that covered the countryside for months had obscured the sun, allowing only a grimy, gray light to filter through. As Gamaliel hunted, Evaine made a lunch of dried fruit and some young roots she dug in the undergrowth. They couldn't afford to waste time. The early darkness in the evenings had already delayed them too much, since they couldn't travel very far in one day. They rested only as long as necessary, then moved on.

As the pair trudged through the dismal woods, Evaine used the time to plan her strategy against the pool of darkness. She had already cleansed four pools over the last two years. Although these encounters gave her important knowledge about the evil magic of these waters, each pool was different. There was no guarantee that any of the cleansing rituals she knew would work on any one specific pool.

The intellectual and magical challenge of destroying these pools outweighed her fear of them. Evaine was not one for taking risks, but the sorceress fully accepted the possibility that each pool might lead to her demise. But her hatred of these foul waters ran deep, and she always took every possible precaution.

Time moved quickly for Evaine, lost in her planning. Only a few hours wore past before the sky began to darken. When it was too dark to go any farther, Gamaliel left Evaine's side to roam ahead, looking for enough of a clearing to roll out the blankets and build a fire safely. In less than half an hour, he returned and led the way to a small, grassy patch beneath some young aspen trees.

"Great spot, Gamaliel. It even looks reasonably comfortable. I'll start setting up, and you can look for water." The cat rubbed against her leg, his great weight nearly knocking her off her feet, before bounding off into the trees.

The pair went about the routine of setting up camp. After Evaine studied her spells, the sorceress and her cat turned in early.

They had been fortunate not to encounter any monsters during the day. Evaine hadn't needed any of her spells, and that meant only a short session with her spellbook that evening. She needed to wake up early in the morning to cast the magic that would help her locate the next pool. The sooner she was asleep, the better. Gamaliel had instructions to wake her before dawn. Both were sound asleep only moments after curling up.

Evaine awoke in darkness. Gamaliel was tucked in a ball at her side, the blankets tangled around him. The sorceress shivered in the chilly, damp air. Squinting through the trees, she searched for a sign of the dawn. The sky was completely dark.

Evaine shifted the sleeping cat, then burrowed into the bedroll. She dozed off snuggling against the warm feline.

The sorceress woke again after about an hour. The sky had lightened slightly. Evaine knew that dawn was not far off. She slid out of the blankets and, using dry pine branches, coaxed the coals of the campfire into a blaze. Then she crawled back into the bedroll. She had stoked up a huge blaze, the flames leaping over four feet in the air. Now she waited until the wood burned down to hot embers.

While the fire roared, Evaine closed her eyes and prepared her mind for the spell she was about to cast. It was a taxing incantation that required all her concentration and energy. She preferred casting it early in the morning, when her mind was fresh and the world was still sleepy. The energy of thousands of busy humans across the continent could sometimes interfere with this type of magic. This wasn't a simple fireball or teleportation spell.

No, the sorceress was preparing to cast a specialized type of scrying magic that would allow her to locate the pool of darkness in Phlan. She knew of no other sorceress who was capable of casting the spell. It had taken her years of experimentation to perfect the technique. She had survived many near-disasters in the process, including losing her familiar, the barn owl. That loss and her grief had set her back several months, but this scrying spell and the missions it allowed her to complete were too important to abandon.

Evaine breathed deeply. She opened her eyes to check the fire, then returned to the process of cleansing her mind and focusing her thoughts. She began to whisper a chant that was as old as magic itself, a chant she had been taught as an apprentice. It was the first thing revealed to apprentices, to teach them to clear their minds of distraction and focus their attention. Used by a practiced, talented sorceress, the verses allowed the most powerful of magics to be summoned.

Evaine continued the chant until the fire was ready. Still murmuring the language of the chant, she arose slowly and began to rake the coals into a circle. When the embers were ready, she repeated two more verses of the chant, then cast the spell.

Gamaliel had awakened. He lay motionless, not twitching so much as a whisker. The light from the coals reflected in his green eyes. He had seen Evaine cast this spell before, and he understood the danger inherent in the amount of energy she channeled. He had once made the mistake of disturbing her during the casting of the spell. Fortunately for both of them, the error happened before Evaine had made the connection with the pool she was seeking. Had the incident occurred any later, she might have been rendered permanently insane. Only through her exceptional willpower was she able to disperse the spell's energy and escape without harm. She lay in bed for two weeks after that incident, slipping in and out of consciousness. Gamaliel had learned a valuable lesson. Against the very nature of his feline psyche, the cat had learned self-control.

Now Gamaliel lay on the bedroll, silent and unmoving, his eyes following Evaine's movements. He watched as she circled the hot coals, first to the right, then to the left. She paused, began a new chant, sprinkled purified white sand into the fire, and circled the embers three times. She stopped again and dropped onto the coals the golden feather of a couatl, donated to her willingly by the magical winged serpent. She circled three more times. Next it was the blood of a red dragon followed by seawater, each followed by three trips around the firepit. She now cast icons representing the four elements—

earth, air, fire, and water—into the coals. At last the fire was purified and she could begin.

For the next hour, Evaine added mystical elements to the coals, stirred them and divided them according to a precise ritual, whispering, murmuring, and shouting arcane passages. Gamaliel barely moved a muscle on the bedroll. All his senses were completely alert to any motion, sound, or scent in the trees. He would allow nothing to disturb his mistress.

After an hour of spellcasting, Evaine dropped to her knees next to the fire. She drew from a pocket a crystal of quartz, one of the earth's purest substances. The crystal was easily as big as her palm. She laid it carefully on a forked stick, then gently deposited the crystal in the center of the coals. She uttered another series of incantations, then drew the crystal from the fire with the branch. It was hot, but not hot enough to alter the crystalline structure.

Evaine carefully sat cross-legged and laid a padded cloth in her lap. She placed the crystal on the pad and fell silent. With her elbows on her knees and her head cupped in her hands, Evaine began to concentrate.

In her mind, the sorceress saw herself seated near the coals. Her other self began to rise in the air, and from above she saw her corporeal form, Gamaliel, and the clearing beneath her. She rose more and more rapidly, then her mind began to fly at breakneck speed over the tops of the trees. The countryside became a blur. Her mind was led by the power of the pool. Allowing one's mind to be carried along by a force of evil was a terrifying prospect, but Evaine's discipline and mental focus kept her in control.

The next thing Evaine knew, her mental image was whizzing through clouds. Then she found herself plummeting toward the earth, toward a large and unfamiliar body of water. Crude tents were set up around the perimeter of the bay, but Evaine's image was falling too fast for her to be able to identify any landmarks. Something was terribly wrong. The last time she had checked on the pool, it had been sequestered in an underground cave. Her breathing became rapid. Sweat beaded on her forehead as she struggled to maintain control, pushing away panic.

Evaine's mental projection broke the surface of the water, plunging through the deepest part of the bay. What she saw startled and puzzled her. The bottom of the sea was completely barren of plants and aquatic life. She saw no weeds, no water grasses, no fish, no turtles. All around her was nothing but a water-filled crater, as if the hole had been dug by some inexplicable force and filled in with water. She was completely confused by what she saw. And there was no sign of the evil pool.

Evaine forced her mind to rise to the surface of the bay and break free of the water. Her view changed as she escaped the depths of the water and was able to survey the surrounding countryside. From her previous magical observations of Phlan, this certainly looked familiar. She had practically memorized the roll of the distant hills and the farms that surrounded the Moonsea. She knew that Phlan was supposed to be in this vicinity, but where was it? Had her spell gone wrong?

At that instant, the quartz crystal in Evaine's lap shattered.

# ♣ 6 ♣

# Unpleasant Surprises

After leaving the dwarves, Ren stopped in a tiny hamlet for a few supplies, then turned toward the Stojanow River. There were plenty of roads that led to Phlan, but all wound through the mountains, and although the routes were good, they took at least three days longer than the route Ren had planned.

He had traveled along the river many times and knew its terrain well. Although the trail could be rough, even disappearing in the underbrush from time to time, a ranger on horseback had little trouble following it. So Ren spurred his horse toward the river and rode as hard as the terrain would allow. Three days of riding brought him to the Dragonspine Mountains. A swift brook rushed and gurgled with the heavy rain that had hit the region for the last month.

Two days later, the brook linked up with the Stojanow River. It, too, was a rushing torrent, swollen with the heavy rains. Ren and his horse pressed along the muddy banks, through day after day of rain and gray skies. Yet after all those weeks of tracking and ambushing orcs, he was relieved to be traveling the wilderness without clear and present danger.

The river slowly curved and weaved to the south, and would eventually empty into the Moonsea. Phlan would be perched in its familiar crook at the end of the river.

As Ren rode the river trail, he remembered traveling this way ten years ago. Back then, this had been a favorite route for the many ogre and orc armies trying to wrest Phlan from the merchants of the city. Humans avoided the river at all costs.

In the days when the river had been overrun by monster armies, the water had been a polluted syrup. Vegetation for hundreds of yards on either side withered and died at the river's touch and from the stench that arose from the pollution. Not a single fish, tadpole, or weed lived in the water. But the recovery the river had made since that horrible time was incredible. Now the water was alive with fish, birds, frogs, and snakes.

A few more days down the river put Ren halfway to Phlan. As he rode over a rise, he sighted Sorcerer's Island in the distance. He rode down the hill toward the edge of the water. The island used to stick out like a cancerous growth. Happily, the land had completely renewed itself. Fish now jumped in the clear water, white birches and small pines grew all around, and many muskrat warrens were visible at the water's edge.

A silver pyramid that had once been the evil sorcerer's stronghold stood in the center of the island. It was ugly and out of place, but no longer pumped foul poisons into the river. In fact, the pyramid was heavily overgrown with vines and weeds.

Ren patted his horse's neck as he gazed at the island. "That was quite a battle, Stolen, old boy. It was the three of us against the evil, crazed wizard. We depended heavily on Shal in that fight, because it takes a wizard to fight a wizard. But Tarl and I were at her back, and by the gods, no monster harmed her that day. What a tussle the three of us had. You can't imagine what it's like to be slimed by a six-foot-tall frog with teeth."

Ren dismounted and led the horse to the edge of the water so it could drink its fill. He still hesitated at letting himself drink from the lake. The image of that once sulphurous quagmire was burned deeply in his memory.

The ranger opened his saddlebags and took out a couple of apples for himself and his steed. He knew he spoiled the huge gray horse terribly, but war-horses didn't live long, and Ren especially liked this one.

"Stolen, those were some of the best days of my life. Even though Shal, Tarl, and I put ourselves through tremendous risks, we knew we were doing the right thing. The wizard living in that silver monstrosity was experimenting with life and death and creating the most abominable, deformed monsters. As a result of his experiments, poison was being dumped into the river so his monsters could swim downstream and take over all the cities on the Moonsea. Shal, Tarl, and I came up from Phlan to find out what was causing the pollution and the influx of hellish creatures. When we encountered the mage, we knew right away he was evil and crazy. We fought and killed him and finally burned his tower."

Ren waved his arms as he told the story to his horse, but the animal was more interested in the apples in its master's hand. Ren laughed and held out the apple, and Stolen snatched it away.

"Right, boy, you don't care about wizards and poisoned rivers. All you care about is a good fight and an even better dinner. But seeing this river makes me remember. Back then, I worried whether my life was going in the right direction. Now I know I did the right thing.

"Maybe I've been worried for nothing. Shal, Tarl, and I are going to have a good laugh over those dreams I had and then I can get back to my valley. Let's hurry to Phlan. It should be only two days from here."

Ren swung onto Stolen's back, feeling much better about the journey. He was looking forward to seeing Tarl and Shal; it had been too long since he'd visited them. He shouldn't have let a stupid dream worry him so much. He knew people whose dreams foretold the future, but never in his life had he been prescient.

Just the other night, Ren had been startled by another nightmare, this one about pit fiends, abishai, erinyes, and a huge red tower. He knew such fiends existed, but he also knew that such creatures rarely, if ever, made an alliance. Ren had decided it was probably his imagination or something he ate.

As they moved along the trail, Stolen sensed his master's urgency and pushed himself hard. Ren hardly had to encourage him. They traveled all day and well into the night, then camped and started early the following day. They didn't quite make it to Phlan by nightfall, but riding along the river in the dark, the ranger could make out the lights of the city far in the distance. He made camp, cleaned himself and his gear, and gave Stolen a hearty brushing. He wouldn't allow himself to show up on Shal and Tarl's doorstep looking like a hobo. Ren wasn't prideful about his appearance, but he liked to be clean.

His thoughts again drifted to the old days. Years ago, he'd briefly thought of asking Shal to be his wife. He didn't begrudge Tarl his luck, but Ren wished that things might have gone a little differently. More and more, he found himself wishing for someone to share his life. But he realized that Shal wasn't the woman for him. She reminded him far too much of Tempest, and he would never have been sure whether he married Shal out of love for her or as a surrogate for Tempest.

As he lay under the cloudy sky, his heart still burned for his long-lost Tempest. He could still see her in his mind. She was tall, so quick and agile. She wore her hair in a long braid, but when she wasn't trying to steal jewels or pick a pocket, her long red tresses fell loose to her hips. Tempest had been Ren's first love. She had consumed him so completely that he'd temporarily abandoned the lifestyle of a ranger to become a thief. Her death had been a blow from which Ren had never really recovered. He deliberately tried not to think of her, yet he was reminded of her all the time. In the foolishness of youth, the pair had thought themselves indestructible, but they had learned otherwise. Other women had shared his life after that bold female, but none had filled his heart like Tempest. Ren fell asleep dreaming sweet dreams of her.

Arising before dawn, Ren dressed in shining elven chain mail and mounted a freshly brushed and curried Stolen. They galloped into the Quivering Forest and traveled for an hour, smelling the fresh green woods around them. Even though this was the rainy season, Ren hadn't seen the sun in five weeks. But the new spring growth in the forest was the thickest he had ever seen. He inhaled deeply and savored the smell of wet earth and blooming trees.

Rounding what he knew was the final bend in the river before reaching Phlan, Ren and Stolen emerged from the woods. The ranger reined in his horse in shock. He sat for long minutes, dumbfounded, gazing at the scene before him.

Phlan wasn't there.

There should have been huge walls patrolled by armed guards; there should have been towers and battlements; and Denlor's Tower should have been visible looming over the city. Instead, as far as he could see, only a sooty smear of multicolored tents stood against the backdrop of the crystal clear Moonsea. Where Phlan had once stood, there was now a bay. The city was gone.

Ren spurred his horse forward. Beyond the tents, the ranger could see a few merchant ships and fishing boats tied to what looked like a hastily constructed dock.

Stolen trotted along the edge of the river as Ren searched for a place to cross. Riding closer to the tent city, the ranger noticed some type of rafting operation that hadn't been there on his last visit to Phlan. As he neared, he saw armed guards working a rope winch.

"Good morning, troopers," Ren hailed the three. He forced himself to sound pleasant despite his rotten mood. "Uh, when did Phlan disappear?"

"The gods took the city a month and a week ago," one of the rough troopers said gruffly.

The winch hauled a large raft back from the tent city and over to Ren's side of the river.

"By the gods, seems like yesterday," another trooper added. "The only people you'll see in New Phlan are those who were away from the city on the night of the storm." Stolen nickered a warning and backed up. Ren patted the horse's neck.

A sandy-haired guard, older than the others, approached the ranger. "Quite a beast you have there. Don't think I ever saw a horse that large or that gray. What business do you have in New Phlan?" His tone was hostile. The other two troopers loosened their weapons and stood behind their leader.

"My name is Ren o' the Blade. Perhaps you've heard of me?" The ranger used his most polite tone, the one he reserved for guards who thought they were bigger than life.

The three exchanged glances, backing away at the mention of Ren's name. After the battles he had won with Shal and Tarl many years ago, there weren't many people in Phlan who *didn't* know the names of the trio. The ranger could tell that these three were no different. They knew of his reputation, all right. The scowling looks on their faces changed to ones of respect, then worry. The three glanced at each other, then the leader cleared his throat and addressed Ren.

"Will you be looking for the cleric Tarl and the sorceress Shal? They were in their tower when the gods took the city. The people of Phlan, including your friends, haven't been heard from since that night." The older trooper was the only one brave enough to explain and risk upsetting the ranger.

"What's your name, trooper?"

"Shelly, noble ranger. I have been appointed by the council of New Phlan to operate this ferry service. We usually charge whatever one can pay for the ride, but we'll cross you for free. It's the least we can do for a hero of Phlan." The trooper's look was pleading. Deep down, he was hoping that Ren might help locate the city.

The ranger stared hard at the three. He tried to assess whether they were really who they said they were. Maybe they were thieves trying to rob honest citizens trying to get into Phlan. Then Ren realized he was glaring and softened his look. "Who did you say operates this ferry?"

"The council, sir. The profits go to feed the homeless— in case you were wondering."

The ranger was convinced. He dismounted and led Stolen onto the huge raft. The craft was so enormous the logs didn't even dip into the water when the huge war-horse stepped on. Shelly followed the pair onto the raft.

"Tell me, Shelly, how much would you have tried to charge me?"

The raft started to move as the other two troopers cranked the winch.

The sandy-haired warrior hesitated nervously, then drew himself up. "Why, I would have insisted on at least a gold piece for a fine-looking warrior like yourself, sir."

Ren grinned and tossed two gold coins to the man. Slapping him on the back, Ren tried to sound friendly. "Thank you for the information, Shelly. See that the homeless get this."

Shelly was obviously pleased by this gesture. He softened up a bit and no longer seemed as jumpy around the legendary ranger. "Many thanks, sir. And watch out for the first councilman. Lord Bartholomew is a rough one, Ren o' the Blade!" the old guard offered.

During the rest of the short journey, Ren asked Shelly if he knew anything else about the city's disappearance. The trooper knew little more than silly rumors, and the ranger realized that most of the sparse information was only idle chatter.

The tent city that sprawled before Ren was a huge, dismal thing. A large corral for horses stood to the north of the city. The wretched smell made it obvious that horse droppings were regularly tossed into the river. Greasy cooking fires sent plumes of smoke up over the village. Most of the tents along the river were little more than ceilings of canvas with open sides or blankets propped against ladders or wooden planks. Ren hoped there were some answers to be found, but his mood worsened as he looked about. He seriously doubted that anything useful would be found in New Phlan. His heart felt heavy in his chest. Even Stolen seemed somber.

As the raft approached the bank, ten troopers stood ready to meet it. They were led by a tall knight wearing plate mail armor. The knight's crest proclaimed him to be of the Wainwright clan, but Ren had met other members of the Wainwright family and found them much more refined than this gruff-looking fellow. Before even a polite hello could be offered, the leader began bellowing orders at Ren.

"By the order of the great and noble Lord Bartholomew and the council of New Phlan, your horse must be stabled with the other mounts of the city."

The ranger didn't like the tone of this fool. Ren's patience had worn thin. He wasn't in the mood for delays, not when an entire city was missing.

Shelly came to his aid. "Lord Wainwright, you know not who you bark at. This fine gent is none other than Ren o' the Blade. He's come to help us get our city back." Ren winced at the confidence in Shelly's voice, but the man spoke well.

Shelly continued. "Back your men off, Lord, before Ren o' the Blade has to prove his name once more in the new city of Phlan." Ren opened his mouth, then closed it, waiting to see what would happen.

He couldn't tell if it was his reputation or the bold proclamations of the old trooper or maybe the stomping of his nervous war-horse that elicited the desired effect, but the ten troopers backed up. The tall knight didn't move an inch.

The leader obviously wasn't going to be pushed around, but he wasn't getting any support from his troopers. Turning to the raft, Lord Wainwright saw the ranger's big grin.

"Lord Bartholomew discovered that animals were making New Phlan a diseased place. He has ordered them all penned. Your horse will be well cared for. But if it's a fight you want, you can be *well cared for*, too."

Ren laughed inwardly at the tall knight's bravado. He

was probably a real coward who ran from anything more than a bar brawl. But it wouldn't be very polite to cut a fellow like him in half. New Phlan would likely need every healthy defender it had.

"I have no desire for a fight," Ren answered sincerely. "But I do have something more gentlemanly to ask of a member of clan Wainwright. I fought alongside your cousins on the old walls of Phlan and found them to be heroic and brave. May I suggest that if you wish to live as long as your cousins, you explain your orders to innocent people before you deliver them? I believe it will dispose them to obeying rather than challenging you."

"My lord," the now-smiling knight said, "from the look of your two-handed sword, your chain mail, and the daggers trying to hide in your boots, I judge you haven't been innocent for quite some time."

The tall knight's men got a good laugh out of the joke. The ranger nodded in deference to Lord Wainwright's clever observation. Waving acceptance, the warrior led his mount to the makeshift corral a hundred yards away.

Ren located an empty area and took a few moments to unload his gear. He fed and watered Stolen, patted the beast, and ordered the war-horse to be behave. Stolen was the biggest horse in the corral, and the ranger departed without concern for the animal.

Ren glanced around, hating what he saw. Walking aimlessly up and down the river, the ranger could see there was little method to the arrangement of New Phlan. Three wide dirt paths spread to the east and west, but the tents along these paths formed side alleys and dead ends. Everywhere he looked, he saw people looking poor, destitute, and dirty. Phlan had been a prosperous city of many merchants. New Phlan needed a lot of help if it was even going to survive.

The city watch was in force—a good sign. At least some attempts were being made at law and order. Each squad of men was led by a knight in plate mail. From the dents and scrapes on their armor and shields, they looked to be earning their pay the hard way.

Venturing into the middle of the city, Ren found one tent a little larger and cleaner than the rest. He instantly recognized the Scales of Balance, symbol of the god Tyr, on a crest at the flap of the tent. Although Ren wasn't a worshiper of the god of justice, he knew Tarl was. The ranger entered and found three warrior priests trying to help the poor souls crowding into the tent seeking food and healing. Feeling sorry for the three over-worked clerics, Ren put aside the scores of questions filling his mind and pitched in.

After several hours of distributing healing potions and food, there was a lull in the activity. One of the clerics addressed him for the first time.

"Thank you, stranger. Your help is appreciated. You aren't of our faith, are you?"

The ranger extended a hand. "My name is Ren o' the Blade. One of my friends was a priest in your service. His name was Tarl, and he lived in Phlan before the city disappeared. Do you know of him?"

"We all know Tarl," the cleric answered. His voice reflected respect for Ren's friend. "He was a tower of strength and courage in Phlan. I fought many a battle at his side. But you should speak with Brother Anton. He'll return shortly. He might be able to tell you more about what has happened in the city. In the meantime, please dine with us and stay the night."

Ren grinned. "That's an offer I can't refuse. Brother Anton was recovering from a wound during my first visit in Phlan ten years ago. I am happy to hear he is still alive. I'll return after I check on my horse at the corral."

The city was nearly dark. Ren hurried to the corral, and in no time, watered and curried Stolen, giving him an extra ration of oats. The big mount was nervous and chafing at the boredom of the corral.

"You big lout. You know you won't be stuck here long. I'll give you a good hard ride tomorrow. We've been busy the last few weeks, and there'll soon be plenty more action for you. I don't know where our friends have gone, but you and I will find them if our search takes us to the ends of Toril."

Ren shook his head as he left the enclosure, trying hard to credit his own words. If the gods had actually taken Phlan, finding his friend would be a tall order.

A giant of a man was waiting for the ranger in front of the lighted tent of Tyr. Anton had been weak and barely walking the last time Ren had seen him, years ago. Now the man was strong and robust, reaching out to hug Ren.

"It's good to see you, ranger," the warrior-cleric said with a rib-crushing hug. "Tarl and Shal aren't dead, my boy. I know that for sure, but I know little else. Come into the tent and share the evening meal with us."

Ren was barely able to contain himself. Anton just nodded and smiled, talking about the events of the day. He had traveled from tent to tent, helping families to put their lives back together.

Two of the priests of Tyr were gone on a council mission to gather trees from the forest to begin rebuilding the city. Five more of the brothers were with a larger contingent sent to quarry stone from the Dragonspine Mountains. Phlan wouldn't be Phlan without new walls to protect the city. Ren couldn't help but marvel at their optimism. They all spoke of *rebuilding* the city; as far as Ren could see, there was nothing to rebuild *from.* They were entirely starting over.

Finally, Ren could stand the suspense no longer. "Anton, what of Tarl and Shal? How do you know they aren't dead?"

"Oh, I imagine you can feel it, too. You and I hold them deep in our hearts. We would know if they died. Our hearts would know it."

Anton's tone was somber as he continued. "I have communed with Tyr about our friends and our city. Our god has graciously granted me the knowledge that Tarl is alive. Tarl was given the gift of summoning the Warhammer of Tyr. During the night the city disappeared, a small gathering of our order took the hammer on the Ceremony of Spring. We were far from the city when the storm broke and ripped Phlan from us. But the hammer was summoned right out of our midst, and Tarl was the only one among us with that power."

Ren choked at this news. "I saw him do it! It was in a dream I had over a month ago. I saw Tarl and Shal fighting for their lives after something horrible had happened to the city. Until today, I'd hoped it was only a dream." Ren was agitated, and Anton encouraged him to relate the details of his strange dream. When he had finished, Ren turned to the cleric in earnest. "I have to find them, Anton. Can you help?"

"I'll do what I can, Ren, but I can't leave Phlan. I have to help the refugees here. But I have a feeling that the answers to some of your questions lie here in the city. Keep looking, and with the aid of Tyr, you will learn the fate of your friends."

Brother Anton grew more serious as he counseled the desperate Ren. "I must warn you, brother, that what you find may well be worse than anything you have lived through." Then Anton's fatherly nature took over. "Now get some rest, boy. You'll do our friends no good if you aren't at your best."

If Ren hadn't been so worried, he would have been amused at being called "boy" by this giant of a man. The ranger was almost forty years old, and rarely thought of himself as young. But he was comforted a little by Anton's compassion. Ren eventually fell into an uneasy sleep.

Up at dawn, as was his habit, the ranger helped the clerics for part of the morning, but Anton soon pushed him out of the tent.

"Ren, my lad, get out and among the people of this troubled city. Steer clear of the town guards. They're an honest lot, but they have a tough job and take their work seriously. Now out with you."

The seven-foot-tall Anton was hard to refuse. Ren sighed and left with a smile before Anton could toss him out of the tent, setting out to explore the sad city.

New Phlan could hardly be called a city—it was less than a hamlet, even though hundreds of people filled the shores of the Moonsea. Merchants hawked their wares, but without enthusiasm. Children played in the muddy dirt paths, but without energy. It was as if something had sucked the life out of the place.

Ren had fetched Stolen to give him some exercise. As he started out, a contingent of four city watchmen approached. They were led by a knight with a hawk's crest on his shield. Ren didn't recognize the heraldic emblem.

"Are you Ren o' the Blade?" the leader barked.

Ren wondered if all the town guards failed their lessons in etiquette and making friends.

"What's a simple ranger done to attract the attention of the town watch?" he responded.

"Lord Bartholomew has ordered us to find Ren o' the

Blade and bring him to the council. If you are this man, come along with us."

"I'm the man you're looking for, but I have other things to do," Ren replied. "I'll try to visit the council this afternoon."

The knight looked ready to fight, but there was no such enthusiasm among the other guards. The leader fairly seethed as he responded to Ren's boldness. "I will tell lord Bartholomew all that has transpired here. You had better find yourself at the council tent this afternoon or you will be sorry this conversation ended the way it did. I will personally make sure you are sufficiently regretful." The knight spun around and pushed his way through his men.

"Another friend gone, Stolen. Some days you just can't please anyone."

Seated high on Stolen's back, the ranger waded into the river until he was far to the north of the encampment. This section had been the campgrounds for countless invading armies in the old wars. The land was a flat plane with all timber and obstructions long ago removed. The poorest of the poor now lived here, north of New Phlan. These were the people living under the sky. Only the gods knew what they would do when winter came. Frost and sickness would kill most of them.

Happy to be out of the stable, Stolen rode hard. Ren merely guided him. They traveled to the southwest, circling wide around Phlan. The ranger wanted to reach Stormy Bay before noon. The fresh air felt good after the squalor of the city.

Arriving at the bay sooner than he had expected, Ren's attention was drawn to a campfire. Two druids rose to meet him.

"Finally, you've come! The fish is almost ruined," said a

tall man. He turned from Ren and bent over a campfire to examine several bass sizzling in a large pan.

The woman directed her attention to Ren. "Please don't mind him. My cousin has a passion for food. We guessed you would get here by lunchtime. I am so happy we were right."

Ren stared. He was completely surprised that these people thought they knew him, but he also stared for another reason. The woman was nothing less than gorgeous. Short in stature but with an ample figure filling her druid robes, her skin was browned from the sun and her long brown hair fell in a shower around her hips. She had a way of looking at Ren that made him strangely uncomfortable.

"I am called Ren o' the Blade," he said, feeling self-conscious. "You must be mistaking me for someone else. You couldn't have known I was going to be here. I didn't know myself until I started riding." The ranger dismounted, wanting to get a better look at these two strangers.

Stolen bowed his head to the woman, something that surprised Ren, especially since the war-horse had never been trained to do such a thing. The woman produced a huge apple from somewhere in her robes and offered it to the horse. Stolen accepted it, enamored of the woman, much to Ren's dismay.

Without looking up from his cooking fire, the other druid spoke. "Please forgive my manners for not greeting you properly." He moved a pan of fish off the fire and straightened up to face Ren. "My name is Andoralson, and this lady is my cousin, Talenthia. We have been sent to help you find Phlan and return it to its proper place. What plans do you have?"

The woman scowled at her cousin, looking exasperated. "You could wait until he's had his lunch. He doesn't even know us. We owe him an explanation, at the very least."

Ren looked back and forth at the two strangers, completely confused and not knowing what to think. The ranger couldn't decide whether to trust them, although he found himself wanting to like them.

Stolen, on the other hand, knelt in the grass near the woman. Ren sighed; his steed looked more like a wide-eyed puppy than a noble war-horse. But animals usually had a sense about such things. Beside that, the fish smelled great. Fresh cooked food was something he could appreciate. He decided to give in, at least for now.

Ren reached into Stolen's saddlebags and brought out a large flask. "Um, I think this wine from Vaasa should go well with your fish," he said, still not quite comfortable.

"Just the thing to complete the meal," Talenthia said with a smile. She produced three wondrously crafted wooden chalices from a wicker hamper.

Serving up the fish on huge leaves, Andoralson told their story. "We've been sent here by our god, Sylvanus. Until now, my cousin and I have been traveling Faerun looking for a forest to call our own. But in many recent dreams, the plight of Phlan was made known to us. Phlan's disappearance has disturbed the equity of nature. Sylvanus tells us you have the best chance of restoring Phlan and restoring the balance."

Ren was still somewhat stunned. Talenthia handed him a leaf loaded with fish, winking at the ranger. Her robes parted slightly as she moved, and Ren noticed green chain mail under her gown. How the woman could show such a fine figure weighted down under chain mail, Ren couldn't guess. But he didn't mind speculating.

The ranger held his fish in his hands, wondering what to say. "I—I don't understand what you're talking about," he stammered. "I have no plan. I only want to find out what's happened to my friends."

"But we believe the evil gods have stolen Phlan. We must do what we can to set things right." Talenthia's voice was pleading.

The last thing Ren wanted was to attract the attention of angry gods. "I'm a ranger, and I love the land as much as you do, but I care nothing for the affairs of gods. Besides, I prefer to work alone."

This last was said in deliberate rebuff to the pair before him. The man appeared to be a capable adventurer, but Ren didn't like his lecturing tone. The woman was far too distracting to be anything but trouble on the trail.

"I don't believe you have the proper frame of mind, ranger," Andoralson said. He savored every bite of fish as if it were some exotic food. For some reason, Ren found this annoying.

"What my cousin means is that we have been *ordered* to help you. We only want to restore nature's balance. You can understand that, can't you?" Talenthia was difficult for Ren to resist, but resist he continued to do.

The ranger wiped his hands on the grass. "I want to thank you both for the delicious meal, but I must go visit with the town council. I appreciate your offer, but you and your god will have to find Phlan without me. I don't have any plans right now, but I like to move as opportunities arise. You two would just slow me down."

The ranger gave them the friendliest smile he could muster, mounted Stolen, and waved good-bye.

Talenthia watched until Ren and his horse became specks in the distance. "Wasn't he handsome, Andoralson? I'm so glad Sylvanus sent us to help him."

"Talenthia, why must you always flirt? If they're tall and have a little gray hair, you fall all over them." Her cousin was obviously irritated, but he attempted to put his feelings aside. "He appears very confident. I like the fact that he didn't jump at our offer. We obviously have to prove ourselves to this one. The town council session ought to do it, don't you think?"

"Just what we need, Cousin. We should pack our gear and get moving." The woman's eyes twinkled. "And don't act as if you've never flirted before!" Her cousin blushed.

The druids spoke a magical syllable and were instantly transformed into huge golden eagles. Lifting into the air, they set out for the council. They would arrive there long before Ren.

\* \* \* \* \*

The ranger was deeply troubled. He tried to put the pair of druids out of his thoughts, but the woman's figure kept slipping into his mind. Gods, she was beautiful.

"Stolen, let's get back to the tents. I want to be in New Phlan long before the sun sets!"

The huge horse galloped across the grasslands at its best speed. Its massive, rippling muscles tirelessly carried the pair across the land.

Stolen slowed as they approached the river. Ren urged him to leap into the water. Rider and mount landed with a gigantic splash. Both enjoyed the cool relief.

Ren wiped the sweaty foam off Stolen. "What a great beast you are," Ren told the animal as he cleaned the horse in the waters of the river. He led Stolen to the bank. The horse balked slightly when it saw that it was headed for the corral, but Ren's urging got the animal moving.

Heading for the gate, the ranger sensed more than saw another group of guards waiting among the tents. He could have avoided them, but such cowardly behavior wasn't his way. He preferred direct confrontations. He threw his saddle and other gear onto the pile of equipment at the side of the corral and handed the stable boy a silver coin.

"Take good care of my horse and feed him an extra ration of oats tonight. There is a chance I won't be visiting him for a while."

Ren saw the boy's eyes widen as he looked at the coin and then beyond the ranger. The fighter turned to face several knights and a horde of town watchmen.

"Ren o' the Blade. You will come with us to Lord Bartholomew. My commander didn't say what condition you had to be in, and we would all welcome a fight." The rough leader of the knights gripped his sword eagerly.

"Am I charged with a crime?" Ren asked evenly. Some of the guards had surrounded him, but they kept their distance. A crowd of tent-dwellers had formed around the entire group. Some showed open hostility toward the guards, but most of them just looked on, curious.

"Resisting arrest, refusing an order from a councilman, obstructing justice, and a hundred others. Besides, I don't really need a charge to pummel you senseless, ranger. How do you want it?"

"I'll come quietly," Ren responded. Then he raised his voice to all the people gathered nearby. "You all know me. I fought on the walls of Phlan and killed the bronze dragon that plagued your city. I do not deserve to be treated like a common thief. I will come now, but I will take the hand of the first man who tries to bind me." With this, Ren started walking. In a heartbeat, a faintly glowing dagger appeared in his hand for all to see. In the next moment, the dagger disappeared. The simple sleight of hand was enough to impress many of the onlookers and several of the guards.

"We don't need to bind you," the lead knight called out. It seemed to be an attempt to counteract Ren's statement. "My men and I are more than capable of bringing you to justice."

Ren strolled along, head high. He smirked, wondering who was bringing whom, but kept silent.

Deep in the heart of ramshackle New Phlan, Ren was ushered to a mounded palisade of wood and earth. What the ranger saw was a keep of sorts, meant to be a last ditch defense if the tent city was attacked. Ren was impressed. He was ordered into the center of the compound, where he discovered a large white tent. Inside, he met the new council of Phlan.

"Why has this ranger been brought to me wearing weapons?" The speaker was a tall, thin knight in expensive, gleaming armor. He was obviously nobility, and Ren knew he faced Lord Bartholomew. The other councilmen were seated around a large table. Ren saw Anton sitting in the tenth councilman's seat, and for the first time since the encounter with the guards, he found some joy in the impossible situation. The cleric of Tyr would not fail the ranger.

"I wasn't brought to you, Lord. I came myself. I am wearing my weapons because I was not made aware of any charge against me. Has the council of Phlan changed so much that an innocent man must stand like a criminal, unarmed, before them?"

"What I have heard of you seems to be true, Ren o' the Blade. I am Lord Bartholomew, first councilman of New Phlan. My city needs brave heroes like yourself to help rebuild. I would make you one of my highest lords."

"I didn't come here to become a gate guard of a town with no gates. I have come for information regarding my two friends. Maybe you have heard of them—the warrior cleric Tarl and the wizard Shal Bal?"

"Bah, they were of old Phlan. The gods took the city for their own reasons. We have to think of the future. We have to build New Phlan into a greater city than the old one ever was. Now, are you with us or against us?"

Ren was stunned. This man was actually ready to forget Phlan. Lord Bartholomew was too pushy for his taste. This first councilman was a far cry from the type of leader the new city would need.

Anton tried to signal Ren to remain calm, but the ranger didn't care right now who he offended. "I'm going after my friends wherever the quest takes me. I will not be stopped."

"Stopped? I will do much more than stop you if I must, ranger. You can be chained to a work crew. You can be sold to serve on a merchant ship. I will have you working for Phlan or—"

"Have you ever seen an enraged squirrel attack a wood cutter?" a deep voice cut through the tirade.

"Or have you seen what happens when dock rats get unbearably hungry?" said an enchantingly feminine voice.

Two druids had slipped through the throng of guards as if they didn't exist, gliding up to Ren. The brown robes they had worn earlier had been replaced with dazzling white robes. There seemed to be a pale green aura to the fabric, but the robes were so white they were hard to look at.

"Rats, squirrels, what are you talking about? Guards, remove these—"

"Oh, I wouldn't try that," said Talenthia. "We druids have a way with animals. Or aren't you aware of such powers?"

A huge black rat, bigger than a man's boot, leaped up onto the chamber table, and seven more surrounded the first councilman.

"Please let me explain before my cousin turns the rats on this entire tent. I am Andoralson, a druid and worshiper of Sylvanus. This is Talenthia. If you harm our friend Ren or do anything to hinder him, you will be amazed and terrified at what happens. The animals of the forest will prevent you from taking the lumber you need. The mules you drive to bring back the stone of the Dragonspine Mountains will refuse to budge. The fish of the sea will never enter your nets. Have I left anything out, Talenthia? Ren?" After a moment of stunned silence in the tent, the druid added, "The three of us will be leaving now."

Anton was the only councilman looking at all pleased. The cleric made no attempt to conceal the big grin on his face. He gave the three a wave of encouragement.

"No, I think that covers everything, Andoralson. We must be going. We may be in town for a few more days. See that these fine, strong troops don't bother us, Lord Bartholomew. Ren, come with us." Talenthia took the surprised ranger by the arm and led him away. As they left the tent, she whispered, "I am so glad everything worked out. Things could have gotten messy. Now what do we do?"

"I don't have the slightest idea," Ren said, looking into her deep gray eyes. He couldn't remember a time when he had been more confused.

# ❧ 7 ❧

# Phlan Under Siege

The battle plans were ready. Troops were assembled and trained. Monsters were recruited, bribed, and in position. All varieties of spellcasters—both clerics and wizards—were ready to unleash magical fury on the unsuspecting city.

Phlan was about to be attacked again.

At the center of this swarm of activity was a cackling, evil, overconfident wizard. Red robes flowed around him as he galloped among the troops on his horrifying black horse, a nightmare. Catching sight of his battle commander, he trotted over to issue final instructions. Marcus was exhilarated by the thought of the upcoming conflict.

"Commander Brittle, with the forces we now command, we can't lose. The pathetic citizens of Phlan will soon know what it is to have their lives ripped from their grasp." Marcus laughed an evil, grating howl.

The battle commander turned toward his superior. Neck and spine bones creaked and cracked as the skeletal warrior moved. The clicking of bones and the rattle of armor was audible above the sounds of battle preparations. Marcus grinned. Undead creatures fascinated him. He was delighted to have skeletons, ghouls, wights, and other undead making up nearly half his army. These creatures weren't harmed by the injuries that could devastate a human; they didn't bleed and were immune to many spells. Marcus had spells to simulate such effects, but these benefits came naturally to undead creatures. The wizard grinned again.

Brittle listened to his leader with feigned respect. A thousand years ago, he had been a mighty human commander of an army of hundreds of thousands. Buried peacefully until recently, he had been awakened and animated by Tanetal to serve this crazed wizard.

The undead warrior wasn't impressed by the forces passing in review, but he would do his best to serve. There was always the chance to move up in rank if those above him became casualties of war. But even Marcus's position didn't pique his interest. The ragged assembly of warriors, monsters, and spellcasters was neither disciplined nor properly trained. Great numbers of creatures had been assembled, nearly twice the population of Phlan, but Brittle doubted their effectiveness. Time would tell.

This red-robed wizard was arrogant and overconfident. He organized a terrific military parade, but simply wasn't a strategist.

If the skeleton had been capable of breathing, Brittle would have sighed. Instead, he faked interest in the wizard's babbling. Skeletal warriors couldn't be choosy about whom they served.

"The gates of Phlan must fall in this attack. The gates *will* fall in this attack. There are thousands of men out there ready to die for me. After the gates are dust, we will sweep into the city and decimate the rabble trying to defend their homes. But remember, as tempting as it may be, we can't kill them all. Most of the pathetic humans must be captured and taken to the dark pool. I have some enticing rewards planned for my commanders who prove themselves today." Marcus's eyes gleamed.

Brittle was irritated. He had heard all these plans before, over and over. All seven feet of his undead body crackled with mystical energy.

The bony commander knew what would really happen. The mercenaries would run at the first sign of real resistance. Even the piles of gold the pit fiend had promised them after a victory wouldn't be enough to make them hold rank. Against Marcus's wishes, Brittle had placed better troops behind the puny humans to cut off the inevitable retreat and force the mercenaries to keep fighting.

"Look at those ogres, trolls, and orcs. There must be a thousand of them. With these monsters as the backbone of my army, I know we can't lose today. I wish I'd had these troops a month ago when we first attacked Phlan. All I had were those dozen fiends, just like Bane gave the attackers of the other cities. The troops of Phlan crushed them and the other armies I hurled at their walls. But I'm not going to lose this time. By the gods, this army is ten times stronger than the last one."

The crazed red mage was right about one thing, the skeletal warrior thought. The ogres, orcs, and trolls were the best troops he commanded. They would carry the day if anything could.

"Look there, Brittle," Marcus said, pointing, "why aren't those two hundred skeletons in the front lines with the rest of the undead troops?"

Brittle's answer was short and curt. The less he said, the less his chances of revealing his contempt for the wizard. "Reserves. In any battle, reserves are crucial." Then, staring down at his leader, the skeleton took the opportunity to end Marcus's lecturing. "I must go now to lead the ogres into battle. With your permission?"

"Of course—go, you tower of bones. Do me proud, and I will command the pit fiend to restore you to life. I will personally lead the reserve forces into the fight when needed. You needn't worry about them. They will be well commanded."

A shudder slithered up the fleshless spine of the skeletal warrior. The thought of this bag of water leading anything didn't please him. In centuries past, Brittle had controlled a hundred wizards like Marcus and had forced them to do little more than ensure clear weather. Now, he was forced to follow such a man's orders.

Although the skeletal commander hoped the mage wouldn't lead the reserve units to disaster, Brittle gave up the notion of depending on that portion of the army to do anything worthwhile. He marched down the hill to lead the waiting army.

Up on the rise, Marcus was still giddy with anticipation. His armies had to win today. Bane wouldn't tolerate many more delays. In the few communications the pit fiend had had with the god, Marcus learned that some of the other captured cities had also managed to resist the god's grasp. He was relieved that Phlan wasn't the only city holding out. One town filled with spellcasters had even managed to transport itself back to Faerun. The Red Wizard hoped the distraction of the other cities would help fend off the god's wrath until Marcus could conquer Phlan.

The wizard's mood was dampened slightly as he surveyed his troops. "Where is that fourth squad of mercenaries? I thought we counted about fifteen hundred human troops coming up to the tower. I hope that pit fiend didn't eat them or something. It would be just like him to eat the best troops. Well. No matter. It's time to put the fear of Red Wizards in the hearts of my enemies. *Xanotos, kartaalomi, tysrius flarigraasi!*"

The upper third of the huge cave was suddenly filled with a ball of fire thousands of yards tall and wide. The blinding light of the magical flames blasted forth as bright as the sun. The inferno at the top of the cavern gradually began to form familiar images and scenes.

The flames writhed and created blood-red towers and gates identical to the walls and towers of Phlan, which rested a mile below on the floor of the cavern. More flames took the forms of molten figures of men, orcs, ogres, and trolls, taller and more powerful than the real things. The scorching armies charged against the flaming towers and walls high in the sky. A magical battle began between the flaming forces representing Phlan's guards on the walls and the molten armies of the Red Wizard. In seconds, the molten forces tore down the gates and broke through the walls, streaming into the city like a river of lava.

"A splendid effect!" sighed Marcus. The spell was a bit more than he had planned, but if his magical show of power frightened the defenders and inspired his own troops, his efforts were well worth the cost of his magical reserves.

Waves of searing heat blasted down on the Red Wizard's army. The trolls, particularly vulnerable to fire, cowered in fear. The orcs, ogres, and humans stood at sweaty attention, frightened by the display. Hundreds of skeletons raised hollow eye sockets to the flames, showing no expression on their fleshless faces, but nonetheless impressed.

"Stupid wizard," hissed Brittle, "now I have to use the ogres to get the trolls moving. And he's destroyed any element of surprise we might have had."

The skeletal leader commanded powerful ogres to move toward the gibbering trolls. Trolls were awesome fighters and difficult to kill, but fire prevented them from regenerating damaged limbs. The lumbering green creatures feared fire above all things. Gods help him, if Brittle survived this fight, the enchanted commander wouldn't ask to be made human again. Thinking unspeakable thoughts, the skeleton imagined it would ask for the heart of the wizard instead. The undead leader snorted a dry chuckle at the thought as he directed the army to attack the gates of Phlan.

\* \* \* \* \*

The defenders of Phlan were unimpressed by the magical display. None knew why their town had been taken by the gods and sent to this place of evil. None knew when their torture would end. But all knew how to fight, and the force rising against them wouldn't be much trouble. They had endured worse.

"Think they'll attack over here, Ston?" Tulen asked, spitting a chaw of tobacco over the wall.

"Naaa, looks like they're goin' after the Death Gates again. You think they'd learn after the last time. Them trolls are nasty, though. My brother Dorel got eaten by a troll in the hill giant battle we had a few years back."

"Shouldn't be much of a problem this time, Ston. That cleric Tarl sent a bunch of boar skins full of blessed oil over to the gate the other day. That's one smart priest if you ask me."

"I know what you mean. That sorceress wife of his has been cooking up all kinds of magical defenses. And, boy, is she something to look at." Ston snorted a laugh.

"I hear tell our wizards and clerics can't figure out

where the gods stuck us. Whaddya think?"

"I guess I'm not surprised none. Wizard stuff ain't normal. But they've usually got an answer for everything. If the gods want us in Faerun or in the Nine Hells, well, then that's where we'll have to be. Mark my words, we'll be back fishing on the Moonsea before the year's out. Tarl has the Warhammer of Tyr, and his god is a tough one to trifle with. If we hold off these attacks, we'll be fine, you betcha."

"Looks like things are heating up over there. What say you and me hustle over and join in the fun?"

"Commander Billings would have our butts for breakfast if we tried leaving our posts. The gate attack could be a diversion for something bigger somewheres else. Remember the fire giant battle? The army of giants that attacked here and a hundred umber hulks burrowed underground and attacked on the other side of the city? Nobody ever saw 'em coming. Now, where would we be if some of those wall defenders had left their wall and come over here to share in the fun?"

"Damnation, you're right. Hate to admit it. What say after our shift here, we go and ask old Billings to be transferred over to the Death Gates. You and me being sixty years old should have some say in where we defend Phlan."

"Now there's an idea. Especially if that ugly Red Wizard is going to lead any more armies against us."

At the Death Gates, the battle was warming up. Marcus's mercenary troops, hauling ladders and siege engines, slowly approached the walls around the gate. The northernmost entry into the city, this main entrance had been built and rebuilt over the stormy, war-torn history of Phlan. Now, this gate was larger and better fortified than any normal gate.

Two huge gatehouses of red Dragonspine stone stood a hundred feet apart and jutted out a hundred feet beyond the walls. The three-story towers were crowded with archers, and equipped with cauldrons of burning oil and small catapults. The double-door gates rose thirty feet. Each was made of aged oak, bound with thick bands of iron to strengthen the doors. The effort necessary to open and close the gates required huge counterweights and pulleys.

Behind these towers, a deadly passage connected with another set of towers embedded in Phlan's walls. The passage could be showered with arrows or burning oil by the defenders of the city. Even if the attackers broke through the outer doors, they faced the passage of death and another set of double-door gates lined with arrow slits, allowing the defenders to pepper the passage with feathered death.

The last assault by Marcus and his army had barely scratched the first pair of gates, but the wizard was convinced the battle would be different this time. The siege towers rolled grimly toward the walls. In the last attack, rolling towers like these had been burned by catapult fire attacks before they'd reached within a hundred yards of the gate. Now, flaming shot bounced off the magically protected surfaces of the steadily moving siege engines.

"They're fireproof, fools," Marcus shouted from behind his army. He ordered his nightmare into the sky and watched the battle from a hundred feet off the ground, remaining far enough away to be out of range of most spells and stray catapult loads. "You won't be burning my siege towers again!"

Hordes of ogres pushed the engines of destruction. The six siege towers moved faster and faster toward the walls. A hundred heavily armored troops were hidden in each tower. The ogres and the men inside became more and more eager to face the defenders of Phlan. When the siege towers closed in on the walls, small bridges would be lowered. The troops inside could stream over the protective wall, attacking Phlan's troops.

Six loud crashes erupted suddenly, and the towers fell, crushing hundreds of men unlucky enough to be in the vicinity.

"What in the name of Bane himself?" Marcus couldn't believe his eyes.

A chorus of cheers arose on the walls.

"Did you see that, Ston? It worked! I told you it would! The wizards dug a bunch of pits fifty yards from the walls, and every tower smashed into one. Wahoo!" Tulen hopped up and down with glee.

Marcus fumed. Now he could see the clay-lined pits that had been cleverly covered so the weight of a few men wouldn't spring them. The full weight of a heavy siege tower was needed to break the covering. The wizard's flameproof towers lay in splinters.

"They'll pay! Those fools will pay for every day of delay they've caused me. I'll burn them in eternal fires!" Marcus began to wheeze and tried to calm himself. "This is a just minor setback. My own little surprise will get them. Just wait and see."

Marcus watched from on high as arrows, crossbow bolts, and catapult rocks rained down on the mercenary troops as they rushed the gate, spurred on by the fearsome troops behind them. For a while, they made headway behind the army's mantelets. These mobile wooden walls rolled ahead of the troops and absorbed most of the deadly missiles. But as the attackers got closer, many of the heavy crossbow bolts found their way through or around the mantelets to find soft flesh behind the wood. The mercenary numbers were quickly reduced.

None of the defenders paid much attention to six axe-wielding troopers running slightly ahead of the other mercenaries. These warriors looked like all the others, but the missiles that approached them bounced inches away from their battle-hardened bodies. To the defenders on the walls above, the shots simply looked poorly aimed.

The axemen easily reached the first gate. Instead of hacking at the oak walls, they dropped their axes and drew small scrolls out of silver tubes. Each warrior glowed with magical protections as he read spells specially designed to blast open the gates.

Too late the defenders recognized the men for the spellcasters they were. A sheet of burning oil poured from the top of the gate in an attempt to burn the mages or at least foil their spells. The oil poured off an invisible magical barrier and fell to either side of the spellcasters. The Death Gates opened, groaning, and the attackers rushed into the tunnel. The next gate was in sight. With leaders such as these, surely the enemy couldn't fail.

Three hundred of Marcus's mercenaries that remained outside the gates ran into the tunnel. Anything had to be better than the rain of death outside. Orcs, ogres, and trolls rushed in, hurling rocks, arrows, and sling bullets at the defenders. The fighting grew more intense.

In the tunnel of death, three of every five men died from arrow wounds as they tried to approach the second gate, which stood only a hundred feet away. The six wizards reached the gate without so much as a scratch. Their spells found the locks and bars of the inner gate.

As the portal swung open, the mercenary swarm smelled victory.

From their position on the wall, Ston and Tulen could see the gates open, exposing the broad inner streets of Phlan to the enemy. Filling the streets, prepared to greet the enemy, were wave after wave of pikemen all set to receive the charge. At the front was their leader, a warrior-cleric wielding a glowing blue hammer.

"Welcome to Phlan!" Tarl shouted.

Brittle recognized the gates for the death trap they truly were. He had laid siege to such places in ages past. His human troops had been directed to make the initial attack so he could get his elite army close enough to execute his own tactics. At his command, the ogres pushed the trolls toward the walls on either side of the gate. Brittle strode ahead of his troops to the red walls, attracting hundreds of arrows and crossbow bolts, all bouncing harmlessly off his enchanted bones. Another dry chuckle testified to the advantage of not having flesh.

Watching from on high, Marcus couldn't believe what the fool, Brittle, was doing. The remainder of the troops could stroll right into Phlan! Instead, the ogres were herding the trolls to the walls where they could be easily shot by arrows.

"Roast his bones, that fool Brittle. Now I have to go in and save him and my army."

The Red Wizard commanded his nightmare to circle over the troops at the rear. Swooping down over the warrior skeletons, the nightmare snorted smoke, its red eyes blazing. Marcus bellowed at the reserves and ordered them forward. A clattering army of armored bones creaked across the field. As they moved, Marcus cast spell after spell of protection. Little flames of magic burned over the bodies of all the skeletons. Other spells increased the speed of his small force, allowing them to swing their weapons faster. The wizard hid himself in a tower of intense flames. As he commanded his troops into the valley and toward the gates, he lost sight of what the rest of his army was doing.

The ogres had teamed up and were tossing trolls to the tops of the walls. The trolls landed hard, but weren't harmed by the impact. In the entire history of Phlan, this tactic had never been used against the stone walls. Within moments, fifty green, seven-foot-tall trolls were clawing and biting the defenders.

While the trolls waged their battle, ogres and orcs raised the long-forgotten ladders and climbed up onto the walls without resistance. Brittle was the last to climb up. His toothy mouth grinned at his exceptional strategy.

Tarl and the Warhammer of Tyr battled the enemy spellcasters while pikemen decimated the mercenaries. The strategy had been practiced often by the Death Gate guards. Tarl gave the signal for a sheet of burning oil to fall behind the attackers, cutting off their retreat. Then the cleric moved in for close combat with the six enchanted wizards. Hundreds of pikemen slaughtered mercenaries to the last man. Neither side considered surrender. In this battle to the death, there could be only one survivor.

Far above Tarl's head, Phlan's spellcasters stood on an enchanted rainbow. Using a spell that had required decades of research, the men and women stood astride a ten-foot swath of energy. Beneath the feet of every priest and wizard, the path matched the chosen color of the spellcaster's energy. Ten-foot blocks of green, blue, orange, yellow, purple and a myriad of subtle hues alternated in the path of protective magic. Lightning bolts, balls of fire, swarms of magical hornets, showers of ice, and other enchantments rained down onto shrieking monsters.

Ston shouted to Tulen over the clashing and ringing of the battle. "You should see it, Tulen! The magic stuff is broiling everything it hits! And the trolls are getting hacked to little green pieces! Ooh, there goes an arm! There goes another arm—and a head! Come on, guys, set them on fire before they regenerate! You know it doesn't take trolls long to pull themselves together!"

Most of the trolls were chopped down before the ogres and orcs even got into the battle. A dozen warriors were assigned the task of dousing the trolls' remains in oil and setting them ablaze. The stench was nauseating.

But soon the ogres were smashing into the organized lines of defenders on the wall. As the armored, pig-faced orcs entered the battle, Brittle felt a surge of confidence. Casualties were high, but his troops were holding rank and showed no sign of retreat. The frenzy was so thick that he no longer worried about his troops routing.

Then Brittle noticed something he hadn't expected. Another red stone wall stood a hundred yards farther into the city, and another, and another farther in. This blasted city was ringed with walls! Brittle hoped the Red Wizard had some brilliant fallback.

Meanwhile, Marcus was enchanting himself with magical strength. Astride his steed, he led the skeletons to the outer red stone towers. He couldn't imagine failure.

"*Ubinosis erronazanz blutuphonkrar!*"

The gates that had stopped him before were blown to bits, crushing ten skeletons.

"There! Those gates won't be a problem again." The wizard smirked.

Arrows, crossbow bolts, and rocks all turned to dust as they struck the magical flaming barriers around the

Red Wizard and his steed.

Black magical flames burst from Marcus's fingertips and burned the bodies of the dead mercenaries to ashes. The floor of the deadly passage, choked with bodies moments ago, was now covered in black soot. All Marcus could see now was the open gate ahead of him. Finally, victory would be his.

"This is how war should be—with me in triumph! Where is Brittle, that fool? He could learn from this!"

Marcus rode proudly into the city of Phlan on his snorting nightmare, a sulfurous cloud surrounding him. To his left and right stood massive squads of defenders. But they were too far away for Marcus's spells of destruction to reach.

Only a lone man, a warrior-priest, stood before him.

"I've seen you before, priest. You caused me trouble in the last battle!"

Tarl saw only a pillar of flame, but knew the Red Wizard spoke from within. He looked around the city quickly to assess the situation. Everywhere, Phlan's defenders ably challenged the hordes of monsters and soldiers. Far above him, the magical ribbon wove across the sky, rainbow energies surging down on the enemy. Tarl picked out Shal's shade of purple and sighed, knowing that she was safe and her efforts were making a difference. He turned back to the Red Wizard.

"What have you done to the city of Phlan?" Tarl shouted. Sweat coated his forehead as he swung at a few undead soldiers who got close enough to worry him.

"Puny human! My warriors will destroy you!" Marcus ordered his skeletons forward to attack the priest.

As the mass of clacking, enchanted bones approached the cleric, he lifted his hammer. The holy relic glowed with a blinding blue radiance. Tyr's power was strong in

Tarl. The nearest attacking skeletons instantly turned to dust at his feet. He knew no fear. Rank after rank of skeletons approached and were destroyed in mere seconds. A heap of dusty armor and weapons lay at the feet of the cleric as he gazed into the center of the flaming pillar.

"Answer my questions now, wizard, or feel the might of my god!" Tarl moved toward the pillar of flame.

A magical parchment in Marcus's hand burst into flame as it launched a fireball, a circle of fire, and a mass of writhing, burning tentacles at the cleric. The priest was blotted from sight by the powerful, dark flames, but his hammer absorbed every bit of the fire magic and glowed brighter for the forces that were contained.

To his horror, Marcus had discovered that the blue weapon was capable of absorbing any nearby spell on command. His tower of flame and all his protections vanished as the damnable cleric approached.

The furious Red Wizard yanked at the reins of his mount, launching himself over the wall in a streak of flames. As he flew upward into the sky, purple and orange streaks blazed after him and surrounded him. Marcus retreated from Phlan, leaving his troops to fend for themselves.

The bright, streaking path of the cowardly wizard's retreat caught the attention of Ston and Tulen. They slapped each other on the back and hopped around on the wall, cackling in delight. Marcus's flashy exit was also noticed by Brittle.

"By the gods," the skeletal leader hissed. "We'd have won this battle!"

Brittle and the ogres had cleared the defenders from the center gateway. The trolls were destroyed, but the orcs still were fighting with vigor. Yet Phlanish reinforcements were on the way, and Brittle could see spellcasters floating toward the gates.

"Retreat! Leap from the walls!" Brittle took his own advice and jumped down. He'd be damned if he would allow himself to be destroyed twice in a thousand years—especially because his commander was an idiot and a coward. If he ever got his bony hands on that Red Wizard, there would be a real reckoning.

\* \* \* \* \*

An enraged, wild-eyed Marcus screamed profanities as he burst into the spellcasting chamber of his red tower. The massive pit fiend calmly sat cross-legged, levitating a few inches off a glowing pattern on the floor.

Some of the wizard's rage and frustration lessened at the comical sight of his fiend looking small and silly, floating above the floor. But then the creature stood up, still floating, and there was nothing comical about the beast anymore. The smell of stale blood filled the room, and the massive monster stretched from wingtip to toe. The fiend was a horrid monster even among its own kind. Marcus noted that the creature seemed even bigger and more powerful now than it had when it had first entered this world at his summons.

"How have you lost now? *Latenat!*" the fiend hissed, dripping green goo that sizzled as it struck the black stone floor.

The offended wizard stared sternly at the pit fiend, then held out his hand. A ball of black mist masked a large object in the wizard's grasp—the fiend's heart. The creature bowed its head. Marcus held the key to the fiend's existence on the Prime Material Plane—its name—and the one thing that could be used to destroy it utterly—its unbeating heart. If the wizard wished to, he could send the pit fiend screaming back to the Nine Hells or even destroy him outright at any time.

"I led a perfect battle!" Marcus shrieked and paced about the casting chamber. Tiny red flames sparked and vanished on the wizard's cloak as the room became filled with magical light. The room grew brighter and brighter, and the pit fiend seemed to shrink a bit. Marcus knew that fiends preferred the dark.

"It is time you realize what type of foe we face down there," the wizard ranted. "I have led too many unsuccessful attacks against Phlan. That thrice-damned place is a city always ready for battle. This time we actually broke through the gates, but got no farther. Next time you are going down there to aid the attack yourself."

"I thought we agreed that I would defend this tower and concentrate on gaining us more power. You're supposed to be leading the armies. *Latenat!*" The pit fiend was careful about the tone in his voice.

"I don't care what we agreed on! Phlan must be conquered, and the troops you've given me aren't strong enough. Bane is going to own both our souls! Then where will we be?"

"I will go back where I came from, no better, no worse. You, on the other hand, can expect to find yourself transformed by an amazingly painful process into a larva. You will then be thrown into a ten-mile-high mountain of scummy larva much like yourself. You will then be toyed with or devoured by some minions that you will find most unpleasant. *Latenat!*" The fiend's tone was matter-of-fact, but inside he was secretly gloating.

"Know, my master, that I have been in contact with clerics of the great Moander. A branch of their sect is now on its way with a new army for you to command— an army of troops that won't be affected by arrows or stones. This army will be sure to break down all the walls of Phlan and give us the souls we need.

"I have fulfilled my part of our bargain. I have sent some of the mercenary troops into the dark pool to appease Bane. These humans were fools. I told them they would be made invincible by the enchanted pool's ebony waters. They never realized they were destined to feed Bane. He was grateful and appeased, at least temporarily. He told me to compliment you on your progress. What more, master, can I do for you? *Latenat!*"

Marcus still seethed. "Until now, you have bungled everything except this last bit of news, but at least that was well done. I am now going to my throne room to wait until this fresh army arrives. I will send out magical spies to find the best places to attack Phlan. What I need is more information about the city."

Marcus ordered the black mist that contained the demon's heart to disappear into a pocket dimension. The fiend wished it could learn where its heart was kept. In the meantime, the wizard had complete control over it.

Marcus departed. After the day's battle, he deserved a rest. He would call on his winged, female companion to help him relax. As he floated to his throne room, he thought to ask Tanetal to summon more creatures like the erinyes, but he decided to wait until all this unpleasantness was over.

"The life of the future ruler of the world can be so difficult," Marcus sighed and felt sorry for himself for a moment. Then he fell into a daydream about his glorious future.

Upstairs, Tanetal contemplated his situation.

"Fool! I am such a fool for not killing him long before this. *Latenat!*" The fiend moved around the room, extinguishing the magical fires and lights Marcus had lit.

Some of the flames were exceptionally difficult to quench, even for the fiend. The Red Wizard had become even more powerful than Tanetal had suspected.

"But I haven't taught him *everything*. If Phlan doesn't fall soon, that little human idiot will be the one suffering under the beams of Bane's glare. *Latenat!*"

Tanetal would have to speak with Bane again, to grovel and explain the failure in conquering Phlan. The fiend sighed a slobbering sigh as it anticipated the unpleasant idea.

Still, the pit fiend held out hope. When the mercenaries had been sacrificed in the pool of darkness, he had absorbed some of the soul energy and gained power. Perhaps it had been enough to give him power to stand up to the god of strife.

He would be careful not to reveal too much of his own power in the next meeting with Bane. The god would be suspicious. Bane was a jealous lord, so Tanetal's best hope was to gather a strong army, overwhelm Phlan, and provide the god with many souls for the pool.

The beast grunted. "Yes, little human. I will call Bane once again. But the god will know who is in control here. *Latenat!*" He hissed as the last of the magical lights were extinguished.

# ❦ 8 ❦

# Pool of Mystery

In the dim light of dawn, Evaine's spell to locate the pool ended abruptly. Her traveling mind was instantly dumped into her brain. In the woods once more, she realized her face had been dusted by the white powder of the pulverized crystal, but she was otherwise unharmed. She looked up toward Gamaliel.

The cat was already on his feet. *If I didn't know what a strain you'd just been through, I'd tease you about looking like a carnival clown. But you need rest.*

Without a word, Evaine brushed the dust from her face into the cloth in her lap. She carefully gathered the corners of the fabric, then held it up to Gamaliel, who took the cloth in his mouth and deposited it carefully into a metal cup near the bedroll. The powder would be used as a component for another spell.

The cat returned to his mistress, allowing her to lean on him to rise to her feet. Then he led her to the bedroll. She slid to the ground. Gamaliel grasped a corner of the blanket in his teeth and pulled it up to Evaine's shoulders. He muzzled her cheek and ear, purring. *Are you going to be all right?*

Evaine didn't open her eyes, but answered the cat. "Yeah, Gam, I'll be fine. I just need to rest. Take care of things for me, will you?"

Gamaliel stretched out on the blanket alongside

Evaine. His front paws lay extended in front of him. *Don't worry about anything, mistress,* he said, nuzzling her hair. *We've been here before.*

Evaine was already asleep. Gamaliel knew she might sleep for a long time. His job was to protect his mistress as long as necessary.

The sorceress awoke in complete darkness. The coals left in the firepit had died, but she saw two points of light in the dark. "Gam? I sure hope that's you."

The cat was at her side in an instant, ready to mother her. *You slept nearly a full day. It'll be dawn in another hour. Here's the waterskin and some dried fruit. You'd better eat something so you can begin to recover.* The cat dropped the items into Evaine's hands. She followed his orders without question.

After a few minutes, Evaine felt better. Her mind was clearing, and her body was regaining energy. "Gam? Thanks for looking after me. Sometimes I don't know what I'd do without you."

*I know. Sometimes I don't know what you'd do without me either,* answered the cat. Now that Evaine was recovering, Gamaliel had reverted to his usual teasing self.

Evaine just laughed. She couldn't find it in herself to be upset with the cat—she was too accustomed to his attitude. In fact, she often thought to herself that she wouldn't have him any other way, but she'd never admit that to the feline.

"I'm going to lie here until the sky lightens, Gam. Have you eaten anything? Why don't you find yourself some breakfast? I'll be fine." Evaine really was feeling better and knew her companion must be hungry.

Gamaliel hesitated, but then decided that it wouldn't take long to hunt up some food. He rubbed her hair with his nose, then crept into the woods.

Evaine dozed. When she awoke, Gamaliel was polishing off a large trout. She wondered why he never tired of eating fish. She watched as the cat finished the last scraps, then meticulously began to wash himself. It was a careful, perfect habit that Evaine never tired of seeing. In her life of adventure and challenges, simple, normal routines were a comfort.

As Gamaliel finished, Evaine rose and stacked tinder and kindling onto what used to be the fire. She spoke a single word of magic, and a bright green flame appeared on the tip of her finger. She held it to the tinder, and, in moments, the wood was ablaze.

*Are you sure you should be doing that? You've had a rough time. A person can handle only so much magic, you know.*

"Are you kidding? This is nothing. I hardly have to think about this trick anymore. I can remember when I first learned this spell. I was so impressed with myself that I did it all the time. But now it's almost second nature." She smiled. "Don't worry, Gam, I'll be fine. But I won't be spying on the pool for at least a week. That spell would be too much." Much as she hated to admit it, Evaine was drained by the pool spell. The incident would have killed a weaker wizard.

*So what happened, anyway? It didn't look like your scrying went well. You looked as if something went wrong.* Gamaliel was eager to hear the story, but knew he had to wait until she was ready to tell it.

Evaine sighed. "Something did go wrong, I think. I really don't understand it." She looked at the cat in the growing light and suddenly noticed great ragged scratches on the side of his face and along one shoulder. "Gamaliel, what happened to you? You look like you were in a war! What went on while I was asleep?" Evaine instantly arose and picked up her pack, rummaging for a healing ointment.

*Oh, it was nothing, really. The four wolves ran off as soon as they got their noses singed on your protective spell. It was the pair of owlbears that gave me a little trouble.* Gamaliel was obviously proud of his victory, and his feigned modesty made Evaine laugh.

"Mister Tough, eh, kitty? You amaze me sometimes. How did the creatures get through the ward, anyway?" Evaine rubbed the ointment into the cat's wounds. The scratches healed before her eyes.

*The first three got cooked when they touched the ward. That broke the spell, though, and the other two just sauntered in. I was ready for them, of course, and made short work of them. And to answer your next question, I dragged the bodies into the woods. They didn't smell too nice, and I didn't think the first thing you should see upon awakening was a pile of disgusting bodies.* Gamaliel tilted his head proudly.

Evaine scratched the cat's head vigorously. "You're worth you're weight in catnip, Gam. I guess fate was on my side when I hooked up with you." All the wounds that were covered with the magical ointment had closed completely. "Feel better, Gamaliel? I think I got all the scratches." The feline responded by rubbing his face against her shoulder and purring.

"We'd best get ready to hit the trail," Evaine noted. "After we're packed, show me where you put the owlbears. Their feathers make great spell components." She stirred the fire, leveling out a small heap of coals. After setting a metal cup filled with water on the coals, she went about packing her gear. Evaine carefully gathered the quartz powder and poured it into a vial, shaking out the cloth, then tucked it away.

By the time the water boiled, Evaine had everything packed. She carefully removed the cup from the fire and added an herbal mixture. Leaving it to steep, she followed Gamaliel to the stream to fill the waterskins. By the time she returned, the brew was ready.

The herbal mixture was her own recipe. It was a combination of soothing and healing herbs that smelled like mint and raspberries. She drank it as hot as she could bear, then dropped the cup into her pack. Gamaliel was already brushing their footprints from the camp.

Evaine gathered her pack and scanned the area. Everything looked to be in order, and she was feeling much better already. Gamaliel finished hiding their footprints. Seeing that his mistress was ready, he led the way toward the owlbears. After the sorceress had gathered what she needed in the way of owlbear feathers, Evaine told Gamaliel what had happened in her spell. While they talked, the sorceress puzzled over the meaning of the spell.

"Gam, you've been with me long enough to know how the spell should have worked. Normally, the pool pulls my mind along until I arrive at its location. Then I can see precisely where it is and what conditions surround it. And usually, I can learn something of the evil nature of the pool."

She frowned and paused. "But this time, I didn't even see the pool. I didn't even see Phlan. If I had to guess, I'd say that some catastrophe of epic proportions had befallen the city. I'm almost afraid to speculate. I guess I'll just have to wait until we reach the city."

Gamaliel didn't always understand magic, but he knew his mistress. He always offered his support. *It isn't often that you question the outcome or success of your spells,*

*Evaine. You're careful, and I've rarely seen your magic go awry. Trust your instincts. They're usually right.*

"But that's part of the problem, Gam. I'm not sure what my instincts are telling me right now. I want to believe my magic, but is it possible for a whole city to disappear?"

Gamaliel didn't respond, but rubbed against Evaine's leg. They both knew it was time to go. Gamaliel led the way. His mistress followed silently, puzzling about the results of her spell.

They trudged through the woods for two hours, until Gamaliel stopped suddenly in his tracks. Evaine didn't say a word, but stopped instantly, watching the cat. Her hand moved automatically to the lining of her cloak. Its many pockets held her spell components.

Gamaliel's ears twitched, honing in on the faintest sounds. His nostrils flared as he sniffed for the scent of whatever was out there. Evaine heard nothing but the wind in the trees.

Then, without warning, Gamaliel spun and dug his haunches into the soft earth. In a split second he was airborne, sailing over Evaine's head at *something* behind her. Evaine ducked and spun in time to see the cat's front paws land on the chest of a seven-foot-tall creature swinging an axe over its head. Gam knocked it to the ground, taking another monster behind it to the earth as well. These were ugly creatures with yellow-brown fur and snouts like bears. Their pointed ears stuck straight up, mimicking the giant fangs that protruded from their jaws. Gamaliel was a flurry of fangs and claws, and in moments, the lead creature stopped moving. The thing barely knew what had hit him.

Meanwhile, Evaine was summoning energies and scorching the attackers. She had fought bugbears before and knew that speed was the trick to overcoming them. All totaled, nine creatures had crashed out of the bushes and were circling Evaine and the cat. Gamaliel was finishing off the second bugbear he had pinned, leaving seven still on their feet.

The sorceress recited the words of a short but powerful spell. Eighteen green magical jets leaped out of her fingertips, whizzing toward the creatures. Finding their targets, the missiles seared through armor and flesh, enveloping each creature in a green aura for a split-second. The smell of singed fur and flesh filled the air. Five bugbears were each hit by three missiles, killing two of them instantly. A fifth monster was hit by two missiles, wounding it seriously. The sixth monster was only scratched.

Gamaliel had killed his second bugbear. He checked on Evaine's success and immediately leaped at the least wounded monster. Sorceress and familiar had been through so many battles together that neither needed to consult the other before acting. They instinctively knew what they should do next. The cat always chose the creature that posed the greatest immediate risk to his mistress.

Gam knocked the bugbear to the ground, but not before the monster's axe sliced into the cat's shoulder. Gamaliel hissed in pain, but his attack never slowed. He tore into the grotesque creature.

Evaine managed to dodge the swings of the three creatures that now tried to circle her. The magical ring of protection turned away several axe strikes. She cast another spell and promptly disappeared from sight.

The monsters stood stupefied for a moment, wondering what to do next. Their prey had seemingly escaped. But Evaine had turned invisible, rushing out of the center of the trio. She knew better than to have the enemy at her back.

Evaine reappeared several feet down the path. She shouted to get the creatures' attention. As they turned to face her, a miniature hailstorm erupted over the heads of the bugbears. It lasted only a few minutes, but the pelting ice killed the three weakest creatures.

The remaining monster charged Evaine, its axe held high. She dodged, but found herself trapped in the thick underbrush. As the axe started its downswing, Evaine grimaced, closing her eyes. She heard a whump, but felt nothing. Opening her eyes, Evaine saw the bugbear flat on its belly with Gamaliel's jaws at the back of its neck. She reached for her dagger, but the monster had stopped moving.

Evaine slumped to the ground, panting. Gamaliel rolled onto his side, his wounded shoulder staining his fur dark red. The sorceress located a small vial in her pack, then hurried to the cat's side and took his muzzle in her hand. "You know what this is, Gam. It'll fix you right up. Open your mouth."

The cat blinked, but didn't protest as he opened his jaws. Evaine's entire hand fit easily into his mouth. She emptied the contents of the vial into the back of his throat. The feline swallowed, and his wound immediately began to heal. In moments, there was no sign of the injury.

The pair sat on the ground, breathing heavily, for several minutes. They finally rose and began checking the bodies for coins or useful items.

The task of rifling bodies was always unpleasant. The bugbears were grimy and bloody, and smelled of filth and rotting meat, but the sorceress accepted income wherever it presented itself. Spell components could be expensive. A few coins were always welcome.

By the time Evaine finished searching her victims, she had found a dozen gemstones and was able to fill a small pouch with silver and a few gold pieces. "We came out ahead, Gamaliel," she informed the cat. "There's enough money here to buy two horses with enough left over for the ferry across the Moonsea. Not bad."

Gamaliel looked up at his mistress. *I don't suppose there's enough change left over for a nice ration of catnip, is there? It's been a while since you bought me any.*

Evaine just laughed. "Gamaliel, the first catnip I see growing in the wild or available for sale at an apothecary is yours. I promise. You've earned it."

The cat purred, rubbed against her leg, and the two set off through the woods once again.

*By the way, mistress, why is it that you didn't blast the whole lot of those ugly brutes with a lightning bolt? You could have killed them all with one spell.* Gamaliel was already twenty yards ahead of the sorceress, but that didn't affect his telepathy.

"I considered that option, but I was afraid I'd either fry you along with the bugbears, or set the woods on fire. So I opted for some less spectacular spells. And it was still an easy battle."

The cat made his approval known and slinked through the underbrush.

Another night of camping passed uneventfully. Evaine and Gamaliel set up as usual, turned in early, and were back on the trail at first light. Evaine expected to link up with one of the major roads to Phlan late in the day. On the way she intended to buy two horses. She didn't want to search for the road after dark.

The pair traveled quickly, with only a few stops for water and rest. By midafternoon, they broke through the trees and found themselves at the edge of a dirt road wide enough for two carts to pass in opposite directions. Evaine knew they had arrived at the right spot.

Before leaving the woods, Evaine took a long look at Gamaliel. She decided it would be better not to be seen with a giant cat, as it would attract too much attention. With a sigh, she said to her companion, "Gam, I think you'd better change. We'll be safer if people think you're human."

The cat hissed in protest.

"Come on, Gamaliel, you know it's necessary," Evaine demanded. "Besides, it's human form I want, not house-cat. That's the form you really hate. This isn't going to kill you." The feline knew that change was the intelligent choice, and stopped grousing. He stepped away from Evaine, closing his eyes.

The pendant around the cat's neck began to glow a pale green. Gamaliel's tawny shape blurred. His furry body seemed to swirl and writhe, and then came into focus again. No longer was a cat standing in the woods, but a tall, wiry human male wearing clothing made of soft animal skins. The man had intense green eyes and sandy, shoulder-length hair. He moved with a smooth, fluid grace. On his hands were dark brown, kidskin gloves. Fingertips with sharp, tough claws protruded from the ends of the gloves. An enormous sword in a suede sheath was strapped to his back.

"Ah, now there's a warrior," Evaine said admiringly. "You're a beautiful cat, Gam, but you're a darn nice look-ing human. You'll get used to this shape again in no time."

Gamaliel said nothing, but followed his mistress out of the woods. They joined up with the road and saw that it was frequented by farmers, peasants, and pilgrims. The road wasn't crowded but was certainly busy.

Evaine kept her eyes open for anyone with horses to sell. She passed on a few nags, but eventually spotted a pair of horses that looked healthy and well cared for. Before approaching the owner, she cast a quick mind-reading spell that allowed her to learn whether the horses were stolen.

She negotiated with the horse trader for a few minutes, reading his thoughts and learning that the horses were indeed in good health. They were his own and were for sale simply because his family needed the money. Evaine negotiated a good price, and in a few minutes, horses and money had traded hands. She and Gamaliel mounted the horses and galloped down the road.

By nightfall, the pair arrived at the ferry that would carry them over the Moonsea to Phlan. A nearby inn had a vacant room for the night, a luxury Evaine welcomed after a week in the woods. She and Gamaliel stabled the horses, got themselves settled, and prepared for a comfortable night's sleep.

"We made it, Gamaliel. We'll be in Phlan tomorrow. It should be easy going from here on in."

Gamaliel replied with a peculiar purr that never sounded quite right coming from his human body.

# ❧ 9 ❧

# Confusing Meetings

Ren stood in the streets of New Phlan, staring out at the Moonsea. Closing his eyes, he rubbed his forehead as hard as he could, wishing he could wipe away his confusion. Phlan was gone, Shal and Tarl were gone, and the new city council wanted him for a lackey. To make things worse, two druids who claimed to know him were following him around like baby ducks.

After leaving the council chambers, he had spent the past hour wandering the alleys of New Phlan. As often as he tried to change the subject or lose the druids among the tents, they always caught up to him or managed to turn the discussion back to the pool of darkness.

The ranger opened his eyes. Two faces stared at him quizzically. Ren groaned.

"Look, I know I owe you a favor for getting me out of the council meeting, but I work alone." Ren was thoroughly irritated and couldn't believe the pleading sound of his own voice. But at the same time, he felt as if he belonged with these two druids for some odd reason. To his displeasure, he remembered he'd had the same feeling the first time he met Tarl and Shal.

Talenthia took Ren's hand. "But Sylvanus wants us—"

"I know, I know. You've told me a hundred times. I don't mean any disrespect to your god, but he'll just have to find another mission for you. I don't have any grand plan. But when I decide what to do, I want to move fast. You'd just slow me down." Ren shook his hand free, striding toward the corral. A workout with Stolen might help him to clear his head.

The druids followed. They had been ordered to help the ranger, and help him they would—whether he liked it or not.

The trio hurried through the alleys. Everywhere they looked, people begged from their makeshift tents. The citizens who had once been lively and energetic were now lethargic and dispirited from hunger and sadness. It was more than Ren, Talenthia, and Andoralson could bear.

As Talenthia watched Ren's reaction to the poverty around them, she tried to reassure him. "Ren, we know how you feel about these people. We all want to help them, and the best way to make these people happy is to restore Phlan. You have that power, and we're here to help you."

Andoralson clamped a hand on Ren's shoulder and stopped him. "This isn't any easier for Talenthia and me. We have been directed by our god to help you. We intend to follow our orders."

Ren paused, weighing what the druids had said. Maybe he was being too stubborn. He could see these two were powerful priests of their sect. They seemed as if they could take care of themselves. Would it hurt to have some help?

"All right. I can't think of a solid reason to refuse your offer. If you agree to follow my orders, we'll work together." The ranger rubbed his forehead again. "Do you have any idea where old Phlan went?"

The cousins exchanged troubled looks. "No," Talenthia began, "we tried to use our magic when we first heard of

Phlan's troubles, but something is blocking our spells. Sylvanus wouldn't have sent us here if answers weren't forthcoming. We found you easily. Andoralson and I both believe that we'll link up with another to aid our quest."

Ren rolled his eyes but said nothing. "Let's head for the corral. I need to look in on my horse. Do you have horses there?"

The druids grinned at each other, sharing some secret joke.

"No, we don't have horses. We move about by, uh, *other* means. But I would love to visit that big horse of yours. He's a beautiful beast. I'd like him to tell me a few things about you." Talenthia's eyes sparkled as she teased Ren. The ranger made a face. He knew that druids had the ability to speak with animals.

"Talenthia, we have more important things to do," Andoralson scolded.

She pouted at her cousin, but grabbed Ren's arm. They all walked toward the river. On the way, Talenthia explained that she had talked with dozens of forest creatures about the disappearance of Phlan, but had learned nothing.

Cooking fires burned outside the ramshackle tents. The companions took their time walking to the corral, but as they approached the raft landing, an argument attracted their attention.

"But I'm not staying! Can't you get that through your thick skull?" A petite sorceress dressed in a green tunic and deerskin leggings was losing patience with Lord Wainwright and his squad of guards. A tall barbarian warrior at her side was saying more with his posture than with words.

"I'll bet she's a powerful spellcaster, Talenthia. Do you

notice the rhythm of her voice and the way she pro-
nounces her words?"

"I do. And do you notice something unusual about the
barbarian? I can't put my finger on it, but there's more to
him than meets the eye. He's ready to spring to defend
her any second."

All this was lost on Ren. From his vantage, all he had
noticed were the sorceress's long braid of red hair and
her dazzling green eyes. He laughed a little as he watched the scene unfold. "This must be a bad week for that
poor knight," Ren chuckled to Talenthia. "First I gave him
grief, and now that sorceress, who looks like she could
blast them all to cinders if she wanted, is doing the same
thing. I wonder if I should give the knight a hand, just to
make up for my rough treatment yesterday?"

The argument grew louder as everyone watched. A
crowd began to gather, but onlookers made room for
the trio in front of the pack. Many of the people recognized Ren from the previous day. Whispers went
through the crowd pointing out Ren's presence, and the
onlookers' attention was split between Ren and the on-
going argument on the raft. The ranger would never
have acknowledged the attention he was getting, but in
Phlan, he was truly a figure of awe.

The sorceress was now speaking to the knight in simple sentences, perhaps thinking that his thick brain
needed some help. "These are pack animals. They need
to carry my supplies. How can I load them up if they're
in a corral a mile away from the supplies I'm buying?"

The sorceress had a point, but the Wainwrights
weren't known for their grasp of logic.

"Mistress, you must do what everyone else does. Corral your mounts and bring the supplies to them. Your
man here looks strong enough to carry any number of

supplies. Now be a nice little wizard and do as I say."
With that, the knight put his hands on her shoulders to
forcibly guide her off the raft.

The woman twisted against his grip, and in less than
the blink of an eye, an emerald spark the size of a grape-
fruit arced from her body to the metallic gauntlet of the
knight. It blew him backward ten feet, right into his
men. He lay stunned, looking at his smoking glove. The
other guards promptly drew their weapons.

The barbarian at the sorceress's side clutched a massive sword, ready to defend the woman. She simply
waited, though the look on her face said, "There's more
where that came from."

Ren knew the ten men were probably ready to die in
order to obey their leader. This won't do, he decided. No,
this won't do at all.

"Gentlemen. Lady. Please put up your weapons!"

Followed by the druids, Ren pushed his way into the
mass of guards. All heads turned at the sound of his
voice.

As the ranger helped the knight to his feet, he said,
"We have to stop meeting like this, my friend." A scorch
mark the length of the knight's chain mail gauntlet
caught his attention. Lifting the knight's visor, Ren saw
the dazed warrior looking around confusedly.

Talenthia was suddenly at Ren's side, casting a healing
spell on the knight. His wound was instantly healed, his
mind quickly cleared.

Andoralson stood behind his cousin, casting a strange
illusionary spell that created great sparks and blasts of
fire flashing in the sky above the crowd. The people
moved away in fear and awe. The guards froze. The sorceress was staring at the three strangers. She had produced a magical staff and was obviously ready for any

type of action. Her companion's lips were curled in a hiss, but he stood his ground.

The druids each cast a spell of protection as they separated and hurried to either side of the troops. Ren smiled in spite of himself. It was almost as if they had been fighting with him for years.

"*Enangusfusisus!*" Andoralson cast another spell. Suddenly there were five duplicates of him, moving toward the guards.

The confused watchmen were trying to look everywhere at once. Druids casting spells, a sorceress zapping their leader, and a barbarian ready to cleave them apart—it was all just too much. They looked at each other as if to say, "I'll surrender if you will!" To further complicate the matter, a former hero of Phlan was against them. They knew when they were beaten.

Lord Wainwright had completely lost control of the situation, and he knew it. He struggled to regain what little dignity he could. "Never mind the illusions, troops. Mistress, I admit I shouldn't have touched you, and I apologize."

The spellcaster sighed, giving him a nod in acknowledgement of his apology.

Wainright cleared his throat. "But your barbarian friend will please sheath his weapon and you will take your horses to the corral. If you don't comply, I can't take responsibility for the blood that will spill."

The sorceress sized up the troops, knowing they could never stand up to her magic and Gamaliel's sword. "This should have never gotten this far," she responded evenly. "If you insist, I'll stable my animals. Where is the corral, please?"

When the barbarian sheathed his weapon, Ren nodded to the druids. They turned to slip out of the crowd.

The sorceress maintained her composure, but smiled to herself as the throng opened to let the three strangers by. She observed looks of respect on the faces of the people as the ranger passed.

As she prepared to leave the raft, the spellcaster made an attempt to be gracious to the knight. "Good warrior, you have my apology for my hasty actions. Can you tell me who that ranger was?" She flashed her friendliest smile at him.

Pleased by this change of attitude, Lord Wainwright spoke up. "Oh, that was Ren 'o the Blade. He's famous throughout Phlan. He and his friends discovered the pool of radiance ten years ago and killed the dragon that guarded it. They made Phlan a safer place to live—until the thrice-damned gods took our city away, that is."

The knight steeled his courage and added, "You know, mistress, the marketplace will be closing, it nearly being dark and all. I have a large tent you could sleep in, and my squire could make room for your man."

The sorceress's smile faded. "What a kind offer. But I am afraid Gamaliel and I will have to refuse. We will corral our horses as you have instructed. Thank you, Sir Knight."

Evaine and Gamaliel passed through the parted crowd, the stares of the villagers following them. Wizard and barbarian led the animals toward the corral.

"Gamaliel, you heard that oafish knight. That warrior knew of the pool of darkness before—when it was a pool of radiance. Of all the pools we've hunted, I've seen only one pool of radiance. I must learn how this one was changed into a pool of darkness. We have to find that Ren fellow and ask him some questions." Her companion listened to her words, but said nothing.

A crowd surrounded the corral. The fence was ringed

with torches, making it easy to approach in the fading light. As the pair approached with their mounts, some of the watchers opened the gate and a stable hand hurried over to help with their equipment. The woman correctly guessed that the story of the raft incident had already made its way to the corral. Every effort was being made to be cordial to the sorceress.

*Gamaliel,* Evaine mentally communicated to her friend, *the druids and that warrior are here. Try to keep the druids busy while I talk to Ren. I won't be long.*

*Careful, Evaine. I smell powerful magic on all of them.*

She scowled at the barbarian. *Gamaliel, you worry too much. I need to talk to him, to get information. Now get going.*

"Druids," Gamaliel called out, "would you be so kind as to look at our horses? I think they may have the fever."

Evaine smiled at her clever companion, so smart for a cat. She knew her horses were healthy, but the nature-loving druids would be busy checking them over for at least a short time.

Ren was brushing down the biggest war-horse Evaine had ever seen.

"Ranger, my name is Evaine. I want to thank you for stopping what could have been an ugly situation."

"Think nothing of it, my lady. I am called Ren by my friends. What brings you to New Phlan?"

An uncomfortable silence hung between them for a moment. "Uh, the knight at the raft told me you knew of the pool of radiance. I've always been fascinated by the stories of such waters, but I've always wondered if they really exist."

Ren stopped his work to look searchingly into the eyes of this strange sorceress. "Oh, they exist, all right. Take it from one who's seen a pool firsthand. I had the honor of freeing this city from the corrupted dragon that was using the pool of radiance."

"I'm interested for study purposes only," she said, noting the ranger's stare. Evaine was glad he wasn't a spellcaster; she figured her chances were good that he couldn't see through her lie. "I had to come to Phlan when I heard there was a pool here. I thought I'd have a look for myself, but the pool is gone, apparently, along with the city. I'd still like to locate it, if there's any chance of doing so."

Suddenly Ren became excited at what Evaine was saying. "Would you be interested in a little quest to find the pool?" She nodded. "Talenthia, Andoralson, come over here! I think we've found someone to join our mission."

The druids hurried over, followed by the lanky barbarian. Ren introduced Evaine, and she in turn introduced Gamaliel. They all started talking at once, but Evaine stopped them. "Let me guess," she insisted. "It's a little hobby of mine. Let me see. You, Ren, are a ranger at heart but you also know the ways of the thief. You admire women but haven't settled down with one yet. You're a hero in Phlan—but that was easy to guess, because the knight told me most of the story. You've been away from the city for a long time, and you have returned only recently.

"Talenthia and Andoralson. You're both druids, but Andoralson also commands the magic of illusions. You're related—let's see, not brother and sister. How about cousins? You were sent to Phlan by your god. You travel by means of your shapechanging abilities. And you only met Ren within the last few days. How did I score?" the sorceress asked.

The trio looked at her, dumbfounded. "You've used your magic to spy on us!" Andoralson accused her.

Evaine was amused. "Don't be silly. Until a half-hour ago, I'd never seen any of you."

"Mind magic. You can read our thoughts," Talenthia suggested.

"Nope. Trying to read the three of you at once would give me a terrific headache."

"Well, maybe you're just plain smart," Ren offered. He hadn't a clue about this woman's abilities, but he didn't want to be left out of the game.

Evaine touched her finger to the tip of her nose. "The ranger wins. I observed you carefully and made some simple deductions. Ren for example, walks with a light step—as if he's walking in the woods—but he's agile and quick and has the moves of a thief. The way he speaks to Talenthia and myself, it's obvious that he respects women and enjoys their company."

The ranger nodded his agreement.

"Also, Ren has spent a lot of time outdoors from the look of his tanned skin. If he were a resident of Phlan, he'd either be missing with the city or have his own tent.

"The druids. You don't show any romantic feelings toward each other, and there's a slight family resemblance. You don't talk like siblings. Cousins, that's my best guess."

The druids smiled at her cleverness.

"I've seen Andoralson's illusion magic. That was easy. You don't have horses, so I can only assume that you shapechange. Had you trekked through the woods or down the roads to Phlan, I think your robes would be dirty and tattered. You're in the city because your god sent you. That's also easy. Most druids don't hang around in cities by choice. You belong in the wilds.

"Ren's only been in town a few days, and you still don't know a lot about each other. That's why I guessed that you'd just met. Well?" Evaine waited for their reaction.

Ren burst out laughing. After all the depression and sadness he'd seen in the last few days, this woman was a breath of fresh air. She wasn't rattled by the day's events, and she still had her wits about her. He was astonished by her insights.

"Right you are, lady. You didn't miss on a single point. Would you care to guess my birthdate now?" Ren was still laughing.

"No, thanks, Ren. That's not something I can guess just by looking at you." Evaine chuckled at the ranger's amusement.

The druids were too amazed to speak. But they couldn't help themselves and now joined in the good humor. Gamaliel didn't laugh, but rubbed a hand on Evaine's shoulder. She patted his hand affectionately.

"Okay, you've figured us out. How about telling us a bit about yourselves?" Ren coaxed.

"Not much to tell, really. I came to Phlan looking for a few unusual spell components. I prefer traveling to sitting home in a dusty lab experimenting, but once in a while I need an obscure substance for some research. Gamaliel always comes along. He's quite a fighter and likes to make sure that I'm safe. We've been together quite a number of years."

Ren and the druids were left with no doubt that the barbarian was an able protector. His graceful gait and intense demeanor were evidence of discipline and concentration. His lack of armor was not a sign of weakness; rather, on this human, armor would have seemed awkward. The barbarian's heavy blade and sharp-taloned gloves spoke of skill in combat, with or without a weapon.

The group left the stable, exchanging stories briefly. Ren explained his mission to find Shal, Tarl, and the city, and the cousins explained that they had been sent by Sylvanus to assist Ren. The conversation was like one between old friends.

The barbarian whispered something in his mistress's ear.

"You're right, Gamaliel. I think they're okay, too. Think I should tell them?" The warrior nodded.

Evaine's smile faded, and her tone became serious. "I don't make it a habit of telling all my secrets to strangers, but I think I'm safe with the three of you. We both have something the other wants." The trio listened intently.

"I didn't tell you the whole truth about the pools of darkness. I've made it my life's quest to find and destroy those waters of evil. I know that pools of radiance can transform into pools of darkness. A pool of darkness is nothing less than a powerful tool of evil. The one in Phlan vanished when the city vanished. I have to learn more about what happened to the pool of radiance ten years ago. Maybe whatever you did caused the pool to change. Maybe not. But any information you can give me could help me discover where the pool has relocated.

"I've tracked and destroyed four pools in the past five years. I know many special spells that help me locate and then purify the evil waters. My magic has revealed strange visions. I know you want Phlan back, and I want that pool. I'm certain that if we find one, we'll find the other."

The trio again stared at her, dumbfounded. Ren was the first to choke out a reply.

"Evaine, are you telling us you have a means to find the pool that was in Phlan?"

"I think so. First, we must leave this pitiful city. In four more days, I plan to cast another location spell for the pool. The spell is extremely dangerous, and I can't cast it more than once in seven days."

Ren was elated at this news. For the first time since he had arrived in Phlan, there was some hope of finding Tarl and Shal. "I'll do anything to find my friends. You can count on the druids' help, as well."

An odd smile crept over Evaine's face. "This is the strangest thing. Ordinarily, I work only with Gamaliel. But somehow, I feel that fate has something slightly different in mind for me this time. I feel like I can't say no."

Andoralson laughed.

Talenthia sighed in exasperation. "Why is it that all you strong, silent types work alone? If everyone worked alone, nothing would be any fun, now would it?" Andoralson patted his cousin's shoulder.

"We have a lot of work ahead of us. There are plans to be made and supplies to be bought. If Evaine can find the pool in four days, we'd better be ready to move fast." The druid's tone was serious, but the impending adventure put a glimmer in his gray eyes.

Ren began herding the group toward the tent held by the worshipers of Tyr. "It's already dark, I'm hungry, and we need a place to sleep. Brother Anton has offered me lodging; I'm sure he won't mind a few more. I suggest we get settled so we can get an early start. Any objections?"

Evaine wasn't used to lodging with a crowd, but she was too tired to object.

Brother Anton welcomed the group warmly. He found space for all of them to roll out blankets and bedrolls, and offered them a warm meal. As tired as they all were, they were too excited to sleep. They lay awake in the dark until well after midnight, exchanging whispered ideas and plans. When they finally dozed off, none slept soundly. The danger that lay ahead crept into their dreams.

# ❧ 10 ❧

# Battle of Undeath

"North?"

"That's right, north. We aren't going to have a debate every time I want to cast a spell, are we?"

"No. You're the wizard, and I'm the muscle on this mission, but the woodsman in me always wants to know why a certain direction is chosen."

"And the druid in me would like to go northeast into all those beautiful forests," Talenthia chimed in as she spurred her horse next to Ren's.

"If we're voting, I'd opt for south. Ocean voyages are much easier on one's riding muscles," Andoralson said from the back of the group. No one paid attention to the druid.

Gamaliel said nothing, but expected that before long, they would be heading north.

The past three days had been full of such arguments as the five new companions made preparations to leave Phlan. The group had argued over supplies, directions, plans, clothing, and mode of travel. The druids had to be convinced to buy horses rather than rely on their abilities to transform into animals. They all shouted, screamed, laughed, and swore at each other. Egos were bruised. Feelings were hurt. But here they were, packed, organized, and on the road.

They were only a few hours out of the tent city and

heading for some predetermined place known only to Evaine. Talenthia was convinced they were on a wild goose chase. Ren was willing to believe the sorceress, but he was still skeptical.

Gamaliel was the only steadying force in an otherwise chaotic mix of personalities. Although he didn't speak often, when the discussions got too loud and too far from the topic at hand, the warrior's voice quickly brought everyone to their senses. Although he always sided with Evaine, the others trusted his instincts.

Now he trotted along on his horse, slightly ahead of Evaine. As always, he stayed close to the sorceress. No one understood their relationship. It was obvious to everyone that the barbarian adored the woman and would protect her with his life. He seemed to be constantly on edge around the rest of the group, as if inside his body a tight spring was ready to explode. His behavior made Talenthia hope that Evaine didn't harbor any romantic interest toward Ren.

The argument continued between Ren and Evaine.

"My spell should find the pool of darkness, but it functions more efficiently if it's cast away from the life energies of the city. We're all in this mission together. I'll cooperate fully with the group, but I can't take the time to explain everything I have to do."

Ren raised his hand to make a point, but Gamaliel was in motion before he had the chance. The barbarian leaped off his horse and drew his sword in one smooth move. He stood perfectly motionless, facing north, though all anyone could see were miles of grassland. Gamaliel lifted his head and sniffed at the air.

With the barbarian positioned between Evaine and what he thought was danger, Andoralson started casting several protective spells. Something was wrong, and it had to be important to make the big warrior so uneasy.

"What is it?" Ren asked, drawing his blade.

"Listen!" Gamaliel ordered.

The party fell silent. Under the dark thunderclouds, a slight breeze drifted in from the Moonsea, far to the south. The wind shifted. Distant sounds of chanting and clashing weapons were audible.

"Someone's singing and fighting at the same time?" Talenthia tried to make a joke.

"That's no song, that's a war chant." Ren spurred his horse toward the noise. "Men of Tyr sing such chants, but only when they're in battle and think they're going to die! Follow me!"

Talenthia, eager to follow the ranger's lead, spurred her horse after Ren's.

Evaine and Gamaliel didn't move.

"Well," Andoralson asked as he rode up to Evaine, "you heard what the fearless leader ordered. What's stopping you?"

"I never rush into battle, ever. If that sword-swinging lout wants to hurl himself into a trap, that's up to him, but it's not my style. And you?"

"Oh, I'm with Ren because I can tell he's lucky. My god has ordered me to aid him. But I always do things my way, too." Without another word, he spurred his mount far to the right of the others. As he did so a blue mist surrounded Andoralson and his horse.

Wondering how they had gotten into this, Evaine sighed in frustration. "Well, Gamaliel, there's no getting around it. If we're going to use Ren to find the pool, we have to tag along."

"You don't like the big ranger much, do you, mistress?"

She and Gamaliel galloped after the group, their horses nearly in step. "No, my feelings aren't a matter of liking," she told him. "I trusted him right away. It's just that he has so many rough edges. There is no logic to the man, just raw emotion. I don't understand his type. Let's hope he doesn't get us into something you and I can't get us out of."

Evaine and Gamaliel galloped through the woods. The sounds of battle grew louder as they approached a secluded clearing. Broken tombstones littered the field, and the ruins of a small, ancient temple lay at the north of the graveyard. Five crumbling mausoleums stood like stone guardians around the weedy perimeter.

The raging battle was an awful sight. A tall warrior, armored from head to toe, stood in front of the largest mausoleum. The door to the stone structure had been ripped off its hinges. The knight stood surrounded by undead creatures that were erupting out of their graves.

Ren and Talenthia held their ground in the thick of the swarm, fighting off heavily armored skeletons. Andoralson waded into a nearby group of zombie warriors whose skin and clothing hung in tatters.

The huge knight in the middle of the fray chanted praises to his god, Tyr. Something about the knight suggested to Evaine that he was a paladin, a warrior eternally devoted to the cause of good, but there was something peculiar about the way he fought. His style of fighting made her uneasy, although she couldn't put her feeling into words.

The sorceress dismounted, turned her horse toward the woods, and slapped its flank. Gamaliel did exactly the same, and the horses trotted into the woods together. Evaine never cast spells from the back of an animal. A mere twitch could ruin a spell or hurtle its effects toward a comrade.

The sorceress's senses tingled. She quickly decided on

a course of action that would turn the tide of battle without endangering her comrades.

"Gamaliel, creep up to the edge of the battle and keep these monsters at bay while I prepare a few spells."

"Mistress, I hope these friends are worth our effort— but I will do as you command."

Evaine smiled grimly, amused by his attitude. She told herself to chide him later for being so catty. For now, there was work to be done.

Still on his horse, Ren rode deeper into the battle. Summing up the situation, he decided to aid the outnumbered knight. He crashed Stolen through a throng of skeletons and took off several heads, calling out, "Need some help, warrior?"

The knight before him was covered in a finely wrought suit of plate mail. Glowing gauntlets and a magical helmet completed the suit. Ren was impressed by the craftsmanship of the armor, but there was no time for admiration. The knight sang his reply to Ren while in the middle of his death chant to Tyr.

*"Freely offered aid from an able fighter,*
*Gladly accepted, makes this knight's work lighter."*

During the old battles on the walls of Phlan, Ren had heard such chants from the warrior-clerics of Tyr. Ballads composed in battle were a last chance to prove devotion and praise their deity. Such songs were raised only when a worshiper of Tyr truly believed he was about to die. Ren didn't question why this knight was chanting. The odds looked grim.

Talenthia called down bolts of lighting. Each one destroyed two or three of the skeletons and zombies. But the vile creatures continued to rise out of their graves in ever-widening circles around the mausoleums.

"Retreat!" Andoralson screamed, charging into the battle. He threw a handful of dust into the grass around his horse. A bluish purple haze arose, blanketing the grasses ahead of him, moving in a rippling wave toward the undead warriors. The tinted grass twisted into ropy tentacles, reaching for the loathsome zombies and dragging them, still struggling, to the ground. The bodies of the walking dead were crushed to powder.

Near the edge of the battle, Gamaliel's voice also boomed "Retreat!" as his weapon chopped one skeleton after another in half.

Evaine launched two lightning bolts of her own, cutting wide paths into the steadily growing mass of undead. The monsters that weren't fighting Ren and his allies were lining up to battle the knight, who stood like a great, rooted statue at the open door of the tomb.

Looking over the battle, Ren saw that too many creatures were rising from the ground, and they were no longer just skeletons and zombies. Hideous creatures of shadow, misty wraiths with glowing red eyes, and ghostly spectres were also answering the call of battle.

The graveyard filled with green streaks and blue sparks as Evaine and Andoralson cast one spell after another at the undead monsters. Sparks bounced in the grass. Monster after monster succumbed to magical blasts.

Both spellcasters turned their attacks to the wraiths and spectres. These ghastly things were far more deadly than the other creatures and easier to kill magically than by swordplay. If they didn't act swiftly, one of their companions might become victims of the monsters' spectral talons. Ren spurred Stolen. Crunching through the mounds of bones and dashing to the warrior's side, he shouted, "Knight, retreat!"

A reply came in the knight's chant.

*"I wait the coming, the coming of one,*
*The thousand-year old one, when battle will be done."*

Ren's frustration at the knight's refusal quickly turned to horror. A deep, throbbing voice filled the air.

"Then wait no longer, chanting fool!" A black mist rose from the ground just outside the clearing. "You and I will finish this, Miltiades. This time *I* will win."

The mist swirled, forming the night-black ghost of a ghastly warrior. The spectral fighter rode a nightmare horse of writhing, dark smoke. The beast pawed the earth with vaporous hooves. Huge chunks of grassy earth flew in all directions. The ghost, vaguely human, drew a saber of extraordinary length. The weapon glowed as black fire danced up and down its blade. The sword looked to dispense death at a touch.

Every undead creature in the graveyard turned and bowed to the mist warrior. Taking advantage of the sudden lull in the battle, Talenthia and Andoralson tore into the monsters, swinging weapons furiously, destroying three or four creatures with every blow.

Evaine and Gamaliel stood nearest the night-black ghost. Wave upon wave of evil radiated from the eyes and body of the spectral warrior and its mount. Evaine conjured numerous spells of protection, creating layers of green magic around herself and Gamaliel.

The ghost warrior stared at the huge knight in plate mail armor. "Miltiades," it groaned, its voice guttural. "Do we fight alone, paladin, or shall I empower my army to kill your friends?"

"We fight alone, ancient one. The living beings will not

interfere." This last was directed at Ren.

The ranger nodded in agreement. "So be it, paladin." But Ren and Stolen continued destroying the horde of skeletons by bashing them with steel-shod hooves and Ren's magical blade.

Following their lead, Gamaliel waded into the still-kneeling masses of undead, cutting and chopping. No creatures would remain to attack if the knight lost.

Evaine created missiles of magical energy. Streams of green sparks spewed from her fingertips, killing over a dozen zombies at a time. The creatures did not fight, they knelt meekly, oblivious to their certain doom.

Miltiades, the mysterious knight, marched to the edge of the clearing to face the ghost warrior. The warrior of Tyr no longer chanted.

The knight's shield blazed with a blue glow; the symbol of Tyr engraved upon it glowed golden. Miltiades's war helmet hummed with a protective power all its own, bathing the knight in a foggy blue mist. An enormous sword—one that most men would have had to wield with two hands—was easily swung in one hand by the knight. The blade was etched end to end in runes.

The ghost warrior calmly sat astride his vaporous mount, his saber dripping black fire.

The knight of Tyr struck first. Rolling low, he cut the legs out from under the ghost horse. His sword blasted a shower of blue sparks as the blade severed the front legs of the mount. The beast fell forward and the ghost warrior tumbled to the ground, then rolled up on his feet. The horse vanished with a blood-curdling cry of pain.

"Puts us on more even footing, Zarl!"

"Though you are a paladin, you never were an honorable fighter, Miltiades. Let us finish this."

Blades crashed as the two swung and parried. Miltiades was engulfed in a blue aura that hummed when it touched the ghost's black mist. The battle was evenly matched. Neither landed a blow for long minutes.

The rest of the group found it difficult to keep their attention on the undead creatures that surrounded them. None had ever seen a battle like the fight between these two mysterious warriors. But the five companions finally succeeded in destroying the hundreds of undead in the graveyard. In minutes, bones and withered body parts lay ankle-deep all over the clearing. Ren, the druids, Gamaliel, and Evaine were all exhausted and gasping for breath after the massacre.

The five retreated to the opposite end of the clearing to watch the final battle. Evaine magically levitated herself and Gamaliel to the roof of one of the mausoleums to gain a better view.

The two enemies were beginning to land their blows. Every time the black blade struck, bits of ebony flame left the sword to strike the paladin or sizzle to the ground. Wherever the flames landed, the grass withered and the moist topsoil turned to dust.

Both combatants expended themselves fully, taking titanic swipes at each other with their enchanted blades. Both were remarkably skilled, but this battle was not one of finesse and swordplay. Each wanted the other dead with a fury. Every ounce of muscle and energy was poured into the battle.

Unencumbered by a physical body, the ghost warrior moved faster and faster, circling around the knight. The black flaming sword landed too often, ringing against the paladin's armor. Each strike seemed softened by the blue mist coming from the knight's war helmet. But the blue mist was fading; it grew thinner and thinner with every strike, as the protective energies of the helmet were eaten away by the flames of the black sword.

"He's going to lose! I'm casting a—"

"No!" Ren shouted, grabbing at Evaine's foot, which dangled over the side of the mausoleum. Gamaliel, even quicker, pounced off the structure to tower between the spellcaster and Ren. His big hands found Ren's neck. "You must never touch her!"

Evaine leaped off the crypt and yanked at Gamaliel. "You can't attack Ren!" The barbarian realized what he was doing and dropped his grip instantly. Ren choked, but he hadn't been harmed. The ranger reeled back, trying to find his words.

"If we don't do something, the paladin will die," Evaine insisted.

Ren glared deep into Gamaliel's eyes. For the first time, he noticed their deep golden color and catlike pupils. But the revelation was lost in his fury.

"This is an affair of honor," the ranger croaked through bruised vocal cords. "Whatever happens, you must not interfere. We can fight and defeat this creature together if the paladin falls, but first we must give the paladin a chance to win."

The battle between the strange warriors raged. The paladin knew he was losing. He wasn't fast enough to keep up with the steadily moving ghost. More and more of the evil blade strikes found their marks. In a desperate move, the paladin threw down his magical shield and gripped his weapon with both hands.

The ghost shouted with glee and swung his blade to cut into the discarded shield. Black flame met holy power and, with a loud ringing, the shield was split in two. But the ruined halves of the shield stuck fast to the blade. The ghost's misty face showed his shock and anger as he awkwardly tried to recover his weapon. The paladin struck, cleaving the ghost from head to thigh.

The only audible sound to mark the passing of the ghost was a soft, "No, not again." The warrior spirit shriveled into a thin black mist and evaporated.

The paladin fell to his knees, gripping the broken remains of the shield. Instead of a cry of joy at his victory, the knight murmured, "What have I done? What have I done with the gift of Tyr? I should have known Zarl would attack the shield when I threw it down."

"What would have happened if you hadn't thrown down the shield?" Ren now crouched quietly in the grass behind the knight. The others stood behind him.

The paladin turned to look at the five strangers. "After my destruction, Zarl would have easily defeated all of you. He would have then used his evil to raise an indestructible undead army and sweep the continent. His goal would have been to destroy every living thing in Faerun, even if it took a thousand years. He was evil and destructive in life, and he remains so in death."

Andoralson expressed his compassion for the knight. "I believe Tyr would think one holy relic was worth the lives of millions of people. Don't you agree?"

Talenthia bent down to help the paladin to his feet. "Take off that heavy helm and let me see your wounds. I'd be happy to heal you, if you'll allow me."

The paladin rose, but gently removed Talenthia's hands from his arms. "In all honor, I must tell you my story first. When I take off my helm, do you all promise to let me finish my tale?"

The companions glanced at each other, but all nodded in silence. After the scene that had just unfolded, they were curious. Ren looked at the smoldering black blade still lying on the ground and wondered what fantastic story lay behind it.

Miltiades lifted his war helm. Talenthia gasped. A barely audible growl arose in Gamaliel's throat. The group saw the head of a horrible skeleton. Like his foe, the paladin was also undead!

"I am a paladin of Tyr. I died a thousand years ago. Please listen before you think of destroying me."

The pleading sound of the knight's voice was hard to ignore. A face with empty eye sockets and withered skin turned to Ren; the knight knew instinctively that the others would take the ranger's lead. Wisps of hair still clung to the parchment skin on the knight's head. Bones creaked as the undead paladin moved.

Ren sat on the grass, motioning the others to do the same.

"We want to listen to you, but I have never heard of paladins rising again to serve their god."

"I understand your doubts, and I thank you for this chance. As I said, I died a thousand years ago. In life, I served my god Tyr faithfully and wholeheartedly. I fought the enemies of my faith across all of Faerun. Because I was so successful, other followers of Tyr gave me the Holy Shield of Tyr, my magical war helm, and this runic sword of Tyr.

"The land on which we stand was much different a thousand years ago. A city stood a few miles to the north. I was its steward and war champion. For fifty years, I had the honor of guarding its gates. The city of Turell knew much strife, but we were always victorious.

"All the residents followed the ways of Tyr and all the citizens were warriors as well as craftsmen. But the year before I died, a horde led by the terrible warrior-wizard Zarl laid siege to my city. For over a year, we resisted. Week after week I challenged and defeated the most powerful warriors of the horde in combat before the city gates. But Zarl would never face me in battle.

"My city and the besiegers were both on the brink of ruin. We were desperate, and after much prayer, I decided to sneak into the camp of Zarl and try to take in stealth what he wouldn't allow me to take in honorable battle. My city was at stake. I killed him, but in turn I was killed by his men. They buried me here and surrounded me with a thousand of the most powerful members of the evil army. Then they charged into my city and leveled it. Not a single stone stood after they were through. Turell was literally wiped off the map.

"The army took Zarl's body back to their lands, but his spirit remained in the earth next to my resting place. Because I didn't boldly go into the camp and challenge Zarl in battle, Tyr refused me the rest granted to heroes slain in honorable battle. I was cursed by my god. For one thousand years, my spirit has roamed these lands, awaiting the day when Tyr would raise me for one last quest.

"Only hours ago, Tyr's radiance raised me. At the same time, Bane's power raised the dead around me. All across the Moonsea lands, horrible legions of undead are awakening—I can sense it. In my spirit form, I saw Phlan stolen by Bane's power. Now Tyr has summoned me to venture forth and help return Phlan to its home on the Moonsea. If I can prove myself to Tyr, I will finally be granted eternal peace."

Silence fell over the five companions. All were surprised and deeply moved by his saga.

Andoralson spoke first. "Is your mission truly to restore Phlan?"

The warrior responded with the pride of a man on a holy quest. "Yes. Tyr has raised me to face Bane's minions and wrest Phlan from their grasp. If I must complete my mission alone, I am prepared to do so."

Evaine, Ren, and the others exchanged questioning glances. All seemed to be thinking the same thing. Ren spoke up.

"Noble warrior, we have all come together for our own reasons but with a common cause. We all seek to restore Phlan. I have dear friends missing along with the city. Talenthia and Andoralson have been ordered by Sylvanus to assist me. Evaine seeks the pool of darkness that lies within the city. She plans to destroy it because . . ." Ren realized for the first time that he didn't know why the sorceress sought the pool. He looked to Evaine for an explanation.

Evaine's eyes met Ren's, but her cheeks were flushed with hidden emotions. Her voice was steady, but the others could see that it was an effort for her to maintain control. "Let's just say that I have a very old and very personal reason for hunting the pools. I prefer not to discuss it. But you know by now that my loyalties are sound and my dedication is unwavering." Gamaliel patted the sorceress's shoulder. None of the group had yet seen such a show of emotion in the logical sorceress.

"I think I speak for everyone when I say you are welcome in our group. If you'd like to join us, that is." Ren rose from the grass and reached out a hand to the paladin.

"Not so fast, ranger." Evaine's calculating mind had again taken over, and she rose to her feet. "No offense, paladin, but with the world in chaos as it is, you must understand our caution." She turned to the druids. "My magics tell me this one didn't lie when he told his story. But we must be sure. Andoralson, can you tell if this paladin is still lawful and good in his faith to Tyr?"

"Easily done, sorceress," the druid said with a smile. He waved a hand and whispered an arcane sentence. Miltiades was quickly outlined in a golden glow. "He is still dedicated in his faith, but he has none of the normal powers of a paladin. He is now some type of spectral warrior."

"Logically speaking, you may be a hindrance to us any time we encounter other people. They'll immediately assume you're evil. No offense, of course, but we must consider the good of the mission." Evaine turned away from the group and walked toward the woods where she had sent the horses. Gamaliel followed her closely.

"Wait a minute, my lady," Andoralson's words stopped her. "No one will know our new friend isn't the noble paladin he seems to be. Observe."

After a few gestures and words issued from the druid, a magical illusion swirled around the skeletal form of the paladin. Miltiades removed his gauntlets, and instead of skeletal bones, perfectly formed hands appeared. The paladin's head became the visage of a noble man with flowing dark hair.

"I like your style, Cousin," Talenthia chirped. "I've seen this type of magic before. My cousin's illusions fool almost everyone. Evaine, I think a creature favored by Tyr will be an advantage to our group. Won't you reconsider?"

"It appears I don't have much choice. You have removed my objection. Let's give it a try." She paused and turned to the paladin. "But if your presence turns out to be harmful, I think we should reconsider our alliance. No offense to you, Miltiades, or your god."

"None taken on my part, sorceress. I appreciate your caution. I will be no trouble—in fact, you will be glad I am coming along. I must go now to my tomb to collect several items useful for our journey."

Gamaliel again growled faintly, but Evaine flashed him

a look that instantly quieted the barbarian.

The five companions followed the warrior to the tomb.

The small crypt contained two chambers. The first was an entryway, empty except for a disc-shaped brazier lit with a steady golden flame. The silvery container matched the size of a small shield. Its metal was engraved with runic symbols. Although several inches deep, the brazier was not designed to burn coals; instead, the flame issued from a coin-sized hole in the center of the device.

Evaine cried out in surprise. She had heard of braziers that had the power to double and sometimes triple the strength of a magical spell. Miltiades knew immediately what the sorceress was thinking.

"The evil army discovered this flame as they were building my tomb. They were about to place my body in a log hut and burn the hut to the ground, but Tyr had other plans. He wished me to remain whole for my future quest. He caused the flame to leap from the ground. It created a magical vision with instructions for the members of the horde. Being superstitious creatures, they obeyed the message of the vision and built this tomb.

"I believe the brazier can make your spells more powerful, Evaine. In my spirit wanderings over the centuries, I have learned of other such devices with similar properties.

"I'm sure you will wish to bring the brazier along on our journey. Notice the small platinum cap attached to the brazier with a fine chain. If the cap is placed over the flame, the flame will be temporarily extinguished and the device can be moved safely. The fire will relight when the cap is again removed, but it will light only a limited number of times. No one in this world knows how much magic remains. It may never light again—or, it may relight a hundred times more."

The knight bowed to the sorceress. "I will allow you to use the brazier if you promise that it be returned to a temple of Tyr after our mission is accomplished."

Evaine was clearly excited. "This is just the thing we need! A brazier like this can enhance my magic and improve our chances of finding the pool! Tomorrow, I'll be ready to cast the spell. Miltiades, this is truly a wondrous gift from your god. Please thank him for me. Be assured it is in good hands."

Gamaliel handed his mistress a green silk handkerchief with a fine gold cord along its edges. The knight lifted the brazier. Evaine spread the handkerchief under the device. Miltiades placed the golden cap over the flame, and Evaine spoke a word of magic. Gathering the corners of the handkerchief upward and pulling on the golden cord, the brazier disappeared into a tiny, green silk pouch. Evaine slipped the cord over her wrist.

"Miltiades, I promise the brazier will be returned to one of Tyr's temples after Phlan has been restored."

Miltiades's illusionary face smiled. "Please follow me. I have some items here for all of you. I think Tyr would wish you to have them." The knight led the way deeper into the tomb.

The scent of lilacs wafted up from inside the dank crypt. At one side of the chamber lay a small pile of equipment.

"The evil army had a strange sense of honor," Miltiades explained. "Because I defeated Zarl in battle, I was entombed with all his important possessions. I think there are some useful items for all of us."

The paladin sorted through the pile, handing items to

his astonished companions.

"Andoralson, please take this oak shield. Its protective power is great. You will not be struck by arrows, rocks, or catapult fire while you carry it.

"Talenthia, this is a magical chalice of healing. By filling it with water or wine, you may create a healing potion once each week.

"Ren, this is magical barding for your horse. Part of its magic is that it adjusts to fit any mount, even your magnificent beast. It is feather-light, and your horse won't even know he's wearing it. The spells on this barding will protect your mount from all magical attacks.

"For you, Evaine, is this ring. It allows you to see creatures hidden from sight. You will know the presence of invisible creatures, those hidden by darkness, and those hidden by any magical means.

"And for the fine Gamaliel." The paladin dug deeper into the stack of equipment. "You obviously don't fear magic the way some barbarians do. For you, I have a magical ring that will never allow you to be poisoned. Whether you breathe poison vapor, consume food or liquid, or are struck by a tainted weapon, the poison will not harm you."

Miltiades looked pleased with himself. The group admired their gifts with surprised looks, and at once, all murmured their thanks.

"Now, now, do not thank me. These are gifts from Tyr as much as they are from myself. I wish to be a valuable part of your group. Tyr will watch over all of us. Now, we should prepare for our journey."

Gamaliel led the way out of the chamber. The sky was growing dark. Knowing his mistress's habits, the barbarian spoke. "We'd better find a place to camp. It'll be dark soon, and we need a safe place to sleep. I assume you'll want to build a fire."

No one was in favor of sleeping in the graveyard, and Evaine explained she would need a place clear of the evil influences of such a site for her spell. She instructed Gamaliel to run ahead and find a clearing for them. He bolted out of the graveyard and was gone before the sorceress could explain.

"Gamaliel's a fast runner and an excellent tracker. He'll find a campsite in no time. And he may even have dinner for us by the time we arrive." Talenthia scowled, thinking that the sorceress was probably just bragging. Ren and Andoralson doubted anyone could be that efficient, but said nothing.

Evaine continued. "Is the ghost's black blade still lying in the grass? We can't just leave it here for anyone to find. Miltiades, what should we do with it?"

The knight spoke solemnly. "The blade certainly should be hidden, but no one may touch it. The safest place for it will be inside my tomb."

Without a word, Evaine strode to the site of the battle. The smoldering blade still lay in the blackened grass. The sorceress spoke a few words, and a green mist flowed from her hands. The vapor enveloped the sword and raised it a few feet off the ground. Concentrating, Evaine slowly walked toward the tomb with the blade suspended in the air ahead of her. She entered the tomb and promptly reappeared. "Is there anything else that should be done to safeguard that sword?"

Miltiades nodded and asked the other men to assist him at the entrance to the crypt. The doors were pushed shut with an unearthly creaking noise.

Gamaliel suddenly appeared at the edge of the graveyard. "I've found our campsight. Follow me." The companions gathered their horses and set out on foot after the barbarian. In moments, they arrived at a secluded clearing. The babbling of a stream filled the air. Two huge jackrabbits, freshly caught, lay at the center of the clearing.

*Anything else I can do?* Gamaliel silently asked Evaine.

The sorceress shook her head and chuckled. She knew he had transformed into a giant cat the instant he was out of sight. The others wondered what she found so funny, but were afraid to ask.

"If you'll be coming with us, Miltiades, you'll be needing a horse. Evaine, do you have anything in your magical bag of tricks that'll give him a horse?" Ren's voice was joking, but he wouldn't have been surprised if she had produced a steed.

"No need, ranger. I have my mount." The paladin reached into a pocket and drew out a miniature stallion carved of ivory. He held it out to Evaine, who grinned and nodded, then he set the figurine on the ground and spoke a word of magic. In a white flash, a fully saddled stallion appeared in the clearing. Talenthia eagerly admired the horse, then Miltiades reduced it to a statuette again and slipped it into a pocket.

The group quickly divided up the work of gathering firewood and preparing the rabbits. Evaine announced that as soon as everyone was settled, she would place a spell of protection around the site. Ren asked for volunteers to take turns on nightwatch.

"That won't be necessary," Miltiades stated. "I do not need sleep. I will be awake the entire night, and I am more than happy to serve as your guard." The exhausted party accepted the knight's offer gratefully. Still, Evaine was glad to have Gamaliel around—just in case.

When the meal was finished and everyone was settled, Evaine asked for attention. She would be casting her spell at dawn and insisted on explaining the procedure and giving instructions.

"This is one of the most dangerous spells a wizard can cast. It is not dangerous to the five of you, but it could kill me or render me insane. If anything goes wrong, I guarantee the result will be disaster.

"If no creatures approach overnight, the ward that I place around this camp will still be in place in the morning. Do not enter or leave the clearing or you will be fried to a cinder before you know what has hit you. I require this safeguard because I can't have monsters wandering into camp in the middle of the spell.

"Ordinarily, I must build a fire and purify it. The brazier will allow me to skip that step and conserve some of my energy.

"Once I begin casting, I cannot have any distractions. You must not speak and you must not walk around. If my concentration is broken, we'll all be sorry.

"I will be gazing into a crystal for the greater portion of the spell. My body and brain will be present, but my mind's eye will be elsewhere. Even if you think I'm in trouble, do not disturb me. Follow Gamaliel's lead if you think I need help. He has seen me cast the spell dozens of times."

The barbarian nodded grimly, and the others silently noted their agreement.

"When the spell ends," the sorceress continued, "the crystal will shatter, but I won't be injured. Gamaliel will take over from there. Follow his instructions; my life will depend on him.

"I will be nearly unconscious all day following the spell. Don't think you can wake me, throw me on a horse, and hit the road. I will have almost no powers, and you'll put us all in danger if you drag me along. All you can do is let me sleep and regain my strength. We can start out again the second morning. Any questions?"

Andoralson snickered. "Can you write down the instructions for this spell so I can try it sometime?" Talenthia's elbow landed squarely in her cousin's ribs.

Evaine's green eyes blazed at the druid. "I know you command some magic, but if you were to try this spell you would spend the rest of your natural life in a coma or hopelessly insane. Your brain would be plagued by monsters of your imagination so horrible that you could do nothing but scream and writhe in your bed. You would die a thousand horrible deaths in your mind and you would be so tortured that you'd wish for death. But you couldn't even ask to be put out of your misery." She scowled, almost daring the druid to ask another snide question.

Andoralson looked sheepish. Miltiades had hung on her every word. Despite her original feelings about the paladin, Evaine had the feeling she was going to appreciate having Miltiades around.

"Ren, I'm going to need you awake and alert during the spell," Evaine said after a moment. "I need you to concentrate on the pool with every ounce of energy you have. It will help me make contact and get a solid fix on its whereabouts." Ren nodded his cooperation, and the sorceress felt somewhat relieved. "I know I can depend on you with the lives of your friends at stake."

Evaine stood and paced the perimeter of the clearing. An emerald mist followed her, dissipating quickly. With the ward in place, the sorceress sat down to study. A few hours later, all the companions were in their bedrolls and sleeping fitfully.

Gamaliel awoke Evaine just before dawn. Miltiades stoically stood guard over the camp as she retrieved the brazier from its miniature bag and removed the platinum cap. To her relief, a bright flame sprang forth.

The sorceress spent nearly half an hour clearing her mind with meditation exercises. When she was ready, she signaled Gamaliel to awaken Ren and the others. The barbarian led the ranger to a position near the brazier, and whispered to the others to keep their distance.

Evaine drew a large crystal from a pocket and performed the same ritual she had used at the campfire a few days earlier. After the crystal was heated by the magical flame, she laid the stone in her lap and began to concentrate.

"Hey, what's that roc—" Andoralson blurted out.

Gamaliel was sailing through the air at the druid before he could finish his sentence. The barbarian knocked him to the ground, pinning his chest, and clamped an enormous hand over Andoralson's mouth. "Keep your mouth shut or I'll shut it for you!" Gamaliel whispered with a snarl. His tone was so menacing that the druid didn't so much as blink. Ren, Talenthia, and Miltiades sat motionless.

Thanks to Gamaliel, Evaine hadn't noticed the interruption. Her mind now sailed up over the treetops and toward the pool. Her breathing was rapid and regular, her body was engulfed in a pale green mist. All the others could do was wait.

Gamaliel eventually allowed Andoralson to sit up. But he sat glowering at the druid throughout the rest of the spell.

After what felt like hours, the crystal in Evaine's lap shattered into dust. Gamaliel leaped to her side. She was breathing hard, drenched in sweat, but otherwise healthy. Gamaliel collected the crystal dust, helped his mistress to her bedroll, and saw that she was safely asleep.

Talenthia was the first to whisper to the barbarian. "Is she alright? Is there anything I can do?"

Gamaliel responded calmly. "She'll be fine. All we can do now is wait for her to awaken. We won't know the outcome of the spell until she's ready to tell us. In the meantime, you can do as you like. She's sound asleep, so you're not likely to awaken her." The barbarian seated himself near the sorceress's side with a waterskin, a tin cup, Evaine's herbal mixture, and several clean cloths close at hand.

Around midnight, the sorceress stirred. Gamaliel was still at her side, watching every move. Evaine opened her eyes abruptly and was relieved to see the barbarian's face peering down at her. "What day is it?" she whispered.

"It's the middle of the night, the same day you cast the spell. You've been asleep, oh, about seventeen hours." The barbarian dabbed her face with a wet cloth.

"Good. That's not very long. I should be ready to hit the trail in the morning. I feel strong. I think the magical brazier made a difference. And Ren's presence allowed me to focus on the pool quickly."

Although the pair whispered in the dark, Talenthia and Ren awakened. Andoralson snored in his bedroll, but his cousin shook him awake. Miltiades watched silently, but stoked up the campfire, expecting that Evaine would be telling her story very soon.

Gamaliel raked aside some hot coals and set out a cup of water to boil. The others dragged themselves and their blankets close to the fire. The night air was damp and chill, and the flames were a welcome relief.

Evaine propped herself up and sipped some water. The others looked on, not speaking, waiting for her report. Finally, the sorceress spoke.

"I know you're all eager to hear what happened, but I must warn you, I think we're in deeper trouble than we expected."

"Wonderful," Andoralson murmured. Talenthia silenced him with a stare.

"I should first explain to you how the spell works," Evaine said. "Although I was sitting here where you could see me and I was partially conscious of what was going on around me, a large portion of my mind left my body and flew in the direction of the pool, unencumbered. The travel is lightning fast. I must allow myself to succumb to the power of the pool and let it pull me along. That's partly why the spell is so exhausting; while I'm letting myself be pulled by the pool, I must maintain control of my mind and soul."

The sorceress took another sip of water. "It seems that something is blocking or shielding the pool. Ordinarily, as my mind is whizzing through the air, I can see the countryside blurring along below me. This time, the pool pulled me to the southwest near where my old master lived, where I first studied magic. I continued on for several hundred miles in that direction.

"It was there that I discovered a region of incredible blackness. I've seen some of these only lately—areas of the countryside enveloped in black, impenetrable clouds. But I've never seen one this large or this dark. These are places of intense evil, but I can't imagine what could be generating a zone this large. As I said, I think we're getting into something more terrible than I'd expected.

"I circled the area several times, and from the pull of the spell, I could tell that the pool of darkness lay within. There was no way for me to enter the dark zone and guarantee a safe return."

Evaine paused while Gamaliel mixed the mint and raspberry tea and handed it to her. Miltiades stirred the fire which crackled brightly in the blackness of the woods. The sorceress continued.

"I toured the surrounding countryside briefly to get the lay of the land and perhaps find a safe route for our journey. In the process, I found another tiny black zone, deep in a nearby forest. This gave me an idea.

"The tiny zone of blackness is the home of an old acquaintance of my mentor. At least it used to be his home. I never met the man, but Sebastian spoke of him often. They used to visit each other and argue over spells and trick each other into favors. The two hated each other, but each appreciated the other's powers. It was a rivalry both loved.

"Although I've never met this other wizard, it's worth a try to find out if he still exists. It's a dangerous venture—I'm sure he won't welcome strangers—but if I can prove that I knew Sebastian, maybe he'll listen. Maybe he can even help us. Either way, his home is on the way to the dark zone. It won't take us much time to stop there. And right now, I think it's the only chance we have for a solid clue."

Finally, Ren spoke. "I think we're all having mixed feelings about this mission, especially seeking out a being of evil." He was greeted by nodding heads all around. "But right now, it's our only choice. Why don't we all get back to sleep. We can discuss this in the morning."

No one had to be told twice. Bedrolls were again rolled out. In silence, everyone settled in as the fire burned down.

As he took up his silent watch, Miltiades smiled. All the bedrolls were a little closer to the fire than before.

# ❦ 11 ❦

## Eerie Parley

The atmosphere inside Denlor's Tower was heating up. But it wasn't enemy wizards or warriors applying the pressure.

"You can pout, you can sulk, you can even wear that blue silky thing you wear when you want something special, but you aren't going on this raid."

"Tarl, I'm not going into the council chambers until we get this settled."

"Good. You can stay here until Phlan is teleported back to the Moonsea. I'll talk to the councilmen."

Shal's eyes blazed at her husband's words. The pair left the tower and headed for the council chambers.

Few citizens moved about the city today. Most were either stationed on the wall or gathering food for the hungry defenders. Of those who were near the council, all looked on as two prominent personalities of Phlan argued in front of the chamber doors. The sight was worth watching.

The woman, who was over six feet tall with beautifully sculpted muscles, wrung her hands and pleaded with her husband not to go into battle without her. A slightly shorter warrior-priest of Tyr, dressed in full battle armor, was trying to calm his wife.

Tarl grew more and more exasperated. "You and I have battled the horrors and evils that have assaulted Phlan in this cavern for over a month now. There is no end in sight. My only desire is to see you safe."

The sorceress gripped her husband's hand. "Do you think I want you any less safe? Is the Warhammer of Tyr going to keep you alive forever? There's only one way this argument is going to end. I'm going wherever you go. You can't stop me."

Tarl gazed at his wife with admiration and frustration. He shook his head in defeat and opened the door for her. By the gods, he loved this woman.

First Councilman Kroegel rose to meet the pair. "So glad you could attend our meeting. In these troubled times, it is comforting to have loyal citizens to defend Phlan."

Tarl bowed to His Holiness, Seventh Councilman Wahl. He was pleasurably reminded that a cleric of Tyr had held a seat on the council for the last hundred years. Tarl had been offered the seat, but he shunned politics. Administrative duties didn't appeal to his free spirit. Bishop Wahl was an excellent alternative; he and Tarl had always seen eye to eye on matters in the past.

Fifth Councilwoman Bordish motioned to several comfortable padded benches. "We've called you here to discuss an effort at peace."

"We're here to talk about a raid into the cavern, not about peace," Tarl said, jumping up and pacing before the Council of Ten. "How can you even think of talking peace? We've been attacked repeatedly and our homes have been moved to gods-only-know-where. If whoever did this had any intention of negotiating, don't you think we'd know by now? I don't see that we're in any position to bargain!"

"Sit down, Tarl," Bishop Wahl replied gently. "I posed the same concern to the council over the past two days.

They want to attempt a truce, and I want you to lead the contingent making the attempt. If something goes wrong, the envoys at least have a chance of making it back to the city."

"With Tarl and I along, you can be sure of that," Shal said, smiling to her husband.

"You can't go," Tarl hissed under his breath. He gave her a silent stare that meant they would talk privately later. He turned to the council. "I will lead your peace mission. I want Thorvid of Porter, Alaric the White, and Pomanz as companions. I also want my opinion entered in the official record that this isn't going to work. I think the effort is doomed."

"Your fears are noted," sneered Fourth Councilwoman Eldred. "But the men you picked are all knights. How do you expect to talk peace with only warriors at your back?"

"I'll do all the talking. Those men are along to provide muscle if we're attacked. We'll leave within the hour. Please alert the knights I have named and ask them to wait at the Death Gates."

Husband and wife walked out of the council chambers, hurrying toward Denlor's Tower.

"Shal, I know you're angry and I know you want to come along. But I have a more important job for you. I'm going to try this peace attempt, but I'm sure it'll fail. I need you standing by to save this delegation when we're attacked."

The sorceress's mood softened. She smiled at her husband as they headed down the cobbled street. "I suspected you had some plan in mind. I appreciate the idea of riding in like an avenging angel when you get in trouble. I'll watch you magically and jump in when I'm needed. Just make sure nothing happens to you until I get there."

The couple walked arm in arm to their tower to prepare once again for war.

An hour later, Tarl and his party stood before the Death Gates, ready to leave. The cleric scowled at the truce flags his men carried.

\*　\*　\*　\*　\*

Above the cavern that held Phlan hostage, high in the vermilion-stoned tower, the Red Wizard seethed.

"Truce flags? They can't surrender! I just finished lining up all the forest creatures sent by that fiendish god Moander. If Phlan surrenders, I can't pull down the walls," Marcus raved. "Tell them to go back to their pathetic city and suffer my wrath for resisting!" Red robes swirled as the fuming mage paced his chamber.

The mercenary commander who brought the message had turned to leave when a commanding voice shouted, "Stop! *Latenat*!"

"Fiend, don't hinder me now! Keep to your room and I will handle the war down below," Marcus said, conversing with the air around him.

The mercenary hadn't moved, but was silently confirming his opinion that no amount of gold was worth this job.

"Marcus," the voice continued calmly, "we are ordered to deliver as many souls as possible from Phlan into the pool of darkness. Do you suppose when you use the trees of Moander, the very trees of death I gave you, that a few of those souls might be lost in the battle? *Latenat*!"

"Yes, a few of the rabble can be expected to perish. On the other hand, after the dust clears, Phlan will be defeated, which accomplishes my personal goals. That's what's really important, after all."

The throne room suddenly became filled with the smell of blood. The now-terrified mercenary observed a distinct dimming of the lights in the chamber. A chill ran up his spine.

"Maaar-cus," the voice became honey-sweet. "Would you please dismiss your commander? *Latenat!*"

"Yes, of course." The Red Wizard of Thay waved the mercenary away. "I will get back to you momentarily with my decisions. Leave me now."

The warrior of Bane departed in relief. He noticed a dark object growing in the wizard's hand, but didn't want to be around long enough to learn what it was.

In the red-gold throne room, the pit fiend appeared, accompanied by a loud thunderclap.

"Master, do you still wish to become a demigod on this plane? *Latenat!*"

"Of course, fool. I haven't gone to all this effort to have my plans upset."

"Knowing this is your will, how can you expect me to make you all-powerful? You have left me only the souls of a washer woman and a baker boy to absorb through the pool! *Latenat!*"

"What do you mean, fiend? Make your thoughts known, I order you!" Marcus held the black heart out for the fiend to see and covet.

The pit fiend ignored the implied threat and stomped his twelve-foot body up to the throne of the wizard. The monster glared into his eyes.

"The more people you kill, the fewer souls remain for our purposes. Do you think you could use that famous cunning Red Wizards are known for and trick these people? Let them believe they can leave the city, according to their free will. Entice the populace into the pool of darkness. *Latenat!*"

Green drool splashed from the fiend's fangs and splattered on the red-gold floor of the throne room. The sticky, acidic poison hissed and sparked red. This time, however, the acid left no trace.

Marcus smiled. He had grown disgusted with the condition of the floor of his spellcasting chamber and had silently vowed that such oozing pockmarks wouldn't mar his throne room any longer. With some effort, he had devised a spell to protect the floor from all types of slimes. The Red Wizard, pleased with his game, gave the fiend a wide grin, thinking, It's the little victories that really count, after all.

Marcus addressed his powerful servant. "Yes, I can trick this city of fools. But this game would be more fun if I could defeat Phlan with the armies you gave me. Unfortunately, you are right, my fine fiend. Souls are more important to our futures. Consider this trickery done. Now, go back to the spellcasting chamber. You are stinking up my beautiful throne room!"

"As you wish, master," the deep voice grated as the fiend teleported out of the room.

"Fiends are such childlike creatures," Marcus sighed, before arising to see to arrangements.

Alone in the throne room, the erinyes hopped out of her alcove to stretch her feathered wings. The creature flopped down in Marcus's throne to lounge undisturbed. Having heard the entire conversation, she amused herself by dreaming of ways to vent her "childish" impulses on the entrails of the Red Wizard.

\* \* \* \* \*

"A strange forest we ride through, my lord. I don't remember a forest growing in this part of the cavern before."

Eyeing the trees, the knight Thorvid sheathed his sword and unhooked a large battle-axe from his saddle. The four men on horseback slowly trotted through a forest of twisted, moldering trees. Moss dangled and swayed eerily from mottled brown branches.

"These trees are damn disturbing," Tarl observed, drawing forth the Warhammer of Tyr. The ancient relic emitted a blaze of holy radiance. "My old comrade, Ren o' the Blade, could have told us just what these trees are and what all that slimy fungus is on their branches. I know I've never smelled its like before. The stench is almost like the rotting smell of undead creatures.

"Is it possible that whoever transported us here practiced first on trees, and this is what happens when a forest exists underground too long?" Thorvid asked.

Tarl shuddered at the thought. "Pomanz, your father was a forester, wasn't he? Have you ever seen anything like this?"

"I never have, and I don't mind saying that I'll be glad when we're clear of them." Pomanz sheathed his saber in exchange for his battle-axe. The three knights had battled together too many years to ignore each other's hunches. If these trees were capable of attack, axes would slay them faster than swords. "And there's something unnatural here. There's no wind, yet the branches seem to wave in a breeze."

"I don't remember hearing about a forest in any of the scouting reports," Alaric observed, swinging his axe in wide arcs to stretch his muscles.

Suddenly, the radiance of Tyr's hammer glowed brighter and shone on a clearing ahead of the foursome. Bathed in the hammer's glow, a Red Wizard of Thay stood before them. Gold-trimmed red robes flowed about the sorcerer, making him appear to hover over the ground. Black hair spilled down his back, matching a closely-trimmed beard. Steely eyes glared out from under bushy eyebrows. The wizard was an imposing sight, yet Tarl and his men were unimpressed.

"Welcome to my lands, noble knights," Marcus sneered. "Judging from your flags of surrender, can I assume you intend to turn Phlan over to me?"

The four warriors spread out in a line in front of the wizard. The horses stamped nervously, tearing up the earth and uncovering tough tree roots just under the surface.

"Whom do I have the honor of addressing?" Tarl asked in his most polite tone.

"Why, foolish priest, I am Marcus, Red Wizard of Thay and your host. I am the man who singlehandedly transported Phlan to its current resting place. Now that the pleasantries are over, I ask again—have you come to surrender Phlan to me?"

The three knights left the negotiating to Tarl. Thorvid watched the trail behind them; Alaric watched the trees to the left; Pomanz guarded their right.

"You are very brave, Lord Marcus, to meet our truce parley without guards. We have come at the request of Phlan's Council of Ten to talk terms of peace." Tarl was barely able to contain his anger at the effrontery of the mage he faced, but much more than his pride was at stake. He was committed to play peacemaker.

The wizard answered haughtily. "I need no guards to protect me from your sort. As for terms of peace—there are none. I want your city. That's why I transported all of Phlan's buildings here. But all of the citizens may go, taking any goods they can carry. Take my message back to your Council of Ten." Marcus turned to leave.

"Ignoring the fact that no one has the right to steal a city, where exactly are we?" Tarl asked.

The wizard turned to the riders, irritated. From the glare in his eyes, he clearly found them unworthy of his audience. "You are in a great cavern beneath my red tower. You are still in Faerun—at least physically. You may take my generous offer to leave safely or you may die. Now be gone."

Thorvid raised his battle-axe. "Why, you arrogant son of—" Tarl seized the knight's arm, even as he struggled to contain his own anger. Taking a deep breath, Tarl addressed the wizard.

"Before I take your offer back to my people for discussion, I would like to see how we'll get out of this cavern. And I need your guarantee of safety for the people of Phlan."

"Why, of course. Your wish is reasonable. You won't be able to take your horses up my stairs, but do come along." The wizard floated on puffs of red flame down a wide trail between the trees.

Tightening their grips on their weapons, the four warriors fought to control their skittish mounts as they rode behind the wizard.

After perhaps fifty yards, the forest opened up at the side of the cavern. A section of the cave wall melted away in a red mist, revealing a wide staircase spiraling upward.

"Only you, priest, need to see the exit out of my tower. Send the rest of your rabble back to the city."

"Where our lord goes, we follow," Pomanz declared, keeping a wary eye for signs of any trap.

To keep the peace, Tarl was about to agree with the Red Wizard's request, but the wizard suddenly flew into a rage. He fairly bellowed at the four men.

"Knight, know that I am Marcus, a mage of extraordinary power. You are nothing compared to my might. You will do as I say or I will destroy you." The wizard produced a sparking, popping ball of crimson energy in his right hand. His red robes writhed about him.

"There will be no combat. We are under flags of parley. Surely, even the Red Wizards of Thay recognize such conventions of war."

"Oh, we recognize them all right. This is our answer to such knightly foolishness." A wave of his left hand caused the two white flags to ignite and crumble to ash.

"Wizard, you go too far!" Tarl shouted, raising his glowing hammer.

Another wave of the mage's hand caused the ground to rumble underfoot. "No! I have not gone nearly far enough! You can all meet my pool of darkness or face my thorny horrors in the forest. There is no surrender and no escape. My pit fiend was stupid to think I could get anything from you this way. Good-bye."

The wizard blinked out in a blast of red flame.

"Something's happening behind us!" Thorvid shouted.

The forest was writhing and shifting. Every tree was becoming a horribly twisted parody of a human. Tree limbs turned into giant arms; roots heaved from the ground, growing into huge legs; trunks twisted with loud groans into massive, pulsing chests and heads.

Tarl hurriedly searched for an escape. They could go up the stairs into the darkness and whatever trap Marcus had prepared, or they could meet the tree monsters head on.

"Tarl!" Pomanz pointed to the right.

The mystical light in the cavern showed a narrow path through the forest. The companions spurred their mounts into the narrow gap between the trees and the edge of the cavern.

A mile-wide swath of groaning, twisting trees slowly encroached on the path at the cavern wall, squeezing it tighter and tighter. The warriors threw aside lances and equipment to lighten the loads on the galloping horses, but each man could see they weren't moving fast enough to escape. Tarl led the charge toward the perimeter. "This would be a good time, Shal!" he screamed.

Back in the red tower, Marcus and the pit fiend watched the wild ride from a crystal scrying sphere.

"If she's coming to save them, your trees won't be able to stop the cleric and his friends. *Latenat!*"

"I know, but maybe the minions of Moander can ruin one or two of them. Look—his hammer isn't even bruising the bark. Moander certainly has a talent for perverting things of nature." The wizard rubbed his hands with glee.

"Couldn't you have tried harder to trick them into moving up the stairs? *Latenat!*" The fiend was disgusted with the failure of the parley.

"No, this is much better. Tomorrow, or perhaps in a few days, after I have rested, I will lead those tree minions in a final attack on the city. We will pull down the walls once and forever. But we'll be careful, of course, to capture the defenders and not kill too many of them. Then Phlan and all its souls will be ours."

Marcus paced the chamber in delight, anticipating the glorious future. Tanetal rubbed his greasy forehead, wondering what Bane would do with them when all the plans failed. The fiend stared into the scrying crystal.

Tarl and the warriors thundered along the narrow corridor next to the cavern wall. Responding to a magical voice in his head, the ranger screamed to the others. "Hold your breath until the mist clears!" A purple haze materialized at the edge of the trees and drifted into the forest. The moving branches temporarily halted, but as the haze faded, the trees resumed their encroachment.

A wall of ice and snow blasted out of the sky, forming a frozen drift at the edge of the forest. The trees slowed their squirming, and the fungus that dripped from the branches froze solid and fell off in huge chunks. Within moments, the ice began to melt and a cloud of steam arose. The trees resumed their unnatural assault.

Finally, a pinpoint of light appeared above Tarl's head. Growing brighter and brighter, the speck swelled to a ball larger than a warrior's helmet. It followed the cleric as it blazed forth with the intensity of the sun.

The unholy forest recoiled at the blinding light. Trees and plants ahead of Tarl all veered away as he approached. The four riders thundered onward, now unhindered. Less than five minutes later, they burst from the forest to charge across the grassy plain, their mounts streaked with white foam from the hard ride. Tarl called out to his unseen wife. "Nice going, Shal!"

Up in Denlor's Tower, the sorceress smiled in relief.

The reaction in the enemy camp was much different. In Marcus's tower, the fiend slammed his fist into the crystal sphere, smashing it to powder.

# ☙ 12 ☙

## Disturbing Clues

"Fair travelers, we would approach!" A voice rang through the woods, warning the sleeping camp of incoming strangers.

Miltiades, always awake, stood guard. Ren had awakened early to share the morning watch. They heard scuffling sounds in the woods long before the voice announced the presence of travelers. Overhead, dark stormclouds still rumbled and swirled, but the sky had lightened with the sunrise. Three men astride huge wolves trotted into camp.

Minutes earlier, Gamaliel had sensed their coming and awakened his mistress and the rest of the party.

"Friendly faces are welcome, but be warned, we are a formidable band," Ren replied to their hail.

Dismounting, the three strode toward the group. They were a rough lot with shaggy black hair and torn, homespun clothing. None showed any weapons—a fact the companions found unusual for woodland travelers. No weapons, that is, except for the three enormous wolves.

"I am Artur Bladeson." The biggest of the three men gave Ren a toothy grin. "These cubs behind me are my cousins, Wuldor and Donar Arcnos. We are traveling to Vaasa to visit relatives in Moortown. Can you tell us of any trouble in the lands between there and here?"

On the opposite side of the camp, the druids talked in

hushed tones. "Look how the wolves are growling at Miltiades," Talenthia whispered to Andoralson. "Could they be sensing your illusion magic?"

"No, but they could be detecting that he's an undead creature. I'll have to work on putting scent into my illusions. I don't usually bother. I hope you noticed those wolves aren't really wolves."

Meanwhile, Evaine and the barbarian sized up the strangers.

*Mistress,* Gamaliel mentally communicated, *those men do not smell human. And those huge wolves are just waiting for the chance to attack.* He stood facing the three men like a pillar of stone, blocking their view of Evaine.

*Ren senses something strange, too. I can tell by his posture. There's no question he's on the defensive. Let's follow his lead,* Evaine silently told her comrade.

The wolves continued to growl at Miltiades, all the while shooting wary glances at Gamaliel.

"Brutus, Tog, Garf, shut up! These fine people have invited us into their camp. The least we can do is be civil. Wuldor, take those curs away and settle them down."

Wuldor smelled like wet fur. Ren couldn't help but crinkle his nose as the man passed.

"I don't think I've ever seen wolves used as mounts before. Are you druids?" Ren tried to break the uneasiness between the two sides.

The three men laughed in an odd, barking manner.

"Druids," Donar said, choking with laughter. "No disrespect to those two over there, but even druids couldn't tame our three pets. We live with these beasts, and they do what we tell them."

"Your friends don't talk much," Artur said, warming his hands by the fire.

"They just woke up," Ren said evenly. He walked to the opposite side of an already blazing fire and added more logs. He felt compelled to get these men on their way as soon as possible. "The paths to Vaasa are clear—I just came from there. Phlan has suffered the wrath of the gods and has disappeared. Only a patch of tents marks the place where the city once stood. But you shouldn't have much trouble passing through. What do you know of Zhentil Keep and Yulash?"

"I heard that Phlan was gone," said Artur, "but I figured it to be a rumor. You've seen it, then?" Ren nodded. Artur's gaze shifted about the camp. "You people seem a little tense. Let's share some food. There's no reason we can't be friends, eh?" he said, trying to act more congenial than he looked. All the companions instinctively felt he was hiding something.

Wuldor, still tending to the wolves, spoke to Ren. "If you're traveling south, stay away from Zhentil Keep. Something has stirred up the evil in that gods-cursed city. We lost a brother there when we tried to conduct some business for our master. Some frenzied priests of Bane attacked us without reason."

None of this surprised Ren. Zhentil Keep was always a place to avoid, and Wuldor described what might well have been daily events.

Wuldor was slapping the wolves and casting strange glances toward the campfire. "Something is odd about the forests and trails to the south of Zhentil Keep. We tore through them because they didn't smell or feel right. There's a growing evil."

"Yulash, on the other hand, is fine. No problems," Donar said, taking packs of meat from his saddlebags. He quickly whittled a branch into a spit and hung some meat over the fire for roasting.

*Do you see what kind of meat that is, Gam?* Evaine silently voiced to the barbarian.

*I smell what kind of meat it is. Should we attack now?* The barbarian's eyes shifted from pale green to a deep golden color.

*Let me get Ren away from them. When I give the signal, I'll go for the humans—you attack the wolves. Maybe we can disable one or two of them before they have a chance to metamorphose,* she told the barbarian. She raised her voice and spoke to the druids. "Talenthia, I think you should prepare your new chalice for our friends' visit. You know, the one that makes that wonderful wine." Evaine hoped the two would pick up on her hint.

The sorceress mentally readied a spell. "Ren, could you help me for a moment? That clumsy barbarian has the straps of my backpack all tied in knots."

The ranger arose, giving Gamaliel a puzzled look. He pulled a dagger from his boot and stepped toward Evaine. But as he did so, she rounded the campfire and yelled, "Attack!"

Eighteen missiles of magical energy shot from her hands and struck Artur's chest, albeit with little effect. The camp was suddenly filled with the shouts of the companions and the flash of spells. But the three strangers and their wolves reacted almost in slow motion.

Artur rose from his place by the fire. As he stood, he transformed, as did his cousins, into a werewolf. Dark fur sprouted all over their bodies. Each man grew in height, expanding muscles rippling along their arms and legs. The change was nearly instantaneous, but these monsters weren't in any hurry. They relied on the horrifying transformations to help frighten their victims.

The three wolves grew from huge, four-legged shapes

into large and deadly half-human forms, known through Faerun as wolfweres. The three new creatures launched themselves at Evaine, knowing the spellcaster was the greatest threat to them. The creature that had been Wuldor, now eight feet tall, moved to block Gamaliel.

The barbarian's sword landed solidly on the wolfwere causing little more than a scratch.

"Watch out! They're wolfweres!" Ren shouted, slashing at two of the transformed wolves with his magical daggers. The weapons bit deep and diverted the lunges of two of the wolf-men, but the third one smashed into Evaine full force.

Worried about Gamaliel and Ren, Evaine was so caught up in her spellcasting that she didn't notice the attack from behind her. The wolfwere's front paws bashed into her skull and sent her to the ground with a thud. She lay motionless.

Gamaliel's roar of rage could be heard for miles through the woods as he transformed into his true form, the giant cat. Two lightning-quick swipes with his eight-inch claws struck the monster that had attacked his mistress. Its spine was instantly severed, and Gamaliel tossed the wolfwere ten feet into the air. The monster landed, twitched, then was still. Blood oozed from its back and mouth.

Miltiades, knowing only silver or enchanted blades could harm a werewolf, was attacking with brute strength. The undead paladin locked arms with what had been Artur and tried to strangle the life out of the creature. As the werewolf reached to do the same, the paladin's illusionary flesh turned back into enchanted bones.

Artur howled in fright as Miltiades snapped his woolly neck.

Wuldor leaped at Andoralson, but the creature's crusty claws struck—not the druid—but an illusion. Two mystical flaming scimitars, created by magic and guided by the druids, flew forth and bit deep into Wuldor's flesh, seeking his heart, burning his fur, and sending him thrashing to the ground.

Ren rolled in the grass, locked in a life-and-death duel. The wolfwere ripped at his throat, but the ranger wedged his chain mail-protected arm into the jaws of the beast while his other hand jabbed with Right to find a vital organ in the huge lycanthrope. Blood splattered the campsite as the weapon found its mark repeatedly. The creature exerted its full energy trying to tear Ren's arm out of its socket.

Still guarding Evaine's body, Gamaliel sank his fangs and claws into the body of the werewolf that had been Donar.

Andoralson, hidden by several illusions, used phantasm magic on another of the wolfweres. The creature's brain played an image of its most horrible fear. The wolfwere died under the attack of mystical fangs, never realizing that the fangs were only in its mind.

Ren's dagger finally found its mark. He threw the dead body of his attacker to the ground and leaped to his feet. His arm was numb and limp, but no monsters were left alive.

All the other companions—except Miltiades—lay in the grass, panting. The undead paladin, never tiring, began dragging the bodies into the woods. Six bloody trails in the grass were soon all that remained as traces of the vanquished.

Catching his breath, Ren turned to see Evaine still lying on the ground. A tawny cat, larger than a full-grown tiger, stood guard over her. Blood slowly oozed from a large gash in the sorceress's head. The ranger limped over to her. The giant feline fluffed out his tail and hissed.

"Ren, don't!" Talenthia shouted. "Gamaliel, or whatever he is now, is in a battle frenzy. He probably doesn't even recognize you. You can bet he'll attack anything or anyone trying to touch Evaine."

"We have to do something. She could die if we don't get her head bandaged." Ren's face reddened in frustration.

"I can try to distract Gamaliel while all of you attend to Evaine. If all of you try together, you can work fast. I don't think the cat can do much to my dead bones," Miltiades offered.

"Don't be so sure," Andoralson warned. He circled wide around cat and sorceress to get a better look at Evaine. "Whatever magic operates on this beast gives it greater strength. If that cat crushed your bones, I doubt that even my cousin could heal you. Let Talenthia and I try to calm Gamaliel." The huge feline simply hissed at the druid, revealing six-inch fangs.

The druids tried everything to coax Gamaliel away from Evaine, but the big cat didn't move an inch. He aloofly watched their attempts, hissing loudly. The cousins tried spells of charming, friendship, illusion, and animal-repelling, all to no avail.

"That's one unusual animal Evaine has there. He's stubborn, but gods, he's beautiful, isn't he? I can see why Evaine is so fond of him."

Andoralson agreed with his cousin. "He really is magnificent. But right now, he's more trouble than anything." Gamaliel's golden eyes glared at the druid, then the cat lifted his nose in pride and looked away.

"Talenthia, I can't tell if it's the magical collar the cat wears or Gamaliel's innate magical resistance that allows him to ignore our spells. Can you get a better fix on him?" Talenthia concentrated and tried a spell, but shook her head. "Sorry."

Ren kept an eye on Evaine, standing as close as Gamaliel would allow. "It looks like her bleeding has stopped, and her breathing sounds more normal. She'll probably wake up naturally in a few hours."

"What do you think we should do, just wait until she comes around?" Andoralson didn't like the idea, but didn't have any other suggestions.

"We don't have much choice," Ren replied, shaking his head. "Miltiades, you and I should burn the bodies of those creatures. The two of you, pick through their equipment and see if you can learn anything about them. All we can do is hope that Evaine is all right and wakes up on her own. But if her wound gets any worse, or if she looks like she's in danger, I'll take a hand in moving Gamaliel myself. I've fought large cats like him before." The deadly look he gave Gamaliel told everyone he would kill the cat to save Evaine if necessary. The glare Gamaliel returned told Ren he would be in for trouble if he tried. "Well, uh, not *exactly* like this cat," Ren admitted. He motioned to the others to get busy, but Miltiades asked a question.

"What were those wolf creatures, anyway? The ones that started out as wolves and changed into humanlike things? I've battled werewolves before, but never creatures like those."

Andoralson explained. "Wolfweres. When werewolves and wolves mate, their offspring are more wolf than man. The creatures are more intelligent than normal wolves and can change shape to look like werewolves whenever they want. They're incredibly powerful and are ferocious killers. Once they're stirred up, they fight to the death—as you now know from experience.

"What surprised me is that the wolfweres allowed themselves to be mastered by the werewolves. I've always heard that the two creatures hate each other. Perhaps this growing evil in our land is perverting nature more than we suspect."

Talenthia shivered at her cousin's observations. Andoralson squeezed her in a comforting hug, then pointed her toward the woods where the bodies of the horrid creatures lay waiting. The foursome separated and busied themselves with chores.

Hours passed. Evaine didn't awaken, but didn't worsen either. Gamaliel refused to budge. He made his mistress comfortable in the grass and gently licked her wound. Still she did not stir. The wolf bodies had all been burned and the druids were done picking through the possessions they had gathered. Ren and Miltiades had cleaned their armor and sharpened all their blades.

Many hours later, as the companions roasted rabbits for supper, Evaine stirred and sent Gamaliel a mental message.

*Ohh, Gam, what happened? I've got such a headache.*

*A wolfwere hit you from behind and knocked you unconscious. You've been out for hours, and I've been guarding you from everyone.* The giant animal purred, rubbing his huge tongue along her neck.

Despite her pain, the sorceress giggled out loud, attracting the attention of the others. *Hey, that tickles!* she said silently. *Ouch, don't make me laugh.* She opened her eyes to find everyone looking worriedly at her.

"I see you've met the real Gamaliel. My familiar should be a little nicer now that I'm awake. Talenthia, can you do anything for this pain? My head is splitting." The druid hesitated, looking worriedly at the cat. The sorceress ordered Gamaliel to lie down.

A stern-faced Ren watched the attractive druid work her magic on Evaine. "I can understand why you didn't tell us about your familiar. I would have done the same thing in your place. But the creature's loyalty in guarding you prevented our helping you and could have endangered your life."

"He won't prevent you from touching me again. I'll make sure of that," she said, rubbing the brown fur between her giant cat's ears. "What happened after I was knocked out?"

"Oh, nothing much," Talenthia replied, finished with her healing. The ever-cheerful druid made light of the serious battle. "We destroyed three werewolves and three wolfweres. I checked to make sure none of us, including you and the cat, got the lycanthropy sickness."

"How did you know those creatures were evil lycanthropes, anyway?" Andoralson asked. He handed Evaine some sweet-smelling fruit juice in a wooden chalice.

"We could all tell they were odd somehow. But when they pulled out that fresh meat, I knew what type of evil they were. The meat was human. Gamaliel knew by the smell. He and I can communicate mentally, if you haven't guessed that already. I would have given you all more warning, but I truly thought my missile spell would kill their leader. The creature must have been unusually powerful."

"Yes, it was. Snapping that creature's neck was more difficult than I anticipated," Miltiades noted. "But we discovered many interesting things about them while you were knocked out."

"Oh yes, you're going to love what we found," Talenthia said sarcastically. She strolled over to Ren to check his healed wound for a fourth time. "Give her the parchment they were carrying."

Andoralson handed over a small, official-looking fold-
er with a broken wax seal. The tiny runes on the seal
were in an ancient, magical script, one Evaine had
learned as an apprentice. The script proclaimed the
holder of the document to be a trusted ambassador. An
ambassador of what, she couldn't tell, because part of
the seal had fallen away. She read the scroll aloud.

*To the lords and mercenary captains reading this
scroll, I, Lord Marcus, bid you greeting.*

*The bearer of this document is a trusted servant of my
new realm. He is empowered to hire and negotiate in my
name for troops and mercenaries who would consider
declaring fealty to me in my red tower.*

*The rewards such warriors may earn are vast. In my
service, the battles are brief and the booty great. Those
who would join should travel west of what was once
Hillsfar along the coast of the Moonsea. All soldiers will
be met by other servants of mine and escorted to my
tower.*

*Lord Marcus, Red Wizard of Thay*

The ranger sought Evaine's opinion. "I dreamed of a
red tower just before I arrived in Phlan. I didn't think it
bore any significance. Could Phlan's pool of darkness be
connected somehow to this tower?"

Evaine thought for a few moments. "The large area of
darkness that I saw in my spell is located west of Hillsfar.
Considering what I know of such places, it's entirely possible that the tower could be within the darkness, along
with the pool. But that doesn't account for the missing
city.

"We should continue riding toward the smaller patch

of darkness. I'm convinced it's connected to the larger evil, and it'll provide important clues." She smiled. "Besides, my home is a few days' ride south of Zhentil Keep. It's a stone cottage hidden in the edges of the elven forest. We can all rest there and discuss our strategy. I can cast another spell to locate the pool. Being that close to the area of blackness should give me more clues about what we are facing.

"I still own many of Sebastian's possessions. If the small blackness is indeed the home of my mentor's adversary, those items will help prove who I am and enlist the aid of the old wizard. Unless anyone objects, that's how I'd like us to proceed."

"Evaine," Ren said, stripping off his weapons to create an amazing pile of daggers and short swords, "could you ask Gamaliel to turn into a human again? Now that you've assured him we won't be harming you, I'd like to talk to him alone for a moment."

Gamaliel blurred and transformed before Evaine could ask. He rose to his feet to look at Ren. The glares they shot at each other might have been poisoned darts.

"Follow me, please. But first, I'd appreciate it if you'd remove your gloves." Ren requested.

Ren stared at the barbarian for a moment, then turned and walked into the woods without looking back to see if Gamaliel followed.

*I can't imagine what he wants, Gamaliel, but please try to be polite. We have to work with this ranger, even if we don't particularly like him.* Evaine pleaded with him mentally.

*As you wish,* the barbarian agreed, then turned to follow Ren.

Casting a worried look into the forest, Evaine retrieved a brush from her backpack and began untangling her hair.

"This Marcus character seems to be trying to raise a huge army," Evaine said, thinking out loud.

"Yes," Andoralson agreed. He checked the rabbits that sizzled over the fire and brushed a sticky concoction over the meat. The scents of herbs and roasting meat were delightful. "With the Moonsea region so stirred up, I don't think he's going to get more than a couple of hundred, maybe even a thousand troops. But an army like that could take advantage of the chaos in the region. Gods only know what this Red Wizard could do to the balance of life around here."

"Miltiades, what could you do with a thousand troops? Especially with the condition the Moonsea is in now?" Evaine had grown to respect the warrior's battle sense. She was beginning to like the undead paladin. He didn't speak much, but he had an intelligence and discipline Evaine appreciated and admired.

"With a thousand good troops, I could conquer all the tent cities of the Moonsea. But without the real cities, the ones the gods have stolen, it would be only a series of hollow victories. If I were on a mission of conquest, I'd certainly want more than hundreds of poor refugees.

"There is more to this Marcus than meets the eye. If he were earnestly trying to hire mercenaries, he would have sent more reliable ambassadors than those lycanthropes. He's either a miserable strategist or he just wants a few armies for some brief attack." The paladin was obviously puzzled.

Evaine and Miltiades continued their discussion about the mysterious wizard while Andoralson flittered about the campsite, muttering about overcooked meat and listening for the return of Ren and Gamaliel. Irritated by their absence, he served up the rabbits, quite proud of his cooking despite his annoyance. The remaining two servings he placed near the fire.

Half an hour later, with supper finished and their portions overcooked, two bruised and battered men limped out of the woods. Ren's hands bore bleeding scrapes and he sported a large cut along his neck. Gamaliel was almost unrecognizable behind two blackened eyes.

"What have you two been doing?" Evaine shrieked.

"*I* was being polite," Gamaliel said innocently. His eyes blazed a bright green but were tinged with gold.

*You're annoyed with the ranger, but you enjoyed your fight, didn't you?* Evaine silently communicated.

*Not to worry, mistress. I'm only slightly wounded, and the ranger finally realizes that I'm not one to be trifled with.* Evaine snickered at the haughty tone in his mental message.

"Let's just say that we men understand each other a little better," Ren smiled, revealing a split lip.

*Ha. He probably thinks he won, too!*

Evaine couldn't help but laugh out loud at Gamaliel's silent sneer.

After considerable scolding and patching of wounds, Andoralson served the remaining portions of the rabbit. "If you'd been here on time, you could have had a delicious supper. But now you'll have to settle for rabbit jerky." The druid huffed in disgust. Ren and Gamaliel had both eaten worse, and thought the meat was wonderful despite its chewiness.

As the two men ate, the rest of the group inventoried their supplies and added the few useful items of equipment left by the werewolves. The spoils from defeated enemies were always welcomed.

The five companions crawled into their bedrolls under the dark, threatening sky. Thunder rumbled in the distance. Miltiades took up his normal watch. All slept fitfully, dreaming of the unknown horrors that awaited them.

At dawn, all were awake and packed for the trail. Transformed again into a giant cat, Gamaliel obliterated their tracks. Miltiades summoned his magical ivory steed, and the companions started out through the woods determinedly.

They rode under the troubled sky for several days, following the coast of the Moonsea. They braved a steady, chilly rainfall the entire second day. As they approached within a few miles of Zhentil Keep, the group made a wide arc around the dark city.

Zhentil Keep sat like a blood-gorged spider on the western edge of the Moonsea. The walled city was easy to avoid, and fording the Tesh River was little trouble. While the others had to swim against the current, leading their horses across, Miltiades and his enchanted ivory mount simply walked along the river bottom and emerged wet on the other side.

Beyond the evil city, a wide road wound to the south. Evaine had insisted on taking that route, but on the first day of travel, the druids became concerned.

"It's rained here far more than normal, even for the conditions around here the last few months. The ground has become unusually swampy," Andoralson said.

"Notice the fiddlehead ferns, the jewelweed, and the jimsonweed. They don't grow in this type of environment. Something is seriously disturbing the balance of nature here." The druids looked more and more worried as the expedition pressed on. The druids were convinced they were witnessing harbingers of greater danger.

Ren rode far ahead of the group, explaining that he

wanted to scout. He refused to admit to himself that he was trying to hide his mood.

With a thud of horse's hooves, Evaine galloped ahead to ride at Ren's side.

"What's bothering you, Ren?" the sorceress asked.

"Using your magic to read my mind, wizard? Why don't you tell *me* what I'm thinking?"

Evaine ignored his surly reply. "I know you and I got off to a rough start. We'll probably never be close friends, but we certainly could be loyal comrades. Everyone can sense your nervousness. What's wrong?"

Ren could no longer hide his frustration. "We're getting farther and farther away from the Moonsea and that red tower. That's what's wrong. Every minute I delay, my friends could be dying. You're the wizard, and I agreed to follow your lead in matters of magic, so we're going south when everything in me screams to find that large area of darkness, wade into the evil, and rescue my friends no matter what the cost. *That's* what's wrong." The frustration and concern on his face spoke more than his words.

The sorceress spoke calmly. "The same urges driving you to forge bravely into the darkness and danger tell me we must be patient and learn what we're facing. That means investigating the smaller blackness first. Let me tell you a story, and maybe it will convince you.

"Most people who want to learn the ways of magic apprentice themselves to powerful wizards. Some attend formal schools. In my case, I apprenticed myself to a wizard who lived just a few days' ride from here. Sebastian was incredibly skilled in the magics of conjuration and summoning. I learned amazing powers from him.

"One day, after researching a spell for over a year, my kindly, brown-haired mentor left his home and laboratory to cast an experimental spell. He said he would return in a week. Twelve days later, he dragged himself up to our doorstep, white-haired and looking seventy years old. He had attempted some type of summoning spell that went wrong. Life was never the same after that. He was still kind and giving, but he refused to talk about that one particular spell.

"The things he taught me from then on were powerful defensive magics. He wouldn't admit it, but I think he expected us to be attacked somehow. Three years later, I buried him. I never learned what happened during his disappearance, but I'm certain that whatever dwells in that small patch of darkness is involved. His old friend might be able to tell us something. As a warrior, you realize that knowing your enemy can mean the difference between winning and losing a battle."

Looking to Ren, Evaine could see the indecision on his face. "I'll make a deal with you. We'll ride to my home tomorrow. We'll need two days more to get to the small patch of darkness. The day after that, no matter what I find there, we head straight for the red tower, wherever it lies, and I promise that Gamaliel and I will follow your orders to the letter. Now, can you ask for more than that?"

Ren sighed. "It's a fair bargain." He tried to soften his expression. "From what I've noticed of you, you're obviously one who plans carefully. I can't say I've disagreed with your leadership so far."

They smiled at each other, comfortable in their agreement. Slowing the horses, ranger and sorceress waited for the others to catch up. A silent party rode hard until sunset.

# ❧ 13 ❧

# Tower of Evil

Over two months had passed since the smallest ray of sunlight had touched Faerun. Over two months had passed since Phlan had disappeared. The group rode solemnly through drooping forests. Only Talenthia maintained her cheerfulness.

"Yes, yes, I know, my honeys. We'll do what we can for you. Fly along now, and don't worry," the druid chirped to the fluttering cloud of sparrows, jays, and robins circling about her as they rode.

"Isn't that the third flock of concerned birds you've talked to today, Cousin?" asked Andoralson. He was partial to snakes and cats, and birds didn't talk to him much. Talenthia was constantly chatting with birds or petting bugs and spiders.

"Yes, dear Cousin, and the poor darlings are frantic. That last robin is ready to lay her eggs and doesn't even have a nest yet. They all say the same thing. The forest in this area is turning horrible and evil. The trees and plants are dying, and it looks as if none will bear fruit this season. What are we going to do about this, ranger?"

Ren reined Stolen to a halt. "Talenthia, I share your concern about the forest. Even I can tell something isn't right about these woods, and the evil goes much further than too much rain and too little sunshine. But as long as you wish to help, and I believe that's what Sylvanus had in mind for you, you must stick to the common goal. I can't go around righting such wrongs until my friends are saved. When that happens, you have my word that I'll come back here with you and do whatever I can. Does that sound fair?"

"For now, handsome, for now. What's with her royal highness and her cat buddy?" Talenthia asked, pointing to the pair going off the trail far ahead of the group. The druid still wondered if Evaine had any designs on Ren.

"Her cottage is off this road. Wizards of all types have a strange attraction to building secluded homes," Ren replied.

"I would have picked a better spot. There are only birches and scrub trees around here. Give me a good oak or redwood grove any day," Andoralson grumbled, mostly to himself. The others were far ahead and off the path, catching up with Gamaliel and Evaine.

The ranger discovered the sorceress and barbarian standing in front of a small, crumbling stone cottage. Half the structure was caved in, and chairs and tables had obviously been tossed out of windows and doors.

Evaine picked up a chair leg and sighed. "I guess if you leave your home often enough, things like this are bound to happen." Her tone was emotionless, but shock at the destruction showed on her face.

"It was ogres, about a week ago, from the look of the tracks," Ren announced. Two blackened ogre skulls, already picked clean by wildlife, confirmed his report. "Looks like these two were blasted by lightning."

Evaine smiled grimly. "I expect my guards and warding spells probably blasted quite a few of them as they invaded. I hope what they found was worth the effort."

"Allow me to enter first, miss. Enemies may lurk within. I will alert you when I know your home is safe." Miltiades bowed low to Evaine, and the sorceress nodded. His courtly manners were hard to resist.

At the paladin's signal, the group entered what remained of the small tower. Almost everything had been tossed out of the lower room. On a small pedestal in the center of the chamber rested a piece of parchment. Evaine read the note aloud:

" 'To the former owner of this structure. My troops have destroyed this place at my orders. I am the new ruler of these lands. You may join my armies forming on the Moonsea or you may die. Know, however, that great rewards await those who serve me. No wizard who is not in my service will be allowed to live in my domains.' " She grimaced. "It's signed by Lord Marcus."

"He's on to us!" Talenthia cried. "He knows we killed his werewolves!" The druid began wringing her hands and pacing the room.

"Oh, be quiet. He does *not* know we killed them." Evaine fairly glowed with rage. "The gall of that man." Suddenly, her tone became icy and determined. "Well, Gamaliel, you and I must pay a visit to this Marcus to discuss what has happened to our home. Maybe we'll do a little tower-smashing of our own."

Andoralson calmed his cousin. "I think you can count us in on your visit," he said quietly.

"Oh, I think we'll all be in on that party," Ren agreed. "Will you still be able to cast your spell to find the pool?"

"I'm sure I can. I don't think there's much to worry about," she said, striding to the east wall of the chamber. It looked fairly solid. "Especially if the attackers were ogres. If so, they wouldn't have been able to find this."

With a wave of her hand, a sparkling green outline of a door took shape on the wall. The door frame crackled with sparks and energy; the light pulsed with a faint, rhythmic drumming noise.

Evaine smiled at the rest of them. "Please excuse the drumming sound. The noise you hear is the enhanced sound of my heartbeat. I've been told it's quite disturbing to friends entering my spellcasting chamber for the first time. We'll be entering a pocket dimension. Naturally, I attached the room to my lifeforce when the chamber was created. Please come in." She and Gamaliel walked through the strange door.

Ren and Miltiades looked at each other, then cautiously walked in behind her. Talenthia and Andoralson stood in amazement outside the magical chamber, inspecting the energies filling the door frame.

"I didn't see any walls large enough for this huge chamber when I walked around the tower. I don't think I would have missed such a bulge, do you?"

Andoralson chuckled. His cousin could control weather and heal the worst injuries, but she was still naive about wizardly magic. "I expect that the bulge, as you call it, is a magical enchantment I've never been able to master. Dimensional magics are fascinating. I wish I could cast spells like this, but I haven't a clue as to the control necessary for such energies. I once tried to create a chamber the size of an egg, and I couldn't cast another spell for a week. This chamber is bigger than most peasant cottages. And attaching her lifeforce to a pocket dimension is tricky business. I bet the entire chamber shrinks if she's injured or sick." The druid couldn't hide his admiration for the chamber.

Talenthia stood mesmerized by the emerald crackles of energy pulsing like a heartbeat. Looking into the green chamber, she could see the others listening to Evaine. But to her senses, the room seemed far too unnatural.

"Go ahead," she murmured. "I think I'll stand guard here. You can never tell when those ogres might be back."

"Sure, Talenthia. That's probably a good idea." Andoralson sensed his cousin's uneasiness. As he entered, he found Evaine explaining the next step in casting the location spell.

"And if you'll give me a lock of your hair, Ren, I'll be able to use your energies to connect more directly with the pool of darkness. I'll read my notes on the spell tonight and cast the magic early tomorrow. Now, let's make camp in what's left of my home while I see what I can find in the wreckage."

Ren tried to help Gamaliel set things right, but the vast amount of destruction made it a useless effort. The tower would need to be completely rebuilt, and unless powerful magics or master stonemasons were employed, Evaine's home would never be restored.

Miltiades volunteered his services to help Evaine salvage her belongings and hunt for missing items. The undead paladin's quiet nature helped the sorceress channel her anger and her sense of loss.

Andoralson and Evaine called upon numerous spells to secure the first floor. The wooden doors and shutters were mended, the stones sufficiently melded to hold the walls in place. It was no guarantee of safety, but at least it would keep out some of the wandering creatures of the woods.

The companions were all exhausted by the time they rolled out their blankets in front of Evaine's fireplace. Despite the day's unpleasant surprises, everyone slept soundly, safe inside the stone walls.

As the cloudy sky began to lighten with the morning, Evaine was completing her spell preparations. Everyone but Talenthia gathered in the casting chamber to watch the sorceress. She set up many warding spells around the perimeter of the room. Andoralson added to the protections with some spells of his own.

"Never hurts to be too careful," the druid explained, smiling to Evaine.

Around mid-morning, Evaine set up the magical brazier. To her great relief, the flame lit instantly upon removing the platinum cap. She began casting the pool-finding spell with a passion in her eyes and voice. Her powers were strong within her own pocket dimension.

Evaine lay the quartz crystal on the enchanted flame and spoke lengthy arcane passages, her voice rising and falling rhythmically. Reaching for the crystal, she laid it on the cloth in her lap and lapsed into concentration.

Her mind's eye easily left her body. Her essence rose above the ruined tower to survey the land for miles around. This time, the magic of the brazier, Evaine's strong center of power, and Ren's link to the pool combined to create a faint light forming a path. The magical light began at the tower and cut over the forest and into the inky blackness just a few miles ahead.

Evaine chose to ignore the light at first. Instead of following its path, she directed her essence toward the smaller patch of darkness. The large mass of blackness had grown so enormous since the last time the sorceress cast her spell that the two evil auras were now only miles apart.

She gathered her strength to pierce the smaller of the ebony mists. The darkness was permeated by intense evil. The sorceress's instincts screamed at her not to touch the vile cloud, but she fought against her will to tap the blackness and learn more about its nature. Then she turned her attention to the larger field. Although she was wrought with fear, she knew that she had to compare the two black fields. Approaching the larger cloud, Evaine learned the painful truth—that their evil natures were exactly the same.

Tapping every particle of energy she could muster, Evaine turned now toward the lighted path. It opened a space in the larger darkness, and Evaine's vision floated along with the light to the beam's end.

Along the path, the sorceress sensed vague outlines of the surrounding landscape. The light led her to a red tower. Could this be the tower of Lord Marcus? she silently asked herself. The power of the illumination pulled her through the tower walls and into an underground chamber. The beam ended abruptly in a crescent-shaped pool of inky blackness. No reflection danced on the surface of the liquid in the pool.

The darkness beckoned to Evaine's soul. The pool's power was terrifying, but it was a sensation familiar to the wizard.

"Who has invaded my tower?" A voice boomed into the dark room, startling Evaine.

"Interesting," the voice continued in a different tone. "I've never seen a detection spell of this type. What's this? A little soul has entered my domain. So pure, so filled with the light of goodness. Bah! Talk to me, little thing. *Latenat*!"

Evaine was shocked. No one had ever sensed her presence before while she was under this spell. Mustering her confidence, she posed a vital question. "How did this pool of darkness come to be in this tower?"

"Oh, you shouldn't play with such pools," the grating voice boomed. "They are bad things—evil things, my little one. Come, come to me in my chambers above the pool. We can talk about many things—yourself, pools, spells, power. Power—there is something I like to talk about. Would you like to become all-powerful? I can make that happen. *Latenat!*" Despite the overly sweet, condescending tone, Evaine knew that the speaker was a creature of blackest evil.

She concentrated on sensing where the presence was, but the horrid darkness around her forced her to draw back into the light of her own spell.

"Little light thing, I am so sorry. My darkness bothers you. Let me move back my protections and we can talk. I have nothing to hide but so much to offer you, cute little soul. *Latenat!*"

Instantly, the darkness was pushed back. Evaine was suddenly aware of the entirety of the red tower. The energy of the pool of darkness was overwhelming. Then, she was struck by a surge of life energy—Phlan. The city lay beneath the tower in an impossibly huge magical cavern.

Evaine was stunned. The implications were phenomenal. The powers necessary for such a feat—placing an entire city in a cavern—were beyond those of any mortal mage.

The sorceress struggled to maintain her mental energy. The surges from Phlan's souls and the evil pool were almost overpowering. And there was still that voice—someone or something able to discern her movements. Such detection had never been possible.

"Look at you. Darting here and there all over my tower, but never coming close to me. I am trying to be a pleasant host, but you are not being very nice. Why don't you stop squirming around and come to me? *Latenat!*"

A tentacle of inky blackness writhed from the top of

the tower into the chamber, reaching for Evaine's essence.

The sorceress leaped away with all her power. She didn't know what the tentacle would do, but she wasn't going to find out. Evaine refocused her mind, concentrated on her tower, and willed the spell to be ended. In a heartbeat, she was back within her body and her magical protections. Panting and sweating, she waved a hand to cancel the spells around her. She beckoned Gamaliel. He brought her the water she mentally requested.

Wind and rain pummeled the broken tower. The protections around her spellcasting chamber had prevented water from getting in, but the rest of the tower was a wet mess.

Andoralson had left the spellcasting chamber earlier, and now the two druids stood outside, near the battered front door. Both gestured simultaneously into the sky. Not a drop of rain touched their cloaks.

"What are they doing out there?" Evaine gasped. She struggled to fight exhaustion.

Ren shouted over the noise of the storm. "When you started your spell, Talenthia noticed a swirl of dark thunderclouds forming above our heads. Only moments ago, huge bolts of lightning started blasting down on the tower. Is your spell connected to what's happening out there?"

"Anything's possible with the strange weather we've had lately. My spell could have drawn the storm like a beacon. But if that was true, the effect should have stopped when I canceled my spell."

Boom!

Lighting struck and was deflected. Against Gamaliel's urgings, Evaine dragged herself outside with the others to see what was happening.

"Nice little storm we have here. I—" Talenthia's words were lost in the thunder.

Boom!

Talenthia gestured quickly, and the lightning strike was forced aside into the meadow near the tower. In the bright flash, all the companions saw smoke rise from the ground. The grass was filled with deep, charred depressions.

"Cousin, it's time to stop this nonsense for a while." Talenthia could barely be heard over the roaring wind.

"Great idea. I'll take your lead."

The two joined hands and raised their oak staves into the air. The pounding rain stopped, and a cool breeze blew up and swirled around the tower and the meadow. The druids' cloaks were whipped by the breeze; their staves swirled round and round above their heads, emitting a humming noise. The clouds above twisted and spun away. Then the sun broke through.

Clouds were visible in every direction, but in a wide oval above their heads, the warm noonday sun beat down from a bright blue patch of sky.

"Well, that's much better," Andoralson said with a satisfied smirk. "I expect our patch of blue will last only a few hours. Talenthia and I were able to slow the lightning today, but I expect the next attack will be stronger and will get through our best defenses. We'd best be off at first light. Evaine, you can rest. Tell us what you discovered as we move along the trail."

No one argued. They all knew they had to press onward as quickly as safety allowed.

# ☙ 14 ❧

# War of Wizardry

"*Tactics,* Captain Brittle! *Tactics* win battles and carry the day!" The Red Wizard of Thay was especially arrogant and overconfident this morning. "And tactics, you bag of bones, is what you sadly lack."

If Brittle, the undead lord, had possessed lungs, he would have sighed in frustration. He had been summoned from the grave by a pit fiend because of his legendary fame for leading all types of armies into all types of battles. His victories and rare defeats a thousand years before were still discussed with admiration in all parts of Faerun. Written accounts of his battles were prized by both good and evil generals. Brittle knew more about tactics and combat operations than any creature alive on Toril. Or dead, for that matter. Somehow, a weak human, less than forty years old, who had spent most of his years reading crumbling tomes of magic in the libraries of Thay didn't impress him.

"Let's review my battle plan one more time, shall we?"

Brittle clenched his bony fists with a faint scraping and creaking. Along with half a dozen clerics of Bane, eight assorted mages, and the pit fiend, he was part of an assembly convening in what Marcus called his war chamber. Others would have called it a converted bedroom. Marcus circled and gestured around the pit fiend's magical creation—an exact, ten-foot-long diorama of the walled city of Phlan.

"I will lead the two main attacks against the walls of Phlan with the minions of Moander. We will attack from two angles in sort of a clawlike action."

"A pincer maneuver," Brittle interrupted.

"Ah, yes. Right. A pincer maneuver," Marcus stammered. "You, Brittle, will lead your three hundred skeletal warriors under the water, through the bay, and into the city, but naturally, your attack will not be the main thrust of the battle."

"Mine is the diversionary action."

"Correct. Yours is the, ah, diversion. One of my units will try to get around the main body of defenders and attack from the side."

"In a flanking maneuver?" Brittle noted flatly.

"Yes, yes, in a flanking action," Marcus said, creating a rod of flame to mark several spots on the model's walls. "If all goes well, the other half of my army should be able to create a weak spot in the walls and climb over to let everyone else in."

"You intend to probe the wall in force, is that correct?" Brittle asked.

"Why do you keep interrupting my war council, Brittle? Just do what you are told, and all of my plans should proceed in good order."

The skeletal commander could no longer contain his irritation. "Lord Marcus, any one of these operations would serve your purpose of getting into the city. But trying all of them at once is foolish—worse than foolish, suicide. I would advise you to give up all these groping tactics and simply make a frontal charge at the walls. With the power of the minions of Moander and all the hundreds of other troops at your command, one solid, direct attack should carry the day."

"It is clear to me, Captain Brittle, that you know nothing about military matters. I don't know how you got your reputation as a brilliant commander."

Brittle's hollow eye sockets stared at Marcus in bony silence.

Marcus turned to his pit fiend. "Escort this insolent being to his troops. See that he doesn't bother me again."

The evil creature flapped toward the skeletal warrior. Both left the room. As the pit fiend led Brittle out of the upper chambers, he lay a taloned hand on the skeleton's shoulder. A burst of magical black sparks sprayed from the talon and swirled around the skeletal body.

"Brittle, I know your talents as a leader. With my magic, I have now released you and your skeletal army from all control Marcus holds over you. You and I both know that tragedies sometimes happen in battle—often, sadly, to the leaders of armies. Go forth, Lord Brittle, and make war as you did in centuries past. *Latenat!*"

With a thunderous boom, the fiend teleported himself back to the heart of the tower.

*　*　*　*　*

At the edge of the accursed, twisted forest, Marcus's troops were gathering. The landscape was covered with green flesh, matted fur, and bony skeletal shapes of monsters of every size and description. Fangs dripped, voices screeched, and weapons rattled as the evil horrors anticipated the slaughter ahead.

Once again, Marcus flew into battle on his black nightmare. He roamed above his troops, reviewing them one last time while he shouted orders from on high.

"You ogres and trolls—move in front of the clerics and wizards. Your orders are to protect them with your lives!" Marcus had no trouble being heard above the din of his army. He had magically enhanced his voice. Even at a whisper, his voice was a bellow.

A little more than a mile-wide swath of Moander's minions stood before Marcus. The treelike creatures were the result of powerful, corrupting magic that rendered them deadly fighters. They moved more slowly than a normal man, but numerous magical protections were built into their bodies.

Marcus smirked from on high. And what's best, he decided, is that they do anything I command with just a thought! He shifted gleefully in his saddle.

Marcus ordered five of the tree-minions to charge Phlan's walls.

"I will invent my own tactics. In a thousand years, the world will be writing about *my* battle style. I'll show Brittle how a battle is *really* fought. I won't even wait until his skeletons come out of the bay."

Sensing his inevitable victory, Marcus ordered the entire army to surge forward. "If I'm lucky, I can win this battle before lunch and enjoy the company of the erinyes this afternoon. I wonder if Tanetal can make the sun shine over the tower. I think I'd like a little sunlight streaming in for a change."

Marcus mentally ordered his tree-minion army to split into two units as they advanced. The living part of his army, the spellcasters, clerics, monsters, and human mercenaries, followed far behind the tree-creatures of Moander.

\* \* \* \* \*

A mile distant, atop the walls of Phlan, a cleric was taking advantage of a special detection spell. He could easily hear Marcus's enhanced voice babbling at his troops. The cleric sent word to Tarl and the other leaders of Phlan's defenses, who ordered the troops at the bay to be reinforced with more clerics. Extra warriors were ordered to fill positions on the northern walls.

The defenders of Phlan weren't impressed by Marcus's maneuvers.

"Hey, Ston—lookit these weird tree-things they're sending at us this time!"

"Yeah, I heard about those the other day. The guys who went to bargain for peace told all about 'em. They smell like the inside of a moldy ale keg, and they might even spit poison gas. Be careful, Tulen old buddy, or you might get turned into some kinda tree fungus before this battle is over." Ston snorted in laughter.

Nearby, on the same wall, two wizards were preparing to launch their spells.

"Whaddya think—lightning or fireballs on those slimy beggars? Course, we could always try freezing 'em." The mage was digging through his pockets, looking for charred scraps of paper, a vial of sulphur, and the other materials that would power his spells.

His companion nervously exercised his fingers, stretching each digit and cracking knuckles loudly. "Those things are awfully wet and slippery. It's hard to get a good look at them. Wait—see those five coming way ahead of the rest? Why don't you blast a fireball at the one on the right, and I'll try a lightning bolt on the one at the left."

The two wizards timed their attacks carefully. Twin bursts of magic, one a fiery yellow sphere and the other an orange streak of lightning, darted from the wall. The magics exploded on the minions of Moander, knocking them to the ground. The mages slapped each other on the back, congratulating themselves. "Hurray, both worked! We're geniuses!"

A few yards down the wall, the grizzled old Tulen spit over the crenellations and sneered in amusement at the two young spellcasters. "Look again, geniuses."

The other three tree-creatures had stopped moving, silently waiting for their two leafy brothers to rise. When they did, the five continued their march as if nothing had happened.

Ston and Tulen were snorting with laughter. "We warriors ain't much for magic, but watch what our buddies are gonna do." Ston was directing their attention down the wall toward several catapults. In accordance with the commands barked out by the catapult captain, each unit adjusted its weapon. The captain bellowed out the order to fire.

A series of loud squeaks and thuds announced the launch of ten separate catapults. In a heartbeat, the moldering tree-things were buried under a pile of gigantic rocks.

Not a twig twitched under the rock piles. This time, Ston and Tulen slapped each other on the back, congratulating their comrades. "Nice shooting, boys! Now that's what I call the magic of old Bessy, old Mamie, old Daisy, and all the other faithful old gals. We got plenty more rocks where they came from, you betchy! Heh, heh, heh. You young fellers should put away those wands and think about joining up with the catapulters. They might take you, too, if your aim is good."

The wizards attempted to look dignified. Although the demonstration of rocks was impressive, the mages weren't about to trade in their spellbooks for crowbars.

A flutter of violet robes drifted out of the sky behind the two mages. Flustered, the two men turned to stammer out an explanation. "Shal! We were only—that is, we—"

The sorceress chuckled and raised a hand for silence. "Nothing to worry about. Now listen carefully. These are your instructions for defending against the siege. . . ."

* * * * *

Marcus still circled high above his troops, astride the pitch-black nightmare. Such a position exposed him to arrows and magical attacks, but he trusted his numerous protection spells. Marcus was alive with anticipation, his blood tingling in his veins. He ordered the nightmare to fly faster, as if that would bring victory more quickly. The wind whipped the wizard's hair, billowing his red robes. The speed enhanced Marcus's euphoria.

As he passed over the battlefield, his attention turned to Phlan, off in the distance. The magical lights of the cavern shone down on the black walls of the city. "Well, that's peculiar," Marcus noted from on high. The walls, which had formerly been a deep red, were now a dull black. The outer defensive wall as well as the second ring of walls were all mysteriously darkened. The wizard shrugged it off. "Whatever you pathetic souls are planning, it won't matter. Your fate is sealed."

At that very moment, an invisible, menacing force of powerful skeletons marched under the sea toward Phlan. The unbreathing creatures would arise on the shores of the Moonsea and take the city completely by surprise. Marcus congratulated himself for thinking of this brilliant idea—even if Commander Brittle would have disputed whose idea it really had been.

When Phlan had been torn from the earth and deposited in the cavern, all of the bay alongside the city and a large section of the Moonsea had been magically stolen with it. The fish and other creatures inhabiting these waters were the only sources of food the defenders of Phlan could depend on.

But now, the bay was filled with warriors, each twice as powerful as the ordinary skeletons raised by evil spellcasters. Each was magically intelligent, unlike their automaton counterparts. Marcus had used extraordinarily powerful enchantments in creating these units. The effort was worth it; they would be deadly in battle. Even the most devout clerics, normally empowered to turn skeletons to dust, would find these mystical warriors nearly impossible to destroy.

\* \* \* \* \*

The observations of a clever priest had alerted Phlan's defenders to the unseen danger in the bay. Tarl had ordered troops to wait in position along the beaches. Hundreds of eyes watched for the telltale ripples in the water that would signal the beginning of the assault.

Suddenly, a helmet arose out of the bay. The alarm was shouted down the beach.

But instead of three hundred bony horrors rising out of the water, only Commander Brittle strode onto the sand. The enchanted warrior strutted boldly up to the first assembly of clerical defenders. These men bravely raised their holy symbols and ordered the skeleton to return to the dust from whence it came.

"Put away your toys, weaklings. They won't work on me. Besides, I've come to make you an offer."

Many of the clerics raised their hammers and flails to attack the skeleton, but one of the younger priests, eager to parley, stepped forward, asking, "What terms do you bring us? What guarantees do you make?"

\* \* \* \* \*

On the other side of the city, the battle was boiling.

The tree-minions of Moander, reduced by a few hundred by the weight of catapult rocks, boldly advanced to the walls of the city. Rooted feet stomped forward in menacing strides. Each tree-thing stood over ten feet tall and dripped an oozing, fetid, poisonous sap. Each creature bore a layer of fungus spores that puffed up in a sickly cloud every time it was hit. Each plant-horror was armed with branchy javelins.

"Masks up! Beware the javelins!" The cry echoed down the wall from captains and warriors alike. Each man pulled a woolen mask over his head to prevent the spores from being inhaled.

Shal had ordered the masks prepared immediately after she'd rescued Tarl and his comrades from the evil forest. After learning of the spores and poisons emitted by the trees, she had experimented with numerous forms of headgear to protect the warriors. The women of Phlan had spent every minute of the day and night spinning, weaving, and sewing the masks. All the wizards of Phlan had been ordered to magically heat sand and create thin glass lenses to allow the wearers to see. Within a few days, every warrior, cleric, and wizard in Phlan was outfitted with a special mask.

Dozens of these outfitted wizards—from apprentices to grand masters—were strung along the walls. Protected by the crenellations and the shields of assisting warriors, they cast their deadliest blasts. Shal and two other mages floated along the top of the wall, directing the efforts into a unified attack and casting their own potent energies.

Fire spells in the forms of waves, sheets, and exploding spheres blazed forth in a terrifying but beautiful rainbow. The searing heat that would have roasted an ordinary army to cinders proved ineffective against the tree-monsters. The wizards changed tactics and instead cast narrow cones of blazing fire that hung in the air for long minutes, broiling the horrid tree-minions. The sustained flames dried the poisonous wet ooze of the trees, charred bark and leaves, and roasted the creatures to ash. The unearthly stench that arose smelled like something straight from the Nine Hells. The minions shrieked and writhed, trying to move forward. But the huge, squirming tree-monsters soon turned to twisted pillars of ash.

Marcus watched from on high, furious. "How dare they use such flame against my army!" He bellowed in fury, forgetting that his magically enhanced voice could be heard all over the battlefield. "I'll teach them what real magic is. Those pathetic mages may think they're powerful, but let them taste the magic of a Red Wizard of Thay!" His crimson robes billowed as he reined the snorting nightmare around and swooped down over the heads of his spellcasters.

"You wizards and clerics, advance on those infidels and dispel their pitiful magics. What do you think I'm paying you for? Get busy!" Marcus's voice boomed instructions.

*　*　*　*　*

Ston, Tulen, and the other defenders on the wall snorted throaty laughs upon hearing the rantings of the enemy leader. Few things were better than knowing your foe was unhappy with the turn of the battle.

An ancient, grizzled warrior named Rakmar lifted his mask to spit over the wall, aiming at one of the minions. He was well over seventy years old and should have been retired to easier work, but Rakmar had a special duty in the most critical battles. No one could rival Rakmar's skill in the task he had performed for over forty years. He ordered his team to ready their catapult for an extra-long shot. Then his graveled voice barked out the order his men had been waiting for all day. "Load Big Brors into the dish, boys. I'm going to hit me some wizards." The men cheered and busied themselves around the catapult.

Big Brors was rolled out. It was an enormous, cone-shaped sculpture of solid granite. Ten men were needed to load it into the catapult. No one could aim Brors like Rakmar. The old warrior had a sixth sense about that weapon of granite death.

Rakmar patted the cone fondly. Over its many years of battle, the boys of the catapult team had lovingly named the huge rock and had chiseled and painted personal mementoes on its coarse surface. Now the warrior ran a callused hand over forty years of memories and victories. Used in every battle, Big Brors was always collected after the skirmish was over and returned to this same catapult unit.

Rakmar carefully checked the position of the granite cone in its cradle. With the experience of four decades, the old warrior scurried around the catapult, adjusting cranks and levers, checking and rechecking, until he was sure everything was just right. Grunting in satisfaction, he stepped back and told the boys to wait for the signal to fire.

Ston and Tulen took turns watching their post and the catapult team, anticipating the rock's flight and glorious devastation. The catapulters stood silently and nervously, awaiting their moment of glory.

*     *     *     *     *

Back on Marcus's side of the field, wizards and clerics surged forward. They were not a united group; it was every man for himself as each wizard hustled to be the first to create a spectacular effect that would attract the attention and gratitude of Marcus. Fellow spellcasters were as much the enemy to these selfish men and women as were the citizens of Phlan. Their desire for fame prevented them from working as a team and instead fostered a dire rivalry.

One evil wizard, Thar Kuul, had risen to a high station in the red mage's forces. He despised Marcus and thought him a fool, but the Red Wizard of Thay was the best chance for power anywhere in Faerun. Thar would play anyone's game if it meant success in the end. This dark wizard had even coerced the pit fiend into teaching him some powerful spells. After several lengthy conversations with the fiend, Thar Kuul had decided he would some day take control of the fiend from Marcus and dispose of the little Red Wizard. That was an endeavor for the future. Right now, he had to play obedient servant.

Thar charged forward in determination. He would show the clerics and wizards around him what a truly talented wizard could do. He had selected his most powerful and most spectacular spells for the occasion.

As the dark wizard neared Phlan's walls, he immediately noticed the blackened stone. Oil, he assumed. The defenders obviously planned to torch the walls during the assault. But he knew a spell that would extinguish that effect before the pathetic defenders even knew what happened. Striding ahead of the pack of spellcasters and moving around the stupid ogres in his path, Thar Kuul murmured and gestured. The five walls of fire that stood as barriers to the tree-minions were instantly snuffed out.

"There, that alone should get Marcus's attention. Now I can cast the spell that will—"

He looked up suddenly as a whistling sound caught his attention. But the wizard never saw what hit him. In his haste to outshine his companions, Thar had made himself a target. His scheming brain was now pinned to the ground by a two-hundred pound, cone-shaped rock.

Marcus was concentrating deeply on the battle, growing agitated. His tree-minions were pounding on the stone walls, but the trees' tentacles were slipping and couldn't get a firm grip. Worse, the trees were dying by the scores as fire, burning oil, arrows, and rocks rained down on them.

Marcus refused to be daunted. "No matter. There are untold numbers of tactical maneuvers to destroy walls. I'll order the flanking movement, then personally supervise the storming of the wall."

He turned the nightmare toward the mercenary contingent of his army, bellowing out orders. His enhanced voice was impossible to ignore. "You humans and ogres—advance on the northern gate and stir things up there. If the fight gets too dangerous, retreat. I plan to personally lead the remainder of the army as it breaches the wall!" The mass of sword-swinging monsters and mercenaries instantly mobilized.

Back on the wall of Phlan, a chuckling cleric gave new instructions to waiting messengers.

Marcus mentally ordered the tree-minions to form living ladders of vegetation. Hundreds of the tree-creatures wound themselves together and thousands of evil soldiers began to climb slowly upward and onto the walls of Phlan. Tarl shouted orders for the clerics to attempt spells of control on the trees, but to no avail. Defenders slashed away with swords and spears to no effect. Halberds and axes chopped into mouldy bark, but too many monsters were scaling the walls.

Trumpets were sounded and entire wall sections abandoned. Tarl now shouted the order for Phlan's secret defense tactic.

As the mass of Moander's tree-minions crawled over the walls in victory, Marcus shouted at them gleefully.

"I've done it! I've beaten them! Now I, Marcus of Thay, own that city. My troops will scale all the walls. By tomorrow, I will be a demigod and these pathetic humans will bow to me!"

\*   \*   \*   \*   \*

Far below Marcus, a brown-robed wizard had witnessed Thar's death. Porter was next in line for command, and now he rejoiced at his good fortune. He planned to lead the wizards to the outer limits of catapult range, allow the defenders to fire one volley, then order a retreat. But as his unit approached the gate, he was surprised that not a single arrow greeted them.

Porter scanned the walls, seeing no one. During their approach, he had seen hundreds of defenders running from the gates to help defend against the tree-minions. The wall was all but deserted now, even though that seemed unlikely.

"Mage Whills, fly up there and scan the towers. Make

sure your spell against arrows is working."

Whills took a moment to activate a spell, then flew onto the wall above the Death Gates. "No one here, sir. They're all fighting Moander's lot!"

Porter was furious. This brief attack wasn't supposed to end like this. There was nothing here to fight! He wanted to retreat, but knew what would happen. Marcus would be furious if one of his leaders challenged his strategy.

The massive Death Gates were intact, magically reconstructed after Marcus's last attack. The doors were locked. Two quick spells popped them open with two loud thuds. Porter had made his decision.

"Alright, men! Let's charge in and see what we find. Ogres, trolls, advance! We're right behind you."

As thousands of pounds of monster flesh surged into the long tunnel, a telepathic message reached the men and wizards under the trap doors of the empty towers on both sides of Death Gates. A warrior-priest of Tyr swinging a glowing blue hammer was the first to leap out of the hidden trap door. Hundreds of warriors surged out of the hidden rooms, raining death on the monsters in the tunnel. Tarl's hammer seemed to take on a life of its own, striking on every swing and killing with every blow.

\* \* \* \* \*

In his ecstasy, Marcus barely noticed the woman astride a magnificent horse riding toward him in the sky. The female and her mount were both bathed in a faint, violet glow. "Who dares come to spoil my victory?"

"I dare!" Shal screamed, "You stole my city and you have assaulted my people. Today, you die!"

She raised her arm, and a sparkling purple bolt of energy arced from her hand to strike Marcus.

It bounced away harmlessly.

"*Tarnelth, whocsom, pellarz!*" Marcus's voice boomed.

Gale-force winds buffeted Shal and her magical horse. Her hair and cloak whipped about, but the battering winds caused no real harm. The beast snorted, yet easily controlled its flight.

A flick of Shal's wrist created a dark purple mist under the nightmare's hooves. The swirling, turbulent vapor looked oily and deadly even to the Red Wizard. Marcus turned the nightmare and flew higher, thinking he would escape the mist. But the vapors followed as if they had a mind of their own.

A red fireball and a lightning bolt surged out of his hands toward Shal, whizzing past harmlessly.

The sorceress was shocked at his ability to cast two spells at once, but didn't show her surprise to the enemy. She told herself to investigate that talent later.

Through the winds that still buffeted her, Shal cast disintegration magic at the nightmare. The powerful spell turned the corrupt creature to dust. Marcus hadn't bothered to protect his mount against such spells. He began to sink into the purple mist beneath him.

A quick wave of his hand stopped his fall, and the wizard now hovered on wings of flame. He grimaced and shrieked the words of a new spell. Behind Shal, an inky spectral form took shape.

Expecting the worst, the sorceress took her best shot and cast her most powerful spell.

"I'm blind!" Marcus screamed in fear. "*Gallen tor supto!*"

Marcus vanished. In his panic, he had teleported himself back to the red tower.

The deadly purple fog dissipated harmlessly.

What had been a desperate moment for Phlan was turning in its favor. Shal had temporarily defeated Marcus, leaving the monsters, tree-minions, and hired soldiers without a leader. Brittle was busy following his own course of action.

The minions of Moander, once perfect warriors, were now snapping like dry kindling. Although tireless and deadly, they lacked intelligence. When ordered to scale the wall, they had succeeded with some effort. The entire army now stood between the outer and inner walls—walls coated with black, sticky oil. Now those same walls were set ablaze by the defenders of Phlan. The intense heat dried and cracked the protective ooze coating the trees, withered leaves, and ignited branches. As the mindless minions stood between the two walls, branches and trunks ignited, charred, and toppled.

A deafening clatter and rattling arose. Three hundred and one skeletons swinging huge axes in their bony hands rushed to the attack. The skeletons gave no thought to the fungus or poisons of the tree-monsters. They ignored the searing heat of the flaming walls; the stone-hard bones of their skeletal frames felt nothing. Every warrior chopped at the minions of Moander while the abominable tree-creatures mindlessly waited for orders that should have come, but never did.

Marcus had abandoned his troops, leaving them to die on the field. High in the red tower, the wizard's rantings, still magically enhanced, were punctuated only by the insults he hurled at the pit fiend. He ordered the fiend to restore his vision. The tower shook to its foundation, rattling the city of Phlan far below.

# ❦ 15 ❦

## Encroaching Evil

"That's the whole story. I found the pool hidden in a dark chamber in the red tower, and some horrid, evil entity spoke to me. I haven't been that terrified in ten years. I didn't think anything was capable of detecting me while under that spell. Now I won't rest until I learn what that gods-forsaken horror was."

The companions rode in silence for long minutes. All were stunned by Evaine's experience while under her spell. At every turn, it seemed that their mission became more mysterious and dangerous.

Evaine herself broke the silence. "Although we now know where the pool is hidden, we still don't know exactly where Phlan is. I sensed its energy, so I think we can assume it's near the tower. But we still have too many unanswered questions. For that reason, I propose we investigate the smaller cloud of darkness. I still think it's our best chance of learning enough to get through this bizarre quest alive."

The horses were trotting along at a quick pace, led through the dense woods by Ren and Stolen. They had purposely avoided the main roads to reduce any chance of being tracked. Ren called a sudden halt.

"We're certain the red tower conceals the pool of darkness. There's a good chance it hides Phlan as well. So at the risk of seeming insistent—why shouldn't we head toward the greater evil and clean it out?" Ren asked.

"Even if you insist, Ren, I won't follow you into the inky darkness surrounding the red tower. I'm not sure I'll come out of there alive a second time. Checking out the smaller evil only puts us a day off schedule." Evaine's voice revealed only composure and logic.

"My friends could be dead in another day! How can I take that chance? We have to get to the red tower soon! Who knows what horrors they might be facing?" Ren's face turned red as he tried to control his emotions. Stolen whinnied quietly.

"I know you're worried." Evaine turned to the others. "This is a tough decision. Since all our lives are at stake, I think we should put this to a vote. What say you?"

Andoralson spoke first. "I can see both sides of your arguments," he said. "Ren, I know you're concerned, but I think we should take a day and follow Evaine's instincts. Then, no matter what we find, we'll head for the red tower." The druid looked around, waiting for the others to respond.

Miltiades was next. "Tyr has given me a mission. How I accomplish that mission is part of his test. All successful military commanders understand that knowing the enemy's secrets can determine the outcome of a battle. I believe we should follow Evaine."

Talenthia was visibly torn over this decision. She wanted to side with Ren, but she was frightened. "I guess I have to agree with my cousin. Evaine hasn't led us astray yet, so if she wants to check out the other area, and it doesn't take too long, let's do it. I wouldn't want to charge into a trap like a pack of scared rabbits. Sorry, Ren." The druid guided her horse over near the ranger and slipped a trembling hand into his.

Gamaliel, in his favored cat form, was perched on a

tree stump near Evaine, listening carefully. Without even asking, the group knew his vote.

Ren grasped Talenthia's hand tightly. His anguish was visible as he rubbed his forehead. "Alright. I guess I lose this one. Let's keep moving. We'll stop for a rest and something to eat in a few hours, then we'll ride hard until dark. At dawn, we'll move out again. I can only hope, for all our sakes, that this side trip works out for the best. Evaine, at our current pace, when do you think we'll reach our destination?"

"If we don't run into any trouble, we can be there shortly after noon tomorrow. We're closer than you think."

Wordlessly Ren turned Stolen and led the gallop through the woods. The others fell in behind. Evaine led Gam's tethered horse, and the giant cat silently darted through the underbrush, his pink nose alert to anything unusual.

The party rode hard, and the day passed quickly. Twice Gamaliel stopped the group to listen for intruders in the woods. The first time, they discovered three small wolf cubs playing in the grass. The second time, Gamaliel stalked ahead and spied a troop of fourteen gnolls. Everyone waited silently until the gnolls were well out of range. Their caution saved them time and untold energy.

As the companions traversed the woods, each was lost in his or her own thoughts. Ren had become increasingly agitated and short-tempered, Talenthia increasingly somber. She was frightened by the terrible events surrounding the journey. Andoralson tried to maintain an outward appearance of confidence, but inside, he was shaken.

Evaine remained focused on the task at hand, but she became increasingly more serious. She no longer joked or laughed around the others, but instead buried herself in her spellbook whenever possible. The others still wondered what secret drove her to pursue the pools.

Only Gamaliel and Miltiades maintained their equable dispositions. The cat remained protective of his mistress and sensitive to her moods, but the kitten in him kept him lighthearted. His spurts of playfulness—pouncing on leaves and batting at moths—were often the only humor to break up the somber mood. The paladin, stoic as ever, was the anchor holding this rocking shipload of adventurers together. Miltiades became a self-appointed morale officer and bolstered the small band at every chance.

As darkness filled the woods, Gamaliel scouted ahead for a place to camp. The companions quickly settled into their familiar routine. Supper was quiet and all turned in early, lying close to the fire and each other. Gamaliel snuggled his giant, furry form against Evaine's back. The ever-stoic Miltiades kept a vigilant watch.

Gamaliel awoke at dawn and roused his mistress. He stalked into the woods to find breakfast while the sorceress lay deep in thought. She had to find the pool of darkness. She had to diffuse its evil energy. But this one frightened her more than any of the pools she had encountered before. What bothered her most was that she didn't know why it troubled her so.

Impatient to meet whatever lay ahead, Evaine flung back the blanket and rose to awaken the others. Gamaliel soon returned with two pheasants and turned them over to Andoralson.

The meal cheered them a little, and Miltiades, experienced at inspiring troops before a battle, again offered words of encouragement.

"All of you are expecting the worst. You are defeated

before the battle even begins. Lighten your mental loads and your bodies will also be lighter. A man who is weighted down in battle is an easy target, like a wounded animal."

No one discounted the wisdom of his words. By the time they had mounted up, all were feeling considerably lighter and more fully prepared to face their nameless foe.

The journey through the forest was easy. Ren and the druids took turns leading the way, and they always seemed able to find animal trails or at least the lightest brush to push through. As the morning wore on and the companions approached the evil cloud, the nature of the forest changed for the worst. Talenthia noticed it first. Slumping over in her saddle, she was overcome by waves of unhealthy energy. Tears welled in her eyes.

"Andoralson, can't you feel the forest suffering from evil? The blessings of nature are in danger. These trees are in pain." Talenthia wept, feeling the presence of evil forcing itself into the hearts and souls of the trees.

Ren called a halt.

"Notice the birds, Ren," Andoralson said soberly. "Crows and ravens, but no robins, sparrows, or finches. This has become a forest of evil."

Talenthia held back her tears long enough to speak. "What has the power to corrupt a forest this way?"

Andoralson tried to comfort her. "I don't know, Cousin—I just don't know. But we must press on."

Talenthia held back her sobs, dismounted, and cast a spell of detection magic all around.

"Talenthia, we have to move on," Ren said gently. She ignored the ranger until the spell was complete, then spoke with new determination.

"You all go on, due north. The center of evil is there. I'll catch up. Don't argue—and don't worry about me. Perhaps I can do some good here while you carry on."

The group tried to convince her to accompany them, but Talenthia sat in the grass as if she was rooted there. Finally, the others mounted up and moved on.

*　*　*　*　*

The shadowy forest closed in around them. Huge, ancient oak trees rose high into the cloudy sky, but instead of proudly guarding the forest, they were weakened by strangling red vines that looked like blood-filled veins twisting along trunks and branches. The forest floor became increasingly buried in fungi of all types. Clouds of damp spores rose with every step of a horse's hoof. The companions wrapped rags around their mouths and noses to keep from breathing the fumes. Evaine fashioned a muzzle over Gamaliel's sensitive nose.

They emerged into a small clearing. Toppled stones, dark and smooth and as tall as a man, lay scattered in a vague circle.

"By the gods, what have they done?" Andoralson shouted in horror. Leaping off his horse, he rushed to the stones, knelt on the bare earth, and gently caressed one of the larger stones. "This was the grove of a druid. Miltiades, please help me raise these stones again. Ren, take Evaine and Gamaliel and ride ahead. I'll only be a few moments and then we'll follow. I can't leave until this is set right."

Ren wasn't about to split the group up any further. "Druid, we can't wait. We have to keep moving if we're going to combat this evil, the thing at the very heart of all this destruction."

"No, Ren, you and Evaine go on. I can't leave until I

correct what has been defiled. Such desecration must be cured or this part of the forest could be forever cursed. Please, let me do this!"

All could see the anguish overcoming Andoralson. Miltiades volunteered to stay with the druid and watch over him as he prepared his rites. The ranger looked at Evaine, then nodded. Against his better judgment, he turned his horse to the north.

They rode for only a few minutes before Ren's rage overcame him. "Damn! I feel like this evil is doing its best to split us up and stop us! Is that possible, Evaine?"

The sorceress sighed. "That's what evil does, Ren. It breaks up friendships, it tears apart lovers, it turns sister against brother. It can do so in the subtlest of ways. It needn't come in the form of serpents or evil armies. It can come as greed and jealousy. We must be careful not to let it influence us."

\* \* \* \* \*

Talenthia was still filled with the pain of the forest. She walked to a small rise encircled by tired, dying oaks. "My god, great Sylvanus, this forest is passing away. There is so much hurt, so much pain." She fell to her knees. The tears poured down her face, for the pain of the forest cut to her very soul.

"What can I do? Compassionate Sylvanus, what can I, your humble servant, do?" Talenthia rocked back and forth on her knees, repeating her plea. Her hands clawed at the earth, scratched at the dead grass and soil. "This is not right! This is death encroaching on life. By Sylvanus's might, I will not let death triumph!" The druid screamed into the empty forest, her pain turning to anger.

Smashing the ground with her fingers, Talenthia clawed deep into the earth. The black soil was richer here. A ray of hope glimmered in her thoughts. The evil had not penetrated the lifeblood of the woods. She closed her eyes and prayed, giving up her soul to the forest. Talenthia willingly freed her life essence. Her only thought was to capture the life that was being sucked out of the land and return it to the forest.

The woods around her, the repressed children of nature, responded.

A silent, intangible wave emanated from the kneeling druid. As it radiated outward, the grass, undergrowth, and trees rustled as they were touched by the healing rays. The blood-red, choking vines shriveled away, and the vegetation absorbed the moisture it so desperately needed. Grass and trees turned a vibrant green, wilted buds flowered and bloomed on the newly freed plants. The fresh scent of moist earth and sweet blossoms filled the air. Talenthia emanated a healthy energy that allowed the forest to thrive again.

The druid weakened, but her mind was in ecstasy as she surrendered her essence for what she loved best.

Branches rustled noisily as new sap flowed. Freed of their evil bonds, the trees creaked a song of gratitude. The crusty fungus that coated trunks and branches flaked away and dissolved. The songs of crickets and junebugs arose from the underbrush.

Talenthia still knelt, pouring every ounce of energy into her healing. A white mist arose ahead of her, then took the shape of a graceful unicorn. "Daughter, you have done enough. You must stop." The unicorn's message silently reached Talenthia's weary mind.

For the first time, the druid looked up to witness the transformation she had commanded. As far as she could see, the glade around her was verdant and lush. An evil darkness still permeated the area beyond her healing, but the forest was not entirely lost. It might still be saved.

"Silvanus, my god, my spiritual father, I thank you for the power you have given me. Will this transformation endure?"

"No, my daughter. In a few weeks, the evil will seep back into the haven you have created. I can do nothing to prevent that. But you have been given a quest that you must pursue. You cannot give any more of yourself and still hope to complete your mission."

"Woodland father, this forest suffers so."

"Yes, my child. But you cannot gather enough energy to cure it permanently. The evil that taints it is too great."

"If I remain here, father, will this land, the land I gladly sacrifice myself for, remain healthy and fertile?"

"No mortal has the power to maintain the forest against the evil that would destroy it. If you remain here, this island in the woods will remain healthy. Your energy will be drained from you and you will die along with the forest." The unicorn met her gaze with wise, sad eyes. "Only if I allow you to transcend death and assume the guardian form can you hope to cure these woods. In doing so, you would be abandoning your quest."

"I have lived my entire life for a chance such as this."

"Ah, but have you considered what your life would be if you accepted the task? You would never leave this forest, being rooted here physically and spiritually. Men who see you will look upon you as a beautiful grove in the forest, nothing more. You will spend your days alone amid the silence of the trees."

"But I will shelter the animals and my limbs will be home to the birds and their young. My power will feed the trees and flowers. The animals will love me and be my friends. Without this, they will all die horrid, poisoned deaths." The druid's tone was pleading, but respectful of her god.

Sylvanus consented. "You have shown me that your heart and head are in agreement. I will grant your wish." The unicorn gracefully stepped forward and bowed its head, touching Talenthia's shoulder with the tip of its horn.

Talenthia gave herself up to the power of her god. Her body became a milky mist rising into the air, spreading wide and taking the shape of a graceful willow tree. The white cloud settled into place and became firm. Color began to spread from the tree's roots, working up the trunk and outward to soft green leaves. Smooth, tan bark and silky branches marked the completion of the transformation. The tree rustled with joy. From beneath its roots, a clear spring bubbled from the earth and its waters trickled down the hill. Talenthia's healing chalice was transformed with her. Now it would permanently nourish the starving forest. For all eternity, this hill would be blessed.

The unicorn gently touched its horn to the tree. Branches and leaves encircled it in a tender hug. After a moment, the unicorn dissolved into white mist and disappeared.

* * * * *

Miles away, Andoralson was completing an ancient rite to purify the land and the stones of the druid's circle. With the stones raised and in place, Miltiades respectfully stood guard.

After a final sprinkling of mistletoe among the stones

to seal the rite, the druid paused and attempted to contact his cousin. Reaching out with his nature magic, he immediately sensed a new, rich presence in the forest.

"Talenthia, what have you done?" He shook his head as he realized what had happened. Although the forest around the ring of stones still shook with pain, the hill where he'd left Talenthia now gave off an exuberant energy, a feeling of joy and serenity.

"Well done, Cousin. I must admit, I didn't think you had it in you." He shed a tear for himself, knowing how much he would miss her, but felt happy that she had found a permanent mission for her life. "When our quest is done, I will return and help you restore this forest."

"Is something wrong, noble druid?" Miltiades asked gently.

"Something is very wrong for us, but it is very right for my cousin. Talenthia won't be joining us to complete this quest. She has been given other duties by our god." Moving to his horse, he told the paladin, "We'd better find Ren and the others."

As they departed the druid's grove, a greenish white mist gathered protectively around the stones Andoralson had consecrated. No evil would threaten this glade in the druid's absence.

\* \* \* \* \*

Evaine, Gamaliel, and Ren were miles ahead of the others. They moved as quickly as the brambles allowed. Evaine had the disturbing feeling something was waiting for them and guiding them. The sorceress tried to brush off the perception and kept the thought to herself. They traveled easily down a path that seemed to grow wider and flatter as they moved ahead.

The forest around them was increasingly tainted with evil. The trees were drooping, bent, and choked with red vines. The path was filled with dark, spore-clogged fungi that made breathing difficult despite the damp rags on the travelers' faces. The grotesque weeds and dark, humming insects told of a forest turned harsh and unfriendly.

Just after midday, the path opened into a small clearing just large enough for a single cottage. Ren and Evaine both found themselves wishing the others had caught up to them.

"I don't believe what I'm seeing." Ren pulled his horse to a halt and drew his sword.

"Neither do I, but I sense no illusions at work here," Evaine said, trying hard to detect any magics.

Ren was truly agitated by what he saw. "Look at this. A cozy cottage with white smoke coming from the chimney. A babbling brook of clear spring water is flowing along the back. In another second, a little old lady with a bent back will open the door and sweep out the dust from her floor. Then she'll invite us in for cake and milk."

"Will a tall woman of fifty winters serve instead?" a voice asked behind them.

Whirling, the trio saw a lovely, aged woman. She wore a flowing, white woolen gown whose color matched her short, curly hair. She held a large basket filled with mushrooms, which Evaine noticed were of both the edible and deadly varieties.

"I've been picking mushrooms. Please, rest your horses near the spring and come inside. I so seldom have visitors."

Gamaliel hissed, his golden eyes blazing. He stayed close to Evaine, waiting for her next move.

The sorceress cast a spell of detection magic as unobtrusively as she could. Faint, emerald energy flowed from her hands, encircling the woman and the cottage in their magical glow.

The woman's pleasant demeanor vanished. "Is that any way to treat your hostess? Your puny magics won't work here, girl. This is my glade, and my essence fills this forest. Now, we can have a nice little chat, or you can all be destroyed. Why are you here?"

"We have more than just magic working for us," Ren said, dismounting. Unlike Gamaliel and Evaine, Ren was attracted to this woman and trusted her immediately. She was truly lovely and seemed perfectly harmless. Ren felt that her eyes looked into his heart and touched his soul. He knew that beauty could hide all sorts of evil, but still, she was fascinating.

Evaine spoke to the cat, watching Ren carefully. "Come on, Tooth. We should be polite and accept this lady's hospitality."

The white-haired woman's mood softened and she eyed Ren closely. "I am called Lanula. What are your names?"

"The ranger is called Blade, I am Coran, and this is my pet, Tooth." Evaine lied.

Ren stood by, looking slightly puzzled. He couldn't understand why Evaine had given this charming woman false names, but he let her speak. He knew magic was involved somehow, and he firmly believed in leaving such matters to the wizards.

Lanula bent down to scratch Gamaliel's ears before he had a chance to back away. "Such a pretty cat you are, Tooth. Why don't you use your pendant and talk with us?"

The feline found himself instantly changing to a

barbarian.

"That's better. You are so much more handsome this way." The woman's voice dripped honey.

*Gam, why did you do that?* Evaine mentally asked her surprised companion.

The cat's voice in her mind sounded slightly panicked. *I don't know! She asked me to change, and it seemed like the natural thing to do. She acts like a nice creature, but she has a strange type of control. I still can't smell anything. Are you sure she's evil?*

Evaine didn't like this. Drawing on some old defensive spells her mentor had taught her, she quickly summoned a pale green aura around herself and her two male companions.

Lanula stood in her doorway, amused. "You are a whelp of Sebastian's, aren't you?"

Evaine was irritated by the woman's attitude, but she forced herself to remain composed. This was either the creature she sought—her mentor's rival—or a dangerous trick.

Looking the men squarely in the face, Lanula posed seductively and summoned them. "Come, Tooth. Come, Blade. Enter my cottage and let me warm your tired bodies by the fire."

Ren smiled and walked right up to the woman.

Gamaliel shook his head, hesitating before moving toward the door. Evaine sensed him struggling to maintain control.

The sorceress refused to budge. She folded her arms across her chest. "This will stop right now. I know you for what you are," Evaine said in the most forceful voice she could muster. *Sebastian, you old dog! You kept company with a creature like this?* the sorceress thought to herself.

Evaine stood alone. She might have to fight for the lives of her two friends, for if they entered this creature's home, they might never come out again. "You're a succubus. Now I remember one of the last things Sebastian told me before he died. Lunlaa!" Evaine shouted, drawing her magical staff in front of her. "Lunlaa, show yourself for what you really are!"

"Aaaagh," the woman snarled. Her hair grew long and turned raven black as her features and muscles bulged. "It seems—owwwww," she cried as huge bat wings burst from her back. "It seems you have found me out, ahhh!" With a final groan of both pleasure and pain, her eyes glowed with red energy and her delicate human hands and feet turned to equally delicate talons and claws. The abominable creature flapped and hopped around Evaine, but the sorceress would not be intimidated.

Through the use of her name, the beautiful woman who had stood before them had been forced to transform into the lush, seductive creature that held men spellbound—a succubus.

The creature laughed a grating, hissing laugh. "You may have forced me to transform, but you can't send me back. Only Sebastian possessed that power, and he chose never to use it." Lunlaa now circled the men, pinching Ren's arm and squealing in delight.

Evaine refused to back down. "I know what you gave Sebastian and what you took from him. I could destroy you here and now!" The sorceress began gathering the energies that would explode a fireball around the creature.

"Harm me and your friends will fight you!" the creature cackled.

Evaine could see that Ren and Gamaliel were completely spellbound by what they still saw as a delicate human female. They were bewitched and couldn't see her horrible natural form. They stood like statues, mouths agape. Evaine knew Gamaliel was incapable of attacking her, but Ren was another matter.

Gamaliel still struggled for control. *Mistress . . . can't kill her . . . get help . . . her help . . .*

"You didn't come here to fight me," Lunlaa purred all too sweetly. Now she smiled at Ren and patted Gamaliel's shoulder. "We have a common enemy dwelling in the red tower. I will tell you how to kill him if we can be friends. I can help you in this quest in more ways than you expected. There is much you don't know about the darkness that surrounds that tower." The succubus was clearly enjoying her game.

"Why should you help us? How do I know we can trust you?"

"The pit fiend that made the tower is a fiend of unusual power, and he grows stronger all the time. The pit fiend would kill a poor succubus like me. And his influence will soon encroach upon my territory. What's a poor succubus to do but enlist the help of gentle adventurers like yourselves? Let us call a truce of sorts. I will tell you and your friends what you need to know, and you will leave me alone. Do we have a bargain?"

Evaine gritted her teeth. "I accept. But only because I intend to destroy the pool of darkness, no matter what it takes. I will be back to deal with you. I have friends who aren't so easily charmed by your powers."

The succubus cackled again. "You are wise and mature beyond your years. A lesser mind would have tried to destroy me here and now. And would have died trying.

"As for your friends. One of them has succumbed to my powers already. The other, a fine specimen, I will allow to pass, even though I'd like him for my personal collection. The third means nothing to me. I will release these two men to you." Ren and Gamaliel were oblivious to the meaning of the creature's words.

The succubus sighed. "I will quickly tell you what you need to know to destroy the tower and the pit fiend. Then you must leave me."

Concentrating to keep her mind free of the evil influence, Evaine spent the next hour listening to the succubus. By the time she led Gamaliel and Ren to their horses, she knew of the abishai they would face once they got near the tower, of the nature of the darkness filling the land around the tower, and about the pit fiend's greatest weakness.

Evaine ordered Gamaliel to turn into a cat once again, then sent him to scout for Andoralson and Miltiades. They headed them off before they reached the cabin of the succubus. Evaine didn't want to risk the chance of the druid falling under the evil woman's spell.

She related the whole story to Andoralson and Miltiades as they rode.

In turn, Andoralson told of his cousin's transformation. Talenthia's loss was deeply felt by everyone. But Andoralson insisted she would be happy in her decision because it was everything she had ever wanted from life. Knowing that her sacrifice was her greatest wish helped lift the sadness of her passing, but only a little.

# ❦ 16 ❦

## Dangerous Visit

The day had been exhausting, both mentally and physically. Even Gamaliel, with his feline energy, was dragging himself from task to task. The group had ridden until darkness closed in, then struggled in the blackness to start a fire and make camp. Only Gamaliel's keen eyesight ensured them a safe place to camp and fresh meat for dinner. Now they lolled about the fire, discussing the day's events and planning their strategy for the mission that lay ahead.

The loss of Talenthia, the encounter with the succubus, and the hard ride all had taken their toll. Frustration reigned, but the companions tried to remain calm and rational. If they were going to finish this mission alive, they needed to keep their spirits up. Miltiades cleverly interjected stories of old battles that were won despite terrible odds. His motives were transparent, but his encouragement was appreciated.

Evaine estimated that if they rode hard and were lucky enough to avoid monsters and travelers, they would reach the red tower in three days.

"Will we be too late to save Phlan?" Ren asked. His concern had grown visibly over the past few days. More and more, he wondered whether he would find his friends alive.

"In one respect, the darkness around the tower is a

good sign. It has grown slowly, which would indicate that efforts to defeat Phlan have not succeeded. I believe the mass of darkness would grow significantly faster as more souls are consumed by the pool. This coincides with what the succubus told me—if we believe she told the truth. And the truth of her statements will be tested if and when we discover the three abishai. I expect to see them flying on the horizon early tomorrow. They'll be our first challenge in infiltrating the red tower."

The weary group chatted a while longer as the fire died down to glowing coals. One by one, they drifted off into fitful sleep.

Miltiades, ever vigilant, kept watch, quietly sharpening his sword. He removed his plate mail armor and meticulously polished each piece, then carefully oiled the leather straps. Turning over his breast plate, the paladin sighed as he caught his reflection in the metal. An unfamiliar face, not his usual bony self, stared back at him.

The paladin didn't regret his appearance; rather, he considered it a privilege. After a millennium in the tomb, his god had chosen him for a holy quest and had given him a chance at redemption.

Buckling on his armor, Miltiades arose to pace the perimeter of the camp. He prayed silently to Tyr. "God of might and law, your servant is truly grateful for this chance at redemption. Grant that I may prove myself worthy. Grant that I may unselfishly complete your quest. Grant me strength that I may take no action except in your name and for your glory. Guide this humble servant into your light." The paladin slowly circled the camp, repeating his prayer in a whisper. Completing a sixth circuit, he bowed in reverence to his god, then seated himself on a boulder to resume his watch.

Morning dawned with a chill breeze and the ever-present stormclouds. Andoralson was the first to rise. Gamaliel, tucked behind his mistress on her bedroll, followed the druid's movements with his golden eyes. Seeing that the two of them were awake, Miltiades ducked into the trees for firewood. Andoralson busied himself at the edge of the clearing.

The druid picked away a patch of grass, weeds, and fungi, dug down a few inches, then planted several seeds. After humming a chant and adding blessed water and some sparkling dust, several tender sprouts pushed up from the ground.

Ren was now awake. His curiosity finally got the better of him. "Alright, druid. I watched you go through this ritual at least four times yesterday. Each time you planted some seeds, and, within minutes, a ring of seedlings started to grow. Why do you keep doing this?"

Andoralson looked up at Ren, smiling. He loved any opportunity to enlighten others about the wonders of the forest. The ranger could see he was in for a lecture.

"I'm helping to save the land. I'm not able to sense the mass of darkness Evaine tells us about. I can, however, see what the unknown evils are doing to the forests. The destruction must be stopped. I am following the good example of my cousin and doing my small part." The druid brushed off his hands and took a seat near the fire, helping Miltiades to stoke up a blaze.

"The trees I've just planted will grow magically. If they are not disturbed for a week, they will grow into huge oaks, unusually resistant to fire, disease, and blades of all kinds. Each ring of seven trees will form a grove—a haven of goodness, if you will. The trees will help counter the effects of evil."

Gamaliel jumped abruptly to his feet, sniffing the air.

Evaine announced the cat's message. "Riders coming."

The group readied their weapons, but left them concealed. They casually broke camp as they waited for the riders to approach. Long before the new group could be identified, Ren and the others heard their chanting. Evaine informed the group that Gamaliel smelled incense.

Andoralson cast a quick spell to mentally view the approaching horsemen.

"They're clerics," he observed. "There's a group of seven who follow Ilmater. You'll be able to tell by their gray tunics and tabards. One wears a red skullcap, indicating he is the leader. Take note if he has a gray teardrop tattooed under his left eye. Such a mark means he is a master of unusual power and dedication.

"There are ten other riders who are clerics of Torm. You can tell by the blinding shine on their plate armor, even under these gray skies. One has a blue tint to his plate armor, marking him as their leader. I'd guess him to be very powerful."

Both groups of clerics were loudly singing different chants, apparently oblivious to the clamor their conflicting tunes created. One priest of each sect carried a smoldering censor, filling the air with a trail of smoky incense. The singing didn't stop, even when the clerics discovered the travelers. The companions were on their feet, packing gear into saddlebags.

"Be ye friend or foe?" asked the cleric in the lead. The even tone of his voice and the scourge he hadn't drawn told everyone he didn't expect a fight. The other horsemen crowded into the clearing, arranging themselves so as not to alarm the strangers.

"Friends to those who would be our friends, foes to any who would slow our quest," Ren said, nodding to both groups.

"Well spoken, for a warrior," the cleric commented. The priest with the red skullcap gestured to the others, and his followers stopped their chanting and dismounted. The clerics of Torm held to their saddles but lowered their voices to a faint hum. The leaders of both groups stepped forward.

The cleric in blue plate mail shouted to his followers to cease their chanting. The smoke from the burning incense concentrated in the clearing, tainting the air with the smell of singed hair and stale, bitter herbs. The entire group grimaced as the odor washed over them. Gamaliel bared his teeth in a silent hiss.

"I am Bishop Painel," announced the man wearing the red skullcap. The gray teardrop tattooed under his eye was now visible to Ren and the others. "My priests are on a quest of our own, along with the priests of Torm." Painel deferred to his colleague.

"And I am Starnak, High Bishop of Torm. What is a ragged band such as yourselves doing here? Do you realize how dangerous this land has become?"

Without asking for consent, Painel moved to bless Evaine and the others. Gamaliel leaped between the cleric and his mistress, hissing at the intrusion.

"Good clerics," Ren boomed in his most authoritative voice, "our quest is to find some friends who were stolen along with the entire city of Phlan. We plan to look for answers at a red tower."

The clerics extinguished their pungent incense. The leaders looked upon Ren's group in surprise.

"Isn't this a coincidence?" Painel said calmly as he backed away from Gamaliel. "Our mighty gods have given us the quest of finding a red tower and expunging the evil there. Warrior, won't you introduce us to the rest of your party?"

Ren quickly surveyed the others. "I am called Blade. Yonder is a warrior dedicated to Tyr, known as Ordean." The ranger silently hoped that the clerics couldn't see through the paladin's illusion or sense that he was actually undead. "The lady is a wizard calling herself Anastasia—" Ren smiled, thinking Evaine wasn't the only one who could think fast on her feet "—her familiar, the giant cat, is Fellinor. The druid—"

"This druid can introduce himself. I am called Acer, good clerics. Perhaps we can join forces to approach the red tower. What do you know of this magical structure?"

Evaine observed slight hand gestures among the clerics at the rear of the group. She knew they were probably casting spells of detection.

The sorceress cleared her throat loudly. She hoped she could stop the clerics before they discovered their real names and the truth about Miltiades. "Excuse me, but your spells of detection won't work on us in the cloud of evil in which we find ourselves," she called over the heads of the two leaders. "Magics of searching won't work around the tower, either. You'll just have to trust us."

"Ah, trust—a charming concept, rarely given freely, is it not?" Painel asked. "Shall we compare knowledge of the tower before we decide whether to join forces?"

Four of his clerics began setting up strange poles, each with an iron gauntlet affixed to the top. The two lesser clerics of Ilmater walked between the poles, spreading the ashes from the incense burner.

Clerics are so odd, Ren thought to himself. He could never imagine such a life for himself.

"So, dear lady, please illuminate us on what your group knows," Painel said. A small stool was placed between the poles and the bishop settled onto it with a grunt.

Evaine was not about to spill the whole truth until she knew more about these clerics. She could tell a little of the story, however. "My home was destroyed and a message was left behind stating that a wizard named Marcus was responsible. He is recruiting wizards to join him at the red tower.

"Through some difficult spells, I think I have determined that this Marcus is involved in Phlan's disappearance. We hope to find him and learn what his terms are for the city's return. I could tell you all the details of our journey, but I'm sure a man such as yourself would be bored with the exploits of our little band." Evaine paused, waiting to hear the clerics' reaction. Hoping to bait them, she added, "I've also discovered three abishai guard the area around the tower."

The clerics were obviously intrigued. "We had no idea fiendkind were involved. The situation is much more serious if fiends from other planes are present." Starnak reached into his cloak and drew out a parchment.

"Our clerics have been using every possible means to learn about the interior of the tower. Over a dozen have gone insane, ranting about the voice of evil just before they die tormented deaths. We know of a secret door leading to a spellcasting chamber, and there are many magically locked doors there. This parchment lists the three words used to unlock the door. Be warned, if you get that far. These words came via the rantings of insane clerics. We don't know whether they'll do any real good."

Gamaliel nudged Evaine suddenly. *Despite all this ridiculous incense, mistress, I suddenly detect the odor of sulfur. And a strange presence—similar to dragonfear, but not nearly as strong. Should we be concerned?*

Evaine relayed the information. "My cat detects a

strange smell and presence. I think perhaps the abishai have found us. Prepare for the battle of your lives!"

Ren, Andoralson, and Miltiades immediately reached for weapons. Gamaliel's ears twitched as he listened for the approach of the fiends. The clerics barely moved.

Starnak paused, then raised his gauntleted hand in a clenched fist. Instantly, his clerics drew their weapons. Starnak swirled his hand twice as his followers began a magical chant, causing their weapons to glow with an eerie green luminescence. The clerics of Ilmater were outlined in a white glow.

Starnak addressed the companions. "I'd like to add your group to our circle of protection. Any defenses we can raise against these fiends may increase our odds of survival."

Ren started to accept the offer, but Evaine interrupted. "We have our own special defenses that we prefer to use. We've found them to be most effective against nearly any beast." Ren shot an angry glance at the sorceress, but Evaine ignored him.

"I've heard these types of creatures create an aura of fear as a weapon," Evaine continued.

"Oh, sweet child," Painel said, "If you allow yourselves to be protected by my clerics, fear will get no hold over you. Perhaps you should reconsider our offer."

Evaine disregarded his words, further irritating Ren.

"Um, Acer, can you do anything to locate the beasts that might be preparing to attack us?" The sorceress hoped desperately that Andoralson would catch on to what she and Gamaliel already suspected.

"I can try. If only my cousin were here—she had the chalice whose mist could locate such creatures."

Ren gave the sorceress and druid a confused look, but then gripped his huge sword with both hands, finally understanding the deception. Miltiades stood ready, ancient blade in hand.

The druid quickly spoke the words of a spell. Bluish purple fire poured from his hands and flowed toward the clerics. One by one, the false men evaporated into the magical mist until only three clerics, among them the two leaders, remained in the clearing.

"Now!" Evaine screamed. "Before they transform!"

The flaming stream of energy cast by the druid bent and curved, bathing the three figures in an outline of turquoise light. The three clerics shrieked unearthly screams as their flesh began to peel away.

Their presence discovered, the three creatures writhed and thrashed to free themselves, revealing a green, a black, and a red abishai. Miltiades and Ren landed solid sword blows on the red and the black fiends before they could complete the transformation. Gamaliel bounded around behind the green abishai, leaping on its back, tearing with all four clawed paws and ripping with enormous fangs. The monster let out an unearthly shriek as black ichor flowed down its back.

Even so, the red and the black abishai were able to leap into the air on huge bat wings. The green creature tried to take to the air also, but Gamaliel's hold was firm. Two hundred pounds of cat made flight impossible.

The druid's swirling blue fire continued to outline the creatures brightly, blinding them slightly. As the two monsters circled about the camp, hissing and spitting, Evaine and Andoralson continued to lob powerful spells at the fiends. The abishai screamed in pain as flashes of greenish white light burned into their wings and bodies. Yet the pain barely slowed them.

The red beast dropped out of the air onto Miltiades. The horrible creature's talons and fangs ripped into his plate mail armor as if the metal were soft cheese. Its tail flailed wildly. In the struggle, the illusion around the paladin failed, revealing the skeleton's true appearance. But his unnatural attacker barely noticed.

Evaine spread her fingers and shot eighteen white-hot jets of energy at the fiend grappling with Miltiades. Its shriek of pain pierced the air, spooking the horses. The abishai maintained its hold on the paladin, but Evaine could see that its wings hung in tatters. At least this monster was grounded.

Meanwhile, the black fiend flew straight at Ren. The ranger swung vigorously with his sword, but the abishai's wings pounded him, allowing only one swing to find its mark. Black ooze spurted from the fiend's thigh. Ren was dizzied by the attack but held his ground, gripping his weapon tightly.

Andoralson chanted loudly, trying hard to maintain his concentration. With a snap of his fingers, a searing white jet streaked toward the black abishai, landing squarely between its eyes. The monster roared in pain as its eyes were charred and blinded. It thrashed wildly, one of its claws raking Ren's shoulder. The ranger's chain mail tore open, blood spurting from the wound.

The green abishai spun and whirled, lashing with its tail. But Gamaliel couldn't be shaken. Four enormous paws with razor-sharp claws dug in deeply. Gamaliel alternated tearing and gouging. The fiend's wings hung limp and torn. The cat's ivory belly was stained black with foul-smelling blood. The feline's great jaws opened wide, clamping down on the monster's neck. Gamaliel shook his head with all his might, trying to break his victim's neck, yet the abishai was too large and strong. In a desperate maneuver, the green abishai hurled itself backward onto the snarling cat.

But Gamaliel's lightning reflexes took over, and he managed to vault away. Yet the fiend raked the cat before he escaped. Gamaliel landed solidly on his feet with a loud snarl of pain.

The sorceress's reflexes were at their best also, and before the monster could rise, a green stream of energy surged from her hand and formed a faint jade-colored hemisphere around the fiend. The green creature pounded and clawed at the invisible barrier, but the magical field of force was unyielding.

Ren now battered the black fiend. With his victim blinded, nearly all his swings found their mark. The monster howled an unearthly wail and flailed at its unseen attacker, but Ren was quick to dodge. He escaped injury while chopping at the black monster

Miltiades swung valiantly at the red abishai. Several claw swipes rattled his bones, yet the warrior was unharmed. As Evaine looked up, Andoralson released a spell to blind the monster, but the energy fizzled as it touched the fiend. Evaine loosed her own blinding spell. The energy found its mark, searing the beast's red eyes.

Gamaliel was now clinging to the back of the black abishai, clawing and raking. Its leathery wings hung like shredded paper, its black blood splattered on the ground. With his sword Ren was whacking at the blinded creature. The cat's weight slowed the monster, allowing Ren to deliver a mighty thrust through the fiend's ribs. The blade sunk in deep, and black blood spurted in all directions. The abishai howled and thrashed, striking Gamaliel. The feline snarled in pain and leaped off the monster. Ren drove his sword deeper and the fiend fell backward. In moments, the horrid creature ceased its twitching.

Evaine panicked. "Poison! That thing's tail is probably

poisoned!"

Gamaliel calmed her fears despite his snarls of pain. *I can feel it starting to spread . . . but the ring the paladin gave to me is cleansing it away. I'll be alright*, the cat growled.

The druid was already springing across the clearing toward Gamaliel, one hand fishing for a vial in his pocket. Evaine called out to Andoralson. "Gamaliel's ring, the one Miltiades gave him—it's cured the poison! He says he's out of danger!"

Andoralson pressed his hands to the cat's head. "He's right. The poison is nearly gone." The druid dropped the vial into his pocket and returned to the battle.

Ren and Miltiades were still fighting the red abishai, the toughest of the lot. The green one was still trapped under the magical sphere.

The sorceress turned toward the red abishai. Green eyes blazing, she uttered the words to one of her deadliest spells. Her long, red braid bobbed and swung as she gestured and chanted. Her face fairly glowed as she summoned incredible transformation energies. An emerald sizzle left her fingertips and streamed toward the fiend, encircling it in hissing energy.

Ren and Miltiades backed away from the glowing abishai, now writhing and thrashing. The top of the ugly creature's head turned ash gray, then the dull color spread down the monster's body. Red, leathery flesh turned to charred ash as the spell worked its way down the creature's body. Tattered wings withered and crumbled to the ground. Teeth and claws cracked and dropped off. Limbs bent and twisted like tree roots. Unearthly howls and screams filled the air, further spooking the already terrified horses.

Ren, Andoralson, and Miltiades watched, gasping for

breath, as the once-powerful creature turned to a dry, gray husk. Gamaliel looked up, blinking, still too weak to move. The green swirl of energy spun around the dying abishai, sucking out its life and energy. Finally, the dry husk of the fiend dropped to the ground with a whump, sending a cloud of ash into the air.

The companions looked at each other, panting. Evaine ran to Gamaliel's side. The big cat purred at her touch, despite his pain. "I've got something that'll fix that gash right up. Andoralson, why don't you see to Ren's shoulder? We still have a minute or two before the magical shield wears off and that other abishai is free. We must be ready for him when he breaks loose." Evaine dashed to her horse to find an ointment in her pack.

The druid hurried to Ren's side and quickly began a healing spell. As the ranger's wound closed, Andoralson looked over at Miltiades solicitously. "Are you hurt?"

"No. I'm a bit shaken, but I'm not injured. Slashing claws don't harm bones much," he said wryly. "I'm going to watch the remaining fiend. If Evaine is right, it'll be free any minute." With a creaking and clattering, the bony paladin arose and strode across the clearing. He assumed an attack posture, sword held high, ready for the first strike.

Ren did the same as soon as his shoulder was healed. He took up a position about ten yards away, prepared to launch his magical daggers, Left and Right, at the first sign of the force field weakening. Andoralson stood next to him, ready to cast a spell.

Evaine finished rubbing the ointment into the long gash on the cat's belly. The wound instantly closed and stopped bleeding. In the blink of an eye, the cat rolled to his feet and bounded toward the trapped fiend. Taking a position opposite Miltiades, he dug his back claws into the ground, prepared to pounce.

Evaine also readied herself. Holding a handful of soot and a black gem, she prepared to blast the horrid fiend.

"This is it!" the wizard announced. "The field is dispersing. Get ready to do your worst!"

The faint green field of force shivered slightly, then disappeared. "Now!" Evaine shouted.

Ren's daggers whizzed through the air. Two loud thumps announced they had found their marks in the abishai's chest. The handles quivered as the beast howled in pain.

An emerald streak erupted from Evaine's hand, encircling the monster. The energy sizzled, but then dissipated in a shower of green sparks. The abishai was wounded, but resisted the full effect of the spell.

Andoralson released a blue surge of energy. It divided into thousands of pinpoints of light, like a swarm of turquoise fireflies. The lights swirled around the beast, blinding it and disorienting it. Again, the abishai screamed in pain as each spark burned into leathery flesh. The fiend's own talons ripped into its muscle as it tried to pull out the scorching magic. An acrid, bitter smoke curled around the horrid beast as it teetered and stumbled about the clearing in a bizarre dance.

Gamaliel leaped for the creature's back, claws extended. He landed solidly on the smoking abishai and wasted no time raking and shredding the monster's flesh. Miltiades and Ren faced the green beast, swinging carefully calculated blows at its writhing form. Four hard sword strikes finally brought the wounded creature to its leathery knees, and Gamaliel dealt the final blow by pouncing full-force on the abishai's head, snapping its neck.

Each of the companions dropped into the trampled grass in the clearing, gasping for air. Even Miltiades creaked his body onto the ground. No one spoke for several minutes.

It was Miltiades who broke the silence. "I'm proud to call you my comrades! I had my doubts about this group, but you are an excellent team." The paladin stood and bowed deeply to the group.

"We couldn't have done it without you, warrior. I think I speak for all of us when I say we're proud to have you on this quest." Ren nodded respectfully to Miltiades. The others voiced their agreement.

Evaine rose and grasped the paladin's hand. "If it hadn't been for your magical ring, I might have lost Gam. I can't thank you enough for your generosity."

Andoralson sighed loudly. "I just hope this isn't an indication of what the rest of the day will be like. We haven't even had breakfast yet, and we've battled three abishai! I don't know about anyone else, but I'm starving." The druid arose and loaded wood onto the embers of the campfire. "Gamaliel, if you feel up to hunting us some breakfast, I'll cook *anything* you bring us."

The cat was on his feet in a flash. Evaine laughed. "I hope no one minds fish for breakfast. I know what he's in the mood for. Gamaliel, if you can sniff out a stream, come back for the rest of us. We're all a mess after that battle. Just look at your fur!"

The feline glanced down at his coat to find that he looked like a bedraggled panther. His tawny fur was all but dyed by abishai blood. Gamaliel raised his pink nose high in the air, made a prideful comment to his mistress, then turned toward the woods. Evaine laughed as she translated for the others. "He says he doesn't look like a mess—he looks like a hero!"

# ❧ 17 ❧

# The White Bard

Marcus's red tower shook to its very core. If not for the magic holding the blood-colored stones together, the building would have crumbled.

"My abishai have been killed! *Latenat*!" the pit fiend hissed at Marcus. The creature circled the inner chamber at the top of the tower, half-flying, half-hopping. Its great wings pounded the walls as it paced.

"Killed? How in the world did you allow my guardians to be killed?" Marcus shrieked.

"Arrrgh! Do you think I let them die? I don't know what killed them! Their life essences were snuffed out, and since *you* ordered them to guard your domain, their deaths are on your hands. *Latenat*!"

The wizard's face flushed deep red, beads of sweat erupting on his forehead. "Are you somehow blaming me for this? It was your duty to guard this tower and build armies so I could lead them to victory, conquering Phlan! You have now failed me. We both know what happens to my servants when they fail."

The fiend still bashed about in the black chamber. If not for Marcus's control of the creature's life essence and his knowledge of its true name, the fiend could have squashed the wizard in an instant. Instead, he was forced to obey the human weakling. But he had already tolerated far more than any pit fiend should.

The fiend kept circling and thrashing as Marcus continued his diatribe. The beast was only half-listening to the wizard. He had heard all these rantings too many times before. Then the Red Wizard spoke the pit fiend's name, summoning the creature's heart from the magical dimension where he kept the beating organ.

"On your knees, beast," he said. "I will speak to you, and it will be eye to eye."

In defiance, the winged horror flapped halfway around the chamber one last time, halting in front of Marcus. The Red Wizard raised the fiend's heart and slowly squeezed until a half-dozen drops of black ichor leaked out, splashing onto the granite floor with a sizzle.

The fiend groaned as his knees dropped to the scarred floor. He glared at his tormentor. "What would you have of me . . . master? *Latenat.*"

"For a time, you and I will change roles. I will guard the tower and you will use your puny powers to force Phlan to submit to me. I will summon more clerics and wizards to help in your struggle."

"That won't be necessary," the fiend growled. It struggled to its leathery feet and stalked out of the chamber. "I'll destroy Phlan myself within two days."

Marcus snorted an arrogant laugh as the creature disappeared. "We'll see about that, braggart. Phlan may break you on its walls and teach you a good lesson in the process. Now, I have a little searching to do. I plan to have several unpleasant surprises ready for the dogs who dared to kill my abishai. And those beauties were mine, Tanetal! I don't care what you think!" Marcus shouted at the empty chamber and the closed door.

\* \* \* \* \*

In another tower, an angry voice was also heard. But this time, it was the wizard Shal who was being scolded.

"Shal, you should never have attacked that mage in your condition. That shadow attack nearly killed you. If Cerulean hadn't had the sense to retreat and bring you back to the tower, you would have died horribly."

Shal tried to raise her head to argue, but she dropped back onto her pillow. Her face was the color of barley mush, her skin clammy. Tarl had used the healing power of the Warhammer of Tyr to restore her strength and sanity, but there were some things the hammer couldn't cure so quickly.

Shal looked pleadingly at Celie, who sat at her side, dabbing her face with a moist cloth. A covered basket loaded with poppyseed cakes was perched on the bedside table.

"Don't look at me, missy. Your husband is right to worry. You've been with child only five months, yet it looks now as if you'll be ready to deliver in a few weeks. I don't know much about magic, but I can see what this exertion is doing to you. The way this baby is kicking, he's not going to stay cooped up much longer." The bakerwoman's voice was stern, but her blue eyes were caring and soothing.

Shal realized there was no arguing with Tarl and Celie. The wizard spoke in a whisper. "I thought if I could kill the red mage who was leading the attacks against Phlan, our troubles would be over. I never dreamed he was powerful enough to cast spells like that."

Tarl caressed his wife's forehead, speaking softly to her. "That's all very noble, but you have a child to think about. A few months ago, I wouldn't have questioned you going after him like that. But you know better than anyone the way high-powered spells can age a wizard.

You've already accelerated this pregnancy. What if the baby decided his—or her—time was up while you were flying around up there? I could have lost you both!"

"You're right. It was foolish to take on that crazed wizard all by myself. I'll be more careful." Then to put Tarl's mind at ease, Shal turned to Celie. "Are those poppyseed cakes I'm smelling?" She knew her husband would worry less if she ate something.

Celie broke into a smile and uncovered the basket. Tarl propped Shal up on her pillows.

"You just lie here and rest as long as you can. We destroyed all the tree-minions of Moander that attacked the city. It should be a while before the wizard regroups and brings another of his armies against us."

"Bring me my spellbooks, please? I'm strong enough to start memorizing spells. I've a feeling we're going to need them soon. If that wizard's got half a brain, he's going to change tactics. I need to be ready when he does."

Tarl mocked a snarl at his wife. "No spellbooks for you, young lady. If you promise to rest all day, you can have your books tomorrow. We all need you to be healthy right now. Especially the little one." He patted her bulging abdomen lovingly and felt a solid kick, as if the baby were voicing its agreement.

"Celie, you keep an eye on her. If she tries anything—anything at all—you send for me. Two clerics are waiting right outside the door, and they'll do whatever you ask. I'm going to meet with the council."

These two mean business, Shal decided, a little glumly. Well, I might as well make the best of it. A day of rest and being stuffed with poppyseed cakes certainly couldn't hurt me.

Yet as Tarl reached for the door, all the magical lights in

the cavern went dark. Candles and fires still gave off feeble light, but otherwise the cave was in total blackness.

Tarl cursed as he galloped down the stairs. The city was nearly out of food and its residents were losing hope. Now the lights were gone, and to the cleric, that meant only one thing—another imminent attack. He grabbed a torch and lighted it as he headed for the council. Perhaps, he grudgingly admitted, the people of the city would be better off escaping the cavern and rebuilding elsewhere. He didn't know how much more they could bear.

* * * * *

The angry fiend flew into the cavern and over the city of Phlan, basking in the darkness. He should have doused the lights weeks ago.

"Marcus is a fool. Conquering Phlan has nothing to do with taking its walls. The destruction of this city lies in taking its people. When I gain their souls, they will open their gates."

The fiend flew over the center of the city, past the docks. The winged beast soared to a secluded corner of the cavern's sea, then concentrated for only a few moments, creating one of its best illusions. The horrid black beast writhed and blurred, then emerged as a white bard named Latenat.

His appearance now was of a kindly, middle-aged bard with a short, white beard and flowing white robes. His voice was gentle and melodic, his demeanor peaceful. The monster's true nature was visible only in his stern eyes. But looking into his eyes would be difficult if Latenat did his job right.

The disguised creature conjured a small white sailing

ship and settled himself into the stern. Although the boat was powered magically, the bard picked up an oar and began to row. The sail hung limply in the still air of the dark cavern.

About fifty yards from the south gate, the boat was spotted by Phlan's guards. Fires had been lit all along the beach, and flaming rafts had been set out in the water to reveal the presence of any attackers. An alarm was sounded at the first sight of the boat, yet it was allowed to approach the dock.

A squad of hard-eyed guards awaited the stranger.

"Just where did you come from?" the oldest guard demanded.

"I am the white bard, Latenat. I've been sent by the gods to lead the people of Phlan to freedom," the pit fiend purred.

"And I am the great bunny Tootal, sent by the gods to sink your boat. You got any proof?" the guard snorted.

The bard's voice was smooth and soothing. "My proof is in my songs friend, in my songs. If you'll permit me, I'll sing one for you now."

"Ain't no law against singing that I know of, but your tune better be good, or you'll be eatin' that stringed thing of yours, young fella."

The bard smiled serenely, strummed his lute, and began his song:

> *"I sing a song of praise for Phlan,*
> *The town I've come to free,*
> *I sing a song of hope for you,*
> *The folk I would set free."*

The bard continued, verse after verse, as more guards gathered to hear the song. The magic of the pit fiend's spell wove in and around the people on the dock. Latenat's ballad of hope made the listeners long for their freedom. The fiend's spell seeped into the minds of the weary captives, making them vulnerable to his foul message.

All day and long into the night, the mysterious bard tirelessly sang his songs. His smooth voice never grew weary. He traveled to inns and halls and large manor houses, never asking for payment for his performances. Everywhere crowds of people gathered to hear the minstrel and his compelling tunes. It had been months since anyone in Phlan had heard such fine singing.

His message was always the same. In his lilting voice, the bard encouraged the people of Phlan to make their escape while the battlefield was quiet and empty. A few people scoffed at the idea, but many others started packing, convinced the bard was right. They had been in this cavern far too long. Most citizens didn't know what to think, but they knew anything was better than waiting in the dark for the next deadly attack.

Tanetal's spell was working. His song lingered in the minds of his listeners. The unity of Phlan's people was finally beginning to wobble.

# ❦ 18 ❦

## A Secret Past

The dull light filtering through chalky clouds told the companions that the hour was near noon. But to the battle-weary travelers, the hour felt more like midnight. The early skirmish with the trio of abishai had exhausted Ren, Evaine, and Andoralson. Even Gamaliel, in his barbarian shape, slumped astride his horse rather than scouting ahead in his preferred cat form. Miltiades, always energetic, blazed a trail at the head of the group.

The riders emerged from the forest of sickly trees into a wide clearing. A field that should have been filled with waving grasses, blooming wild flowers, and buzzing bees was instead a sea of gray, brittle weeds. The dead vegetation crunched loudly under the horses' hooves.

As the riders neared the center of the clearing, Ren suddenly shouted a warning. A black, leathery form dipped out of the sky, enormous talons snatching at Evaine. The sorceress ducked her head into the horse's mane just in time to avoid the creature's claws. The beast pulled out of its dive and flapped high into the sky, preparing for another pass.

"Mistress!" Gamaliel called. "It's not real! It's just a trick!" The barbarian nudged his horse alongside the sorceress.

Again, the monster swooped down, aiming for Ren. The ranger had drawn his sword and now swung valiantly at the creature. His swing missed, but the beast's claws found Ren's shoulder. He screamed in pain as the talons tore open his chain mail, carving out a deep gash.

Miltiades turned his horse, galloping up to Ren. "Close your eyes, ranger. What you see is not an abishai. It cannot harm you."

Ren snorted and looked skyward. Reaching into his boots, he drew Right and Left.

The beast was already diving again, this time at Andoralson. The druid held his oak shield high, bracing himself.

Ren raised his arm to launch a dagger, but a bony hand gripped his wrist and yanked it down. "Wait. This will be over soon." The ranger struggled, but the paladin's grasp held firm.

A fiend bigger than the druid's horse smashed into the oak shield. But instead of a deafening thump and the scrape of claws, the clearing fell silent. As Ren watched, the abishai turned to black mist and dissolved.

"What in the Nine Hells?" the ranger cursed. Andoralson reined his horse over to Ren and immediately began healing his shoulder.

"Illusion," Evaine interrupted. "The creature wasn't really there."

"How did you know?"

"Gamaliel figured it out first. The beast didn't smell like an abishai. Those last three we fought reeked of sulphur. I could also tell it wasn't real."

Ren twisted in his saddle to stare at Miltiades. "My dead eyes are difficult to deceive," the undead knight said. "I saw only a shadow of the fiend." The paladin reached out to hold Ren's chain mail and assist Andoralson.

"What about you, druid?" Ren was growing irritated.

"I specialize in the magic of illusions. When Gamaliel tipped us off, I checked for myself and found the fiend to be a fake."

The ranger huffed. "If that beast was such a fake, then why does this wound feel so real? Ouch!" He glared at Andoralson.

Evaine explained. "When you believe an illusion is real, you also believe its behavior to be real. The theory behind the magic is a bit complicated."

"You mean I could have died from something that wasn't there?"

"I'm afraid so. It's been known to happen."

"So why did the beast evaporate when it hit Andoralson's shield?"

The druid spoke up. "That was the oak shield Miltiades gave me from his tomb. It magically repels arrows and other attacks, so I took a chance on the abishai. I guess I got lucky."

The paladin's stern voice scolded the druid. "Luck. Bah. You should thank Tyr for your life." Andoralson nodded his apology to Miltiades.

"We should move on. We've got a long way to go." Gamaliel offered, trying to bring order.

"Apparently that Marcus fellow knows we're coming. This seems to be his way of greeting us." Miltiades nudged his ivory steed to the front of the group, leading the way across the clearing.

Ren made a face. His shoulder still ached. "You've all got a sixth sense about this kind of thing. From now on, give me a signal, or if we're facing other creatures, make some odd comment about oh, what we ate for breakfast or the price of ale in Waterdeep." The ranger sighed wearily.

The group rode hard the rest of the day. Around midafternoon, Evaine broached a subject that concerned her.

"Andoralson, would you mind telling us what magic you've placed on this group? Gamaliel and I have been aware of some kind of spell ever since the fake abishai attacked us." Evaine's curiosity had finally gotten the better of her.

"Well . . . ah, I wanted us to approach the red tower as secretly as possible."

"I understand. I've got my own protective spells at work. But what spell have you used on us?" Evaine wasn't about to let the matter drop.

"The truth is sort of embarrassing—but since you insist, I've placed an illusion around us. We now appear as a herd of wild pigs."

The barbarian snorted in disgust. Miltiades couldn't contain a dry laugh.

"Pigs?" Ren asked in shock. "Why pigs? Why not lions, or buffalo, or even deer?"

"Uh . . . well, the spell requires a bit of hair or a tooth or some part of the animal. I found a few bristles from wild pigs a ways back. I didn't have the hair from any other animals."

The druid was embarrassed, but after his companions got over their surprise, they agreed his logic was excellent. A herd of wild pigs wasn't likely to attract attention.

The weary group rode a few more hours, until darkness. They settled into a small clearing, but despite their exhaustion, the companions were restless with anticipation. They expected to reach the red tower before noon the next day.

With the evening meal finished, everyone set about making preparations for the morning. Ren and Miltiades knocked a few dents out of the paladin's armor, repaired the ranger's chain mail, then set to sharpening their swords. As a cat, Gamaliel didn't need to prepare, but as a barbarian, he needed a sharp blade. The campsite was filled with the *shhhinks* and *shooshes* of three swords against whetstones. Evaine and Andoralson busied themselves taking inventory of spell components and placing them in convenient pockets. The two spellcasters spent extra time placing protective spells around the camp.

When Ren was satisfied with the sharpness of his blade, he pulled his daggers, Left and Right, out of his boots and began working over their long edges. Miltiades picked one up, admiring its weight and balance. "These have saved my life more times than I can count," the ranger explained. "I have a feeling they'll be put to the test tomorrow."

"A thousand years ago, no one knew how to fashion such fine weapons," Miltiades said. "Most weaponsmiths spent their time perfecting the larger, deadlier blades, like swords and lances."

Ren couldn't resist the opportunity to brag. "In the hands of one who's skilled, these daggers are more deadly than a lance. Assuming we all survive the battle tomorrow, I'll be happy to teach you the fine art of throwing such a blade."

"I would like nothing more, Ren, but tomorrow, win or lose, I will forever be put to rest. Those of us who are walking dead sometimes know when our final day and hour will come. If we succeed tomorrow, I will rest in peace and honor. If we fail, I will again lie in unhallowed ground without the grace of my god."

"Wait a minute," Evaine called out in surprise. "You already know you're going to . . . um, cease to exist . . . no matter what you do?"

"Correct. But do not feel sorry for me. I am lucky to have this second chance. I only hope I can accomplish my mission and help all of you in the short time I have left." His voice was full of pride and strength.

The others were silent for a moment. The loyal skeletal warrior had become a trusted friend and ally.

Ren broke the somber moment. "Well, Miltiades, I don't understand what Tyr may have set aside for you, but you've been a good friend to all of us. If we have anything to say about your fate, I know we'd all agree that you've served with faith and honor."

If the warrior had been made of flesh, he would have blushed at the compliment. Instead he returned the praise. "I am lucky to have found friends like you to share my quest. The gods will smile on each of you." Miltiades arose and walked the perimeter of the camp, peering into the dark forest, preparing for his watch.

The companions settled in for the night, but sleep wouldn't come. The red tower loomed in all their thoughts. Ren worried about Shal and Tarl. Evaine tried to focus her thoughts on the dark pool. Miltiades and Andoralson both prayed for strength and guidance. Even Gamaliel slept only in fits, since the nervous energy in the camp was as tangible to him as cold rain. Now in comfortable cat form, he lay motionless on the blanket, blinking in the dim glow of the fire.

Finally, near midnight, the foursome drifted into restless sleep. Miltiades paced the small camp. Nothing would surprise the vigilant paladin.

Suddenly, a voice boomed out from the darkness. Miltiades gripped his sword. Gamaliel was instantly on his feet, ready to pounce, his tail fluffed out.

"Well, my fine pigs. Will you be visiting me tomorrow?"

The others were on their feet as a horrid face made of crimson flames exploded in the night sky. The writhing blaze formed the head of a human wizard.

"Behold your new lord, weaklings. I am Marcus, Red Wizard of Thay. I would expect a revelation such as this to frighten away most travelers. But I think the pigs I see in front of me will be knocking on my door tomorrow, anyway. You are either exceptionally brave or incredibly stupid. If you dare approach my tower, you will prove the latter. I am preparing a warm and highly magical welcome for you, my little piggies."

The image vanished as quickly as it had come. Gamaliel paced the camp, his fur standing on end, his great pink nose sniffing for any trace of the infiltrator. Evaine ordered him to lie down, rubbing his neck to settle him. "Wizards of Thay are well known for their preference for fire spells," she explained to the others. "That was a fairly common fire spell with an illusion thrown in. But what's really interesting is that he managed to affect us from miles away. That's not normal, and it's not easy. Obviously, we don't have the element of surprise." Gamaliel was now purring faintly, his eyes alert.

Miltiades still gripped his sword, scanning the trees for the slightest motion. Andoralson put a kettle of water on the glowing embers. "Since all of us are ready to jump out of our skins, I'm going to brew some herbs. I've got a mixture that might help us calm down and get some sleep. But it won't leave us groggy."

Ren questioned Evaine further about the Red Wizards. She explained that most were self-centered, arrogant, and only interested in personal gain. Their drive and greed made them extremely dangerous. They allowed nothing to stand in their way and wielded potent magic that could cut down enemies in a hurry.

Ren went to his saddlebags to fish out a metal box. "I think I have something that might help us." He opened the box, sorting out a variety of small vials and scrolls.

"These came from a dragon's horde—probably the property of some mage who fell prey to the beast. I've used them only rarely in the last ten years, but I've periodically taken them to an alchemist to learn whether they were still potent. The potions won't work on Miltiades since he can't drink them, but there's a scroll of protection against fire that should do the job. If he reads the scroll when we get to the tower, he'll activate the magic. We can all share the protection if we stay close to him.

"The rest of you should each take one of these little vials. The amber ones are potions of healing. I know you've all probably used them before—they'll heal you as quickly as any spell. The little red vials are potions of fire resistance. Wait until you think you might need it before drinking one, because they don't last long. But they'll protect you from all normal types of fire and most magical ones."

Ren passed two vials to each of his companions and handed the scroll to Miltiades. They were quickly stashed in convenient pockets and pouches. Everyone knew such potions might mean the difference between life and death in the battle to come.

The glowing coals of the fire began to hiss and spit as boiling water splattered over the side of the kettle. Andoralson moved the metal pot, briskly stirring in a handful of herbs. The smells of honey, clover, and orange rind soon overpowered the scent of wood smoke. Hot mugs of steaming tea were passed around.

A puzzled look crossed Ren's face. He stared at Evaine in the firelight. "Evaine, all of us have told the tales of why we're here, but you've always avoided the subject. We've got plenty of time now. How about letting us in on your story?"

Despite the red glow of the fire, the wizard's face grew pale. She stared into her mug as if searching for an answer, then sighed.

"I don't usually tell anyone my reasons for doing anything, but we've been through a lot together. I guess there's no harm in telling you why I'm in this fight." She settled against a tree stump and began her tale.

"I've been casting spells a lot longer than you might think. I may look as if I'm in my mid-thirties, but actually I'm much older.

"I once had incredible powers. I spent my entire life searching for magical tomes, items of strong magic, new spells, and fantastic creatures whose powers I might draw upon. I didn't care about anything but amassing more power. Sure, I would sometimes perform a service for someone who wanted to hire me, but there was always a price—an incredibly steep price.

"Then I learned about pools of radiance and pools of darkness. Being narrow-minded and overconfident, I decided I could harness the energy tied to the pools, or maybe experiment on the waters and create my own pools. I was warned away by sages and wizards of extreme age, but in my pride, I ignored all of their advice." The sorceress sipped at her mug.

"I managed to collect some water from a pool of radiance. What I didn't know was that the pool was in a transformation and was becoming a pool of darkness. The unstable liquid caused all my experiments to backfire, creating horrible side effects. A portion of my lab blew up. I was knocked out with the explosion. I woke up four days later, lying on the floor of my wrecked lab.

"I was only slightly injured, but changed forever. My mind and body were reversed about fifty years. I was once again a twenty-year-old woman. All but my most basic powers were gone and I was forced to start my life over. I could remember the powers I had and what I'd once known, but I had nothing to work with. You can't believe how frustrating it was.

"I sought out one of my former students and asked him to teach me the same things I had taught him. Fortunately, learning spells the second time was easier than the first. Occasionally, snatches of memory would come back." She sighed mournfully. "Over the next ten years, he was able to teach me much of what I had lost. And since then, I've spent my time traveling and learning. I've made the study of magic my life's work, but you'll rarely find me cooped up in library.

"Years later, I learned that the fiend who was transforming the pool sent incredible energies at me through the water I had stolen. The creature tried to kill me, but the unstable waters twisted the magic. Instead, I suffered the loss of my powers.

"I'm still trying to regain skills I once had, but I'm no longer driven by greed to amass power. I seek to learn all I can to enhance my magical powers and destroy those vile pools. There's no reason for such things to exist. They cause nothing but pain and suffering."

Evaine sipped at her cup while the others tried to comprehend her story. Andoralson poured the wizard a second mug of tea, then gingerly asked the question that was nagging him. "Are you telling us you're actually one hundred years old?"

The sorceress looked at him with an embarrassed smile. "That's just about right. I was seventy-eight when the transformation happened, and I estimate I reverted to twenty. That was fourteen years ago."

Andoralson patted her shoulder sympathetically. Evaine clasped his hand affectionately, but discouraged the sad look on his face. "Don't feel sorry for me. I was bitter and angry at first, but I've accepted my situation. I am determined to hunt down these pools. I once sought power for its own sake, but now I have a purpose in life like I've never had before. I suffered a great loss, but I've also gained a great deal. Not many people get to live their lives a second time."

The wizard's gentle tone changed to one of determination. "So now you know why I'm here. I'm going to destroy the pool of darkness hidden in Phlan, and no snotty little wizard or his fiend from the pits of the Nine Hells is going to stop me. After this one is gone, Gamaliel and I will move on to the next one. If it takes the rest of my life, I'll destroy all of those vile puddles."

Evaine drained her mug. Ren idly poked at the fire's glowing embers with a stick. Drowsiness was overtaking all of them. Once again, they climbed into bedrolls.

As they began to get settled, Ren spoke up. "We'll get that wizard for you, Evaine, and the pool, too. And we'll find my friends and rescue Phlan. After tomorrow, there'll be one less magical blight on Faerun."

# ✿ 19 ✿

# Subtle Assault

Since the day it had been torn from its home on the Moonsea, Phlan had been attacked so many times that most of its citizens had lost count. Once again, they were under siege. Only this time, no one knew it.

When the lights in the cavern died, the city was alerted and all guards were summoned to their posts on the walls. Wizards and priests appeared at their stations, preparing to cast their most powerful spells at the enemy. Children were called indoors, shutters were bolted. The city silently waited for the attack.

In the dark stillness of the streets of Phlan, a lone voice was heard. A bard known only as Latenat brought his message of peace and hope to the desperate city. He walked the inroads and avenues of Phlan, singing his message of rescue. In his wake, housewives packed whatever possessions they could carry and dressed their children for a long journey. The end of their imprisonment had finally come. The bard would show them the way out of the wretched cave.

Crowds of hopeful people began filling the streets. Those who had packed for the escape encouraged reluctant neighbors to join them.

As the residents milled about, snatches of the bard's songs could be heard amid excited conversation. The tunes were infectious, and the voices in the streets grew to an incredible din.

On the city walls, distraught guard captains dispatched several dozen warriors to the streets. The citizens were endangering themselves by remaining outdoors. And the clamor was loud enough to drown out the sound of approaching cavalry. In the darkness, the guards had little other than sound to warn them of an attack.

But the warriors who were sent to keep the peace quickly became part of the chaos. Forgetting their tasks, they returned home to pack their valuables and join their families. The bard's infectious song did not discriminate. Following his instructions, the warriors left their weapons at home, collected their money and jewels, and gathered in the streets. More warriors had to be diverted from the walls to the streets.

The bard tirelessly continued his stroll through Phlan, singing his tales of redemption. No one seemed to notice that the bard had been singing for over twenty-four hours without a break.

Little by little, the city walls were drained of warriors. Soon they were no longer defensible.

Finally, the glorious, wondrous bard signaled his flock. The masses began to move toward the Death Gates. The people sang and danced their way through the streets, charmed by the captivating man and bewitched by his songs.

The spellbound crowd called for the gates to be opened. The guards refused, but Latenat began another song. As his melody rose, the warriors forgot their objections. Puzzled, they looked at each other and at the gate machinery.

Then the minstrel's song was interrupted.

A voice rang out, ordering that the Death Gates remain closed. Booted feet pounded along the top of the wall, coming to a halt on the gate. Tarl, gripping the glowing Warhammer of Tyr, planted himself firmly at the head of the throng. He tried his best to appear calm, but his anger was evident.

A few feet behind him, waiting on the stone wall, stood Shal. She was wrapped head to toe in a purple cloak, but to anyone with magical abilities, it was obvious she was also wrapped in strong protective magics. Six other wizards moved along the wall beside her.

The bard ended his song, turning his back on Tarl and Shal. He raised his hands for silence, then addressed the crowd. "Noble people of Phlan, your famous champions are here to lead you and protect you on your way. Let us thank them for their bravery!" A deafening roar erupted as the mob cheered.

Behind Latenat's back, Shal cast a spell to learn something of this strange bard. The purple beams bathed the bard and bounced off his flesh, but revealed nothing of his true nature.

"Noble heroes, it is wonderful to have you join us in our bid for freedom and safety," the bard laughed. A magical suggestion was wrapped in his voice. But the spell had no effect on Tarl, Shal, or the other wizards.

"Noble bard, we haven't been introduced. My name is Tarl, and I represent the Council of Phlan. I would like to know why you've brought my people to this gate."

A hearty laugh arose from the bard, and his syrupy answer lilted up to the cleric.

"Tarl—brother—dear friend—I am the bard Latenat! I've been sent by the gods of fortune to release these people!" Once again, the bard turned away from Tarl and addressed the crowd surrounding him. "These wonderful people of Phlan must be freed from this dreadful cave and from the dangers they face. They must again walk in the sunlight and cultivate the earth the gods have given them!"

A roar again erupted in the streets, and the mob began chanting, "We are freed, we are freed, we are freed!"

Tarl bellowed to be heard over the noise. "I wish you to be free of danger, too! But leaving the walls of the city will not save you from the foes that have attacked us for months! You will march to certain death!"

"Shall I sing a song to answer Tarl?" the bard asked the crowd.

"A song—sing us a song!" the crowd called back.

The bard raised his lute and addressed Tarl.

> "*Noble and fearless stood a fine priest,*
> *His city and people behind him,*
> *They battled and fought but could not slay the beast,*
> *So Tarl led the charge to a new land.*"

Latenat continued, verse after verse, about Tarl and his heroics. So persuasively did the bard sing that even Tarl began to wonder whether it wasn't indeed time for the people of Phlan to leave.

He looked longingly at the men who stood by to raise the gates. Shal knew it was time to step in.

"Tarl, dear husband! Hear my voice and no other!" She turned to the peculiar minstrel. "Sing no more songs, bard or whatever you are. No one is going with you."

Shal levitated herself into the air, a vision of magical power. As Shal glared down at the bard, the bewitched crowd became filled with fear. At one time or another, everyone had seen her power used against armies of monsters. There was no doubt she could blast the crowd to cinders if she wished.

"Come up into the light of truth, bard." The wizard

raised her hand. A purple mist curled and streaked toward the minstrel. When the vapors tried to lift him, they puffed into harmless gas and dissipated.

"I can join you on my own power, if that is what you wish, my dear." He strummed his lute, and the chords of music wove into a silver staircase hovering in the air. Latenat strolled up to Shal as the crowd shouted its pleasure at seeing the two together. The wizard was startled, but hid her surprise.

The crowd hushed. Freedom was within their grasp. Many citizens shifted their packs, adjusting their bags of gold and silver. Surely the gates would be opening at any moment.

"Sweet child, your husband is prepared to join me. Learn from the other women of the city. Be a good little wife."

His condescending attitude only infuriated Shal further.

"Your spells and magical suggestions won't work on me. We can talk and you can leave, or we can fight. It's up to you." Shal's baby kicked hard, but her grimace only made her appear more determined.

"Why, lovely lady, I could never fight *you*. If gentle reason won't work, I can leave these good people to their fates. Perhaps they wouldn't mind living out their lives in this charming cave." The bard's sugary voice disgusted Shal, but his words upset the crowd and the citizens began grumbling among themselves.

"I only wish to . . . Argh!"

Suddenly the bard collapsed to his knees, clutching his chest. His lute fell from the staircase onto the stone street and smashed into hundreds of pieces. Shal's eyes widened. None of her group had used any magic against the bard yet. The sorceress suspected a trick.

"No! Not now!" Now the bard groaned and twisted in pain. Still on his magical stairway, he suddenly transformed into a black, horrifying pit fiend. His batlike wings thrashed on the staircase. Great talons scratched and gouged at the magical structure as the monster hissed and drooled.

The creature that had been the wondrous bard Latenat turned to vapor and vanished. Children screamed and cried. To the people of Phlan who had adored him only moments before, this new apparition filled them with horror and revulsion. Now they wept in terror at the creature's trickery, falsehoods that had nearly led them to tragedy.

Tarl came to his senses and reached for Shal, pulling her close. The people in the streets wailed in anguish. Shal collapsed in relief into her husband's arms as Tarl addressed the crowd.

"Good people of Phlan, we were nearly tricked into losing our city. We have tolerated this wretched cave long enough. It is time to abandon our walls and save ourselves. Our food is nearly gone. The attacks will only get worse. Take home your valuables, pick up your shields and weapons. Open the armories! Let us march out of here and write a new history for Phlan!"

A deafening cheer arose from the crowd. The citizens turned toward their homes with new hope in their hearts.

Still shaking at the thought of what might have been, Tarl swept up his exhausted wife in his arms and carried her toward Denlor's Tower.

# ❧ 20 ❧

# The Pool Beckons

After five hours of sleep, Ren, Evaine, and Andoralson all awoke within moments of each other under a sky that looked bleaker than usual. The druid arose first and stoked the fire. Gamaliel stirred as Evaine slid from her bedroll, but lay on the warm blanket as his mistress brushed and braided her long hair.

Ren watched the wizard weaving her hair. He had seen her do this nearly every morning since they'd met. At a glance, her mane looked brown; but a closer look revealed smoldering red tones. The ranger thought to himself that her hair reflected her personality—a subtle exterior with fires burning underneath. The woman looked harmless, but packed a wallop with her years of wisdom and extraordinary magical powers.

The ranger hauled himself to his feet and checked his saddle, saddlebags, chain mail, and weapons for what seemed like the tenth time since the group had made camp the night before. He wore his polished chain mail, exquisitely crafted by the elves, and the magical cloak that made his form seem to blur, making it difficult for an enemy to strike him. His numerous daggers were sharpened and tucked away in sheaths all over his body. The long bow was packed, and his huge sword hung within easy reach. It would be his most trusted companion in the hours to come.

Miltiades and his ivory steed were ready, as always. The paladin had prepared his armor and sword the night before. Without the need for food or sleep, he now waited calmly as the others checked their gear.

As Miltiades waited, he meditated and prayed to Tyr. He no longer prayed to gain courage, but to show acceptance of his fate. His spirit was growing tired after its lengthy wait for Tyr's call, and he longed for this chance for eternal peace. The undead paladin made one last vow to prove his worth and devotion.

"Tyr," he whispered, bowing his head, "your servant is grateful for this quest. My soul is dedicated to you. Know that I go forth this day to honor your name. I can be victorious only through your guidance, but my failure is my own. Accept the struggles of this humble servant as testimony to his devotion to you." The paladin silently continued his mediation as his companions finished readying themselves.

Evaine and Andoralson inventoried their spell components one final time. The druid chose a patch of grass away from the others, then knelt in prayer to Silvanus. Evaine settled crosslegged on her bedroll and began a ritual of meditation and concentration that would help her focus her magical powers.

Rising from his prayers, Andoralson planted one last ring of magical oak trees, knowing this might be his final chance to leave a mark of good in the world. As he concentrated on the magic, he could sense the other nineteen groves growing tall and strong. The druid would leave a small legacy behind, even if the battle ahead proved to be his last.

Gamaliel was ready for action, tensely pacing the camp in cat form. He started at every rustle of the wind and at every leaf that tumbled into the clearing. His eyes were deeply golden; his pink nose never stopped twitching at the wind. Twice the fur on his tail fluffed out as if a black dragon had swooped into camp.

The cat informed his mistress that he smelled creatures of evil all around them, within a few miles of the perimeter. Both knew they would meet the horrid minions soon enough.

Evaine felt fully prepared, both mentally and physically, for the battle ahead, but she was still wrought with anxiety. Pools of darkness were unpredictable things, and what worked to destroy one might not destroy another. Yet her hatred for the evil waters outweighed her nervousness and stirred her determination.

The sorceress pondered the problem of the pit fiend. She had faced fiends before, but never one of this kind. She knew them to be vastly powerful and resistant to many types of magic. As she loaded her saddlebags, she drew out a slim, silver case containing four large darts wrought from dragon talons. Opening the case, she checked to see that the tip of each was coated with a brown, sticky substance.

"Ren, are you skilled in the use of darts?"

The ranger stopped his pacing long enough to answer. "I've used various types of darts. But when I need a missile weapon, I prefer the bow. Why do you ask?"

"The fiend we're going to face will probably be resistant to magic. I have four darts made from dragon talons. Their tips are harder than tempered steel, and they're coated with a sap that causes paralysis, at least in humans. I'd like you to carry one in case you can get a shot at the fiend. It may weaken the creature and allow my magic to work. If it's paralyzed or even slowed, it will improve all our chances of success." Evaine held out the dart.

The ranger ignored her, leading Stolen out of the grass and mounting the huge horse. Without so much as a glance at the wizard, he answered indignantly, "You're talking about using poison. I don't work that way."

Evaine's answer was equally tense. "I'm talking about using poison on a fiend from the pits of the Nine Hells, not on an opponent in a bar brawl. We're going to need every advantage we can get. If you can land a dart on the monster but I can't, it could mean the difference in this battle."

Ren stared at the dart for a moment, then spurred Stolen forward and took the small missile from Evaine's hand. It was handsomely weighted and the tip was razor-sharp. The image of Tarl and Shal that sprang to mind told him he was doing the right thing. He wondered briefly whether the wizard had planted the thought in his brain.

Evaine and Andoralson mounted their horses, as Gamaliel blurred and transformed into a barbarian. Riding rather than walking would conserve his energy.

The five companions set out through the woods toward the red tower. The evil aura emanating from the structure was like a beacon drawing the group to their fates.

\* \* \* \* \*

An hour of steady riding brought the travelers to a low rise. As they topped it, they could see the red tower of Marcus in the distance, huge stormclouds swirling around it. Marcus had laid out the welcome mat in the form of a cyclone of pure fire, nearly as tall as the tower. It was speeding up the hill toward Evaine and the others.

Miltiades spoke up. "Fire elemental! The rest of you

ride back down the hill the way we came. I can take care of this beast. It'll do less harm to my fleshless body." The paladin was gripping his sword, maneuvering his horse for a charge.

"You'll do no such thing!" Evaine called out. "Your idea is noble, but suicidal. The only way we're going to win this battle is to stick together and fight. We can't let Marcus's pets kill us one by one."

Now it was Andoralson's turn. "That stormcloud will aid us. Prepare yourselves to fight, but don't do anything until we see if this spell has any effect."

The druid began to chant, crushing berries of mistletoe in his palm. Thunder and lightning crashed overhead as the eighty-foot wall of flame sped toward the top of the hill. In moments, the skies had opened and torrents of rain were pouring forth, flooding the hillside. An unearthly cloud of steam arose around the creature. As Andoralson continued to chant, a bolt of lightning leaped from the sky and blasted the cone of flame. The monster wavered, but still came up the hill. Three more bolts of lightning struck it. The writhing blaze shrank to the size of a small hut. As the rain swept down, the creature drowned in the waters the druid had summoned. The last tongue of flame was extinguished only thirty feet from the hilltop.

Ren cheered as the creature dissolved into the mud. The companions waited under the trees for the rain to end. Evaine took advantage of the pause to cast a spell rendering them all invisible, then the group began the trek down the hill.

As the five approached the tower, Evaine announced her observation that the structure appeared to have no doors. But four paths worn through the grass betrayed the possible locations of the entrances. Even as a human,

Gamaliel's sensitive nose was able to choose a path tainted with the scents of men and monsters. A simple spell revealed the tall, golden doors Marcus had concealed. Evaine went to work on opening the magically locked entry.

Three times the door glowed green, but three times the door refused to yield. Ren fished out his lockpicking tools and busied himself with the lock, but the mechanism refused to budge.

"I've got one more spell I can try," Evaine suggested.

Ren scowled at the door, then looked at the others. "Save your energy, Evaine. We're going to need it later. Everybody stand back. I've got an idea."

The ranger mounted Stolen and rode back up the path. After perhaps fifty yards, he turned and ordered the war-horse into a charge straight for the tower. As the beast neared the portal, it reared up on massive haunches and pounded down on the door with powerful forehooves.

The door shuddered and fell inward with a splintering crash, crushing the four mercenary guards who were posted behind the door.

Still invisible, Miltiades took the lead with Ren. Ahead, a long corridor filled with skeletal troops stretched onward, ending with another door. A stench like that of an ancient, moldering tomb nearly overpowered them, but the two warriors spurred their mounts into the massed defenders, hacking and slaying as they pressed on. Bony hands and rusty blades bounced off Miltiades and his magical horse, Stolen's magical barding and Ren's chain mail. Dozens of blows landed on the powerful fighters, but none caused so much as a scratch.

The hundred or so skeletons, the weakest of Marcus's guards, were quick work for the ranger and paladin.

Stolen and the ivory steed kicked and trampled as they went, crushing bone with every hoof.

The warriors' attacks caused their invisibility to fade, but the spell had served long enough to get the group into the tower. Evaine, Gamaliel, Andoralson, and their horses were still invisible, however, although the two warriors had no trouble knowing where they were. Loud crunching and snapping under the horses' hooves announced their presence as they picked their way over heaps of shattered bones and skulls.

Evaine stepped up to the door. Instantly it glowed green. "It's not locked," she whispered. "There's a huge chamber on the other side. I don't detect any movement, but there might be creatures hiding within."

Ren and Miltiades pushed the doors open, spurring their horses forward. The three companions followed closely. All stopped short at the appearance of a fifteen-foot-tall wizard in red robes glaring down at them.

A scraping voice boomed out of the stale air. "Finally you've come! Too bad my guards weren't nearly enough of a challenge for you. Let me see—how would you like to battle a—"

"*Sanddunarum!*" Evaine shrieked. A jade mist arose from her hand and swirled about the giant wizard. The image warped and shifted, then shattered into millions of emerald facets. Ren and the others ducked, but when they looked up, no pieces of the wizard could be seen anywhere.

"Gods be damned!" the real Marcus screamed in frustration at the destruction of his magical trap. All heads turned to see a red-robed mage hidden in an alcove at the rear of the chamber. "Well, brave heroes," he taunted, "join me upstairs—if you dare!" The wizard lifted off the floor and flew up a side stairway. The sound of his evil laughter drifted down in his wake, echoing in the chamber.

All along the sides of the room, portions of the golden stone walls shimmered and dissolved. Twelve alcoves were revealed behind the illusionary walls. Masses of zombies and skeletons poured forth from their hidden niches.

Undaunted, Miltiades charged forward on his ivory steed, swinging and crashing through the undead swarm. An unearthly clattering of blades against bones echoed in the stone chamber. Andoralson cast powerful spells against the walking dead, causing waves of the creatures to wither before him. As the first wave fell, the druid became visible again.

Ren turned Stolen to follow Marcus up the stairs, but Evaine shouted a warning to the ranger. "The pool is hidden underground! If we go up, we're probably walking into the wizard's traps. Ignore him for now. If we destroy the pool, we may destroy him with it." Leaping off her horse, she canceled the spell concealing her mount so the ranger could find her, but remained invisible herself.

Ren hated leaving enemies at his back, but the druid and paladin were efficiently mowing down the undead horde. Bodies were stacking up and clogging the room. He nodded, then took the lead down another set of stairs. The crashing of swords, screams of the wounded, chanting of the druid, and Miltiades's war song reverberated behind them.

The spiraling steps were wide and deep, perfect for fighting, Ren noted. Two complete spirals brought him to a new challenge.

A huge, scaly creature stood blocking his way. The beast was humanoid in shape, but bore the head of a lizard. The sickly green face hissed at them with a forked tongue as it swung a trident taller than Ren.

"Puny human, I am resistant to magic and weapons! I cannot be defeated in battle! Choose your fate—die fighting, or bow and serve me!" The creature stamped the butt of the trident on the cold floor.

Ren stopped short. He gripped his sword, hesitating, deciding his next move. Then a hot green streak blew past his ear. A blinding flash struck the lizard-creature, melting it into a puddle of smoking green ooze and scales. Evaine materialized behind Ren, grinning.

"The dumb beast thought you were alone. Monsters are like traveling peddlers, ranger—their talk is always better than their merchandise. C'mon. Let's keep going." The sorceress darted around the stunned warrior, sprinting down the stairs.

Completing another spiral, they met a second lizard-creature who spouted the same speech. Evaine yawned. Ren raised his sword, but as the beast finished its words, the monster hurtled over backward, smashing to the floor. Gamaliel materialized on top of the thrashing beast, his great jaws wrapped about its neck. A spurt of greenish black blood spewed forth, then the monster's writhing ceased.

Gamaliel looked up proudly and communicated to his mistress. *I converted to a cat while the clod was babbling about his power. Pthew, this one tastes bad.* The feline shook his head and turned down the stairs. A few steps down, the stair opened into an archway leading to a darkened chamber.

*This is it, mistress,* the cat told Evaine. *The pool is right in the center. I can see its noxious glow.*

Evaine reached into a pouch and drew out some brightly glowing coins. She blindly hurled them as hard as she could toward what she guessed were the four corners of the room. As the discs clinked to the floor, the chamber was filled with light. Ahead, in the dank stone cellar, lay the pool of darkness.

Evaine and Ren tiptoed forward. Gamaliel silently stalked up to the pool and hissed.

"It's the same shape as I remember," Ren noted, "that odd, jagged crescent. But ten years ago, it was filled with clear water. Yecch—I don't even want to know what that vile goop is."

Ren warily circled the crescent to examine it. The lights of the room revealed an oily, glistening fluid that seemed to recoil from the light. "See those little indentations around the rim? When I last saw the pool, it had magical ioun stones inlaid in those holes. Now, they're just filled with that same foul liquid." The ranger sighed as he thought of Shal, Tarl, and himself fighting dozens of battles to kill hundreds of monsters all over Phlan. He desperately wished his friends were with him now. He would have been happy just to know they were still alive.

Evaine was already unloading a backpack. "I need five uninterrupted minutes to weave my spell and destroy the pool. Make sure I'm not disturbed." She set out the magical brazier Miltiades had provided and held her breath as she lifted the cap. If the flame lit, it might hasten the spell and buy some time. For a few seconds, the brazier was still. Then a *poof* sounded, and the flame sprang forth. The sorceress arranged a half-dozen vials of strange liquids in front of her.

Before Ren could warn her that he might not be able to protect her during a lengthy spell, she was lost in concentration, kneeling before the viscous waters of the pool.

With little else to do, the ranger scanned the walls for possible hidden entrances. Gamaliel sniffed out the perimeter of the chamber, but neither found any hint of secret passages. Eventually Ren took up a post out of sight of the entry, clutching five of his throwing daggers. Gamaliel stood guard on the opposite side of the archway.

Evaine had been deep in concentration for nearly two minutes when the echo of running steps was heard on the stairs. Weapons and claws ready, Ren and Gamaliel were relieved to see Miltiades and Andoralson burst into the room. They were quickly cautioned against making noise.

"You weren't planning on having this party without us, were you?" the druid whispered. Miltiades used the moments of quiet to activate his scroll of fire protection.

"There'll be plenty of party favors to go around soon enough. Evaine is casting the spell to destroy this pool, but she needs a few more minutes. We have to buy her that time." Ren glanced around the chamber nervously.

"Too late," echoed a scraping voice. The red-robed Marcus appeared on the opposite side of the pool in a swirling crimson mist. "She won't be destroying anything today except herself." He lifted a hand and sent a spray of deep red motes of light at the three men. The energy sizzled in the chamber and bathed the room in an eerie light as it raced toward them with deadly speed.

Ren and Gamaliel sprang toward Evaine to block the blast, but Andoralson waved his hand and diverted the energy into the dark pool. The mystical waters gurgled and absorbed the awesome power of the tiny meteors without apparent effect.

Miltiades stalked toward Marcus, humming a chant of praise to Tyr.

The Red Wizard cackled, underestimating the power of the group that challenged him. He lobbed a searing fireball and a scarlet tangle of sticky webs at the undead paladin. The warrior walked easily through the flames and slashed through the webs with his sword. Then the wizard conjured a sixteen-foot snake that slithered toward Miltiades. Before the warrior could dodge, the serpent wrapped its red coils around the paladin from head to foot.

Andoralson conjured a jet of ice pellets that streaked over the pool toward Marcus, but as the sleet approached the wizard, it was diverted toward the ceiling where it froze solid into a fringe of icicles.

One by one, Ren hurled his daggers at the evil wizard. Each of the blades hurtled directly toward Marcus's heart, but then bounced off an invisible barrier and clattered to the floor. The Red Wizard cackled. "Put away your playthings, boys. You'll be mine before long." Ren swore at the crazed mage.

Andoralson and Marcus continued lobbing spells at one another. Fire, lightning, ice, mud, rocks, insects, and steam were all exchanged over the fetid pool, but all were rendered harmless by spells of defense. Rocks and mud splattered against the far walls. Lightning bolts tore chunks out of the stone. Debris began stacking up on both sides of the pool.

Gamaliel held his ground in front of Evaine, his eyes wide, claws extended. She needed less than two minutes to finish the spell. Already, the edges of the inky pool were beginning to boil in a white froth.

Ren suspected the rest of his ordinary daggers would be repelled by Marcus's magic. It was time to change tactics. From his boot he drew Right, one of his two specially enchanted daggers. As the silver blade streaked toward the Red Wizard, Marcus tossed five miniature hands carved of stone over the pool toward Ren's feet.

The evil wizard ignored Ren's dagger, expecting it to bounce off his magical shields. But the weapon pierced the barriers to bury itself in the wizard's lung.

Marcus crumpled to the floor with a howl. Blood oozed from his chest. Struggling to breathe, he summoned something black into his hand, gripping it tightly.

Gamaliel pounced on the stone hands, swatting two of them into the pool, but the three that remained melded with the floor and grew into hands of black marble, each larger than a bear. Ren and Gamaliel were suddenly grasped by their throats and pulled to the floor by the giant hands. The life was being choked out of them. No amount of scratching, clawing, or wrestling could loosen the stony grips.

The monstrous red snake still surrounded Miltiades. The paladin was no longer visible.

A black marble hand was wrapped around Evaine's throat, pinning her to the floor and choking her. The pool of darkness boiled and frothed, emitting the foul odor of sulfur, but it was unclear whether the sorceress had finished her spell.

Andoralson stood helplessly staring at his friends. Then a tremendous thud echoed behind him. He whirled around to face the archway leading to the stairs.

"*Latenat!*" a gravelly voice bellowed. Before the druid's eyes, an enormous black-winged creature was beginning to materialize.

# ❧ 21 ❧

# Light From Darkness

Andoralson choked as the enormous pit fiend materialized in front of him. Leathery flesh, huge batlike wings, and talons longer than the druid's hand stood between him and the stairway. The creature's eyes blazed a deathly red. The stench of old blood quickly filled the chamber, but the beast surprised the druid by ignoring him. Instead the fiend strode around him to the opposite side of the pool where Marcus lay bleeding. The snarl that arose from the fiend shook the walls and sloshed the foul waters of the pool.

"I had them, you idiot! The people of Phlan were ready to follow me out of the city straight to this pool! How could you be so foolish as to summon me? *Latenat!*" the fiend roared.

A trickle of blood escaped from one corner of the wizard's mouth as he wheezed and struggled for enough air to argue. "I'm dying! Quit your ranting and save me!"

"You have a punctured lung. You're not dying, fool. *Latenat!* Argh!" The fiend hissed as he grasped the dagger to pull it from Marcus's chest. Its touch seared the fiend's tough hide. Tanetal wrapped the wizard's cloak around the hilt and pulled.

Ignored by Marcus and the fiend, Andoralson seized the opportunity and ran to Evaine's side. She was still pinned by the hand, her throat bruised and swollen. Not knowing whether his spell would work, the druid took a chance and directed a swirl of blue energy around the stone fist. In seconds, the rock dissolved into a puddle of mud. The sorceress rolled over, coughing and choking, trying to clear the mud from her face.

SMASH! An ear-splitting shatter erupted next to the druid and wizard. They saw Miltiades, white bones dripping in blood, bashing away at the hand that gripped Ren.

"We thought you were a goner!" Andoralson gasped.

"Not a chance!" the paladin answered without ceasing his swings. "I don't breathe, so I cannot suffocate. These bones are sharp. It was just a matter of time before I sliced my way out of the snake." Another blow shattered the giant hand and released Ren. Miltiades immediately set to work to free Gamaliel.

But the bashing had also caught the attention of the pit fiend. He looked up to see a strange skeletal warrior smashing the black marble hands with the hilt of his sword. His work had released a human and an enormous cat from the marble traps. "What has been happening here? *Latenat!*" he bellowed at Marcus. The wizard could only gurgle in pain.

Tanetal concentrated for a moment, then breathed wisps of evil blackness into the wizard's wound. It wouldn't heal the damage, but it would numb the pain and stop the bleeding for several hours. Marcus instantly regained the strength to shout orders. "Listen, you fool! Do you hear that clamor? Phlan's people are preparing to escape the cavern. Dispose of these weaklings before they spoil everything! They must be dead before my souls find their way to this pool!"

The wizard rose to his knees. "Kill them all now! They've dared to hurt me, and they must all die. They've tampered with my magical pool! You take care of the men. I'll crush the woman and that wretched beast!"

The companions had survived Marcus's last wave of spells, but now, in their weakened state, they faced the pit fiend in addition to the crazed wizard. And Phlan's citizens would soon be in danger.

Still coughing, Evaine rolled to Gamaliel's side and forced a healing potion down the cat's throat. He was healthy enough to stand, but had been weakened terribly by the stone hand.

Andoralson launched the first attack. A storm of tiny, white-hot meteors streaked toward Marcus and the fiend.

Marcus clambered to his feet. "Your spells are nothing to me, weakling." He raised both hands and began to chant.

Tanetal stood his ground, expecting to be unharmed by the magic. Yet he was knocked to the floor with a loud thud. An unearthly shriek rattled the chamber as the hot meteors melted into the fiend's leathery hide. The beast hauled himself to his feet, snarling at his enemies, but the look on his face betrayed surprise.

Ren and Miltiades charged the fiend, whacking and slashing with determination. Their blades sang as they landed on the seven-foot monster. The paladin's shimmering weapon bit deeply into the shoulder of the fiend, releasing a spray of black ooze. Ren's huge sword found its mark but shattered to pieces, rattling across the floor. The ranger pulled Left from his boot without missing a swing. Both men attacked relentlessly to prevent the fiend from using its magic.

When Marcus completed his spell, a cherry-red beam found Evaine, but the magic sizzled harmlessly against her green sphere of protection magic. With Gamaliel in good health, Evaine struggled to her feet, directing her energy at Marcus.

"Wizard, you've blasted me one time too many!" She raised her staff and released a frigid spiral of ice and snow at Marcus.

Her magic was partially negated by the red protections around Marcus, but the cold still harmed him. It ruined the spell he was summoning and slowed him with numbness. Evaine took advantage of his condition, raising her staff again.

A ball of fire, hot as the sun but tinted the cool green of the sea, streaked toward the Red Wizard. Evaine stepped closer to her enemy. Gamaliel slinked along the edge of the wall, so stealthily that he was unnoticed.

Marcus stood his ground, unharmed by the extreme heat. Instead, his bones were warmed by the blast of fire, and he was able to move normally again. Evaine sighed at this unexpected result. Gritting her teeth, she prepared another spell. A greenish white spiral of ice streamed from her hand.

The force knocked Marcus backward into the wall, spoiling another of his spells. He raised a magical golden rod as Evaine neared. "You've caused us enough trouble for one lifetime!" she cried. "This is the end of you!"

Marcus gaped foolishly at the sorceress. He tried to conjure one last spell of protection against her magic. Nearby, Gamaliel's back feet dug in with his claws, then his haunches twitched.

Before Marcus knew what hit him, two hundred pounds of cat landed squarely on his head, snapping his neck. Marcus slumped to the floor with a sickening crunch, his head tilted at a ghastly angle.

Ren, Miltiades, and Andoralson, still battling the pit fiend, were spurred on by the destruction of Marcus.

But the wizard's death had a sudden, unexpected effect on the beast.

With a horrendous roar, the monster drew itself to its full height. "Free! Oh, the power! I'm free at last!" the fiend bellowed. Its skin turned even blacker as the monster reveled in its release from the Red Wizard. It ignored the attackers who still danced and weaved around it.

Miltiades used the chance to chop at the monster's leg. Ren retrieved Right from the floor where the fiend had dropped it, then slashed away with both daggers. The deep cuts burned into Tanetal's black hide. The fiend roared an unintelligible command, lashing out with both clawed fists.

One arm swung wildly, but the other found its mark. Ren took the blow full force in the stomach, hurtled through the air, and crashed against the stone wall. The ranger slid to the floor accompanied by the dreadful snap of breaking bones. Without enough breath to scream in pain, the warrior clamped his left hand on his right forearm. Blood streamed freely from a puncture made by the broken bone that now stuck out of his skin. Ribs were shattered, and his right leg rested limply on the stone, bent nearly backward.

None of the companions could come to his aid. The pit fiend thrashed at them, though in its rage it had moved dangerously close to the pool.

A clatter on the stairs announced the approach of yet another enemy. A grating voice broke through the clamor of combat. "My troops have been slaughtered, and you have the gall to summon me! I won't stand for this any longer, foolish human! You have—"

An irate Brittle rattled around the corner, ranting and hissing. He stopped short as he observed the battle that raged before him.

"Fiend! Is Marcus really dead?"

A roar from the fiend cut his question short. Brittle quickly raised his sword as Miltiades charged forward to face him.

The two skeletal warriors stared at each other for less than a second, then nodded silently in an unspoken greeting of honor. In the next instant, blades flashed and crunched as the two became a whirl of steel and bone.

Evaine and Andoralson directed their most powerful spells at the fiend. Swirls and sparks of green and blue energy illuminated the chamber in an eerie glow. The beast laughed off nearly half the magical attacks. Gamaliel circled around behind the monster, poised himself for a leap, then sailed through the air to land on black wings. Four paws, claws extended, raked and gouged mercilessly.

Andoralson cast an illusion, duplicating himself ten times. The real druid was lost among his images. All eleven conjured illusionary monsters, directing them at Tanetal, but the fiend merely waved them away with his hand. In moments, the druid stood alone. Nearing exhaustion, Andoralson gasped for breath as he raised his hands to cast another spell.

Ren lay slumped against the wall. He struggled to reach a healing potion in his pocket, lifting it to his lips. The blood that poured from his arm and trickled from his chest gradually slowed and stopped. The ranger's bones were still broken, yet his life no longer drained away. Yet he was helpless to do anything.

Brittle and Miltiades continued their deadly dance, matching each other blow for blow, parry for parry. Swords sang and crunched as the pair's exquisite but horrifying choreography led them around the chamber.

Evaine never ceased directing jets, clouds, and streams of emerald energy at the enormous black beast. Nearly half her spells fizzled uselessly away, and no matter how the monster was harmed, its injuries gradually healed within minutes. Evaine racked her brain for some inspiration, but she had little time to think amid her furious spellcasting.

Gamaliel still clung to the fiend's back. Black ichor flowed down the monster's muscled form, puddling at its feet. A stench like stagnant water accompanied the blood.

The skeletons continued their duel. Every few seconds, a sword found its mark and a shard of bone chipped off to sail across the chamber. The two were so embroiled that both were virtually oblivious to their surroundings.

Evaine had nearly completed another spell when she noticed the paladin's danger. By the time she dispatched her magical energy, it was too late even to shout a warning. Both skeletal warriors had stumbled dangerously close to the pool, bobbing, weaving, and dodging. And then it was over. Evaine watched as the pair teetered for a moment, then tumbled into the pool of darkness with a syrupy splash.

The inky fluid bubbled and boiled as the magical water tried to drain the souls of those who battled within. Every few moments, a bony hand or glinting sword tip broke the surface of the vile water, but there was no way to know which warrior had the advantage. It was only clear that the two skeletons battled for their souls. Occasional syrupy blobs splashed over the rim and sizzled on the stone floor, only to ooze back to the pool by sliding up over the edge.

At last a skeletal hand reached out of the pool, gripping the side. Then a second hand grasped the edge, and a bony form began to pull itself out of the murk. Evaine's heart sank as she realized that it wasn't Miltiades, but Brittle. The enemy warrior struggled to haul himself up. But another bony hand reached up and yanked the evil creature back into the pool. Miltiades still lived—but for how long?

The pit fiend laughed in delight. A minute globe of darkest night formed at the tips of the fiend's talons, then slowly drifted toward the druid. In the globe's writhing mists, Andoralson saw his worst nightmares come to life but couldn't tear his eyes away from the evil images.

"No!" he shrieked, toppling to the ground. The druid kicked and struggled, screaming and gibbering at night-mares invading his mind.

Now the fiend reached behind him and plucked the clawing Gamaliel from his back. The giant cat hissed and snarled, gold eyes ablaze, but the fiend tossed him aside like a toy. The feline tried to right himself as he sailed through the air, but landed on the stone with a sickening thump.

Tanetal took a step toward Evaine. "We meet at last, little soul. I desired to meet you ever since I felt your presence in my chamber. The fires of your magic burn oh so brightly. I look forward to tasting your life force. *Latenat!*"

The beast took another step. Evaine launched her poisoned dragon darts at the creature, while Ren hurled his own dart with his left hand. All of them found their target but bounced off the monster's filthy hide, clattering to the floor.

The ranger summoned enough strength to fire Left at the pit fiend. The blade struck and seared into Tanetal's dripping wounds. The beast bellowed in pain, but lumbered closer to the sorceress.

In desperation the wizard launched two more green blasts at the fiend. The first spell merely charred its black wings, while the second fizzled away. The monster's dry chuckle drove her to a fury she had never known.

Evaine tried to get away, but the creature pursued, half-galloping, half-flying. Before she could cast a spell to hide herself, a giant scaly hand had wrapped about her waist. The beast picked her up as if she were a doll. The scent of blood and ichor hung thickly around the creature. It slobbered in delight as it examined the sorceress, contemplating what to do with its new prize. Then the fiend spoke in surprise and curiosity.

"Sweet child, your soul is powerful and old. What have you done to reach this extraordinary age?" The monster gazed at her with new respect, grinning as it realized she was more valuable than it had anticipated.

Evaine struggled in the fiend's grasp, but could do nothing. The fiend's grip was so tight she was forced to gasp for breath.

Looking about, the sorceress saw no help in sight. Andoralson still thrashed and screamed, tortured by his own nightmares. Gamaliel lay unmoving, and Ren could only drag himself across the floor toward the giant cat. Miltiades was trapped in the pool, if indeed he still lived at all.

Evaine screamed as the fiend's dark mind probed her own. It was trying to examine her soul and learn her secrets. The sorceress fought the probe, knowing the fiend's curiosity might serve to buy her time.

A clatter on the stairs crushed her hopes for finding a way out of this disaster. What new enemy or minion approached?

A bright blue light shimmered down the stairs. Within seconds, Evaine saw that the glow came from a gigantic warhammer held aloft by a blond man charging into the fray. On his heels was a red-haired woman in a flowing purple gown.

"Start singing your funeral march, bard!" the man shouted. He swung the hammer high overhead, releasing it toward the fiend. The blue radiance sailed cleanly through the air, thunking squarely into the fiend's chest.

The monster roared, dropping Evaine to the ground. Breathless, she crawled away quickly. Andoralson suddenly quit shrieking and thrashing.

The woman in purple began launching streams of violet energy at the beast. The blue glow of the hammer reduced the fiend's natural resistance, allowing the spells to tear into the monster.

Tanetal roared and bellowed as he faced his new attackers. He charged the blond cleric, swiping with his claws.

From his corner, Ren tried to shout a warning. "Tarl! Shal! Look out for—" But the ranger was too weak. The words evaporated as he coughed and wheezed behind his broken ribs.

The purple wizard launched one more spell. But as the energy left her fingertips, she collapsed to the floor with a loud moan.

Tarl called the hammer back to his hand and began swinging at the fiend. The hammer bounced off the creature, sizzling as it struck the horny skin. But the fiend was barely slowed. It swiped with deadly talons, ripping four gashes into Tarl's arm.

Evaine lay on the stone, panting. She struggled to clear her mind from the monster's probe. There had to be a way to defeat this beast, but what was it? Why couldn't she grasp the answer?

Tarl shrieked as the fiend gripped him about the waist and lifted him off the ground.

"Not so fast, creature of darkness!" A deep voice shouted a warning to the pit fiend. A dripping Miltiades had crawled out of the murky liquid in the pool of darkness. Brittle was nowhere to be seen. As the beast turned to its new challenger, a skeletal hand splashed syrupy foam into its eyes.

Dropping Tarl to the hard stone, the monster clawed at its face, then turned to the paladin, laughing. "Again you challenge me? Foolish creature! Come to me so I can swat you down like the pest you are! Look at your friends, all helpless! Let me squash you now so I can savor you with the rest of my prizes! *Latenat!*"

The paladin gritted his teeth and raised his sword. He stepped forward in determination.

Tarl regained his breath and clambered to his feet.

The pit fiend roared, rattling the entire chamber. Drawing itself to full height, the beast focused its gaze on Evaine. A low humming emanated from its throat. Twin beams of icy blackness shot from the fiend's eyes, engulfing the sorceress. Evaine thrashed and struggled to escape the beams, but she was trapped in the field of evil magic.

Her screams pierced the chamber. Tarl threw the Warhammer of Tyr at the fiend, but the monster barely twitched. Miltiades chopped at the beast, but his blade barely scratched its leathery hide. Evaine was losing the struggle. In the seconds since the magic had overtaken her, her hair became shot with gray and she appeared to age ten years. Her friends watched in horror, powerless to help her.

Andoralson struggled to his feet. "In the name of Sylvanus! Release her, beast from the pit!" The druid threw himself between Evaine and the fiend. The beam of evil magic washed over the druid, engulfing him.

Evaine slumped to the floor. The others stood by as Andoralson aged before their eyes. His hair turned white and deep lines etched his face.

Evaine sat up abruptly to stare at the seemingly invulnerable monster that towered over her companions. The words of the succubus echoed in her ears— something about the creature's name. She had mentioned the first part of a clue, but what was the second part?

Evaine clambered to her feet, shouting at the pit fiend. "Tanetal, creature from the pits of the Nine Hells, I command you in the name of all the true gods to return from whence you came! Tanetal, creature of darkness, I strip you of all powers on this plane! Tanetal, surrender your hold over others of this world and return to your dark abode!"

The pit fiend blinked, and the beams disappeared from its eyes. Andoralson lay twitching on the stone floor. Tanetal stood staring at the sorceress. Wisps of smoke floated up from the stone around it.

Miltiades and Tarl backed slowly away from the fiend, weapons still raised. The smoke rose thickly, engulfing the monster. Tanetal stood helplessly staring at his destroyer. "No! You cannot send me back! I have powers, great powers! I—you—you may command me! Call me back and I will serve you humbly! We will grow strong with the powers of the pool! You do not know the power—"

The fiend's words were lost as a whorl of smoke engulfed it and the stone beneath its feet opened. The once-powerful beast was captured in a supernatural vortex, sucked into a plane of darkness. With a deafening rumble, the chamber shook, the stone floor closed, then all was silent. A final wisp of sulfurous vapor drifted to the ceiling.

The only sound in the chamber was the panting of the exhausted companions.

\* \* \* \* \*

Andoralson lay silently on the stone. His hair had turned a ghastly white, and his skin was drawn and livid. Tarl ran to his aid, but too late. No sign of life was left in the druid.

Tarl bowed his head and began a prayer to Tyr.

"Sylvanus," Miltiades called. "He worshiped Sylvanus."

Tarl nodded and prayed. "He died nobly. His god will have favor on him," he said after a time. The cleric lay his cloak over Andoralson's body.

Ren and Tarl finally looked up and stared at each other for a moment, then simultaneously voiced the same question. "Where on Toril did you come from?" The two chuckled, then immediately Tarl ran to speak prayers of healing to mend his friend's broken bones. As Ren's strength returned, he briefly told Tarl of the past months he had spent searching for Phlan.

Evaine bolted to Gamaliel's side and knelt on the floor. She lifted his great head and cradled him in her lap. The cat whined faintly—he was badly wounded, but would survive. Ren had administered the healing potion in time to save the feline. Tears streamed down the wizard's face as she realized how close she had come to losing her beloved companion. All the magic in the world would not have brought him back.

Miltiades, still dripping with the murk of the pool, gently approached Shal. "Do not be frightened of me, miss," he began. "May a warrior of Tyr offer assistance?" He knelt and offered a bony hand.

Shal looked up, the agony in her face masking her shock at his skeletal appearance. "Tarl," she whispered hoarsely. "The baby. It's time."

As Miltiades relayed the message, Tarl helped Ren to his feet and the pair staggered to Shal's side. Evaine stuffed a cloak under the cat's head and joined the cleric.

Tarl held Shal's hand and helped her stretch out on the floor. Evaine immediately called orders to Miltiades to gather cloaks, blankets, and her traveling pack. Gamaliel mustered the strength to creep over to Shal and lie next to her to keep her warm.

Evaine took charge. "Okay, Shal. Relax, then clear your mind as if you're about to cast a powerful spell. Breathe deeply. The rest of you, keep quiet. She needs to concentrate. Tarl, kneel on the floor and let Shal lie against your lap." The others did as they were told without question.

"There's not much anyone can do at this point. Nature knows best in these matters. But stay near—just in case." Evaine tucked cloaks and blankets around Shal. "Damn! I don't like the idea of a baby coming into this world so close to that blasted pool. But I don't have time to cast the spells to destroy it!" The frustration was visible on her face.

"Maybe there's something I can do," Tarl offered. "Ren, hold Shal for a little while. I just need a moment." The cleric arose and strode over to the pit.

Tarl closed his eyes, communicating with his god. Without opening them, he swung the holy warhammer over his head, then flung it straight down into the foaming liquid. Not a drop sprayed up from the impact; instead, the hammer attracted the murk as it plunged downward.

The blue glow disappeared in the blackness. Tarl stood rooted, eyes closed, at the edge of the pit. Slowly, gradually, a pinpoint of blue broke the surface of the murk. The glow spread to the edges of the pool as the swirling inkiness boiled.

Tarl stood in the azure glow, deep in meditation, for several moments. Then the boiling and gurgling in the pit slowed. The cleric opened his eyes to see the liquid receding into the crescent pit. As he watched, the fetid soup sank lower and lower until the pool was drained. At the bottom, Tarl could make out a hole in the stone, shaped like the holy hammer. A low rumble from deep in the earth vibrated the tower.

"Praise to Tyr!" he shouted. Miltiades bowed his head and murmured a prayer of thanks.

Tarl hurried back to the others, sliding into position behind his wife. A blue glow again appeared in the pit, and the cleric raised his hand to seize the hammer. But instead of returning to Tarl, the hammer appeared in the hand of Miltiades.

"My time has come," he said serenely. "Tyr now summons me to his side. I have redeemed myself in his eyes. Now I will know eternal peace. Thanks to all of you who have been my friends and aided my quest. I will ask Tyr to favor you."

The paladin lifted his eyes to the ceiling. In a heartbeat, his bones and armor dissolved to dust. The glowing warhammer hovered in the air for a moment, then soared upward to punch through the ceilings and exit the tower. The structure rumbled.

The ghostly voice of Miltiades echoed in the chamber. "Tyr's hammer will not return to you, Tarl. But know that your child is destined to search out the artifact in one of Tyr's greatest quests. It will be your job to teach the babe the ways of our god. Know that Tyr smiles on all of you." The voice faded as the chamber shook.

"He will be missed," Evaine said. "But the pool is destroyed and the child will be safe. Now, let's concentrate on helping Shal through this birth."

A worried look darted across Tarl's face. "Have you ever done this before?" he asked the sorceress. His astonishment was evident—a woman he had never met was about to deliver his child.

"Trust me. I'm nearly a hundred years old," Evaine returned. Tarl frowned, but Ren nodded at him in support of her reply. Gamaliel's purring comforted Shal, and she stroked his fur absently.

As Evaine busied herself with Shal's delivery and gave instructions to the others, a glow gradually grew in the room, bathing the companions in a violet light. Shal's labor screams echoed in the chamber and carried up the stairway.

Marcus's red tower rattled and vibrated on all sides of the companions. Inside and out, stones shook loose and smashed to the ground.

# ❧ 22 ❧

# The Future Calls

The magic that Marcus and the fiend had created
months ago to hold Phlan hostage wavered and collapsed without the energy of the pool to sustain it. The
life forces of Phlan's battle-hardened citizens took control and forced the city to be transported back to its
home on the Moonsea. As Phlan was torn from the cavern deep in the earth, Marcus's tower collapsed into a
mound of red dust.

Two days later, after recovering under Shal and Tarl's
hospitality, the companions gathered in front of a warm
fire in Denlor's Tower. Evening was creeping in. Once
again a glorious sunset filled the skies to the west of
Phlan. The clouds and storms had dispersed with the destruction of the pool. The city was filled with a joy and
energy it had not known in a long time.

Sitting in front of the crackling flames, the companions took turns recapping their journey for Shal and Tarl
as they sipped one of Evaine's herbal brews. The scents
of cinnamon, vanilla, and rose hips wafted about the
room, mingled with wood smoke.

In his lap, Tarl held a tiny bundle wrapped in a purple
blanket. A dusting of red hair peeked out of the top of
the wrap, and in rare moments, two eyes as blue as the
Moonsea fluttered open to gaze about. The baby sighed
and gurgled as he relaxed in his father's arms.

"You know, you're going to have to think of a name for your son pretty soon. You can't just call him 'he' for the rest of his life." Ren looked proudly at the baby boy he was privileged to call nephew.

Shal laughed. "We've been so busy with everything that's happened to Phlan that we never had time to think about names. And we weren't expecting him to arrive quite so soon. But he's here now, and he's healthy."

Evaine set down her mug and walked over to Tarl. Kneeling next to his chair, she stroked the baby's head and spoke softly to him. "Your parents are going to have some amazing tales to tell you when you grow up. You've seen more already than most people see in a lifetime." The baby slept contentedly. Evaine looked at Shal. "With all the spells you cast while you were pregnant, this child could have some interesting magical powers. It's not often that a sorceress has a baby." Tarl offered the baby to Evaine, and she gladly tucked him into her arms, rocking him gently. "I don't think there's any question this child has a special destiny."

Gamaliel snoozed in front of the fire. Seeing Evaine with the baby, he rolled onto his back, paws flopping about, expecting to have his tummy rubbed. Shal gladly indulged him. "You're lucky to have him, Evaine. Some wizards get toads for familiars." The cat purred loudly. Humility wasn't part of his nature.

Ren's eyes widened over his mug of tea. "If what Miltiades said is right, the gods have big plans for your son. It must be a little intimidating to know that so much will be expected of him."

Tarl and Shal both nodded vigorously, and the cleric responded. "I have to believe that what he said is true." Sipping at his mug, he grew thoughtful. "You know, when I was first learning the ways of the Tyr, we heard a

lot about the great warrior Miltiades. He's very important in the history of Tyr's church. He was a hero we
were all encouraged to study and emulate. I'm thrilled
that I had the chance to meet him. Your adventures with
the paladin must have been extraordinary."

Ren laughed. "It was more than extraordinary. And it
probably won't surprise you to know that Miltiades
hardly mentioned his valorous deeds. I guess the greatest heroes have modesty woven into their souls. We had
no idea we accompanied such a legend."

The companions chatted on as the sun set and the
stars tiptoed into the night sky. They took turns cuddling
the baby they had all helped bring into the world.

\* \* \* \* \*

Beyond the twinkling skies of Phlan, two gods were
looking down on the peaceful scene with opposite emotions. Bane was filled with rage at losing yet another city.
His followers had failed him and these mere mortals had
defeated some of his most powerful servants.

Bane's only small triumph was the interception of the
enchanted blue hammer. He gloated as he thought of the
special magics he had used to ensure that the holy weapon would never again be wielded in the name of Tyr. He
was convinced the weapon was so well hidden that it
would never again surface on Toril.

Bane tried to stiffen the control he held over his few
remaining cities. But with Phlan released, he felt his grip
ebbing from the regions that should have brought him
power. The massive disruption in his magical web was
too much for even the evil god to mend. One by one, the
cities Bane held captive popped out of their prisons and
returned to fill their voids in the landscape. Dozens of

Bane's minions died horrible deaths at the wrath of their god as the cities slipped away.

In another realm beyond the skies of Toril, Tyr smiled on the group assembled in Denlor's Tower. His followers had served him well, and a new and powerful warrior was now beginning the long journey that would lead him to be a future hero of renown in Tyr's army.

The god chuckled as he sensed Bane's rage at losing the city and his triumph at stealing the hammer. The artifact was of little consequence to Tyr. Finding the hammer would prove to be an appropriate quest for a certain warrior when he came of age. Tyr looked forward to watching Shal and Tarl's child grow.

\* \* \* \* \*

The conversation in the tower turned to future plans for the companions. Shal, Tarl, and the baby would remain in Denlor's Tower, keeping an eye on the city they had grown to love. They could only hope that Phlan's future would prove to be more peaceful than its past.

After a lengthy visit with his old friends, Ren planned to return north to claim the valley he had worked so hard to win. And he still hoped to make the acquaintance of the beautiful druid who lived in the next valley.

Evaine and Gamaliel made plans to leave Phlan at first light. They would first visit the hill where Talenthia had given her life to restore and protect the woodlands. Evaine owed her life to Andoralson, and she hoped to look after the region for the druid, making regular visits to Talenthia's woods. There was also the matter of rebuilding Evaine's tower. And Faerun was still plagued by other pools of darkness. The wizard had no intention of abandoning her quest.

Evaine ɩ:....
among her belongings.
out the magical brazier to Tarɩ. ..
with this artifact of Tyr. I promised to retu...
church after our adventures were over. Can I troub...
you to deliver it to your elders? I don't know whether
any of its magic remains—it may not light again.

Tarl smiled. "I'd be happy to return it. And under the
circumstances, I'll bet that Tyr will light this artifact at
least once more."

As midnight neared, the friends said good night and
trickled away to the guest rooms in the tower.

Evaine packed some of her belongings for the next
morning's journey, then slid into a real bed for the second time in months. As she lay thinking, the giant cat
jumped up to share the bed.

*Mistress,* the cat communicated, *there's something I've
been meaning to ask you.*

The wizard was dozing off, but she prompted the cat
to continue.

*How many babies have you delivered in your long and
adventurous lifetime?* Gam asked.

*Babies? Why, that was my first.*

*But you told Tarl you had done it before.* The cat
stared at her.

*I told him no such thing. I simply told him my age, and
he concluded the rest. I didn't lie to him, but I gave him
an answer that stopped his worrying. Now go to sleep,
Gam. And don't hog the blankets.*

The cat stared at his mistress a moment longer, then
lay his chin on a giant paw. There was no limit to the
surprises buried in this woman.

Soon Gamaliel's purring penetrated the bed and lulled
them both to sleep.

# EPILOGUE

Phlan was back in place. Her citizens immediately busied themselves putting their homes and their lives in order. The Moonsea and its surrounding woodlands once more provided fish, game, timber, and other necessities of life so badly missed in the cavern.

Phlan's council called for a two-day festival to celebrate the city's safe return. Singing and dancing carried late into the night, and by day the streets were filled with tiny stands selling every imaginable food and beverage. The scents of roasted boar, fresh raspberry pies, steamed fish, hot bread, wine, and ale mingled among the sounds of happy voices and raucous singing.

But as the city again settled into a normal routine, the stress and exhaustion of months in captivity began to take its toll. Children and adults alike suffered horrible nightmares of the endless assaults on the city and the horrible creatures that had threatened the lives of innocents. Neighbors bickered among each other, accusing close friends of luring them into the bard's influence. The council was blamed for too much action, too little action, the wrong actions. As the days wore on, the once-unified Phlan edged closer and closer to the brink of civil war.

Phlan was not alone. The other cities Bane had stolen suffered similar hardships. Families split up, friendships were broken. Governments cracked and wobbled. The most important cities on the Moonsea stood on the brink of collapse and devastation.

Bane reveled in the chaos and destruction. The breakdown of the cities would make their citizens easy targets.

Sensing Bane's evil intentions, Tyr scrutinized the cities across the continent. Certainly, some of the inhabitants were evil, but none deserved to fall prey to Bane so easily. The evil god would have to work much harder to conquer the cities. Tyr would not allow his rival to scoop up the innocents without a fair struggle.

Tyr gathered his powers and, one by one, set about curing the cities. Every evening for eight nights, the god sent an azure mist through the streets of the sleeping towns. By a miracle that could come only from a god of justice, Tyr cleansed the memories and souls of thousands of distraught inhabitants. As dawn broke, old wounds were healed and feuds forgotten. Tyr's mercy wiped away the memories of the ordeals. The population of Faerun was at peace once again. It was almost as if nothing had happened.

But the god also knew the incident could not be completely forgotten. A few brave souls would need to remember the horrors Bane had inflicted. A few heroes would be needed to watch for the evil god's influence and be prepared to challenge him.

And so it was that a ranger, a cleric, two wizards, and a magical giant cat retained their memories of the long adventure and victory. In other cities across Faerun, tiny handfuls of similar heroes and clerics of Tyr remembered their struggles and captivity.

Tyr smiled down on his chosen few. Bane would never give up, and no one on Toril could predict his next move. But a few dozen scattered heroes would be ever-vigilant.

# THE FINAL CHAPTER IN THE GREATEST AD&D® COMPUTER FRP SERIES EVER!

*POOL OF RADIANCE, CURSE OF THE AZURE BONDS and SECRET OF THE SILVER BLADES:* together these incredible games have sold more than *600,000* copies so far! And now *POOLS OF DARKNESS* – the final chapter – propels you into alternate dimensions on an enormous quest.

Battle monsters never before encountered. Cast powerful new spells. Achieve character levels well above the 25th level! Transfer your characters from *SECRET OF THE SILVER BLADES*

intact, or create new ones! Either way, you'll love this true <u>masterpiece</u> of the gaming art!

**Available for: IBM and AMIGA.**
Visit your retailer or call 1-800-245-4525, in USA & Canada, for VISA /MC orders. To receive SSI's complete catalog, send $1.00 to:

**STRATEGIC SIMULATIONS, INC.™**
675 Almanor Avenue, Suite 201
Sunnyvale, CA 94086